ORACLE

ALSO BY THOMAS OLDE HEUVELT

HEX
ECHO

THOMAS OLDE HEUVELT

ORACLE

TRANSLATED BY
MOSHE GILULA

NIGHTFIRE

TOR PUBLISHING GROUP
NEW YORK

ORACLE

Copyright © 2024 by Thomas Olde Heuvelt

Translation copyright © 2024 by Moshe Gilula

A Nightfire Book
Published by Tom Doherty Associates / Tor Publishing Group
120 Broadway
New York, NY 10271

www.tornightfire.com

Nightfire™ is a trademark of Macmillan Publishing Group, LLC.

The Library of Congress Cataloging-in-Publication Data is available upon request.

ISBN 978-1-250-75958-0 (hardcover)
ISBN 978-1-250-75960-3 (ebook)

Our books may be purchased in bulk for promotional, educational, or business use. Please contact your local bookseller or the Macmillan Corporate and Premium Sales Department at 1-800-221-7945, extension 5442, or by email at MacmillanSpecialMarkets@macmillan.com.

First published in Great Britain by Hodder & Stoughton, an Hachette UK company

First U.S. Edition: 2024

Printed in the United States of America

0 9 8 7 6 5 4 3 2 1

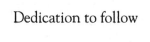

Dedication to follow

1

EVERY MAN'S END

1

It was because of the fog that Luca Wolf and Emma Reich were the first to see the ship in the tulip field. The fog and the fact that they were riding their bikes to school. Later, Luca would wonder how many cars had already passed it by, their drivers blissfully unaware how close they had come to meeting their doom on their morning commute. "The lucky ones," Luca would call them during his questioning. There would be a strong bitterness in his voice, because at thirteen and inspired by the Netflix shows he watched, Luca had quite a penchant for drama. Then he would burst into tears and wish that they too had been as lucky.

Had it been up to Luca they wouldn't even have taken their bikes that day. Looking out his bedroom window that morning, still drowsy with sleep, the world outside was only shapes and suggestions of shapes. A halo of thick mist enveloped the lamp at the far end of the backyard and frost covered the gutter and roof tiles.

He sprawled back onto his bed, opened Snapchat, took a selfie that reflected his ultimate *weltschmerz*, and texted, *Take the bus?* Adding a kiss emoji.

Drama queen, Emma texted back. Her own selfie was dressed and ready to go, looking stunning with her radiant red hair. *Got hockey practice*, she added, so she had to take her bike. Two pink hearts to make up for it, but Luca knew they were only friendship hearts.

Granted, in Luca Wolf's humble opinion, Emma Reich always looked stunning. They had known each other since kindergarten, and even though there had been a brief (and rather childish) fling between them in third grade, Luca got friend-zoned a long time ago. He wasn't boyfriend material anyway. Once they started going to junior high, girls only had eyes for upperclassmen. It was the cruel fate of every thirteen-year-old boy, but Luca had accepted it . . . until recently, when he realized she had started living in his head rent-free.

p*Drama queen*, Emma certainly would have said.

His mom insisted that he put on his parka and mittens, which made him look ridiculous—'Dead ringer for the Michelin Man,' she laughed—but as soon as Luca jumped on his Cannondale and raced down Park Lane, he was thankful he had them. The cold bit into his cheeks, instantly numbing them. Sure, it was your typical Dutch

December, only a couple degrees sub-zero, but autumn had been unusually mild, and Luca wasn't acclimatized to the change. He tightened his hood and pedaled more vigorously to stop the shivering.

It was still dark at dawn and in the fog everything looked strange. Trees and parked cars were unidentifiable shapes until you got really close, and the dull streetlights hovered uncannily among them. The way things emerged from the mist was eerie, Luca thought.

Emma was waiting at the square in front of the summer gelato bar on an oversized Gazelle bike. When she saw him, she put away her phone. 'Hey, Luca!'

'Seriously, screw hockey. I'm freezing to death.'

'Let's go then, you'll warm up soon enough. Nice parka, by the way.'

'Ha ha.'

'No, I mean it.'

Luca could see that she did. Her big, almond-shaped eyes radiated only kindness, and he instantly felt his face flush. In her long, beige coat, woolen scarf, leather gloves and knitted cap, Emma looked anything but ridiculous. Her bike was a hand-me-down from her older sister and completed the picture: she looked grown up. Luca felt embarrassed, first about his own lack of sophistication, then about the effect she was having on him. Around Emma's innate confidence, his brain turned to soup. Every damn time.

The bike ride from their hometown of Katwijk to Northgo High in Noordwijk took thirty minutes, and when the weather was good, they would ride along the boulevard and straight through the dunes. This morning, the lighthouse loomed out of the mist like a ghost, and the invisible, cold presence of the sea seemed somewhat threatening, so they instinctively opted for the inland route. This would take them through the town center, across the canal, then along the lee of the dunes. Once there, a sense of elation came over Luca that he couldn't quite put into words. They were *alone*, but it wasn't just that. The mist locked them into this cold, grey-white morning, along with the impassive silence of the reserve. Its invisible boundary muffled their voices and created an intimate isolation, as if they were sharing a secret.

They discussed the shows they were watching—he *The Witcher*, she *Sex Education*, season two—each trying to convince the other that their choice was superior.

'I don't know,' Emma said, 'I only watched the beginning of *The Witcher*, but—'

'Epic! That mega-spider's face, ha ha!'

'But it doesn't make sense. The swamp is totally quiet. The deer's just grazing on the bank. And then suddenly, this spider leaps out of the water with the Witcher hanging onto its leg, in the middle of some big fight? Where's the credibility?'

'Who cares? That battle slapped!'

'Yeah, but the beginning was just a cheap jump scare. I don't know. I'll finish the books first and maybe then give it a try. But I don't think I'll like it.'

Luca, who hadn't read the *Witcher* books at all and watched the show mainly for the monsters (okay, and the women in medieval combats), had to admit she had a point. Was he superficial for not having noticed it too? But then, watching a chick-flick like *Sex Education* would be over-compensating (although the title had secretly piqued his curiosity).

'Yeah, well, I dunno,' he said, his face deadpan. 'I read the *Sex Education* books, but I think the show lacks their depth. It's just not credible, y'know?'

Emma's face burst into a smile as she tried to shove him. Luca swerved and pedaled ahead of her (allowing him to wipe his runny nose unseen), but inside, he was aglow.

Past the Space Expo, the mist covering the dunes to their left created the impression of a hidden wilderness where you could get lost for days. Maybe forever. His mom called this place Every Man's End, a name that always fired Luca's imagination. There were ample places around here with good names—Thunder Dune, Siren's Hill—and even though the reserve was relatively small and crisscrossed with trails, these names gave the dunes a sense of power.

Finally, they turned away from the dunes and reached the road through the tulip fields to Noordwijk. Emma started discussing their grammar assignment, which was why Luca's attention strayed. A thin layer of ice covered the ditch to the left of the road. Tall, dead grass hung motionlessly over the bank. Usually, you could hear the sound of farming machinery carried from afar. Today, there was absolutely nothing. The silence increased his sense of isolation, but Luca didn't feel elated anymore. Instead, he felt goosebumps all over his back.

He saw something in the mist.

'Whoa,' he said, slowing down.

'What?'

Luca didn't reply but gazed off to the left and Emma followed his eyes. Day had almost entirely broken and the mist assumed the pale grey hue of a dead fish belly. And in that pale light, a shape loomed.

Dark.

Enormous.

2

'Let's talk about the boy,' Diana said. That's how she had introduced herself. No last name. No employer. No recognizable uniform either. Just an expensive, tailored suit that looked as anonymous as the blacked-out nine-seater which had brought them to The Hague, or the bland interrogation room where they were served mugs of coffee—no print on those either. 'Luca Wolf. When did you first see him?'

'When I got to Every Man's End this morning,' Wim Hopman said, as if he were explaining something glaringly obvious to a toddler. 'The bulbs are in the ground, so there isn't much work to do on the land. Must have been quarter to nine or thereabouts when I passed by because I had an appointment with my bean counter in Noordwijk. Give or take ten minutes, but ask Ineke if you want to be sure.'

'It was quarter to nine,' Ineke confirmed. 'And I should know. I've been running the place for twenty-seven years.'

'Praise the Lord for a good marriage,' said Van Driel. That's how *he* had introduced himself. No first name. Broad-shouldered, goatee, smooth skull. Standing behind the interview table with his shirtsleeves rolled, it was abundantly clear he wanted you to see his muscled, ink-clad forearms before you looked up into his humorless eyes. If Diana looked like the CEO of an investment company, Van Driel looked like an ex-marine. Or maybe a hitman.

Ineke might run the house, the kids, and the calendar, but Wim ran the tulip nursery and owned the land that—according to his son Yuri's texts—was now entirely cordoned off with black tarpaulin fences and featured on all the online news feeds. He hadn't had the chance to check the footage for himself, because before he knew it, their driver had held out a container where they were told to deposit their phones— SOP at secured locations, apparently. They had complied without giving it a second thought. That had been a mistake.

'So that's why you drove past the field?' Diana asked.

'Yep. Except you couldn't see a horse's ass with all the fog. Halfway up the road there's a dam crossing the ditch, and that's where I saw the car. Taillights first, engine still running. It's so damn narrow that it blocked the entire road. Probably an accident, I said to myself, because there were four bikes on the shoulder, all on their sides. That would have been a bad one; if he'd hit four of 'em, I mean. It's mostly kids biking to school in the morning. But there was no one there. Not a single soul. And that's when I thought, what the hell is going on?'

'And? What the hell was going on?' Van Driel asked, crossing his arms over his chest.

'Biggest pile of shit on God's green earth, that's what. I didn't ask to be here. Or for you to seize my goddam land.'

Diana ignored this. 'When did you see the boy?'

'I heard him before I saw him,' Wim said. 'The second I got out of the car, I heard moaning. I ran toward it, but it was hard to tell where it was coming from in the mist. Sounds are funny when it's foggy. L'il scary too, not afraid to admit that. And I heard something else.'

'What?'

Wim glanced at his wife, suddenly uncomfortable. Ineke, clearly unsettled, squeezed his hand and turned to their questioners. 'Do you know how that area got its name? Wim's father used to have a copper ship's bell at the front door, which he'd ring to call in the farmhands. He inherited it from his father, who'd got it from *his* father. Many generations ago, some Hopman sailed on a merchant ship. Right, Wim?'

'Right. Mother always rang the bell for us when dinner was ready. She'd swing this thick braided rope on the clapper, with fringes and a tassel and the lot. The old sailors used to call it an "every man's end". It would chime so fiercely that you could hear it across the dunes. The name stuck in these parts. But here's the thing: the bell's been gone for forty years, but that's the sound I heard in the mist this morning.'

'So what did you do?'

'Stood and listened, of course.' This time Wim Hopman didn't want to admit he had gotten more than a little scared. Because what Wim had heard didn't just *sound* like his childhood bell, it *was* that bell. There was no doubt in his mind. Hearing it ring so eerily half a lifetime later had not been a pleasant sensation, not at all. His parents were long gone, the bell with them. How could a sound that had ceased forty years ago suddenly echo again on a cold winter morning . . . and feel so *wrong*?

He cleared his throat. 'Only later did I realize what must have made that sound.'

Van Driel looked at him impassively.

'And then you saw Luca Wolf,' Diana stated.

'That's right. The kid stumbled into me as if the mist just spat him out. Shook the hell out of me.'

'Was he alone?'

'Yep.'

Van Driel put his hands on the table and leaned in, the veins and tendons in his forearms tightening. 'You positive?'

'If Wim says he didn't see anyone else, he didn't see anyone else,' Ineke said. 'Don't treat us like we've done something wrong.' The fear was back in her voice. Wim wasn't sure whether *they* could hear it, but *he* certainly did.

'Of course,' Diana said. 'We just want to get a clear picture.'

But Wim noticed that Van Driel's eyes were no longer just humorless. They now held a merciless appraisal that was much more menacing.

'Later, other people came,' Wim continued, searching for Ineke's hand under the table. She was fidgeting. 'Just a bunch, as I told you before. But when I got there, he was the only one on the scene.'

Van Driel relaxed a bit, and Wim Hopman suddenly understood what this was all about: they needed to know if there were other witnesses. They intended to sweep this whole fucking mess under the carpet.

'How would you describe the state the boy was in?'

'Oh, he was hysterical. What did you expect?'

3

'Holy shit,' Luca said.

There was a ship in the field.

Luca immediately recognized the ginormous shape rising in the mist as the bow, even with the vessel lying on its side. He recognized it . . . but what he saw was so out of place that it simply took a while to register.

'Whoa . . . how did *that* get here?' Emma asked, sounding as perplexed as he felt, and when he didn't answer, 'Do you *see* that?'

'Duh.'

It hadn't been there yesterday. They had taken the same route, and it hadn't been foggy. No way you would miss a thing like that.

They left their bikes at the entrance to the field and continued on foot. This was Flower Country and in April the area would bloom with magnificent rows of colors, swarming with tulip tourists. Now they lay gray and barren. The soil beneath the frozen top layer was soft, making each step feel as if you might sink through the cracked membrane. The silence was oppressive, the mist damp. At first, Emma complained they were going to be late if they dawdled too long, but now she seemed to have completely forgotten about school.

'It doesn't make sense,' she said. 'It looks like it's been washed ashore. But how did it end up on *this* side of the dunes?'

'Beats me.'

'It looks like something from *Pirates of the Caribbean* . . .'

Luca had been thinking of the *Amsterdam* replica anchored in front of the National Maritime Museum, but Emma's suggestion was better. The *Amsterdam* was a fake. This felt old, and *real*. What would you call a ship like this? A galleon? A clipper? Whatever the case, the long bowsprit pierced the mist above them like a sword. Three long masts leaned into the ground from the tipped-over deck; the foremost right at their feet, the rearmost at least forty yards away where the narrow deck converged into the aftercastle, no more than a silhouette. Curving gunwales framed a massive, clog-shaped hull. Peeling paint exposed weather-beaten, blackened wood, but the structure seemed too intact to be considered a wreck. The ship seemed to have simply run aground. Like on a beach. Except it was here, in old MacDonald's flower field, far from any body of open water.

A sound startled Luca. The taut, webbed rigging was softly creaking. One of the torn, raggedy sails flapped in a sudden breeze.

'Look,' Emma said. She walked up to the bow and crouched underneath it. 'See how deep in the ground it is? Must be heavy as hell. The ground is soft, but do you see any drag marks?'

No . . . and that *was* weird. There weren't any traces of people, or lorries, or remnants of a construction site. The ship lay as if it had fallen from the skies.

Luca wet his lips. 'Some time ago I saw a meme of a grand piano that just appeared on a rock in the ocean. Right by the coast, with the waves splashing all over it. No one knew how it got there. Turned out it was some conceptual art project they wanted to go viral. Someone had lowered the piano with a chopper overnight. It was like a symbol for something.'

'For what?'

'Dunno, it was art. But this looks like the same kind of thing. We're supposed to guess how it got here and what it means.'

But Emma shook her head. 'This is no art project, Luca. You can lower a piano from the sky. Not this.' She frowned, and Luca thought her prettier than ever.

'Maybe it was blown here by a storm?'

Emma looked at him incredulously. 'A storm.'

He shivered and buried himself deeper inside his parka. *There* was *a storm here*, he thought. *I just don't know what kind of storm. Or what it spewed out.*

Emma stood up and disappeared behind the bow.

'Emma, wait!'

He ran after her but cracked through a thin layer of ice covering an old tire track. Cold water seeped into his sneaker. Luca cursed and quickly jerked his foot out. When he looked up, he saw Emma watching from behind the bow curve. She had taken off her leather glove and had her hand on the hull.

'Feel this.'

He walked up to her, took off a mitten and copied her . . . but then quickly pulled his hand away. The hull was covered with barnacles, making the surface precariously sharp. Carefully, he reached out again and knocked on a patch of bare wood—one, two, three times.

Three is a magical number, he thought. *People always knock on doors three times without knowing what they are awakening on the other side.*

To be sure, he knocked once more, just to disturb the balance.

The sound wasn't hollow or melodious, as he had expected, but dull, like the ship had absorbed the sound into its massive hull. There was something awful about it, something almost conscious.

'And look,' Emma said. 'No marks on this side either.'

She was right.

They started to walk around the ship.

At the stern they discovered a giant coat of arms in faded red. The image on the woodwork was hard to distinguish, but the engraved letters clearly read: *ORACLE*.

Circling the masts, Luca suddenly felt uneasy. He again noticed that he couldn't hear any of the usual farming equipment, and no sound from the N206 either. Not even the roar of a truck or the growl of a car accelerating. Just the irregular flapping of the sails in the field. And there was something else. Back in the dunes, the mist had held the fresh, pleasant smell of a winter morning. Here, the air was different. Luca associated the oppressive, briny odor with trash cans in fish markets or the smell of the beach on stormy autumn Sundays, when the wind and spume would lash his face, tasting like dead things from the surf.

The ship had brought that smell.

'We've got to report this,' Emma said. 'Who do you call for something like this? The police?'

'Lost and found,' Luca said, making Emma laugh. She seemed not in the least unsettled by their discovery. It only kindled her excitement, which Luca envied. Granted, he got scared—a little. Not something you wanted the girl you liked to know.

Taking the risk she would think of him as a geek, he turned it up a notch. 'Maybe Every Man's End is one of those places where maelstroms spew out. Like in the old seamen's tales where entire ships get sucked in.'

'Yeah! *Davy Jones' Locker*, where Johnny Depp goes mad and thinks he's pulling his ship over the salt plains. That was so funny. Did you see that movie?'

'Sure, but whirlpools are real, you know. People have seen them in the Bermuda Triangle. Get stuck in one, and you'll never get out. Or maybe it's . . .'

. . . *a ghost ship,* he wanted to say, but didn't. They had circled the vessel and were now back at the stern, where Luca stopped dead in his tracks.

On the forecastle, right behind the mast, there was a wooden hatch. It was open.

Emma produced a stifled sound and turned to him, her mouth a grin of disbelief. 'Was that there before?'

'Maybe I shouldn't have knocked.' Luca chuckled nervously, but his voice fell flat in the mist, so he stopped.

'It *must* have been there,' she said, walking past him. 'I wasn't paying attention.'

Luca got the impression she was trying to convince herself more than him. Trying to rationalize something that she couldn't. Because they hadn't seen a hatch. Not an *open* hatch, in any case. He was sure of it.

'Come on, let's check it out,' Emma said.

She walked to the lower edge of the deck hanging about five feet above the ground. A solid wooden rail framed the superstructure, and if you stood on it, you could easily reach the hatch and peek in. Of course, he didn't *want* to peek in, not now, not ever, but he wanted even less for Emma to think he was chicken. So he followed her.

With grace and ease, Emma climbed onto the rail, making sure not to get her feet entangled in the rigging. Then, step-by-step, she shuffled closer and peered through the hatch's opening, her fingers loosely gripping the edge.

'Whoa. You can't see a thing in there.'

Even from below, Luca could hear the ship absorbing the sound of her voice. He took off his mittens and reluctantly tried to hoist himself up onto the wet, weathered rail. He cursed his clumsiness, especially when Emma reached out to hoist him up. He ignored her at first but eventually had to grab her hand to keep his balance.

'Thanks,' he muttered, leaning against the deck and shaking the wetness off his cold hands. His fingers were dark and dirty, with algae, maybe. 'You're taller than me, you know . . .'

Again, he received a blazing smile, as if she hadn't noticed his awkwardness. It gave Luca the courage to shuffle up to her to see what was on the other side of the hatch.

The inside of the *Oracle*'s hull wasn't just dark, it was pitch black. The *Amsterdam* had taught him that the interior of these kinds of ships consisted of cramped, low spaces divided over several levels where adults nowadays would have to duck to fit. But there were no visible outlines of anything. Just black.

'Hello?' Emma called.

No answer, no echo. Only a dull resonance. Luca saw puffs of Emma's breath drift inside and disappear.

The damp smell of old wood was overwhelming, but the nasty, briny stench was more pungent here than around the ship. He was just about to mention it when Emma used both hands to hoist herself up to the edge of the opening and swung her leg inside.

'Emma, what the hell . . .?'

'I want to see. Aren't you curious?'

Bewildered, he watched as she elegantly swept her other leg over the edge and lowered herself down the other side. Her feet must have found a footing in the dark because Luca heard a muffled *clunk*. Now she was leaning out of the ship in a perfect mirror image of herself from ten seconds earlier.

'Emma, I don't think that's a good idea.'

'Oh, come on, you're not afraid, are you?' she coaxed. 'Our little secret?'

That clinched it. Luca started following her example, but then Emma took a step back into the hold and let go of the hatch's edge.

And he saw her face change.

Somewhere within the mist a bell began to toll.

'Wait, come back!' he shouted, suddenly alarmed. 'Emma, get out of there!'

Later, Luca would tell his interviewers that he believed she stopped hearing him as soon as she had entered the *Oracle* and the bell started to toll.

Emma was just inches away, but her expression had gone a complete blank. White breath fell out of her drooping mouth as she looked past him. *Through* him.

That look, that mouth: they would haunt him forever.

'Wait,' she muttered. 'I think somewhere in here there must be . . .' She turned around and disappeared into the dark.

'Emma, come back!'

His lips were trembling. His gaze fixed on the opening. Although he couldn't see her anymore, he could still hear her. Up ahead, to the left of the entrance, the muffled thump of footsteps on wood. They seemed to be moving away from him. Why was she going that way?

The sound of stumbling, as if she bumped into something, a stifled curse. 'You can't see shit in here.'

'Emma?'

Nothing. Luca listened tensely. When her voice sounded again, it was coming from further away, deeper inside the ship. 'Luca? Hey, Luca, give me a shout. I can't find my way out.'

'Here!' he shouted. 'I'm here! Just follow my voice!' Did something just move inside? Could have been his imagination. Why wasn't she coming out? He tried to swallow but there was a lump in his throat. He looked around. The sails on the ground hadn't moved. The webbed rigging stretched under him like fishing net. Further away, the aftercastle, most of it invisible in the mist. The ship's bell tolled and tolled, its haunting sound filling his head.

A *ghost ship*, he thought again, trying to snap out of it.

'Emma, can you hear me?' He pounded the deck a couple times. '*Emma!*'

When he heard her again, the sound came from way to the left, where logic dictated the hold dead-ended into the bow. Yet he could hear Emma advancing through the dark in a place that seemed to be *outside* the ship, still looking for an exit. This induced a sickening sense of disorientation in Luca's guts. His feet started to slip off the rail. He grasped the edge of the hatch, knees shaking, his jeans soaked from leaning against the deck.

One more time, her voice came, faint and far away, and what she said chilled him.

'Wait, is someone else here?' It was the first time he heard a hint of anxiety in her voice. 'Luca, is that you?'

Then it went quiet.

And stayed quiet.

'*Emma!*'

The bell stopped tolling.

From behind Luca, a voice shouted, 'Hooo-ly mackerel! What have we here?'

4

'Did you understand what the boy was trying to tell you?' Diana asked. 'Must have been quite a story.'

'I couldn't make head or tail of it,' Wim Hopman said, shrugging. 'But then I saw that damn boat and stopped paying attention to what he was saying.'

Van Driel nodded. 'When was the last time you visited your fields before this shit-show started?'

'Last night.'

'What time?'

'Must have been around nine-ish, when I was walking Sheep. Sheep is our German shepherd.'

'And you call him Sheep?'

'Got a problem with that?'

'No sir. Your dog. The ship wasn't there then?'

'You think I wouldn't have called someone if I'd found the *Flying Dutchman* stranded on my land?'

'It was dark. Maybe you couldn't see well.'

Wim snorted. 'Not that dark. Greenhouse lights pollute the night skies with orange clouds.'

'How about you?'

Ineke shook her head. 'I didn't leave the house last night. I only realized something was wrong when Wim called me this morning from the field.'

'Your sons are all grown up and live elsewhere, correct?'

That was Diana again, and under the table, Wim could feel Ineke's hand stiffen. They had mentioned their *children*, not their sons. He was absolutely sure of it. And their ages hadn't been mentioned at all. 'How do you know that?'

'Professional intuition.' Diana showed a cheery smile of pearly white teeth. Wim imagined the grin of a shark.

'And neither of you saw or heard anything out of the ordinary,' Van Driel stated—not a question.

'Listen. Our house is smack in the middle of Every Man's End. That ship appeared less than two hundred yards from our bedroom window, and the entrance to that field is right in front of our yard. If anyone had been fucking around with heavy machinery last night, we would have heard it. But you *know* that, right?'

'And why's that?' Van Driel's raised eyebrow showed obvious contempt. It irritated the hell out of Wim Hopman.

'You're asking us if we heard anything that can explain how a ship weighing, let's say eighty tons, shows up on my property. But we didn't. There was no one on my land. If there was, they would have left traces, but there aren't any. Truth is, you people are as stumped as I am. Because you don't *have* an explanation, am I right? Unless the ship has literally fallen out of the sky.'

'Mr. Hopman—'

'But what about *my* rights? I can kiss my harvest goodbye with that circus you've put up there, so maybe answer some of *my* questions, why don't you. Who are you people anyway?'

'We gather intelligence for the Ministry of Defense,' Diana said. 'And don't worry about your finances. We have emergency funds that will compensate you.'

Were they AIVD*? No, they were based twenty miles away in Zoetermeer. Instead, they were in an inconspicuous building in The Hague, although that didn't rule out anything. Only in the underground parking lot had they encountered barriers, but Wim hadn't seen any signs or markings. If the Ministry of Defense was on the case, what in the world had he and his wife gotten involved in?

'I want to speak to a lawyer.'

'That won't be necessary. You're not under arrest.'

'Then my wife and I choose to leave, thank you very much. I want to go home and see what's happening on my property.'

'We'll take you back as soon as—'

'*Now*, please.'

There was a quiet but palpable tension in the room, and it seemed like no one wanted to be the first to speak. Eventually, Ineke did. 'Wim, just tell them what they want to hear. The sooner this will all be over.'

'Wise words, Mrs. Hopman,' Van Driel remarked.

'Then I want my phone. I want to call Yuri. Whom you know is my son.'

'Not just yet.'

'If I'm not under arrest, you have no right to—'

'For Chrissakes, shut your trap.' Van Driel shot forward so fast that the table teetered and Wim and Ineke shrank back. 'You are *not* our guest. You are here to serve the interest of national security. Stop asking questions and start answering some. And stop trying my patience. Am I clear?'

Wim Hopman stared at the man in wide-eyed bewilderment. For the first time, he wondered whether their captors would return them home at all. Technically, they hadn't been arrested, but their participation wasn't entirely a case of free will either. This morning, when the guy in

---

* The AIVD is the Dutch secret service agency, "*Algemene Inlichtingen en Veilihheidsdienst*" (General Intelligence and Sercurity Service).

the suit had verified Wim was the landowner, he had simply requested they step into their van. The crowd of police around them had been too intimidating to refuse.

'Listen,' Diana said, her fingers briefly tugging Van Driel's belt, causing him to retreat. Wim imagined a Rottweiler and its master. 'We want to understand what's going on as much as you do. And we want to find those missing people. You can help them by answering our questions.'

Wim exchanged glances with Ineke, who nodded skittishly. He grunted—tantamount to a concession in Wim's book—and gestured for her to continue.

'When did you realize something was wrong?'

'When the police arrived. The *first* team, I mean.' Okay, that was a bit of a sneer, Wim had to admit.

'Why did that indicate trouble? I get it, but I need you to say it for the record.'

'Because of the kid. He wouldn't stop sobbing, but when the police came, he started to scream. Seriously scream. Throwing a tantrum, really.'

'What did he say?'

'It was hard to make out. It took a while before I even realized he was screaming words. *"The hatch, the hatch"*, that's one thing I heard. And then he kept repeating: *"Don't go in there!"'*

'You hadn't seen anyone go in at that point?'

'No.'

But he would, moments later. Wim had seen enough people go in. He just hadn't seen anyone come out.

'And what did you think?'

'That they should have listened to the kid, dammit.'

5

Luca Wolf flinched and nearly fell off the rail upon hearing the sudden voice below him, but when he looked around, he felt hope flare. It was Ibby Alaoui and Casper Molhuizen, jocks two grades his senior; *sort of* friends from Saturday matches at Quick Boys and summer beach soccer.

'Help!' Luca jumped off the rail, tripped over dangling ropes and ran to them across the brackish soil. 'Emma's in there. Emma's in there, and she's not coming out!'

'Emma *Reich?*' Ibby asked, like there were other Emmas Luca had recently been seen with in town. They stayed put and gaped at the ship.

'Yes, Emma Reich. She went in through the hatch. I think she's lost, I can't see her anymore!'

'Whoa, whoa, whoa, relax, man,' Casper said. 'Did somebody lose their boat?'

'Fuck if I know. It was just there. But Emma—'

'That's some spacey shit right there.' The expression on Casper's face was one of amused disbelief and the kind of misplaced bravado boys his age seemed to trademark. He held up his phone and snapped a picture. 'And Emma's *in* there? Why didn't you go after her?'

'Because I . . .'

He didn't know what to say as Casper put his hands in his armpits. 'Chickened out?'

Luca knew he should be the one going after Emma. If she was lost in there, this was his chance to show her not only that he was brave, but also that he loved her . . . but he *had* chickened out. Something had felt wrong. He couldn't wipe the image of Emma's last look from his mind. Those blank eyes. Her drooping mouth.

'I'm not wearing my contacts,' he said. 'It's fucking dark in there. I'd fall flat on my face.'

'Emma's hot,' Ibby commented, and something dark descended on Luca. 'Let's check it out.'

The boys walked past him on either side, Casper bumping his shoulder: the jock-way of telling him they owned him. They slid their backpacks off before climbing onto the rail. Maybe it was because of that last comment about Emma that Luca, who had never worn contacts, didn't warn them. Instead, he took out his phone and called her. It didn't go through. Didn't even ring. No voicemail either . . . just a recorded message telling him the number was no longer in service.

He tried again. Same shit. Something tingled behind his temples.

Casper leaned into the hatch and called out, 'Yo, Emma?' Then, mumbled, 'Fucking dark in here, no joke.'

'Can you see her?' Luca asked, hoping against hope.

'I can see your mom.' Casper made an obscene gesture with his hips, cracking up Ibby.

One after the other, they climbed inside. As soon as Casper disappeared through the opening, the bell began to toll. Until then, Luca hadn't had a second thought about sending them in because of course the ship wasn't *really* dangerous. Emma must be stumbling around somewhere in the low-ceilinged spaces of the ship's bowels, feeling her way around in the dark for

(*Wait, is someone else here? Luca, is that you?*)

the exit. *Of course* she was still there. Where else could she be? But then that wicked bell began to toll again, and suddenly he got *really* scared.

'Ibby!'

A pale face turned to look at him from inside the hatch, maybe because Ibby was alarmed by something in his voice, or maybe because he had sensed something else. But then his feet apparently found footing and he let go of the opening. His hands were the last of him that Luca saw.

But he could still hear them. He heard their footsteps. Two pairs, walking away from each other.

'Yo, Casper, where are you?' Ibby called, muffled and off to the right. Then, sharper, 'Casper?'

Casper spoke, but it was hard to make out as it came from further away and somehow deeper within the ship. Luca could only distinguish the words *'echo chamber'*. Cheerful hollering followed it, a brief silence, then more hollering. But the whole time, not a single echo could be heard.

An instant later, Ibby and Casper spoke at the same time—not to each other, that much was clear—and Luca couldn't hear what either of them were saying.

Then further silence.

Luca stood rigid staring up at the ship, at the black square of the hatch. When he heard a voice again, it was Casper's and this time it came from right beyond the opening. 'Ibby, this isn't cool, man. Make some noise!'

'Casper!' Luca shouted. 'Casper, I'm right here. Get outta there!'

Something was growing in his chest, something oppressive, swelling up like a balloon and closing off his windpipe. His hands tightened. He couldn't see inside the ship from his worm's-eye view on the ground, but Casper must be close, going off the sound of his voice. If Luca climbed up onto the rail, he would probably be able to see him. But what if he *didn't*? What if he looked inside and found only darkness?

The creaking of taut rope. The soft, raggedy flapping of the sails in the dirt. The constant tolling of the bell. It all seemed *alive*.

'Casper!'

'. . . a little seasick, I think,' a voice mumbled, now much further away to the left, and how was that even possible? How could Casper have moved such a distance in just a heartbeat? And anyway, *was* it even Casper? The voice sounded strange, not at all *like* Casper's, though it *must* have been, because then he heard him say, 'Ibby sank into the cod hold . . .'

That was the last Luca heard from them. The ship's bell tolled for a while, then fell silent. *Whatever happened, it's over now.* The thought festered in Luca's brain like a fungus, inducing panic. He yelled their names, and when no answer came, he tried to call Emma again, and when he still couldn't get through, he started whimpering, stumbling back and forth between the ship and the road for help. Still, each time he drew away, the *Oracle* seemed to disappear into the mist, and he ran back, afraid to lose sight of it with Emma still inside.

Emma's gone. The bell stopped tolling and Emma's gone. The bell stopped tolling and . . .

Eventually, Luca did what any boy in trouble would do: he called his dad.

6

The story Alexander Wolf heard on the phone that morning was rambling at best, but he knew his son well enough to understand by his tone that it was serious. *Bad,* even. The two things he managed to deduce were that Luca was in the Noordwijk flower fields and that Emma had vanished . . . and that *most certainly* sounded bad. So that's why exactly thirteen minutes later his Nissan Qashqai screeched to a halt at Every Man's End, barely avoiding the four bikes at the side of the road. Out jumped not only Alexander, wearing a soccer cap over his uncombed mop of hair, but also Emma's dad, Martin Reich.

The two men ran through the field, each calling out their child's name. Only when Alexander saw the ship loom out of the mist did his son's story start to make sense. He got no time to reflect on it, because that's when they found Luca, who clung to his dad and wouldn't let go.

'Is that where Emma went?' Martin asked. 'Did she go inside?'

'Yes, but you can't go in there, she hasn't come back out, no one has, Casper and Ibby were here too, and—'

Too late, as Martin Reich ran off calling his daughter's name. He climbed nimbly onto the forecastle and disappeared through the hatch without a second thought.

He didn't come back out.

They heard him scream, three times with short intervals. They also heard the bell toll. Confronted with an overload of information, Alexander Wolf followed his instinct: to rush to the rescue. But the moment he let go of his son and ran toward the ship, Luca started to scream too, and in *his* screams, Alexander heard panic. It alarmed him but not enough to abort mission. He was halfway up the rail (which, like father like son, proved considerably more difficult for the Wolfs than for the Reichs) when Luca grabbed him by his foot and pulled him down.

He grazed his shin and landed painfully on his ankle but scrambled back to his feet. Luca clutched his coat and tried to pull him away, whimpering incoherently. Finally, Alexander did something he had never done before: he slapped him (gently), silencing him at once.

'Luca,' he said, holding his son's face between his hands. 'You need to calm down. Martin's in there and needs help. I'm going to look. Why don't you call—'

'No-no-no-no-no . . .' Tears streamed down Luca's cheeks, but Alexander tightened his grip.

'Hush, Luca. I'm just going to have a look. Maybe they're stuck, or maybe they fell. You call 112 and ask for the police.' He glanced briefly at the ship—what was it *doing* here, and who was ringing that damn bell?—then added, 'Tell them to send firemen, too.'

'But Dad, you don't understand! If you go in there, you won't come out . . .'

Alexander Wolf stared at his son for a second or two, then tore himself loose. He couldn't be blamed for justifying what he had witnessed with logic alone—Martin Reich had gone inside, ergo he *must be* inside—and Luca couldn't be blamed for not expressing himself more clearly given the state he was in. As Luca resumed sobbing, Alexander climbed onto the rail and shone his cell phone inside. 'Martin! Emma! Do you need help?'

There was no one there. Seeing how dark it was, the possibility of them having fallen seemed plausible. Alexander would have less trouble finding his way using the light on his phone, but he knew he wasn't superman and would gladly welcome help. So when Luca appeared next to him on the rail, crying, 'Wait, wait, wait . . .' and started to frantically undo a coil of manila dangling from a bolt on the mast, he reckoned it wasn't such a bad idea. He reached out to take the end, but instead, the boy wound it around his waist, tied it off with two knots and threw the rest onto the ground.

'Now you can find your way back,' Luca said in a small, teary voice. The mortal fear Alexander saw in his son's eyes almost made him stop and wait for the storm troopers to arrive. But they had yet to be called, and there were people in need.

'Aye aye, captain,' Alexander said, tapping his son's forehead.

Luca jumped off the rail and clasped the rope with both hands. Once his dad had wormed his way through the opening and disappeared, he didn't pay out. He just let it slide through his hands.

It kept going. And going.

Sometimes it would stop briefly. Sometimes Luca could feel light jerks on the other end. Sometimes he yanked on the rope, not daring to let it go slack, and felt resistance. Then it would go through his hands again.

With just over half of the coil gone, it stopped altogether. So did the bell.

Luca stood alone in the mist, the rope loosely in his hands. He didn't dare pull on it, haunted by a single thought: *Where do people go when the ship makes them disappear?*

Just before hysteria claimed his last coherent thoughts, he had a mental image of a colossal ship cresting restless waves under a starless night and racing clouds. Spume spattered high against the ORACLE inscription on the stern. His dad, Emma, *her* dad, Casper, and Ibby stood on the deck amidships. One by one they fell overboard. Emma and his dad were the last to go. When *she* went, the tips of her beige coat flapped. When *he* went, Luca glimpsed his face turn purple, saw death-patterns crawl up his neck and seal his lips, before he too plunged into the waves and sank into the deep dark . . .

Click—hysteria kicked in. Luca started yanking the rope in, hand over hand. It came out easily, the resistance gone, piling up around his feet. Gravity pulled out the last few yards and the end came through the opening, slid over the rail, and fell at his feet with a thud.

The waist-size loop was still there.

But no trace of his dad.

7

By the time the cops arrived the fog had started to thin and a handful of onlookers had gathered. Some took pictures and posted them online. One was making a video call. Someone tweeted and tagged the local news. And tulip grower Wim Hopman was trying in vain to get everyone the hell off his land.

The police—the *first* team to arrive, as Wim would later testify—came two strong. They were the sixth and seventh to disappear.

Number eight was Bart Dijkstra, who ran the indoor tennis center down the road and got car-blocked on his way to work. He and his girlfriend, Isa Stam, got out to see what was wrong. With no cops emerging, Isa urged Bart to go and see if they needed help. He climbed onto the forecastle and peered inside, when Wim Hopman ran up and said, 'You better not, Bart. There's something fishy going on.'

Dijkstra—athletic type, just shy of thirty—shrugged and said, 'I better had. There are people inside. My mother raised me right.'

And with that, he was gone too.

Wim didn't go in. It was the bell that stopped him. The bell his father had rung to call in the farmhands and his mother to announce supper-time forty years ago. It was tolling again. That's why instead of following the tennis coach, Wim followed the ship's gunwale on the outside, ducking his head under the rigging, to see where it was coming from.

He wouldn't find it, of course. Every time he thought he had singled out its origin—the main mast, the door to the captain's quarters—it seemed to move elsewhere. It was disorienting. And as Isa started to call Bart's name, then *scream* it, Wim was the second person that morning to think of the words *ghost ship*.

The second police team was a genuine squad with three cars and eight cops. More, they came armed. They forced the onlookers back, which Wim eagerly assisted, then forced *him* back, which Wim fiercely protested. Still shouting warnings, he had to watch as the first three officers went through the hatch and into the ship, guns drawn. No one would know whether their weapons had been effective against whatever was hiding in the dark, because no one came back to tell the tale.

The fourth was Yvonne Schrootman, who hesitated. She would later attest that it was something about the expression of the cop in front of her. It was her panic, her flailing, her *authority* that temporarily halted the procession of people disappearing into the ship that morning.

Not much later the fog would burn off entirely, providing residents of the Noordwijk rim a few acres away with a clear view of the *Oracle*, lying there so curiously in the field by the dunes. Shortly after that, the reporters would come. And following them, nose to tail unmarked vans . . . that *kept* coming. With growing concern, Wim Hopman would observe the handful of witnesses being taken away in those vans, and then he and his wife were taken away too.

But before all that, there were the cries for help.

The tolling of the bell.

Yvonne Schrootman screaming into the hatch, 'Boys! Where are you?'

And Luca Wolf, pale-faced and alone in the field, was briefly startled out of the delirium. He stared into the mist and thought, *In the cod hold*.

8

By daybreak the next morning, a huge festival tent, aglow with internal floodlights, had been set up around the *Oracle*. At the same time, almost four thousand miles west, an obsidian Dodge Durango stopped in front of the Lily Arcade Residence in Atlantic City, New Jersey. Here, on the US east coast, it was still eleven-twenty the previous evening.

The woman in the woolen trench coat who stepped from the passenger seat was no older than her mid-thirties but possessed an air of authority. She wasn't a local from the disdainful look she cast upon her surroundings. Maybe she had googled "Is Atlantic City nice?" and now personally saw the first Yelp review confirmed: *Nah, still shabby*. But that seemed improbable as well. She didn't give the impression she got her information from Yelp. She gave the impression she got her information in a briefing.

A massive man emerged from the back, bulging out of his service uniform, sporting an anonymous face. Without a word, he followed the woman across the plaza.

They entered the lobby and walked to the elevator. Not the public elevator, but the one opposite the marble front desk that went straight to the top floor. The red carpet leading up to it muffled the click-clack of the woman's heels. The baffled concierge stared at the visitors as if he wanted to say something but decided against it. Probably a wise decision.

The giant waved a card at the sensor and the doors opened.

'Welcome home, Mr. Al-Nawiri,' the elevator crooned in a mellifluous female voice. Neither of them looked Arabic, but they stepped inside. The doors shut behind them, and the car ascended.

With an equally mellifluous *dong*, it reached the executive floor. They walked into a pleasantly lit hallway hung with drapes, water features and potted plants, displaying the sterile perfection of a luxury retreat on Instagram. You would only notice the eyes of the CCTV system if you knew they were there. They passed three doors set a considerable distance apart and stopped in front of the fourth. No nameplate, just a number: 1404.

The woman pressed the bell.

The man who opened the door (without removing the chain) might have once commanded an air of authority himself but had clearly seen better days. Unshaven, he wore a grey bathrobe and horn-rimmed glasses. Tufts of grey hair outlined an otherwise bald scalp. He exuded the unmistakable smell of peat whisky. The professional smile the woman had just begun to form faded, and she instead pressed her lips together.

'Yes?'

'You're drinking.'

The man stared at her. 'I wasn't told the Big Intervention was on the agenda today. I'm sorry, but *who* are you?' He squinted past her. 'And who gave you access to this floor?'

Pity. *If there is one thing he cherishes more than his cynicism toward the world,* his file had warned her, *it is his blatant disrespect for authority.* A pity, indeed. Ten years of well-paid retirement and this is what had become of him. But reputation was paramount, so the woman in the trench coat decisively extended her hand.

'Glennis Sopamena, United States Military Academy Intelligence at West Point. I need you to come with us. There's an urgent matter we need to discuss.' She gazed down at his robe and the bare, hairy calves beneath it. He was wearing bunny slippers. 'I hope this isn't an inconvenient time.'

The man gazed at her hand through the crack in the door, apparently calculating the consequences of refusal, and judged they weren't good. He was right on the money. Glennis Sopamena had a firm handshake, and he theatrically rubbed his hand and wrist as soon as she let go. But she noticed a twitch in his right eye, and that was good. Very good.

'The Point, huh? Veldheimer and Cox used to be their apostles. Where are Veldheimer and Cox?'

'Retired and dead. I'm overseeing the file now.'

'Cox, dead? Gee, that breaks my poor old heart. Do you need my name on a Hallmark card?'

The woman laughed, a remarkably merry sound, but her face betrayed no emotion whatsoever.

'I don't know why you're here. They always called if they needed anything. The last time was four or five years ago.'

'Excellent. Well?'

'Well what?'

'Are you going to let us in? I believe you still need to get dressed, and I advise you to pack a duffle bag with essentials for three or four days. The clock is ticking, and I'd rather not wait in the hallway.'

'Yeah, well, you know, I'm busy . . .'

She was quiet for a moment. 'Busy?'

'Yeah, that's right. Lots to do.'

'Like what?'

'Well, dinner's on. I need to take the laundry out of the tumbler . . . Oh, and I was reading . . .'

'Reading.'

'Most definitely. *The Duke and I* by Julia Quinn. Know it? It's from that *Bridgerton* series. Very good.'

Silence. Then, 'You smell of alcohol.'

His mouth gaped before he said, 'O . . . *kay* . . .' Then he produced the polite smile of a kindly gramps who has decided not to buy any Girl Scout Cookies this year after all. 'Well, it was lovely to meet you.' He started to shut the door. 'If you don't mind, I'm going to—'

In a flash, the uniformed gorilla, who had until now been standing quietly behind the woman, lunged forward and slapped his hands around the edge of the door. The chain yanked tight and was nearly pulled out of the doorpost. The man in the bathrobe staggered back, shocked, but the woman didn't bat an eyelid. Instead, her face broke into the radiant smile she had intended to show from the get-go. It was a smile that could freeze water. 'Let me remind you that we provided you with this residence. My predecessors are grateful for your past services, but one phone call and I can end our arrangement. You are no longer a free man. You are a recruit, and recruits don't drink. So I won't ask again. Are you going to let us in, or will Bob be obliged to break down this door? I promise you'll regret that.'

The man behind the door looked at the gorilla and nearly choked. 'Seriously, Bob?'

Neither Bob nor Glennis reacted.

Then he raised his eyebrows, smiled, and with an overly courteous gesture, unchained the door. 'Well, well, well, Sunshine and Honey Pie, I don't believe I have a choice, do I?'

'No,' Glennis Sopamena said, as she walked past him and into the condo. 'You don't, Mr. Grim.'

9

All afternoon, Barbara Wolf had felt they had treated her well. Especially Diana. Barbara had no idea how she would have survived the first desperate hours after her husband's disappearance without Diana's calm, unwavering sympathy. She had been professional and comforting, and Barbara had allowed her to be a guiding light. Now she realized that very professionalism had only enabled the woman to take advantage of her despair and put Barbara in the palm of her hand. But now she understood that, it was too late.

Alexander wouldn't have let himself be manipulated, she thought. A piercing, heartsick pain expanded inside her. *Alexander would . . .*

She cut the thought off. With quick, shaky motions, she rinsed the plates she and Jenna had just used for their Vietnamese takeout. Luca's meal was untouched in its foam container on the counter. Just before the food delivery and *after* their big fight, he had slipped into a steaming bath to oust the cold from his bones. Afterwards, a diazepam had knocked him out in one of the bungalow's two bedrooms. Good for him. He needed rest more than anything. Food could wait.

Barbara put the dishes on the rack and dried her hands with a cloth. They were trembling. That was new, her hands had never trembled. Steadying herself on the counter, she stared out the window, concentrating on her breathing. It was dark now. Beyond her reflection, only the arching marram grass on the nearest dune was visible in the glimmer of the porch light. The bungalow stood in the lee of several parallel dunes, the ground between them alternating between sand and stretches of rust-colored, wind-blown saltmarsh grass, pointing everywhere. When they had arrived, it had been impossible to determine east from west. But ninety minutes ago, the blue-grey light had broken into the sickly-pale, orange-yellow glow of sunset behind the house. Found it: the sea.

The glow had also revealed the chain-link fence circling the compound, at least ten feet high, topped with rolls of razor wire and security cameras peering inward.

Following her meditation app's instructions, Barbara exhaled for four seconds. Her hands stopped trembling. She was a nervous wreck, but Jenna was sketching at the coffee table in the den, and Barbara had to be strong for her daughter.

'What are you drawing, honey?' she asked kneeling beside her.

'It's the funny man who picked me up from school today.' Jenna showed her the crayon drawing. It was a black car. The man behind the wheel was a giant next to a stick figure with wiry hair—Jenna's usual depiction of herself. He had a big, open mouth and huge square teeth, making Barbara's skin crawl.

'It's pretty, sweetheart.'

'I want my own crayons. They're much better.'

'It's still pretty.'

But she understood what Jenna at only six intuitively sensed and wished she could tell her she felt the same. The bungalow—the *safehouse*, as that Judas-bitch had called it—was stylish and fully equipped, but it wasn't their home. It possessed the impersonal quality of a photo in an interior design magazine. The books on the shelves meant nothing to her, the laptop wasn't hers, and despite having a Wi-Fi connection, she couldn't access her email or social media accounts (neither could Luca). But the biggest joke was the phone by the door, the *only* phone in the house since they hadn't returned either hers or Luca's. No matter what number you dialed on that phone, you always got Diana.

Next time I talk to her, I'm going to scream. And next time I see her, I'll claw her eyes out.

The food delivery guy had brought them a roller case as well as the takeaway, and when Barbara saw what was inside, her stomach turned. Clothes for all three of them. *Their own* clothes. These people had broken into their home.

The discovery of enough food supplies for at least a week only perpetuated that sickening feeling. How long were they planning on detaining them here? And what legal loophole even allowed them to do so? One thing was sure; Barbara would lose her mind if forced to stay here longer than a day. But what if they hadn't found Alexander by tomorrow?

Jenna interrupted her thoughts. 'After this, I'm going to draw the house,' she said. 'And after that, the dunes. And when Daddy comes back, I'm going to give him all my drawings.'

That brought the pain back full circle. Oh, how she longed for her phone. She wanted to call Alexander, even if it was turned off. She wanted to text him, tell him that she loved him and wanted him to come home.

But all she had left was a hole inside her and the awful realization that they were caged like rats in a Skinner Box.

10

Luca Wolf didn't sleep. He lay in the dark staring up at the ceiling and heard Emma's voice whisper in the corners of the room, *Wait, is someone else there? Luca, is that you?*

That triggered the image of that last blank stare. White puffs of breath like the mist itself rolling from her slack mouth as she looked right through him and he screamed her name.

He sat bolt upright and stared around the room as if expecting an intruder. Nothing. Just him and the king-sized bed, a giant compared to his own semi-double that now stood empty in his room in Katwijk. The comforter tangled below his waist. Emma's voice had been a figment of his tormented mind, but that last scream still resonated in his ears. *Had* he screamed? Probably not. His mom would have been in the room by now if he had.

It was seven-thirty by the digits on the clock on the nightstand. Outside, the wind picked up, rustling through the beach grasses. Luca shivered and pulled the comforter over his shoulders. The cold was trapped in his body; the bath had done little to alleviate it. The events

of that morning had acquired a distant quality after endlessly recount-
ing them to their stupid committee, but alone in the dark, they started
to resurface . . . like a disgusting organism on the seabed awaking from
its slumber to rise unseen.

Just to be sure, and because at thirteen he was still a child (no matter
how hard he tried to hide it from Emma), he lay on the edge of the bed
and checked underneath it. Only a sneaker. The same sneaker that had
cracked through the thin layer of ice on the tire-track that morning in
Every Man's End, submerging his foot in freezing water.

He was about to get back up when he heard the ship's bell toll a
single chime.

Luca nearly toppled over. Clawing the comforter, he shifted his
weight back onto the bed, then looked around again. His heart throbbing in his throat, he turned on the bedside lamp. The room was still
empty. Only, it didn't *feel* empty. The sound of the bell was still rever-
berating in his ears, thin and coppery, as if it had penetrated the bungalow walls, causing the stagnant air to tremble.

He put on his hoody, went to the bathroom and, despite his constant
shivering, splashed cold water onto his face. Then he sat on the toilet
lid and stared at the floor through his fingers. The lid slowly warmed up
under his thighs. He considered going to the den to get a snack, but he
didn't want to face his mom. Not yet anyway. They had a massive fight,
and he had yelled a bunch of nasty things at her. He was ashamed, but
also hurt that she hadn't believed him. That was the heart of the matter.

The story they had tried to sell to his mom was total BS. They were
lying. All four of them. The woman named Diana, who *seemed* nice but
was only there to sugarcoat everything. The younger woman they
dialed in on the video screen, who had said absolutely nothing through
a smile as icy as the crust on the tire-track. Their stupid Dr. Phil with
his textbook blah blah. And the woman in charge, the one with the
weird French name. She was the worst.

She had barged in halfway through their interview wearing a bright
red maxicoat. Her entrance alone was enough to silence everyone and
suck all the oxygen from the room. Luca took one look at her penetrating, sea-grey eyes and felt like a rabbit in the crosshairs of a hawk. Duck
and run, under the table or into a burrow.

'We don't know where the ship came from,' she announced—straight
to business after introducing herself as Eleanor Delveaux, general intelligence, whatever the hell *that* meant. 'We also don't know where your
husband and the other missing people are, but we do know they are no
longer in the ship.'

'But *how?*' Luca blurted out.

Her expression was probably meant to express sympathy but failed miserably. 'Because we've combed it, of course.'

'You went *inside?*'

'Of course, Luca. What did you expect? You said that's where you last saw them, so that's where we started looking.'

He couldn't hide his incredulity. 'But that's impossible . . . everyone who went inside disappeared! Emma, Dad, the cops . . . no one came back!'

'Police officers did indeed go inside, but they aren't missing. We've sent in an array of search teams. Police, firefighters, tracker dogs; they found nothing dangerous inside.'

'But I saw it myself . . .'

'Luca, calm down.' That was his mom, and her soothing tone infuriated him. 'Try to listen to what the lady has to say.'

The woman with the French name smiled a pitying smile. 'I understand your confusion. You saw them go in, but the place was flooded with people. Locals, police, not to mention all the press. You didn't see them come out, so you jumped to the same conclusion as you did earlier this morning: what you thought you'd seen happen to your friends and your father.'

'But what *happened* to Alexander?' His mom's voice sounded shrill and tense. Luca knew she was trying to remain calm for his sake, but he could see the fear in her red-rimmed eyes. 'I mean, where *is* he?'

'We don't know. But none of the missing are inside the ship. We have no reason to doubt your son's words, so we assume that they did indeed go inside. Perhaps, they became disoriented and crawled out on the other end. The ship is huge. In this morning's fog, you couldn't see from stem to stern. It's possible they wandered off. Why they haven't made their whereabouts known and what happened to them after that, we don't know, but forensics are sweeping the dunes as we speak. They will *most certainly* uncover traces of the missing. Make no mistake, as worrisome as it may sound, five people disappearing in the same place at the same time is, in fact, hopeful. It means they're likely to be together.'

Luca opened his mouth, but nothing came out. His head was spinning. The woman's twisted logic dismissed his entire statement and sounded convincing enough to be true. *Could* he have imagined it? But why then did Emma's last expression still haunt him? The way her face was drained of its humanity the moment she went into the ship and the bell had started to toll . . .

'Traumatized children often seek infantile interpretations in stressful situations,' the wannabe Dr. Phil suddenly remarked, and Luca, who didn't know the exact meaning of 'infantile' but got the gist, wanted to scream, *I'm right here!*

Diana and the woman on the screen hadn't spoken at all. They had only looked at him with sweet, comforting smiles—an ice queen smile, in the Zoom lady's case—and that's when it had dawned on Luca. *They've won over mom and think it's only a matter of time before they get me too.*

Never, he now thought.

Luca got off the toilet seat and trudged back to the bedroom that wasn't his, but where the ghosts were still roaming freely. Lost and lonely, they rattled the window in its grooves. It was the wind. No, it was his dad; who had tapped his head with two fingers and said *Aye aye, captain* after Luca had tied the rope around his waist.

The rope that should have ensured that he found his way back.

Why hadn't he tried harder to stop him? The image of his dad disappearing through the hatch was preying on Luca's mind. He had been wearing his AC Milan cap. The black one with the red lining that said ACM—1899. His dad wasn't a fan like Luca, but had bought two after visiting the San Siro stadium in Italy last summer. On the drive back to the campsite where Mom and Jenna had gone swimming in the lake, Luca had asked why his dad had wanted one too, when he didn't even like soccer.

'But *you* like it,' he had said. 'And I like doing things you like. One day you'll do the same for your own kid.'

'So will you put on Jenna's tutu if she wants you to, or is that Mom's job?' Luca had asked and his dad had thrown him a quick, almost invisible wink.

'I think I'd look great in a tutu.'

That had been nice. *Père et fils.*

Luca dropped back onto the pillow wishing he had his cap now. He cupped his hands over his eyes and started crying. He longed for his home, for normality, and felt deeply, intensely guilty. He cried for Emma too, but even though a thirteen-year-old's love burned unbridled, he cried mostly for his dad. He hadn't been able to stop him, and now he was gone.

He must have cried himself to sleep because he jerked awake with a rush of adrenaline when he heard his mom call, 'Luca! Oh God, Luca come here!'

Luca dashed through the bungalow to see what was happening.

The news had broken.

11

Some 40,000 feet over the Atlantic Ocean, at quarter to four in the morning; somewhere Robert Grim absolutely didn't want to be.

He watched indignantly as Ms. Mega Bitch talked into her built-in screen console at the front of the Falcon 7X executive jet's cabin, in a language that sounded . . . Scandinavian? Not German, in any case. The ease with which she switched languages surprised Grim. Her American accent was flawless, and Glennis Sopamena looked about as Scandinavian as a Piña Colada.

Across the aisle Bob the handler (if Bob really was his name) bulged from his white-leathered seat like a hefty BBQ sausage tightly wrapped in cellophane. Maybe he was dozing, but Grim couldn't tell since he was wearing sunglasses.

Grim himself was wide-awake. He hadn't touched the elaborate meal they had put in front of him after takeoff, and he instead longed for a drink. Preying on his mind was the realization that his life as he had known it was, like Atlantic City, in the rearview.

Just four hours earlier, and with similar indignation, he had watched Glennis open the curtains across the panoramic windows that covered the eastern wall of the penthouse. *His* penthouse. Soundproof. Neighbor-proof. A self-imposed no-visitor rule, and for good reason.

'It's a shame to keep the curtains drawn with a view like this,' she said, looking out over the boardwalk and the beach, the sparkle of the Ferris wheel on the pier and the distant lights of the supertankers on the Atlantic. Then she threw off her coat and slumped into a recliner, as if she were Her Majesty The Queen herself. Grim shut his eyes and, with a huge amount of willpower, conjured up a new image, a sublime image: Robert Grim saw her immured behind eight inches of brick and drying plaster.

'Let's say, ten minutes to get dressed and pack?' Glennis cheerfully said. 'We have a long journey ahead of us, and like I said, the clock is ticking.'

'You mind telling me what the hell is going on? And where you plan on taking me?'

'We'll explain on the way. I have no doubt it'll float your boat. It's right up your alley, so to speak.'

He didn't like the sound of that. Not at all. Her passing remark that he was a recruit wasn't lost on him either and was more than a little worrying. But for now, it was important to . . . well, stay put. Or something. He didn't really know *what* to do and that disturbed him.

Meanwhile, Bob blocked the only way out of the main room, like a boulder in front of a cave.

'Say,' Grim said. 'Sunshine over there. Does he speak?'

'He certainly does, but believe me when I say it's in your best interests that he does not.' She was still smiling, but no longer sounded cheerful. 'And you, Mr. Grim, talk too much. You can make this easy or hard on yourself.'

Grim considered a duck-and-run into the hallway, but quashed the thought. He had had a few too many to pull off such a feat. Instead, he offered them a drink. The Blue Label was a hundred and eighty a bottle, but it was their dime, which was in a sense ironic. *Keep him flying. As long as he doesn't start spilling the beans.* It was obvious they had expected him to be done. Hell, *he* had expected him to be done—done and dusted. But the fact that they had come to fetch him from his condo (*draft* him, more like it) had shaken him badly. This wasn't an invitation. It was a mission briefing. And that scared him . . . because he knew what single expertise *he* had to offer.

With a barely perceptible shake of his head, Bob turned down the drink. Glennis snapped that she didn't indulge in libations. As he broke cubes into his own tumbler, she looked at him like a weasel with a bone stuck in its throat. Well, it was a free country. He poured himself a double.

Grim never drank in his old life. There had been too many responsibilities. In his new life, he had none. And there were other reasons. There were always reasons.

After that, he had packed his bag and gone with them. What choice did he have? But there had been no en-route briefing. Instead, they had taken him to Atlantic City Airport. Not the commercial terminal but a remote tarmac, where a private jet stood in solitary splendor in the yellow glow of the floodlights.

'I'm not going in there if that's what you expect,' Grim said, viewing the plane the way one might look at something left behind in a toilet.

'Your file says this is your first time in a plane, and you're getting the VIP treatment instead of Spirit Airlines. People would kill for this.'

Grim, who visualized Glennis wearing cement shoes and sinking to the bottom of an adequately deep lake, remained silent. Their file was correct; he hadn't flown before. In his old life, it had been impossible. In his new life, he had never felt the urge. He was rational enough to not let the idea of flying upset him, but the possibility of where they might take him did.

They would fly him into Stewart International in Newburgh, New York. A car would be waiting to take him south on Route 9W past New

Windsor and Cornwall-on-Hudson, and from there into the Black Rock Forest along the Storm King Highway to . . .

Oh God. Black Rock Forest. There's something wrong in the hills.

But no. Airborne, the Falcon had immediately headed over the Atlantic Ocean and according to the monitor on the bulkhead, they were now somewhere south of Nova Scotia flying in a steady easterly direction.

So Europe. But why?

Glennis came over and sat opposite him. 'Welcome onboard, Mr. Grim. I haven't had the chance to tell you that with the rush earlier. I bear you no ill will for your stubbornness earlier. But have you come to terms with the fact that you're still in our service, according to the agreement you signed with my predecessors?'

'I'm in no one's service. This isn't a draft, it's a kidnapping. And I want to know why.' He hesitated. 'And why me.'

'All will become clear to you shortly. Eleanor Delveaux is in charge of November-6, a special unit within the Dutch secret service agency AIVD. She will brief you over our Dreambox.'

Dutch. Close enough. 'Is that where we're heading? To the Netherlands? Why am I going to the *Netherlands?*'

'That doesn't matter now. What matters is how you will conduct yourself toward Ms. Delveaux. She thrives on a forthrightness that might feel unorthodox to you. Your feelings are, however, of no importance. Ms. Delveaux has little patience for trivial details, so you will curb your usual cynicism. When she asks a question, you answer. When she gives you an order, you obey. When she—'

'—says roll over, I'll roll over. So you're sucking up to some Dutch lady, huh? That's not very American.'

'The Dutch are our allies.'

America doesn't give a damn about its allies unless there are rewards, Grim thought. *You either owe her, or you want something from her.*

'Tell me, Glennis. You said you're running The Point's watch on those woods. Cox and Veldheimer used to call it the "Open Your Eyes" program as a homage to a kid who might have *actually* opened our eyes, had we not been so willfully blind. Talk about cynicism.'

Glennis looked at him impassively. On her face, careful assessment and nothing more.

Grim mouth had gone dry and his hands were trembling. 'What's the deal up there?'

'I'm not at liberty to say. You know that.'

'So you expect me to kiss your ring, but can't give me anything in return? Pretty lame if you ask me.'

'I don't need to remind you that the information you're asking for is classified. Sharing it with third parties is a criminal act.'

'I'm not a third party,' he snapped.

'But you are, Mr. Grim.'

He made a scoffing sound. 'Then I want a drink.'

'Impossible. Protocol forbids me to—'

'Fuck your protocol. You said this was the VIP treatment. You can take me to hell and back for all I care, but without a drink, I'm not doing or saying jack-shit.'

She wavered, not with hesitation but calculation, then nodded to Bob, who immediately disappeared into the galley. Not dozing after all. Grim realized he had engaged in a rash negotiation and quietly cursed himself. The whole thing had caught him off guard, and allowing his aggravation to guide him would be the worst mistake he could make.

Glennis directed him to her seat at the console screen and keyed the touchpad. Bob came back with Grim's whisky, its aroma betraying their knowledge of his favorite Blue Label.

His mouth watered, but that was nothing new. That he suddenly felt wrong about it was.

'Here we go. Remember everything I told you, Grim.'

The screen established a connection and then she popped up. One glance was enough to see that, as far as Eleanor Delveaux was concerned, Glennis hadn't exaggerated. The woman sitting straight up behind her desk wore an expression that would make a wolf slink away with its tail between its legs. She also wore an expensive-looking red suit that framed her thin shoulders and a large faceted ruby ring. Behind her stood a uniformed chrome dome who was in many ways an exact photo-copy of Bob. Naval vet, watch dog, all of the above.

'Hello Ms. Delveaux. Allow me to introduce Robert Grim,' Glennis said. 'Grim, Eleanor Delveaux, Dutch General Intelligence, NOVEMBER-6.'

Delveaux didn't beat around the bush. 'My time is precious, Mr. Grim, so please listen very carefully.'

'Sir, yes sir!' Grim said and saluted with his glass. Ice cubes tinkled in the glimmer of amber at the bottom. Glennis put a hand to her brow, but Delveaux was unmoved.

'Excellent. The precarious nature of your former mission in Black Spring has familiarized you with the operating tactics of secret service agencies like NOVEMBER-6. We are essentially not much different from the West Point division you used to report to. You are acquainted with the application of secrecy in the interest of homeland security. In addition, Ms. Sopamena has led me to believe that you have a unique expertise. Unique in the world, perhaps. And that's why you're here.'

'I don't think I want to know where this is going.'

'I need your help, Grim.' Eleanor Delveaux had likely meant to project a humble or at least respectful tone, but her words sounded snappish, revealing a faintly European accent to her otherwise flawless English. 'There is a lot at stake.'

'Okay.' He planted his glass on the table a bit too forcefully. 'What wormhole did you morons open this time?'

'Yesterday morning, an incident occurred near the Dutch coastal town of Noordwijk. Some children found what seemed to be a replica of a *fluyt*, a type of 17th Century sailing vessel, called the *Oracle*, in a tulip field near the dunes. We presumed it was a replica, because as far as we've been able to establish, the original *Oracle* sank in the North Sea in 1716. However, initial tests indicate that the wood samples are several hundred years old. The Netherlands is proud of its maritime history, Mr. Grim. We keep a replica of the Dutch East India Company's *Amsterdam* in our National Maritime Museum, and a similar replica of the *Batavia* in the port of Lelystad. Our expert says that compared to the *Oracle*, both look like Lego models.'

'And of course, you know of no plans for such a replica,' Grim said, intrigued despite of himself.

'Correct.'

'Then the obvious conclusion is that it isn't.'

'We're considering that. The remains of the *Oracle* have never been found. The documentation on the ship's sinking could be wrong. It could also be a later vessel named after the original *Oracle*. But it doesn't stop there.'

'Because you have no idea how it got there.'

'That's right. We don't.'

'And there are no tracks.'

'I have to admit your deductions are astonishingly accurate.'

'I put out similar fires every day for over thirty years. Nine years in La-La land don't brain bleach that. So you got a magic fucking ship pop up in a tulip field. As miracles go, could you be any more Dutch?'

'This is no laughing matter, Mr. Grim. Some of the children entered the ship through a hatch on its deck. They have vanished. Two of their fathers also went in. They too have vanished.'

'O . . . kay . . . Did anyone go in and look for them?'

'Yes. A civilian and five police officers. They all disappeared. Only then did someone finally stop anyone else from going near it.'

'Oops.'

'None of the people who went in have come back out. They've all disappeared without a trace.'

'Phones?'

'Dead. We sent in cameras and drones. Everything disappears. Even the electronic signal dies in there. We have no explanation for it.'

'When you can't point to a logical explanation for something, it usually means that you haven't found it yet. There's always one eventually.'

'True, until you hit the exception to the rule. Which as I understand was the case with you in Black Spring.'

A photo of the ship popped up on the split screen, looking like something out of Peter Pan or Treasure Island, but tipped over and embedded in ploughed farmland. The image made Grim's stomach tighten.

'There's something else,' she continued. 'The moment something goes through the *Oracle's* hatch, a bell tolls. A ship's bell, we assume, though we haven't been able to analyze it yet, probably because it's coming from inside the ship—even if that may be a bit of a philosophical construct in this case. I was present when we sent in one of the K9s. An expensive animal, same breed as the dog that found Al-Baghdadi.' Delveaux paused and shot a meaningful look at the camera. 'We all heard it bark. At first, at least. Then we heard it *howl*. It was hard to pinpoint where it originated, because it seemed to be coming from everywhere. Then it stopped, and so did the bell.'

Grim had gone pale. It always started with dogs barking. Dogs disappearing. He had to clear his throat to continue. 'What do the media say? Sounds too big to cover it up.'

'We were lucky, if you can apply such a term to these circumstances. There was a heavy fog, a literal smoke screen, and only a handful of witnesses. A few photos popped up on social media, but there was also a press release about an upcoming open-air expo of ancient sea vessels, *Mysteries of the Dutch Seaborne Empire*. The press release was ours.'

'A publicity stunt!' Grim laughed, clapping his hands. 'That's straight out of my book. I should sue you for plagiarism.'

'Your expertise might be unique in its kind, but your methodology proved efficient. It set a precedent.'

New photos appeared on the split screen: news clippings from Dutch websites about the so-called viral campaign with snapshots of the ship. Planted in a field like it had been stranded there, and in this context, it did look like a fake. '*Mysteries of the Dutch Seaborne Empire*' was clever, because why else would you pull off such a stunt in this weather? The snapshots were spectacular. So spectacular that they must have captivated the Dutch public's attention for at least seven seconds before they scrolled to the next headline. Long live the noise of the information age. It drowned out everything the secret services didn't want you to know.

'People are zombies,' Grim said. 'Put up a smokescreen so ballsy and in-your-face and they'll eat it up with a spoon. I bet that exhibition of yours is supposed to open in June? And whaddya know, some last-minute bankruptcy will call the whole thing off.'

'Busted.'

'So what do you want from me?'

Eleanor Delveaux leaned forward, her eyes locked on the camera. 'Your experience, Mr. Grim. I need a veteran. A Mr. Fixit.'

'Moonshine behind you looks like a fine Mr. Fixit. Quite the hot-bloodsy type by the looks of him.' He turned to Glennis. 'Are you sure you don't want a drink?'

The chrome dome at Delveaux's shoulder, who had until now seemed like the world's most inscrutable bouncer, bit his lip, filling Grim with satisfaction. Hearing Glennis groan did too.

But Delveaux was unfazed. 'His name is Van Driel, and I prefer you didn't call him that. You ask where you fit in? You're experienced in damage control. I can tell by your reaction to the remarkable nature of the information I'm relaying to you, despite your . . . intoxication. I want you to lead the research team. You'll have two objectives: determining where the ship came from and how it works.' She pressed her lips together. 'My condition is that you curb your habits. Ms. Sopamena says you have a drinking problem.'

'Cheers,' he said and chugged his whisky. 'Listen, I'm not your man. I know nothing about your problem. Even less than you do.'

'You have hands-on experience with the unexplainable.'

'*One* case. That doesn't make me an expert on the supernatural.'

'In my book, that makes you the *only* expert on the supernatural. Besides, it hasn't been confirmed if we're dealing with something supernatural.'

'You're scared,' Grim suddenly said. 'You're pretending not to be, but I've seen enough fear in my life to recognize it. You're stuck with a riddle you can't solve, and it scares the hell out of you. As it should. Because let me tell you one thing. We never controlled what was happening in Black Spring. We never even *understood* it. All we could do was hide it from the outside world. And meanwhile, it went from bad to worse. These kinds of things,' he said, jabbing his finger at the camera, 'are *dangerous*. In the food chain of the unexplainable, we humans are at the bottom, and it always ends in a feast. With us on the menu.'

'Are you done, Mr. Grim?'

'No. Because the worst part is that your motivation is corrupt. Your so-called research team and its mission, there's one thing I haven't heard you mention.'

'Which is?'

'Finding the missing.'

Eleanor Delveaux looked at him dispassionately.

'What?' Grim snapped.

'Put yourself in my shoes. You're confronted with an object that seems to have manifested out of thin air and doesn't conform to the laws of nature. And you've been assigned to conceal it. *Of course* I want to find those people, but you know more than anyone that the interest of individuals can never outweigh the interest of the common good.'

'Ten individuals,' Grim snapped.

'Eleven, actually.'

'Five of whom are cops. I mean, how on earth did you keep *that* quiet?'

'We didn't. Yesterday at 3pm, there was a fire in a paper depot in the nearby town of Sassenheim. We set that fire. We needed the local press to focus their attention elsewhere. And—'

Grim's mouth opened, closed, and opened again. 'You pronounced them *dead?*'

'Five officers of the Noordwijk police force were the first on the scene and entered the smoking warehouse to make sure it was evacuated when the propane tank blew up. They were killed in the explosion. That's the official story, at least.'

'Jesus fucking Christ!'

'We had to do something. Eleven missing people is too big a story to keep quiet in the Netherlands. The fire, rather than the ship, is the headline news. Smokescreens . . . your words. We've been able to curb news of the other six, at least for now.'

'And what if they're found? Dead cops and all?'

Delveaux's lips twitched briefly. 'We'll cross that bridge when we come to it. Right now, we need to buy time. It's been more than twenty-four hours since they disappeared, and the chance of finding them alive diminishes with each passing minute.'

'You *cannot* know that.' Grim leaned back in his seat. 'Fucking amateurs.'

'All the more reason we want you onboard.'

'What about the witnesses?'

'They're secured.'

'Secured?'

'Incarcerated.'

Robert Grim was flabbergasted. Secret service agencies of small countries like the Netherlands didn't usually possess such executive authority, forced to present their cases to law enforcement or the judicial system. Apparently NOVEMBER-6 did, and Ms. Gestapo Bitch here had immediately switched into *Sicherheit* mode.

He turned away from the screen and stared out the window at the immense black of the Atlantic Ocean. The hand holding his glass was trembling. He felt a strong urge to say something that would end the conversation. After touchdown, he could wait for them to let their guard down and slip away. He had his passport, since 2013 listing 'Poughkeepsie, New York,' not 'Black Spring, New York,' as his place of birth. He could Uber back to Schiphol Airport and take the next plane to nowhere. The Atlantic City penthouse was nothing more than a way station; there were other places he could wait out his life. But Grim could find nothing to say. His curse hadn't ended in Black Spring. He was cursed for life. What reassured him was the fact that Delveaux had started a dialogue. That meant she might have something to offer. Not money: she knew he had plenty. Glennis & Co. had paid him generously to buy his silence.

He turned back to the screen and saw Delveaux impatiently waiting. 'Suppose I cooperate, I have one condition.'

She listened, then looked at Glennis. Glennis said, 'That's negotiable.'

Grim sat quietly for a long time. Then he raised his glass. Found it empty. 'Till death us do part, huh?'

It was directed at Glennis, but it was Eleanor Delveaux who answered: 'Yes. Till death us do part.'

12

By the time the news was over, and Luca was on his laptop digging for information, Barbara Wolf was in a state of hypersensitive anxiety. Any sound—the creaking of rafters in the roof, the rapping of Luca's feet against his chair's swivel casters—was enough to make her jump. She felt as if her veins were wired.

Jenna had gone to bed (thank God) and was dead to the world. With growing dismay, mother and son had watched the coverage of the business park fire in Sassenheim. When they showed the makeshift memorial in front of the police station in Noordwijk, Luca had jumped up and shouted, 'Her! It was her! I knew it!'

The camera lingered on framed photos of the dead cops among the offerings of candles and flowers before cutting to an interview with a grieving bystander.

'The curly-haired officer! She was there this morning; *she went into the ship, Mom!*'

Barbara clenched his wrists like handcuffs and gazed into his eyes. 'Are you absolutely sure, Luca?'

'For real! I'm not a hundred percent sure about the others, because they'd pushed us further back by then, but *she's* the one who came over and asked the farmer and me questions before they went inside. I remember her hair.'

'What about the others? Do you remember anything else?'

'I didn't get a good look . . . Ow, Mom, you're hurting me . . .'

'Were there five of them?'

'What?'

She practically shook him. '*Are you sure five police officers went into the ship?*'

'*Ow!* I think so. First, there were two. Then more came. I don't know how many went in, but I *think* there were five.'

Barbara let go and stared past him. 'Maybe it's a coincidence . . . They said the fire was in the afternoon. There was enough time in between for them to . . . to . . .'

'Aw, come on, you're not buying that, are you?'

No, she wasn't. If five cops died in the same town where five *other* people had so mysteriously disappeared without a trace on the same morning, and Luca could place at least one of them inside the same damn ship he had seen Alexander and the others disappear into, then any belief in a coincidence went out of the window.

So they were lying.

It didn't take long for Luca to find images of the dead officers online. The *AD** website showed them; apparently, Diana Radu's idea of civil liberties allowed current events. It also didn't take long for him to uncover the load of bull they had come up with to explain the sudden appearance of the ship. They were playing a sophisticated game. The

* *Algemeen Dagblad* is a Dutch mainstream newspaper

story had gone viral, but not viral enough to dominate the news or raise critical questions.

No one had linked the ship to the disappearances . . . because there had been no disappearances.

Luca tried googling Emma and Martin Reich, then Ibby and Casper, then Alexander and themselves. Nothing. Barbara stood behind him, clawing his turtleneck with her right hand.

It dawned on her that she had sensed something fishy going on all day, but she hadn't been able to pinpoint what it was. After all, nothing about today's events had turned out to be normal. She had been too preoccupied with Alexander to realize they were on a slippery slope going down *fast*. It started when they entered that weird building in The Hague and the bulky checkpoint worker told her to put her phone, keys and wallet in a tray before sending her through a body scanner. He put her belongings away in a locker and gave her a small key tagged with a number. Protocol, he said. And what did *she* know? Her mind was elsewhere. The key was still in her pocket.

And that was just the beginning. Yes, they were doing all they could to protect her and Luca from the newshounds, so Diana had assured her, which was why they had a safehouse in an undisclosed nearby location where she and her family could lie low. For some reason, it had all seemed to make perfect sense.

Don't worry, Barbara. Every state investigator in the west of the country is on the lookout for Alexander, so it's only a matter of time before we find him. Wouldn't it be nice for you to be nearby when we do?

Except this safehouse came with an electric gate that hermetically sealed the access drive, ever since the delivery van with the tinted windows had left.

In a flash of horror, Barbara cupped her hands over her mouth. She remembered how casually Diana had asked about their planned activities for the day. Just her book club, Barbara had answered. Six friends and two of their hubbies gathering at Bianca's in Valkenburg to discuss their Pick-of-the-Month, this time Colson Whitehead's *The Underground Railroad*.

Suppose Bianca had received a text from Barbara's number that said that she had a headache and would have to skip tonight's session?

Nobody knew where they were.

Nobody knew anything was wrong.

'Try Facebook,' she urged Luca.

'I can't. It's blocked.'

'Try again.'

He did, but to no avail. She told him to try Gmail. Outlook. Yahoo. Twitter. All returned failed connection notifications.

Then she had an idea. 'Go back to the *AD* website.'

Luca did, and some scrolling and clicking led them to a contact form. He looked up and visibly shook at the expression on her face. 'What do you want to do, Mom?'

'Send an SOS. Move over.'

But she had barely squatted next to him when the webpage poofed with the same failed connection notice. Luca frowned, clicked refresh, went back, forward. The *AD* was still there. The contact form wasn't.

'I don't get it. It was just there . . .'

Barbara pinched her closed eyelids with her fingertips and frantically tried to think. 'Try accessing a support page. Some of them use live chat boxes that aren't bots. I think Nordstrom has one.'

Luca opened Nordstrom's webpage. They indeed had. 'What do you want me to say?'

But then Nordstrom went dark too.

'*Pieces of shit!*' she yelled.

'What's happening?'

'Don't you get it? Big Brother is watching us.'

His mouth closed abruptly. Luca needed a moment to process, but then he rolled back his chair. '*Now* do you believe me?'

She got up with creaking knees. Barbara was no longer thinking of a slippery slope but a raging river. They were being swept away in the middle of it, and she hadn't grabbed the lifeline she *should* have seen.

They dangled Alexander in front of you like a carrot, and you jumped at their promise of a swift, happy ending. They dismissed everything else as the fantasy of a confused child. Your child.

But Luca had known all along, and she hadn't believed him. Dear God, what had he witnessed this morning?

Suddenly a fear as sharp as shrapnel tore through her. Her eyes bulged, and she touched her throat with her fingertips. If they were willing to declare the cops *dead* in their grotesque cover story . . . what did that say about their belief in Alexander?

She marched through the bungalow and snatched the button phone from the console. It was a clumsy attempt, and it fell to the floor. Her hands were trembling so badly that it took her two tries to pick it up. She dialed . . . screw it, what difference did it make? She dialed 112 and brought the phone to her ear.

'Good evening, Barbara,' she heard Diana's honey-dripping voice. 'What can I do you for?'

'*Where's Alexander?*'

'I'm sorry to tell you I don't have any updates at this time. Otherwise, you would have heard from us. But the search team has been reinforced with special defense units, and . . .'

'You're not searching at all! The news said that the officers Luca saw go into that ship are dead! *Dead!* What are you not telling me?

On the other side of the room, Luca clenched his fist and bared his teeth. *Give it to 'em, Mom.* Her eyes suddenly welled up and she flashed him the OK sign.

'Oh, that was such a tragedy,' Diana responded without hesitation. 'Who could have imagined? It's a devastating blow to the Noordwijk police force. Yes, two of the officers killed in the fire were indeed present at this morning's incident with the ship. They were under terrible pressure to keep it under wraps; maybe that led them to misjudge the situation.'

'You're lying! It's ludicrous!'

'I can assure you it is not, Barbara. It was a tragic coincident.'

'I don't believe you. And an *exhibition*? Is *that* what you're telling the media?

'But . . .' Diana stalled and sounded so sincere that despite everything Barbara started to doubt herself. 'Didn't they tell you about that? Dammit, I knew I should have stayed for the briefing. My deepest apologies, that's our mistake and should never have occurred.'

'I'm not following . . .'

'Well . . . *of course* we had to come up with something to distract the public, Barbara. Reporters would've been all over it. They would have swarmed the site and trampled the evidence. You know that, right? Finding these people is our top priority, and the last thing we want is to jeopardize the search. I'm sure you share our sentiment. That's why we provided you with the safehouse.'

'This isn't a safehouse, it's a prison.' Her voice quivered, and she hated it. 'Your goal was never to protect us from the media but to protect the media from us.'

'But Barbara . . . surely you understand this is all standard procedure? You're upset and confused. And who can blame you? We have ample experience with people in extremely stressful situations. One slip and you could inadvertently put the entire investigation at risk. How could we possibly take such a risk with Alexander's life at stake?'

Game, set, match. Diana's claims made so much sense that Barbara could feel any resistance leaking out of her like air from a punctured tire.

'You can't take our freedoms away,' she tried again, but without conviction, and Diana knew it.

'Of course not, we're not China. Tomorrow we'll reevaluate the situation, but for now, it's essential that you two get some rest. You've been to hell and back today. If you feel the need to talk, I can arrange for a trauma therapist to come over at any time. Better yet, I'll pop over myself in a bit. Would you like that?'

'Please don't,' Barbara whispered. 'I just want Alexander.'

'Then rest assured that we're doing everything in our power to find him. And that you'll hear from us the moment we have any news.'

'*Find him.* I don't care who you are or what you're up to. But *find* him, please.'

She hung up.

And had to muster the courage to face Luca.

13

Just after 4 p.m. the next day, the Falcon 7X touched down at Schiphol Airport under a pale but clear winter sky and taxied to a windy platform for private jets. Eleanor Delveaux and her chrome dome watchdog were waiting for them on the tarmac beside an obsidian black car—not a Dodge Durango, Robert Grim noticed, but a hybrid Jag.

'You guys have a lot more style than your American counterparts,' he said, nodding to Glennis after she had unfolded the airstairs and started down before him. 'But hey, what else is there to do in Europe than drive around all day looking pretty.'

'Your reputation precedes you Mr. Grim,' Delveaux said.

'Aw!' Grim clapped his hands, chipper as a chickadee. 'Only good things, I hope!'

'A word of advice: don't let it get you into trouble.'

She didn't shake his hand, and Van Driel greeted him with only a curt nod. Whoop-de-doo. What wasn't whoop-de-doo was Glennis' shift in attitude. He had caught a couple hours of sleep on the plane and was now sharp enough to discern that she had gone from self-assured to a subtle but almost weaselly form of anticipation.

'Hello Ms. Delveaux.'

'Glennis.' They exchanged a few words in Dutch.

So you do suck up to her, he thought. *What does she have on you?*

Once they were on the highway, he decided to inquire in a roundabout way and asked how he had appeared on their radar. There were only four of them in the car; after loading their bags in the trunk, Bob stayed behind at the airport.

'It can't be news to you that friendly intelligence services share intel. Due to her Dutch-American heritage, Ms. Sopamena has proved a valuable asset to us in matters of counterterrorism. We like to gather information on anomalies, Mr. Grim. Your past is one of the blips that showed up on our radar. A most remarkable blip, might I add.'

That may have convinced others but not Grim. Not with this kind of remarkability. Good ole' Abe Lincoln himself had bestowed exclusive authority over Black Spring with a special division at West Point. After that, even successive presidents hadn't known about its troubles. The matter had simply been too explosive; the danger of it leaking too great. And after 2012, a whole new load of shit had been added to the pile.

I don't need to tell you the information you're asking for is classified, Glennis had said to him on the plane. *Sharing it with third parties is a criminal act.*

But she had done exactly that. With a foreign spook no less.

Whatever the deal between them, Grim thought it better—safer—to find out what it was asap, because *he* was the leverage.

They delivered him and Glennis to a highway hotel and gave them thirty minutes to freshen up, which Grim used to check out the minibar (only a peewee bottle of Absolut Vodka, which he drank anyway just for the sake of it). After the pit stop, they continued on jammed back roads, stop-and-go all the way. In his sixty-seven years, Grim had never traveled beyond New York and New Jersey, and his first impression of the Netherlands—crowded, flat, neurotically organized and filled to the brim with luminescent greenhouses—didn't make him feel like he had missed much. Good. Robert Grim liked seeing his suspicions confirmed.

By the time they arrived in the ops area (Delveaux called it Every Man's End, which admittedly was a good name), the sky had turned dark and Grim felt like they were a rock band being directed backstage at Coachella. At least until they passed the first corridor behind the shielded barricades, where the regular rent-a-cops had been replaced by clusters of tense-looking marines patrolling what looked like a giant stage tent. Van Driel navigated a trench of steel road plates between the outer perimeter and the tent, passing a multitude of semi-trailers, generators, boom lifts and even a crane. Grim was tempted to ask Delveaux where the burger 'n' beer stalls were but decided not to risk it.

'We never got this kind of budget,' he commented instead, sounding crankier than he intended.

'Cry me a river,' Glennis said.

Some walkie-talkie guy scanned their license plate and gave the OK for the tarpaulin to be opened. They drove inside and for the first time, Grim laid eyes on the ship. The sight shook him, and not just because the area was teeming with armed soldiers and folks in white coats or protective suits, none of whom looked like they knew what they were doing, even after thirty-six hours—a recipe for disaster in Grim's book. No, it was well beyond that. Everyone had seen replicas of old wooden ships, but nothing compared to what he was looking at now. The *Oracle* was astonishingly *real*. You didn't need a PhD in maritime history to see that. She was lying on her side, caught in the glare of floodlights suspended from scaffolds. Yet even the harsh, two-dimensional quality of the light couldn't diminish its grandeur . . . or how out of place it looked.

'Sweet Jesus,' Grim said in a thin voice.

'Quite something, isn't it?'

He glanced at Delveaux. A vague smile played on the corners of her lips, and Grim thought, *You've got something up your sleeve. I don't know what your scheme is, but it's no good.*

Van Driel stopped the Jag and the door was opened from the outside. Eleanor got out, then Grim, with Glennis and Van Driel trailing close behind. A stocky man wearing a lab coat over his suit welcomed them. The pale light of the iPad Pro in his hands reflected in his specs.

'Marc, this is Robert Grim,' Delveaux said. 'Robert, meet Dr. Marc Leffers of the Netherlands Forensic Institute.'

'Pleased to meet you,' Dr. Leffers said.

'Do all of you here speak English?'

'That's our claim to fame, Mr. Grim. English, German, French, you name it. The only language we Dutch don't speak is Russian.' The doc made a curious whinnying sound, which might have been a laugh.

Delveaux rolled her eyes. 'Zippity-zip, Marc. Updates?'

'Still no trace of the missing,' Dr. Leffers said, leading them toward the ship's stem. 'Toxicology has received our wood samples. We have no reason to believe we'll find any chemical or viral contamination, but we're taking no chances. That's why you see all those, um . . . spacemen walking around.' More whinnying. 'But our top story tonight is that we have people inside.'

'You went *in*?' Delveaux asked sharply.

'That's right. As per your instructions, we didn't drill into the hull or the deck, although that will probably be necessary in the long run to determine how the ship works . . . and exactly how *far* it works. No, somebody had the bright idea to open the poop deck hatch instead, all the way over there at the mizzenmast. Any drones we've flown in there have all come out. As did our dogs.'

'That's remarkable.'

They stopped short of the bow and Grim could see the open hatch on the forecastle. Scaffolding with fixed lights and cameras had been erected in front of it, but the area was empty and cordoned off with red-and-white tape. Toward the *Oracle*'s stern, space-suited investigators on more scaffolding were feeding cables and hoses into a second hatch.

Grim looked down at his muddy shoes and thought that the only thing that could have made this spectacle more surreal was if it were April and the whole circus had popped up in a bed of red tulips.

'Remarkable is putting it mildly, Ms. Delveaux. We've established a safe route from the stern hatch through the lower decks, all the way to the front. Drones and dogs first, of course. But from a historical perspective, the ship is truly a marvel. Right behind the hatch over here we found a shelter where the lower-ranking sailors used to be quartered, called the "fo'c'sle". Get this: when Mozart was sent in there from the inside, he sniffed around a bit and darned if he didn't just jump out through the cursed hatch, all barking and wagging.'

'Mozart?' Grim remarked.

'Yes.' He was quiet for a moment. 'Unfortunately, we lost Beethoven.'

'And the media?' Delveaux asked.

Dr. Leffers gazed at her in disbelief. 'You're asking me about the media after I just explained to you that this hatch might be creating a distortion of the space-time continuum? That we've possibly discovered a portal for teleportation?'

'That's fabulous, but let me remind you that it's my responsibility to keep this operation under wraps. If anything leaks, it's not space-time that will be distorted.'

The doc flushed. 'Um, right. No problems today, to my knowledge. Your intelligence staff can brief you further, but as far as I can see, your smokescreen has proved quite effective. The minute it goes commercial, no one wants to give you free publicity anymore.' He heehawed at his own joke.

There was a signal from the technicians at the back. Dr. Leffers touched his screen, and Grim, Glennis, Delveaux and Van Driel gathered around. Apparently, the iPad held a live connection to a man inside the ship, receiving razor-sharp POV images from what was likely a GoPro mounted to a helmet. The camera followed the rhythm of his footfalls through a narrow, tipped-over room with an arched ceiling and straight wooden walls. A torchlight was swaying left and right, and the image followed.

'Look, Peter's in the orlop now. That's where the crew's supplies were stored. And this passageway here leads up to the fo'c'sle in front of us.' He pointed up to the hatch, not taking his eyes off the screen. As the GoPro man continued his expedition, the sounds of stumbling came from the hull. A square of bright light flashed on-screen. Looking up, Grim saw a man in a gasmask and white suit emerge from the dark beyond the hatch. The screen now showed people bent over an iPad. They were looking down at themselves.

'Peter!' Dr. Leffers called, raising his hand. The man in the white suit waved back.

Then it all went south fast.

Grim heard the man say something. In the real world, it sounded muffled from behind the mask but from the various iPads the technicians carried, it was a ricocheting chorus of, '*Alles kits hier.*'

'Everything's okay,' Glennis interpreted for him.

One of Dr. Leffer's coworkers asked him something through a headset—what he was seeing, Glennis translated for Grim. The headset lady was further off to their right, and Grim saw the man lean out through the hatch to face her. If you ignored the hazmat suit, he could be a man leaning out of a window making conversation to a neighbor.

His voice again echoed from the speakers, and by his body language and the way he shrugged his shoulders, Grim guessed it was something like *nothing special, just an ordinary hold.* He couldn't be sure though, because before Glennis had the chance to translate, the man had leaned back into the hatch and the image went dead on all their screens. Someone screamed and this time Grim didn't need an interpreter to get the gist: '*Peter, niet doen!*'

Out of thin air, a bell started to toll.

Three men jumped onto the scaffolding; one of them dropped his iPad, shattering the screen. The scaffolding wobbled under their weight and the floodlights moved like spots in a theatre. Back at the aftercastle, technicians were hastily jumping *off* the scaffolding, causing one to tilt and crash its equipment onto those fleeing below. Grim heard sheer panic in their screams. He saw Dr. Leffers eyeing the now empty hatch in bewilderment. Glennis covered her mouth with her hands. Seemingly calm, Van Driel stood with his hands on his hips, his face expressing wonder if anything. Eleanor Delveaux closed her eyes and bowed her head.

'*Peter, kom terug!*' one of the men on the scaffolding yelled, leaning so far forward into the hatch that the other two had to grab him by the waist and yank him back. '*Peter, hier!*'

The white suits scurried around like a colony of ants. One tripped over rope hanging from the main mast. Another assisted a technician from under the pile of aluminum beams, his ankle apparently broken. A bunch of them were hauling in the cables and hoses through the rear hatch, and two of Peter's coworkers eventually came scrambling out, ripping off their gasmasks and gasping for air.

At the front hatch, the wannabe hero shouted again to Peter and reached in to grab him. But there was no Peter. Just his choked screams of profound terror.

It's the bell, Grim thought, as it tolled amidst all the chaos. *That sound is not of this world. Or rather, not of this time. It's coming straight from ages past, when this foul thing sailed the North Sea bound for who knows where. Maybe the same destination where that poor man Peter is now headed.*

He turned and walked toward the tent's exit on unsteady legs. Delveaux came in pursuit and, despite her high heels, managed to catch up, followed by Glennis on a much wider margin. At least that was praiseworthy.

'Where the hell are you going, Grim?'

He stopped and saw how tired and worn out Delveaux looked. Not afraid though, and that worried him. She very much should be.

'By your own logic,' he said, clearing his throat, 'that man is doomed.'

'I'm sorry. It should never have happened. Leffers' ass is grass. Tomorrow, we'll—'

'Step one,' Grim interrupted her, 'is for you to move this puppet show of yours. To a bunker, an army compound, I don't care. I need a secure testing site equipped with every goddam amenity you can think of.'

'You want us to move the ship?' She turned and looked in dismay at the chaos still unfolding behind them.

'Read my lips. This is a fucking train wreck, and I don't want to lose any more people!' He was no longer able to conceal his rage. 'If there are trucks that can transport Boeing fuselages, you can transport this ship. Take down the masts and wrap it all up with a ribbon and a bow if you have to. I'm not going to be your patsy unless I can guarantee the safety of my team.'

'Understood. It's a fair request.'

'Step two: you can decide whose on the team, but if I don't like them, they're out. Is that clear?'

Impassively, she said, 'I understand from your file that you don't really like anyone, Mr. Grim.'

'All the more reason for you to get cracking. Now, if you'll excuse me . . .'

He continued toward the exit, and now Glennis came forward. 'Where are you going?'

'To the beach,' Grim snapped.

'You can't just—'

But Delveaux grabbed her wrist—*pick your battles.* Without acknowledging the dumbfounded conscript at the entrance, Grim yanked the tarpaulin aside and walked into the night.

Just drink, he thought. *Just drink and you can make it all stop. Including your privileged little life, but that's part of the equation. You know that, right?*

He knew. He was dying for it.

14

It was going on midnight when Luca Wolf slipped out of the strange house in the dunes. Serving as his prison for over twenty-four hours, it was suffocating him, and his mom's increasingly erratic behavior was driving him nuts. She had allowed Jenna and him only a minute or two of airtime in the afternoon, at the back of the house and under close supervision when Diana had come by to report that she had nothing to report. It was unbearable. He *had* to get out.

The sound of the tv was coming from the den. Maybe Mom had fallen asleep in front of it, or maybe she had turned in on the big bed with Jenna, who was thrilled to snuggle up for the second night.

The minute his foot crossed the doorstep, he cold wind attacked him. Luca turtled inside his parka and shut the door behind him. The edges of the pavement were buried under drifts of fine sand that seemed to be crawling in the bitter wind, as if the dunes were gradually conquering back the world those foolish humans had stolen. Luca walked to the driveway, and overhead, the housefront camera followed his every move. Motion-activated. Night vision too? Worth a shot. He turned around and gave it the finger.

It was a clear winter night. The wind had dispersed most of the clouds, and a cold, starry sky watched over him. He didn't take the obvious direction to the entrance gate (pointless) but instead crossed the driveway and started to climb the steep dune on the other side. He had to feel his way as he plodded through the loose sand, sinking into it, and constantly flailing his arms for balance. He could hear the steady thunder of the sea in the distance.

What if his dad never came back?

The past twenty-four hours had given Luca ample time to think, and he simply could not believe they had gone inside the ship to look for him. Somewhere within, whatever fucked-up meaning of the word 'within' was implied, his dad must still be wandering around, alone, probably mad with fear. Would he run into Emma? Or one of the others? What if rescue took too long and he starved to death? What if he *died* and left Luca behind with his mom and sister?

He tried to push the thought away. The marram grass voiced its ghostly whisper and seemed to bend toward him from all directions. He didn't want to cry again. He didn't want to keep replaying that horrible image of his dad falling overboard and disappearing into the waves, his face purple with death-patterns. It had just been his imagination, not a prophecy. Luca upped his pace, now using his hands to grab the saw-toothed blades of grass as the wind around him whispered, *In the cod hold, he's in the cod hold now . . .*

He reached the crest of the dune and stood panting. A hot stitch ran from his waist to his shoulder. The chain-link fence was right in front of him, and he stuck his fingers through the mesh. Beyond, the dunes rolled into an endless wilderness like the sea itself, revealing only pitch-black outlines. The sole interruption in this landscape was the distinct shape of a house, maybe three hundred yards ahead. Luca saw a faint orange-yellowy gleam inside and frowned.

The house was identical to theirs.

He craned his neck, his cheeks almost touching the fence. A silhouette of a man scurried about in front of the same style of panoramic window as in their bungalow. Tall, slightly bent . . . Luca recognized that posture.

Easy kid, calm down . . . what the hell are you doing on my land?

It was impossible to be sure at such a distance, but Luca knew what he knew. He was looking at the farmer he had bumped into after his dad disappeared into the *Oracle*. The tulip grower who had called the cops . . . and then begged the cops not to go in.

How many witnesses are they holding? Luca wondered. *How many safe-houses do they have?*

It had to be a big operation. How else could they keep it a secret? Most likely, the government was involved. Although—and this is where Luca's penchant for drama came into play—not the *regular* government. Even Luca understood that locking up innocent people without a warrant or trial was unconstitutional. A *shadow* government.

If only Emma were here. They could have squabbled about it forever. But wherever Emma was now, Emma couldn't squabble. Wherever she was, it was likely dark and cold, darker and colder even than here, and . . .

Wait, is anyone else there? Luca, is that you?

He killed that thought. Not out here in the dark, no sir. He got moving, following the fence to the left down a steep, dark slope into the lee of the dune. The house in the distance was no longer visible, but every thirty steps or so he spotted the small red eye of a camera. As he descended, the terrain got jumbled with seaberry bushes, forcing him to swerve further away from the fence.

He hit the trail of crushed seashells before he saw it. In front of him, the fence was interrupted by a wooden swing gate. He was surprised to find it ajar.

A shadow emerged from the dark, and Luca yelped. A light flashed. Luca raised his arm and turned away.

'A jolly good evening!' a voice crooned.

The light was lowered, and now Luca saw a giant of a man waiting on the trail on the other side of the gate. A coiled wire spiraled between his ear and the collar of his puffer jacket. A security guard.

'Cripes, you startled me,' Luca said.

'Sorry, pal.'

'I'm not your pal.'

'Suits me.' He grinned, not in the least affected. 'Enjoying a nightly stroll, are we?'

'Yep. And you're gonna tell me I can't stroll here.'

'Now why would I do that?' the guard said, courteously opening the gate wider. 'It's a tad dark, but the stars can show you the way. If you stay on the trail, that is.'

Suspicious, Luca didn't move. 'So I can go on?'

'I don't see why not.'

Without another word, he stepped through the gate and past the guard on the other side. His heart was thumping in his throat. Eyes fixed on the dark in front of him, Luca followed the narrow trail up into the dunes, still expecting the gatekeeper to call out or stop him at any moment. He didn't, but when Luca put fifty feet between them, he heard him speak into his chest mic.

On each side, the trail was now lined with regular barbed wire, and the thicket of undergrowth beyond it too dense to risk straying. Besides, the guard's advice had felt more like a warning, so Luca decided to heed it . . . for now.

Several hundred steps later, he reached the crest of the last dune and looked out over the sea. He froze in his tracks, enthralled by the force of the howling wind that swept his hair back and salted his lips, quickly numbing his face. Tears drew horizontal trails across his temples. It was a moonless night, but the stars and their reflection cast enough light to make out the angry waves assaulting the coast, throwing spume far along the beach.

Luca was a child of the North Sea, and it held no secrets from him. Not a single Sunday of his childhood had gone by without his dad taking him to the beach, together combing it for washed-up treasures like driftwood, fishing nets, ray egg cases (his dad called them mermaid's purses) or coins that had slipped through holes in beach-goers' pockets. They would dwell for hours where the water and land came together and eat ice cream or drink hot cocoa at one of the Katwijk beach pavilions, spreading out their booty on wooden benches. Luca knew the sea stormy and calm, but tonight he sensed a threat he had never felt before, invisible and persuasive. It wasn't in the wind or the steady lashing of the surf, but he couldn't quite nail *what* it was.

He started down the swale to the beach when a dark figure standing motionless in the sand about three hundred feet to his south caught his eye. He could only see the man's outline and the orange glow of a cigarette, so Luca figured he was standing with his back to the wind. To his right—north—he thought he saw another, although it was overcast there and practically pitch dark. *So, the gatekeeper has friends*, Luca thought. They sure as hell wouldn't be so accommodating as to let him pass. This stretch of coastline was apparently his private beach for tonight.

He ambled all the way to the water's edge where the sand was wet and firm and razor clams crunched beneath his sneakers. There he stopped, as salty spume splashed cold in his face. Luca turned and leaned back into the wind, looking up at the stars. There was Orion, the mighty hunter with his illustrious belt. And there, Cassiopeia's W. Luca felt exposed and insignificant beneath them. The depth of the night sky seemed to be tumbling over him, and he staggered. He imagined that ten thousand years ago, on this very shore a boy might have gazed up at the same starlit sky, recognizing the constellations not as Orion or Cassiopeia but as manifestations of his own spirit world. A bird man, a medicine woman with a cane, a mammoth with giant, curved tusks. If you looked long enough, the stars would take on all these forms.

Luca shuddered and buried his hands deep into his pockets. A plaintive cry came from the sea, more human than seagull. It was answered by another to the right. Then they—whatever *they* were—fell silent again, leaving the wind to howl alone.

Something was wrong.

His head was too troubled with the confusing, painful emotions of the past two days to figure out what it was. All he knew was that it was true . . . just like he had known something was wrong when he and Emma had walked around the *Oracle* yesterday morning.

'Dad?' he heard himself say with a hoarse voice, and underneath his parka, the hairs on his neck stood on end.

It was the sea. Shadows, wild in the wind, reached out for him like fingers.

Something was coming.

Luca's mouth went dry. He suppressed the urge to cry for help. Instead, his body broke out in a cold sweat. What had gotten into him? Why that sudden urge to get the hell out of here, far away, quickly?

He stumbled back a few steps and his sneaker hit something, making a hollow *ting*. A bottle was his first thought, but when he kneeled to pick it up, he was surprised to find that it was some sort of tube, covered in battered leather the length of his hand. When he twisted the copper-colored ring at the tip, three brass segments slid out with the crunching sound that his mom called a *sand-on-a-sandwich* when they picnicked on the beach.

A spyglass.

Maybe a birdwatcher had lost it. Or a sailor, ages ago. The nautical term for it was 'monocular', Luca remembered. Under different circumstances, he would have been thrilled with his find, a unique piece for his collection. But now, the spyglass only increased the sprawling sense of doom.

Turn around. Get out of here.

He patted the lens and almost sliced his fingertips on the cracked glass. Still, he raised the spyglass toward his eye.

Don't. You don't want to look through that.

Suddenly he got scared, *really* scared, because he knew what was about to happen. But it was too late.

Squeezing one eye shut, he gazed through the monocular. He shouldn't have been able to see anything but a perfect circle of black blur. But he *could* see. He saw the sea. He saw the rolling waves, he saw the rising tide. He saw ancient constellations bowing over him. And he *heard* something, too.

He heard the sloshing of footfalls in the surf.

Not real, he tried to assure himself, but his heart raced and his breaths grew short. *Not real. Just a gull flapping its wings.*

He lowered the spyglass and stared wide-eyed out over the black water. Nothing. Too dark. He couldn't hear anything either. So he looked through the eyepiece again . . . and now it was unmistakable. Splashing in shallow water. Right in front of him, in the surf. Coming his way fast.

And there was another sound. A deep, dark, rumbling crescendo far out at sea.

Luca wanted to run but couldn't. His legs simply didn't comply, his sneakers seemed to be sucked into the sand. Again, he stared into the night unaided but saw and heard nothing.

For the third time, he looked through the spyglass, and panic hit. *Slosh slosh slosh.* Close. *Fast.* He couldn't *see* anything . . . or could he? Did the water splash unnaturally right in front of him?

Luca would never be sure if he saw a specter that night. But he *did* see something else, a mirage further out on the water. He saw a long, white line of spume in the light of the screaming stars, stretching north to south. A swirling line rolling toward him from the horizon. And he suddenly understood what the rumble was and why it had brought a feeling of threat.

He dropped the spyglass. Luca turned and ran, sneakers digging into the sand, his hair fluttering in front of him as if showing him the way, and he didn't look back at what was following right behind.

15

Luca Wolf wasn't the only one battling his demons in the dunes that night. So was Robert Grim, less than eight miles down the beach. After the debacle at the *Oracle,* he set off at a brisk pace and soon left the ops area far behind him. Following the light of his phone, he found a trail that rose steeply into the dunes. Before he knew it, he was lost, but he didn't care. His head hunched into his collar, he pushed forward and watched the icy wind carry his breath away.

In the hills, the woods, my breath formed little clouds. I was walking back to the former Popolopen Visitor Center from the Grant residence, where bad luck seemed to linger that fall and now had come to a new, tragic low. The preceding days had been subzero dawn-to-dusk, but that night a thaw had set in, and I knew some unspeakable thing was about to unfold. It was still five or six days away, but I knew anyway. Owls were roaming the woods that night. Owls and weasels and . . .

He tried to cut his thoughts short, but too late.

. . . her. She had been there too.

A deep, elementary cold possessed not only his body but his soul. It was ages since he had last thought about these things. Never had the past been fully exorcised, though. The curse Robert Grim had taken with him from Black Spring was the curse of remembering.

He shivered uncontrollably but couldn't shake it off. The wind was still picking up. Every now and then, it would roar over the dunes with such strength that Grim had to turn his back against the blast until it passed. Out here in the dark, he gave his thoughts free reign.

It was Christmas Day 2012 when he escaped from what had bound him to Black Spring his entire life and, at fifty-seven, his life commenced for the second time. The drinking commenced in September of the following year. By then, he had resigned himself to complying with The Point's arrangements. Veldheimer and Cox personally handed them to him in a black leather binder after he had been under twenty-four-seven supervision in a high-security facility for over two months, at first on the academy grounds, then, when they had dared to put miles between him and the source, in Poughkeepsie. They could have claimed that his rehabilitation was their chief concern, but they called a spade a spade. Their intention was to curb any aftereffects . . . and his urge to talk. He hadn't felt that urge, but Grim understood it served him better to keep them guessing.

The binder had contained a new birth certificate and passport, a retirement plan with a generous savings account and the key to the penthouse in Atlantic City.

'This could be your new life,' Veldheimer had said. 'We give you something, you give us something. Think about it, but not for too long.'

He had. There had been two alternatives: he could leave and start over as a John Doe somewhere, or he could call it a day and end his life. He briefly considered the latter—no need to be melodramatic about it. And if he got the travel bug later, he could always indulge himself with the ridiculous sum of money he found in his savings account. It was hush money, yes, but he decided to take it. Paramount was that Atlantic City was far away from Black Spring.

Robert Grim was born on August 17, 1955, the night Atlantic hurricane Diane had flooded the Hudson Valley. In his old life, he used to say that the storm had puked him out, but then he had discovered he didn't like the ocean. The salty air irritated his skin and the constant surge of the waves outside his panoramic window gave him the willies.

But it was better than the alternative. Better than the Hudson Valley. Better than the hills and the woods.

The Black Rock Forest, where that fateful November, the creeks started to bleed as if the earth itself was wounded. I misread all the omens. When things started to go haywire, I was constantly one step behind, making all the wrong decisions. I was playing catch-up and it proved fatal.

The memories never haunted his sleep. They tormented him when he was awake, and that was far worse. First, it was the dead. He saw their faces reflected in the panoramic window, looking out at sea one chrome-colored day. They had all been there, but the boy was the worst, with his purple, swollen face, the rope burns on his neck and the accusing eyes bulging from the pressure on his brain.

'You weren't there to stop me,' he heard a rasping whisper behind him, and Grim swung around. The condo was empty, but he had never felt altogether alone anymore after that. So he drew the curtains and never opened them again.

One day, pulling dirty socks out from under the bed, he heard footsteps and looking under it, he saw emaciated and mud-stained feet on the other side. He couldn't move. He could see the filthy hem of the dress, the claw-like, cleft toenails, the rotting, bruised skin. With a clank, the rusted, iron chains fell to the ground in front of the feet, and Grim screamed.

The next day, he bought a box spring with a frame that reached the floor, so nothing could hide under it. It had felt safer.

Safer . . . maybe, but that won't set you free. That was the voice in his head, his sole constant companion for the last ten years, one he wouldn't mind showering with sarin to silence it.

Because she never left, you see. Not really. No amount of Blue Label will expel her from your memory; no blend can put that genie back in the bottle. You can watch as many cutesy YouTube videos as you like—puppies and bunnies and kittens playing with yarn—and you think they'll make you feel all gooey inside, you think they'll distract you, but eventually, you'll always see dead ermines, floating to the surface of opaque, rank water. Eventually you'll be condemned to relive that dark, terrible night over and over again, and you'll remember it the same every time. Because that night you went to her and—

He cut off the voice before it could continue. Enough. It was pointless to rake up the past. Even Veldheimer and Cox had abandoned their efforts to understand why he had been the last of the Mohicans. Some things couldn't be said and some things you just didn't talk about. Sometimes silence was the best answer.

Grim reached the crest of the dune. To his right, the town of Noordwijk lit up the sky. The beach clubs on the boulevard would be closed at this off-season hour, but somewhere, a hotel bar was probably still open. He considered going to find it. Drinking didn't keep the demons away, but that had never been his reason anyway.

The reason was what Robert Grim called the psychological Doppler effect.

In 2015, he started having gallbladder problems. Yuri Fisher, the young, good-natured gastroenterologist at the Atlanticare HealthPlex, said his drinking problem wasn't necessarily the boogeyman but insisted that he seek help anyway. 'Because your cholesterol is through the roof and your blood pressure is a hate crime. We can take care of the gall-stones, Robert, but the coronary that will knock on your door to wish you a happy sixty-fifth birthday is a different kettle of fish.'

That'll be one more visitor than I'm expecting, Grim thought, but he chirped, 'Then I'll have to feed it some cake, won't I?'

Dr. Fisher chuckled. 'Red velvet. Strokes just love sugar bombs like that. Seriously though, if you want, I can recommend some people trained in substance abuse recovery.'

'If I were to say, "that would be pointless", then you'd probably say, "every sucker who needs help says that" and then I'd say, "but I'm different" and you'd say, "different my ass".'

'Exactly, so why don't we cut to the chase?'

'Except in this case, it really would be pointless.'

'And why's that?'

Robert Grim had looked him straight in the eye and witnessed the psychological Doppler effect at play. He asked Dr. Fisher if he remembered a town by the name of Black Spring.

'Arkansas?' Fisher said.

'No, Black Spring, New York. Near West Point.'

'Oh yeah, I think I've heard of it. My sister lives in Tarrytown.'

'Do you also remember it being in the news a couple years back?'

Dr. Fisher's eyes started to flicker. His expression became puzzled, then bewildered. 'Refresh my memory. What was that all about again? All those people left or something . . .'

'The entire town disappeared. A few thousand people.'

'That was a strange story. Right. Now that you mention it, I do remember seeing something about it on TV.'

'CBS *This Morning?*'

'Yes! Sounds about right.'

'And then you forgot about it.'

'I guess I did.' He sounded dreamy. Confused.

'What would you say if I told you that *everyone* forgot everything Norah O'Donnell and the news reports had to say about it?'

There was an awkward, charged moment in which Dr. Fisher appeared to have either sunk into deep contemplation or to be slowly emerging from general anesthesia. Finally, an amiable smile breached his face. 'Yes, that would be pretty strange when you put it that way.'

He fingered the pages of his calendar, and his eyes started to wander off. Robert Grim told him that a darkness had come to Black Spring, that the town had been perpetually cursed and that it had ended in unspeakable horror. He told the young doctor that as the sole survivor, he now carried a fuckload of survivor guilt and that there was nobody, literally *nobody* he could talk to, because the entire incident was erased from everyone's memory, just like the town itself. Dr. Fisher admitted it was all very strange, then had his assistant find a date for the gallbladder surgery.

This was the psychological Doppler effect. Talk about the disappearance of Black Spring, and a strange, unnatural quirk shifted the frequency of the words halfway between source and listener, like the siren of a passing ambulance. The effect had been extensively documented by The Point, whose operatives were also under its influence, though less so thanks to their *Open Your Eyes* program: constant exposure in order to battle superimposed forgetfulness. Their findings were less than satisfactory. Where Black Spring, New York, had once been, there was a collective blind spot. It was creepy if you thought about it, because if the influence was still that strong . . . what did that say about its *source?*

Now there was a thought Robert Grim didn't want to dwell on.

In any case, he had been telling Dr. Fisher the truth. Anything approximating therapy was absurd at best. So he was alone, in every sense of the word. A shot of whisky at least somewhat numbed the loneliness.

Once again, he looked out over the lights of the town and reckoned his feet were ready to carry him that way, but on impulse, he turned the other way into the dark. He snuggled deep into his coat when he reached the beach. The sea wind carried the long, ethereal notes of a funeral hymn that resonated in his old bones. Was it always to be this opera of doom and gloom in this strange country, where he didn't want to be, where everything felt so unknown and *unwelcome?*

She was also from the Netherlands, remember? She must have piggy-backed on one of old Pete Stuyvesant's first ships. Must have been around 1645, still a child when she settled in the upriver Hudson outposts. Had she travelled with family? Or had she been alone even then? Either way, she was from the Netherlands, and in 1666 . . .

Cut it.

Grim noticed there was fear in his heart. It wasn't the past that triggered it. It was his future. The coronary that Dr. Fisher predicted had never scared him; it had simply failed to arrive. It was the sea that frightened him now. And that accursed ship. Robert Grim wasn't a man to ignore bad omens anymore.

The problem was, in Black Spring he had *been* someone. He often asked himself if he were offered a do-over, would he choose that life again. The answer was plain vanilla 'yes'. All opposing forces—human and otherwise—notwithstanding.

Black Spring had defined him. Now all of that was behind him, and he no longer knew *who* he was.

He stopped at the waterline, just as Luca Wolf did eight miles north. His specs fogged up. The taste of dead seaweed and shellfish on his lips made him queasy. He suddenly understood that he faced a choice: he could walk into the surf, submit himself to the waves, and let the cold take him out; or return to the dunes, never touch another drop of alcohol, and take the job Eleanor Delveaux offered him.

He took a tentative step forward, but the tip of his shoe hit something half-buried in the sand. Grim kneeled and pulled it out with a wet *schhhlop*. It was a damp, black cap. A gust must have swooped it off some beachcomber's head and into the sea. Now it had washed back ashore.

He spun it around his finger then shone the light of his cell on the logo. Not the Mets or the Yankees like you saw stateside, but AC Milan.

A twinge of revulsion made him fling the hat far out into the surf. It stayed afloat for a while before a breaking wave swallowed it up in a roar of spume. Grim couldn't have expressed why this image filled him with such dread, but he turned and ran from it, his windpipe clenched as by an invisible fist, back into the dunes.

INTERMEZZO

MAMMOTH

1

The crippled mammoth rose from the waves and withstood the North Sea's merciless thrashing as if it had been doing so for centuries, but its resistance was to break. It would fall.

Such symbolism was pretty and deserved to be the poetic introduction to the damage report, but the bad thing that happened to Vincent Becker that day on the rig, the fright he got at the bottom of Stairwell C, prevented him from even hinting at such associations. He didn't even tell his wife Corinne who, when Christmas came, asked him where his mind kept wandering off to. Even the kids had noticed something was wrong.

'Work, honey,' Vince told her—not a lie, but not the full truth either. 'You know how hectic it's been. I think some downtime over the holidays is exactly what I need. I'll *try my best* for it to be what I need.'

'Uh-huh,' Corinne said, leaving absolutely no doubt as to what she thought about his built-in proviso. But he *had* tried, and the holidays turned out to be good—great even—although the incident never really left his fevered brain.

Six years prior, work and love had relocated Vince from Britain to the Netherlands. As an inspector for Aurora Offshore, he accompanied the decommissioning company's Damage Assessment Team to Mammoth III that day. It was the last of three trips, and cruising on the chopper toward open seas, he felt relieved that the DAT's job would be done after today. Vince used to love the offshore work, but the endless two-week shift swaps in cramped bunk beds shared with a fellow roustabout had started to take their toll. On Corinne and the kids, too. Days were long and rough, and he hated how fast darkness fell at sea. An operational oil rig lit up twenty-four seven like an industrial Christmas tree, but when the sun sank below the horizon, it seemed to be floating in a pitch-black vacuum. Anyone would get the jitters.

'I want you to look after yourself,' Corinne had said to him the night before. In the light of the bedside lamp, he could see she wasn't looking at him but staring at the ceiling with a pained expression. 'It's a nasty place.'

'You know how strict our safety protocols are, hon. And this will be the last time.'

'All the more reason to be careful. They say that's when accidents happen.'

'That's just superstition.'

'It isn't, though. You think you're done, you stop paying attention. I want you to keep me and the kids at the front of your mind. From the moment you step into that chopper till you set foot back on land.'

'Pinky swear.'

He turned to kiss her but she didn't kiss him back. Instead, she gave him a pensive look. Corinne cherished a moral sense of responsibility that almost comically contradicted her concerns. Like so many rigs on the Dutch continental shelf, Mammoth III ceased production when the oil reserves dried up two years ago. The essential personnel of 160 was scaled down to a maintenance crew of just fourteen (of which Vince had no longer been part), while the colossus waited for the state and parent company Shell to fight out a strategy for its decommissioning. It could have been the perfect moment for Corinne to convince him to leave Aurora altogether. He knew that's what she wanted, and he had even brought it up himself, hoping she wouldn't take him up on it. But she wanted nothing of the sort. When it came to his job, Corinne applied the same set of rules to Vince as she did to Ruben when he was done playing with his Legos: clean up your mess. Down to the last brick.

'Run!' he had smirked. 'Greenpeace has infiltrated the building!'

'So what does Shell want then? Put a plug in it and off you go?'

'Of course not. They can make billions in recycling. But there's more. The underwater pillars are now reefs, perfect habitats for cold-water coral and rare marine life. Remove them, and you disrupt the entire ecosystem.'

'And I'm sure the cost-saving for leaving them where they are isn't at all a factor?'

'Win-win.'

'You certainly know how to sell it, mister. I see your new job is getting to you.'

But it was true. Even the environmentalists agreed. The plan for Mammoth III was to cut its legs just below the surface, have the world's largest construction vessel the *Pioneering Spirit* single-lift the topside off its base and transport it to a ship graveyard in the Rotterdam harbor.

All swell . . . until early November when the whole thing blew up. It happened during routine maintenance on one of the pressure valves. Even though the platform was no longer operational, there was still gas in the reservoirs, and a series of explosions led to a raging fire. Ten engineers escaped in a lifeboat, one was killed in the blast, and three were thrown into the sea fifty yards below when the lower deck collapsed. They were never found. Vince knew the victims; they were friends. Corinne was right to be worried. It could have been him.

Now, as the H160 descended toward the helideck over white-crested swells, Vince's lips dried up. The rig's four steel legs and high frontside really gave the platform the impression of a crippled mammoth. Thank God the drilling wells had been sealed with concrete at the time of the explosion (averting an ecological disaster), but from the air he got a clear view of the gaping hole in the heart of the stacked decks and industrial piping. The accommodation tower supporting the helideck was blackened and had become uninhabitable. Still, that wasn't the real danger. The entire structure had been thrown off-balance. The DAT had discovered ruptures in two of the pillars. Fingers crossed that the unstable rig would survive the winter, because a strong enough hurricane could theoretically topple the whole thing over.

And Vince knew how wild the North Sea could get.

In fact, it was now a race against the clock to figure out how come April, the *Pioneering Spirit* could lift the platform without breaking it in two, while playing a game of Russian roulette with the elements.

Of course, Vince hadn't said *that* to Corinne.

2

The H160 touched down with a soft thud. As soon as the blades stopped, the DAT disembarked. Exposed to the cold wind on the platform, their orange coveralls billowed, but Vince could still hear the pilot letting out a selection of creative expletives.

Guano. Bird shit. The helideck was painted with it.

As Vince gave his briefing at the foot of the staircase, herring gulls coursed overhead. A metallic bang turned seven faces capped with hard hats toward a gull landing on the steel grid, skittishly bobbing its head at the visitors to gauge whether they posed any danger. Either it reckoned they didn't, or its greed was too strong because it hopped to where it had dropped its mussel and hooked its beak into the cracked shell. Vince tried to look away but couldn't. He watched as the gull tore out the flesh until it snapped like a piece of chewing gum. Up went its head, gobbling it down.

'Oysters, anyone?' said Joey, the senior mechanic.

'Fuck you,' the pilot called from the helideck, and the men laughed. The deck was scattered with the remains of clams and crabs. The downwash of a landing chopper could blast them everywhere. Worst case, straight back into your rotors. As the rest of the team got to work, the pilot would have to inspect his blades and hose down the landing zone.

Vince didn't laugh. *A nasty place*, Corinne's words echoed. Under his feet, he could feel the platform swaying, worsened by the explosion beyond its structural limits. From far below came the constant moaning of steel.

I want you to keep me and the kids at the front of your mind. From the moment you step into that chopper till you set foot back on land.

He did so when they got to work, and he did so consistently . . . until he broke his promise. It happened later in the day when the weather had turned. Rain lashed Mammoth III and the northern wind howled through its piping. Corinne would curse him if she found out he separated from the group and had gone exploring on his own, but there was no reason why she ever would. Of all the marital secrets a man could keep, Vincent Becker thought this one rather insignificant.

After all, he was a curious man, especially after a few too many beers had loosened his old platform chief's lips last week at Kamperduin, telling him about the skull and the stowaway.

3

Ab Havinga had invited him to Kamperduin, an old pub by the port, because he knew Vince was advising the DAT. After the explosion, Aurora Offshore had suspended him pending the results of the investigation, but even if they hadn't, Ab wouldn't have shown up for work. That much was glaringly obvious the minute Vince saw him sitting at a table in the back behind two pints of beer. Ab had always been a sturdy fellow, but he looked twenty pounds heavier now.

'Don't just stand there gaping, take your beer. I didn't order it for nothing.'

Vince sat and pulled his glass closer. 'Christ, are you okay, Ab?'

'You know I'm not. They were *my* men and I was responsible for them.' He raised his finger the same way Vince had seen him cut off arguments during his daily control room briefings. 'Don't tell me I wasn't. I'm not afraid of what they'll find, but they sure as hell won't bring back those men.'

Nor your peace of mind, Vince thought, but said nothing. Ab's eyes were sunken and red-rimmed. Not just because of the beer.

'But enough about that. Let's talk about why I asked you here. My mother always said: if there's something gnawing at you, speak now or forever hold your peace. If I don't speak now, I'm afraid I'll take this to my grave. And you're going back there. You can see if there's any truth in it.'

Somewhat perplexed by this statement, which sounded like the prelude to a confession he would rather not hear, Vince took a sip of his beer and listened to what his former platform chief had to say.

Before the accident—this was mid-October—divers had gone down to the reef to inspect the subsurface forest of tanks and wells. On the seabed, they had found the perfectly preserved skull of a woolly mammoth. Such discoveries were low on Aurora's priority list, but Ab had had it brought up anyway, because museums were always interested in such curiosities. It was widely known that after the last ice age, there was a large landmass across the present-day North Sea, stretching all the way from the European mainland to Scotland and teeming with prehistoric wildlife. Especially at Dogger Bank, trawlers had dragged up countless fossils, often damaged by the ravages of time.

'But not this one. I've never seen such a beauty, not even in a museum. And huge! We measured the tusks, they were almost fourteen feet long.' Ab curled his fingers in the air, reminiscent of a clichéd villain in an old film pulling his moustache. 'Must have been a giant bull.'

'So you called Naturalis.'

'Yep. They practically creamed their pants over it, but they were unable to sort out transport, and we were on a minimal crew with other fish to fry.' His voice slurred with alcohol. 'So we wrapped the thing in plastic and stowed it at the bottom of Stairwell C to keep it out of the wind and the rain. It was still there when the place blew up.'

'Then it's probably still there now.'

'True. The fire raged in the central parts of the tower, but the skull was stowed well below that. If Stairwell C didn't collapse and crush it, it should be pretty much undamaged. You could go have a look.'

But Vince heard a quaver in his voice, as if the former platform chief wasn't entirely sure this was a good idea. 'Listen. You're a pragmatist. I don't understand why you're making a big deal about a mammoth skull after everything that's happened.'

'That's not the point,' Ab said. He chugged his glass and Vince saw his hands tremble. *Parkinson's*, he thought, but then, *No. Anxiety.*

'Then what is?'

'Late in October, Scotty approached me. He was one of the two Brits who were killed, you know who I'm talking about, right? He claimed that while making his rounds, he'd seen someone in Stairwell C. Someone not part of the crew.'

'Unlikely.'

'That's what I said, and Scotty thought so, too. That's why he'd hesitated for so long before coming to me. You know how those stairs are all welded grates? Said he'd seen someone three stories down through the grilles, so it was all a bit unclear. But this person wasn't wearing a coverall, of that he was sure, so Scotty decided to report it anyway.'

The orange protective coveralls were mandatory except in the cabins, the gym, or the sauna. If you were caught not wearing one, you got a severe reprimand . . . the first time. Strike two, and you were out.

'So Scotty went down to have a look, but there was no one there. Thought whoever it was must have fled through the corridor when he'd heard him coming. It was the laundry level and we weren't using those cabins, but this person could have easily taken Stairwell B on the far end and gone anywhere. So I tell Scotty it was probably one of his mates and issued a reminder about the coverall rules. I didn't give it much thought after that.' He glanced at Vince but then looked away. 'Until two nights later Jurgen came up with the same story.'

That had also been in Stairwell C. In the wee hours, and apparently Jurgen had been all out of sorts.

'He heard a strange sound. First he thought it was moaning, but then he recognized it as some sort of throat singing. But that's not what upset him the most.'

'Then what did?'

'He was convinced it was a woman.'

Vince's mouth snapped shut. Granted, some women worked in the offshore industry, but they were a very small minority. None had been on Mammoth III's skeleton crew.

'So we woke up the crew, did a head count, and then we combed the rig. I mean, if we had a stowaway on board, I needed to know, right? Unlikely as it was. We searched everywhere, not just the tower. Couldn't find anyone.'

There were three more sightings the following week, two in Stairwell C and one from two men who swore on their mother's grave that they had seen a female figure in strange attire on the lower deck. The crew were all tough and experienced men, but now there was unrest among them.

'More than unrest, actually. They were scared, Vince. You know these boys are reliable. They're not the kind to see ghoulies and ghosties.'

'I know. I also know that when you're at sea for a long time, it starts to affect your mind. The isolation, the fatigue, the long shifts . . . sometimes the walls start closing in.'

'It wasn't like that.'

Suddenly Vince understood why. 'When did *you* see her?'

'Two days before the accident.' Ab reached for the only full glass between them. Vince had barely touched his beer and now watched as Ab chugged it down. He said nothing of it, as Ab didn't seem to notice. 'Outside, in broad daylight. Scotty was there. We were coming down the stairs from the drilling deck when he jabs me and points, "There she is, that's her!" She was standing at the railing, facing the sea, one deck below and some thirty yards away. I finally saw what my men had meant about her getup, about how it was difficult to describe. She wasn't wearing a coverall or a dress. She was wearing the skin of an animal.'

That's when Vince decided the story—dubious at best until that point—was a figment of Ab's imagination. Still, he did him the favor of hearing him out. He had always respected the chief and it wasn't his place to burst the man's bubble.

'She was waving a cane of some sorts at the sea. We stared at her for the better half of a minute before Scotty suddenly shouted, "Hey!" She looked around and I saw her face, just for a second. Then we were flying down the stairs, and when we got there, she was gone. But in that instant when she looked back, I could see her just as clearly as I see you now.'

The woman's face was withered, and the animal skin wasn't just wrapped around her shoulders like a cloak, but around her head the way a shaman would wear antlers or a wolf's head.

'Only this wasn't a wolf skin,' Ab said. 'I don't know how it was possible because she wasn't a particularly large woman, but she was wearing the skin of a woolly mammoth. And I swear to God, there were tusks on both sides of her face.'

4

Ab's story may have been a figment of his imagination, but Vince couldn't shake it off either. That's why he was now staring down through the ruins of Stairwell C.

Turned out the shaft was damaged far beyond his expectation. The difference between it and A and B was shocking. Blackened steel walls opened into a gaping hole lower down, where the explosion had carved a deep wound in the accommodation tower, practically hollowing it out. Stairwell C had apparently functioned as a chimney because, even with the wind now wailing through it, the smell of soot was so overwhelming it took his breath away. The stairs had mostly collapsed into a gloomy mine shaft of twisted pipes and grilles vibrating in the updraft. Making it this far was one thing; going beyond this would be madness.

Nevertheless, Vince stepped over the edge and lowered himself on the rope.

He had his harness, he had his belay device, and he had his ascenders. He was prepared and able, as long as he proceeded slowly. Bit by bit. He kept Corinne and the kids at the front of his mind, just as he had promised.

Vincent Becker was a scientist and as such, took pride in viewing the world with an open mind. No, he didn't believe there had been a woman dressed in animal skin on the rig, and he certainly didn't buy the sailor talk that explained such apparitions as omens of impending doom, not even in light of the accident. What intrigued him was how *Ab* could be so convinced about what he had seen. The trauma of the explosion was a powerful trigger, but his fancies must have needed a catalyst. That catalyst had been the mammoth skull, and now it triggered *his* curiosity as well.

Still, he felt ill at ease as he descended deeper, maneuvering through the jumble of steel. Every time his feet hit the supports of former mid landings and left prints in the soot, echoes rang through the shaft. Somewhere, a safety door banged, and that too echoed. So did the rattling of the rain against the steel walls. Even the rustle of his coverall seemed amplified, creating the impression he was descending into a well full of whispering life.

Halfway down, he knew he wasn't alone.

Someone was watching him.

Startled, he looked down. His eyes were now accustomed to the dark, and he could distinguish the debris of fallen stairs some fifty feet beneath his dangling legs. Nothing moved down there, but the wind was tugging on his coverall, and he started to spin, sending a stab of panic through his guts. He kicked his legs and struggled to gain control.

'Hello?' he called out. 'Is anyone there?'

He stopped shouting because too many echoes answered. Besides, there *couldn't* be anyone there. The damage made this part of the complex inaccessible by any other way, and the DAT was assessing Mammoth's outer decks today.

Had they noticed his absence by now? Probably. They wouldn't raise the alarm right away but any longer, and they would.

For a second, he considered abandoning the plan. It was a fool's errand to begin with. He could clip his ascenders on the rope and climb up. But something stopped him. There, lower down. Something seemed to be etched into the smoke-stained rear wall.

He lowered himself until he could see it.

A mammoth. A group of human figures. No spears, no hunt. They were just standing in a circle around the animal.

Amazed, he looked at the crude outlines in the soot.

Like a cave painting, Vince thought. But then, *Nobody could have drawn that. Nobody's been here after the fire. And nobody could have reached that wall. Not with the stairs blasted away like that.*

Unless Nobody could fly, Vince thought, chuckling. But he quickly cut it when a chorus of echoes chuckled back through the shaft.

He had come this far; he might as well have a look. It would be good for him to know that there was nothing down there so he could file this brief episode away in the denial drawer. So, Vince lowered himself swiftly and expertly, past the gaping hole in the tower through which he could see all the way down to the lower decks and the swirling waves, until his feet landed on a wobbly pile of metal rubble. The lower flights of stairs seemed intact but were showered with big chunks of debris and he had to maneuver carefully to make sure he wouldn't get stuck, or worse, crushed. But secured to the rope, he felt relatively safe, and not long afterwards he reached the bottom, where he untied himself.

Thanks to its relatively sheltered location, the bottom of the stairwell was untouched by the fire, but its high thresholds had turned it into a tub, filled ankle-deep with sooty water. Grey light fell through the reinforced windows. Twisted grilles lay scattered around.

And in the middle of it all was the mammoth's skull.

It was strange to see it in such a deplorable setting instead of a natural history museum, where it belonged. They had put it on a pallet, now immersed in water, and wrapped it entirely with cling film, so that you could only see the shiny, silver-white shape of the head, not the bone itself. The curved tusks threw grotesque shadows on the walls.

For thousands of years, the skull had lain waiting on the bottom of the North Sea, buried in sediment, exposed by the current. Now, they had fished it up and closed its hollow sockets with plastic.

That was quite unbecoming.

And there was something else. A tangle of plastic strips jutted out the left socket, as if mice or rats had burrowed into it. Or were they feathers? Vince sloshed closer and began tearing away the strips, scattering downy plumes in the half-light.

What am I doing? What in the hell am I doing?

He saw a webbed claw. He pulled it, stretching the plastic with a sticky *rippp*. He had to use his knife to cut it loose . . . and held up a large, dead seagull.

Must have gnawed its way in and got stuck. Choked, as if someone pulled a plastic bag over its head. Why?

Because the gull had also wanted to do something about the mammoth's stare.

Vince laughed. Forced himself to. Bollocks, of course . . . except it wasn't. Because, let's face it, hadn't he known all along that it was the mammoth staring back at him? Extinct or not, he had felt the animal's gaze fixed on him from the moment he entered the shaft.

The gull's black little eyes were clouded over and there was blood on its beak. Disgusted, Vince tossed it into a corner, where it splashed in the water and floated wings outspread. Then he too began tearing the plastic off the skull.

Better to set it free.

Afterwards, Vincent Becker wouldn't be able to pinpoint exactly why he did it, only that he had felt compelled somehow, perhaps by his subconscious. Or maybe it had been a rudimentary form of respect, because being wrapped in plastic wasn't an honorable next stage in the existence of this magnificent creature that had once reigned over the plains of Doggerland. So he clawed at the plastic, cut it when necessary and soon exposed the sockets.

No staring eyes, no ulterior life, nothing of the kind. Just dark bone. He waited a while, staring vacantly into the holes.

I swear to God, there were tusks on both sides of her face.

A loud bang echoed through the shaft in Stairwell C, and he jolted. The door. Crawling shadows. Nobody was moving, just the wind.

'Nunyunnini,' it whispered.

All his muscles went limp. For a second, he was convinced he had actually heard that word. What did it mean? *And who had made that wall painting?* He tried to contemplate it, but his mind was all over the place.

With obsessive vigor, he attacked the wrapping, even when the splashing of the water, the rustling of the plastic, and his own out-of-control panting made him queasy all over. If someone or something was hiding in the stairwell, he wouldn't be able to hear it sneak up on him. Tough. Best to get it over with quickly.

Behind him, the gull floated, a fallen angel or a sacrifice, surrounded by the plastic that had choked it.

Eventually, Vince uncovered the entire skull, from the knobbly head to the tips of its tusks. Again, he stopped to look. He had been wrong; there *was* something odd about those empty sockets. He tried to pull his eyes away but realized he couldn't.

The knife dropped from his hand and plunged into the water, but Vince didn't notice.

Only much later, when he heard voices echoing his name and saw flashes of light in the shaft, did he wake up from his stupor. At first, he didn't understand where he was or what he was looking at, and when he did, he thought, *Ab's off his rocker. I didn't see anyone down here.*

5

Vince was the last to go up to the helideck that day, and when he heard a loud metallic crash behind him, he turned on his heels.

A gull had dropped something on the platform. His first hunch was it looked like a longish piece of cold-water coral, but closer inspection revealed it was a bone. A piece of ulna, by the joint at the end of it.

'Becker, get in!' Joey shouted over the roar of the chopper.

Vince gestured that he was coming but didn't budge. On the other end, where the bone was split, a piece of metal jutted out, glistening in the rain.

A *fracture pin,* he thought.

A giant seagull alighted next to it, folding its wings. It gave Vince a quick, threatening look, as if to say, *Mine.* Then its head jerked forward to rip out the bone's marrow.

6

There was no mention of a stowaway in Aurora Offshore's final report. The Coast Guard occasionally sailed out to chase away thrill seekers from abandoned rigs but never this far from the coast, and Vincent Becker hadn't seen anyone on Mammoth III. Nor did it say anything about a paleontological curiosity at the bottom of Stairwell C.

As the holidays neared, the events still plagued Vince's mind. More often than he bargained for, in fact, and usually at night as he listened to the wind, Corinne a lump under the covers beside him. The wind around the house wasn't the same as the wind at sea, thank God, but it still gave him the jitters.

No matter how hard he tried, he would never fully really recall what happened in the hours he had spent at the bottom of the stairwell, before the guys from the DAT came looking for him. It kept getting away from him, as if he were grasping at smoke. Instead, he stared into the distance and imagined his fingers gently caressing fossilized ivory. He would see a large herd of terrestrial animals passing by before his mind's eye, slowly like silhouettes on a prehistoric horizon, and he knew he had to follow them to stay safe from the rising seas.

Then he would hear faraway throat singing and think, *Nunyunnini*.

2

LIMBO

2

LIMBO

1

Initially, Barbara thought a single day of lockdown in the dunes would be enough to drive her crazy. More, she had been so angry that given the chance, she would have taken on her captors bare-handed. After *four* days, that fighting spirit lay shattered, and she would have kissed the soles of their shoes to get out.

The late afternoon of day four was cold and bleak, and the twilight had the color of wet jeans. A man and a woman they hadn't seen face-to-face before stopped by. The woman introduced herself as Glennis and when her paralytic doll-face smile appeared, Barbara recognized her as the woman who had dialed in at Luca's interview. The man introduced himself as Van Driel and wore a fixed expression that could turn angel wings to dust.

'Where's Diana?' Barbara asked.

'Reassigned. From here on, I'll be your go-to. Quickly now, let's not lose any time.'

Like a whirlwind, she led her through the bungalow to collect their few belongings. Then she ushered them all into the black nine-seater waiting with its engine running, ignoring Barbara's pleas for news.

'Where are we going?' Luca asked.

'Efteling*,' Van Driel said. 'Quit yapping.'

Thirty minutes later it was dark. The windows were blacked out, so Barbara didn't realize they had taken them home to Katwijk until after they let her out of the van. Before her stood the house on Park Lane, theirs for the past seventeen years. Only four mornings ago she had woken up inside next to Alexander and they had had breakfast together. Like every morning, they had chatted about the day to come. Alexander had made Luca lunch, and she had made him put on his parka. And they hadn't known. Any day could be the last and you never knew.

'Let's go inside,' Glennis said. 'We're not fans of that well-intended neighborhood watch.' She chuckled, but no one joined in.

'Uncle Jim!' Jenna crowed. She tore her hand loose and ran up to the porch. Barbara froze when she saw the uniformed giant emerge from the shadows by the door. She called her daughter's name, but

* Efteling is a fantasy-themed amusement park in the south of The Netherlands

Jenna leaped into his arms, and he lifted her far above his head, as if she were filled with air.

'Hey, little troublemaker!' he called. His posture reminded her of Lurch from *The Addams Family*, but when he bared his square teeth, she was appalled to recognize the man in Jenna's crayon drawing. This was the creep they had sent to pick up her daughter from school.

'Jenna, come here right now! And *you* . . . put her down.'

'Chop chop,' Glennis said, clutching her arm tightly, not so much that it hurt, but close. It shocked Barbara. That single move established with no uncertainty who was pulling the strings. Barbara had been blindsided by Diana Radu's sudden replacement, as they must have anticipated. Glennis was younger, more hard-bitten, and their fate didn't seem much of her concern. Maybe the same had been true for Diana, but at least her facade had appeared caring. Barbara hated to admit that her resistance had crumbled to the extent that even a mask had given her comfort. One thing was sure: they might have taken them home, but they were still directing this show until the final curtain call.

'Jim will look after Jenna, so we can have our little talk. Don't worry, he's great with kids. Look, they're best friends already.'

'Uncle Jim is so funny,' Jenna laughed and squeezed his nose, at which he blew up his cheeks. To Barbara's horror, her daughter didn't show a shred of distrust toward the stranger. She didn't blame Jenna for that; she blamed herself.

Van Driel had the key to their house and unlocked the door. He found the light switches with the efficiency of someone who had clearly been there before. He probably had. While she and Luca hung their coats, he drew the curtains on both sides of the living room, shutting out the view of the backyard koi pond and any possibly curious neighbors. Jim put Jenna down in the play area, and she proudly showed him her *Frozen* dolls, which he said were magnificent.

'Good.' It was clear a weight had been lifted off Glennis' shoulders now they were inside. 'There's no place like home, right? And what a nice home you have, Barbara. Beautiful lot of koi. No worries, we've been feeding them. How about I make us a big pot of tea?'

She headed for the kitchen before Barbara could answer. It all felt so unreal, she couldn't think straight. 'Um . . . yes, might as well.'

'Mom! Are you just going to let that bitch mess around in dad's kitchen?'

'Luca!'

But Glennis laughed as though this were a particularly good joke. 'I think he likes me!' She winked. 'Can I get you something, Luca?'

Luca shot her a look that rivaled Van Driel's and flashed her the finger. Glennis threw her head back and laughed again, then disappeared into the kitchen.

Rougher than she intended, Barbara grabbed his shoulders and took his face in her hands. 'Luca, I *know* you're angry. So I am. But please, suck it up. Just for now. If we do what they say, this will all be over soon.'

He looked at her, bewildered and disgusted. 'This will never be over. Don't you get it?'

The unadulterated contempt in his voice hurt her. In just four days Luca, her sweet and awkward teenage son who wouldn't hurt a fly, had turned into this bundle of bottled-up rage. And he was right. The kitchen *was* his dad's domain. Alexander was an excellent amateur chef, and it would have broken his heart to see her let them walk all over her like this.

I'm sorry, Alexander. Maybe you would have handled it differently. But I can't. I just can't anymore, and I have to do what's best for the children.

Van Driel ushered them to the couch, as Glennis came back with a tray. On it was a steaming teapot, three mugs, and a glass of coke. She put the tray down and placed the glass in front of Luca. Instantly, his foot shot up and kicked it over. It went into a spin, splashing cola over the coffee table and onto Glennis' tights and heels.

'Dammit, Luca!' Barbara yelled, not angry now but afraid. Glennis didn't budge. Van Driel hurried to the kitchen to get towels. Luca slumped back into the couch, his arms folded and his face like thunder.

'So no coke,' Glennis said. No smile on her face now, and Barbara could see what had been hiding behind it: a cold, relentless machine in the shape of a human. That scared her more than anything else. 'I understand you don't want this relationship to work. But I want *you* to understand something as well, Luca. I want you to understand that I was on your side. I also want you to understand, understand *real well*, that these are Louboutins.'

'Fuck your Louboutins. Next time it'll be hot tea.'

'Luca, *please!*'

Van Driel came back with towels. He mopped the coffee table and floor, while Glennis started dabbing at her pumps. Then he turned to Luca. 'Pull a trick like that again and you'll spend a couple more nights away from home. Only this time in a hospital bed, with a broken arm and two black eyes. I've been trained to inflict injuries in such a way that it looks like an accident.'

Barbara moaned, but it was enough to silence Luca. That was something, at least.

'Right,' Glennis said after she sat down and poured everyone tea. 'Let's assume this was a false start. We brought you home. It seemed like a good idea for you to see it with your own eyes before we present you with your options. Your staying here tonight unsupervised or going back to the safehouse a while longer is completely up to you.'

'First I want to know what you've learned about Alexander,' Barbara said.

'The short answer is not much. I know that's not the answer you've been hoping for. What we *do* know is that neither Alexander nor the others have been anywhere else in the field, other than in the area between the road and the ship. Not anywhere in the dunes either. The forensics are conclusive. They went into the ship, and they never came out. So that's now the focus of our investigation.'

'I *told* you so,' Luca snapped. 'You were lying.'

'We didn't have answers, that's not the same thing. We still don't. Our priority was to prevent a public shockwave, for the sake of those who are missing. Of course we were hesitant to share the little we did know.'

But now you are, Barbara thought, *because you don't want us to play Scooby Doo all over the dunes. You don't want us to draw attention to your little secret.*

'But that brings me straight to the heart of the matter. Believe me when I say that we feel terrible about what you're going through, Barbara. I can hardly fathom how you must feel.'

'You most certainly can't,' she said.

'We all want to find your husband. But we can only do it if we can conduct our investigation discreetly. I emphasize this because I need you to be fully aware of the risk. If the media catches on, it's over. There would be nothing more we could do, and Alexander would be gone forever. Do you understand what I'm saying?'

'I understand.' Barbara's eyes suddenly teared up. Annoyed, she wiped them and said, 'God, I understand. Just don't stop looking. Please don't give up on the father of my children.'

Glennis smiled again, more triumphant than friendly. Or maybe this *was* her version of friendly. Barbara didn't know anymore. In the backroom, Jenna squealed with laughter at the giant's shenanigans. Barbara closed her eyes.

'Now let me tell you a story,' Van Driel said, leaning in. 'You and Alexander have been having marriage issues for quite some time now.

You never reached out to friends or sought counseling because you thought time would work it all out. It didn't. So last weekend, the two of you decided last-minute to take the family to the Ardennes and see what could be salvaged.'

'That's not true!' Luca blurted out. Barbara was too flabbergasted to say anything.

'In this story it is, and don't make me have to tell you again to shut your mouth and listen. You decided on Belgium because that's where you've had good times in the past. Last year's fall break, to be exact. We saw it in your family albums.'

You've been nosing around in my albums? Barbara thought. *Sons of bitches.*

'You left on Tuesday morning. Things seemed to be going well, but Alexander started to feel increasingly unhappy. And last night you got in a bad fight. A shouting match, in fact, and it even woke you up, Luca. You'd never heard your parents yell at each other like that before. Alexander packed his bag and left. The last time you heard from him was a WhatsApp message saying he needed time and that you should go home. Which you did, for the sake of the children. You don't know where he is now. He's gone AWOL.'

'Dad would never abandon us!' Luca said, and now he was crying.

'You'd be surprised what daddies can do,' Van Driel said.

'Excuse me?' Barbara burst out, putting her arm around Luca's shoulders. 'I know damn well you've backed us into a corner and I'll play ball, even though I *despise* you for it. But keep your personal grievances to yourself and don't you *dare* ever threaten my son again!'

Before Van Driel could open his mouth, Glennis intervened. 'This isn't about what Alexander would or wouldn't actually do. This is about you having an explanation for why the children haven't shown up at school for four days, why you haven't been to work, and why Alexander has vanished.'

'But Luca's right! How on earth am I supposed to shovel this load of bull? I'm not an actress!' Again, tears came and this time she couldn't hold them back. 'What am I supposed to tell my friends? What am I supposed to tell my sister?'

'You'll ace it, I'm sure, because you'll be thinking about Alexander. Besides, we've done all the legwork.' Glennis fished Barbara's phone from her purse and put it on the coffee table. Barbara reached for it, but Glennis put her hand on it. 'Soon enough. Trust me when I say we can perfectly mimic people's texting habits. Your sister Loes will be coming to visit you tomorrow morning, assuming we can come to an agreement. She can't wait to put her arms around you.'

Again, Barbara was flabbergasted. 'Couldn't you have come up with something that would have painted a nicer picture? This is *Alexander*, for Christ's sake! Why not just a breakdown? Why couldn't he be in a clinic to recover . . .'

Glennis handed her a tissue. Reluctantly, she took it. 'Impossible, Barbara. Alexander called in sick on Wednesday because he didn't show up for his Tuesday appointments. After that, for all Kramer & Nysingh know, he disappeared off the face of the earth. Which fits our scenario. He's got problems at home and drops the ball. Had we used a medical issue, they would have been compelled to send an occupational physician. You're in the clear because Roselinde and Jill were willing to take over your shifts this week.'

'Alexander would never,' Barbara said, but she understood they had created the perfect cover. No, Alexander wasn't the man for a no-show, but throw in a wild card like marital problems and anything was possible. Alexander was an IP attorney at Kramer & Nysingh in The Hague and Barbara a financial advisor at an insurance broker in Leiden. By the time he came back—*if* he came back—they would be lucky if one of them still had their job.

'At least he's alive in this scenario,' Glennis said with that icy smile of hers, and now Barbara hated her, really hated her, the way Luca did. 'Because that's what we're all counting on, right?'

No, it isn't. Otherwise, you wouldn't have declared those cops dead on day one.

'I know how difficult this is, and we'll walk you through it step by step, so you'll have the story down pat. The less you say the better. People get awkward around marital disputes, so they won't poke around. Loes will tomorrow, naturally. Just say you're not yet ready to talk about it. She'll understand. Her objective will be to give you the care you need, and I advise you to be open to it. Right now, you can use all the support you can get. For specfics, you can turn to me. Day or night. We'll also make a therapist available with whom the both of you can talk openly. I strongly advise you to consider that.'

The accuracy and ease with which Glennis predicted human behavior didn't even surprise Barbara anymore. With a clear display of glee, Van Driel produced two pairs of stapled sheets and handed one of them to Barbara.

'And now . . . the moment of truth! Sign this and you'll all sleep in your own beds tonight.'

Barbara knew how to read contracts and this one was only three pages, so it didn't take long for her to get a grasp of their position: not good. Meanwhile, Van Driel dangled the second copy in front of Luca. 'Let me explain to you what this says, because I don't expect you to read this through. I do expect you to do what it says, so listen carefully. It says here you'll talk to nobody about what happened in the past few days. When we say nobody, we mean nobody. Not the cops, not the media, not anyone in your family and not your friends. If you *do*, we'll find out. Don't think you can outsmart us. We *will* find out. We have ears everywhere. The second we hear anything, we'll come and get you and lock you up. Not in a magnificent holiday rental this time. Your mother will go to jail, and you and your sister will be put in a juvenile detention center where the rooms aren't nearly as nice as those in the dunes. The company even less so. Capeesh?'

Luca leaned in and spat on the contract. The *smack* was ringing in Barbara's ears almost before she was aware that Van Driel's free hand had shot up and slapped him in the face. Luca shrunk back with a smothered scream, his hands cupping his face.

'*Bastard!*' she yelled. She took Luca in her arms, but he froze and yanked himself free. Instead, he stared at the man in stunned disbelief, his cheek glowing bright red.

Van Driel wiped Luca's spit off the contract with the towel Glennis had used for the spilled coke. It left a wet, yellowish-brown stain. 'I warned you. Man, you're annoying. Think you know everything. Bloody hell.'

With an almost solemn face, Glennis glanced from Luca to Barbara, and suddenly Barbara was furious. She snatched Glennis' pen from the table and signed the NDA on the dotted line next to the firm, no-nonsense signature of *E.A. Delveaux, Head of Division NOVEMBER-6*.

'Very well,' Glennis said. 'Luca, since you're a minor, your mother signed for you and your sister as well. Do you understand what that means?'

Luca said nothing.

'The lady asked if you understand,' Van Driel said. 'Acknowledge.'

'I understand,' he muttered.

'Excellent. Now this one.'

He swapped contracts with Barbara. She signed the second copy.

'You can keep that one.' He pointed to the stain. 'Let it be a reminder.'

'Glennis?'

'Yes, Barbara?'

'Call me if you want to walk me through your story. But now, get the hell out of my house and take your watchdogs with you.'

'You got it.'

2

Late afternoon, December 17, Robert Grim was the only living soul in Hangar 3. Nightfall had come entirely too soon for his liking, and now he was leaning against the rail of the skybridge running halfway up along the side of the unit, giving him a bird's eye view of the *Oracle's* deck. He was barely aware of his trembling, white-knuckled hands clutching the rail. He *was* aware of his fear. More so than he was ready to admit.

Supported by wooden scaffolds, the *Oracle* now stood proudly upright. Bright a-glare in the silver spotlights, she looked more maritime museum exhibit than deep cover testing subject, yet she undeniably emanated menace. Stripped of her masts, sprit, sails, and rigging, the bare, clog-shaped barque had been reduced to her essence. But something still seemed hidden beyond this appearance, taunting him. It reminded Grim of a deep-sea anglerfish, with its enchanting lantern, hypnotizing like a will-o'-the-wisp in the inky deep dark, inviting you closer and closer until it was too late. You only noticed the hideous creature lurking behind the light as its face split open into an all razor-teeth mouth. The *Oracle's* mystery was like that. Grim could sense the magnetic attraction that tugged him toward it but was dead scared of what would bite if he dared reach out his hand.

His eyes twitched and he tasted metal. Reaching into his pocket, he took out a bottle of Xanax. Not exactly Blue Label, but they fit the bill. He popped a blue pill into his mouth and swallowed it dry.

No more people had been lost—thank God—but the Peter van Wijk incident on the night of his arrival still preyed on his mind. The split-second the sorry scientist had leaned back into the hatch. The tolling of that doggone bell. Next thing, his screams had died, and Peter? Dead as well, he assumed, like the others. Where? No fucking clue.

Pensive, Grim let his gaze drift from the hatch to the ship's peculiarly narrow and elegant aftercastle. What hadn't yet died was the bell. Even with the ship stripped of all its ornaments, it still tolled every time they sent in rabbits for yet another failed experiment.

Thing was, there was no bell. And yet the fucker kept ringing, single-handedly ruling out the possibility that they were dealing with some sort of unexplained scientific phenomenon. Each time he heard it, he remembered Peter. It scared the living hell out of him, so he kept the probes into the hatch to an absolute minimum.

Wherever it sends things must be teeming with rabbits and Dutch military drones.

Grim let out a high-pitched laugh but quickly bottled it up. The echoes that bounced off the walls of the maintenance hangar sounded more like wailing, and he didn't need that.

With ever-trembling fingers, he snagged another Xanax, swallowed it, and looked at the masts and folded sails on the floor. Delveaux had been terrified that removing them would impair the ship's *structural integrity*, as she put it, but in Grim's book, she was afraid the ship would forget its magic trick. That alone proved the woman had ulterior motives. Dismantling the ship had been key for transport, but it did raise a knotty question: to what extent could you dissect a possessed object before it lost its powers?

The similarities with the famous philosophical thought experiment weren't lost on him, and under different circumstances, he might have found them charming. It went like this: Theseus, mythological hero of the seas, is sailing his ship across the Aegean Sea, but after years of island hopping, he discovers the wood is prone to wear. He replaces a plank. On he goes, sailing a vessel that is obviously still his pride and joy. After a while, he must replace another plank. And another, and another, until several years later, he's replaced all the woodwork, piece by piece. Sails and masts alike. The ship looks exactly the same as when he first set sail, and he's remained its captain the entire time. But *is* it still the same ship? And if not, what was the tipping point?

Even Plato didn't have an answer.

But wait. Suppose they had been keeping all the original planks in a shipyard. Suppose they refurbished them and secretly used them to build a new ship, an *exact* copy of Theseus' ship. Which of the two is the original? The one he now commands, or the new ship in the docks, which our confused hero has never even laid eyes on?

Grim looked down at the scattered parts on the hangar floor with a sense of unease. One by one, they had untangled the ropes and lowered the sails in the fields of Every Man's End on a trial-and-error basis. The rabbits kept disappearing. The bell kept tolling.

At what point *would* the Oracle lose its magic trick? Yet to be determined. And what if they built a second ship using the separated parts . . . would that too make people disappear?

Oh yes. You know how curses go; don't dupe yourself. They spread like an ink blot until everything is besmirched in black.

The skybridge accessed the hangar's adjacent offices. He heard a door opening and Grim turned. Behold, Eleanor Delveaux, a.k.a. the Kraken. Stilettos clicking, she looked impeccable as ever in her bright red maxicoat. At odds with this look, her usually sharp eyes were now sunk in their sockets and her skin wan. Here at Volkel Air Base, Grim had Glennis and twelve other NOVEMBER-6 agents at his disposal, and all who were working on the ship looked like they had come down with something.

'Robert, Glennis told me you took her to The Hague today.'

'Yes, to the National Archives. I needed an interpreter. Would you rather I asked you? Could have added a little candlelight dinner. Maybe some Sade in the background . . .'

'Spill it.'

'Alright, chill your biscuits. The almanacs we ploughed through say the original *Oracle* was built in a shipyard in the town of Hoorn in 1702. Owned by a shipping company in Noortwyck, spelled with T and YCK in old-Dutch, says Glennis, and used in the Baltic Sea trade. As you know, she's said to have sunk in a crashing Nor'wester in 1716. We've dated over a dozen wood samples and can positively conclude that we have the original *Oracle* here, not a replica. We can't explain why the sails are in such mint condition.'

'Nothing new there. What else?'

'I've had a recording made of the bell. Turns out its frequency, amplitude, and waveform, are identical to those of the bronze ship bells forged in the seventeenth and eighteenth centuries. The National Maritime Museum in Amsterdam's got one. Pretty creepy to hear it toll, because you can actually, um . . . *see* a bell.'

'Interesting. Anything else?'

'Maybe. Hard to verify. In 1715 and 1716, there was an apparent smallpox epidemic in the Dutch coastal region. Glennis found a reference claiming the *Oracle* might have been used as a death ship, although no official records can confirm that. Even back then it was only hearsay.'

'A death ship?'

'Yes. In the old days there was little understanding of the spread of infectious diseases, but they did notice that many who'd been in contact with the deceased also got it. So as a protective measure, they loaded the bodies onto ships and dumped them at sea.'

'Whaddya know,' Delveaux marveled, and Grim could see a glimmer in her eye. 'So even back then the *Oracle* made people disappear.'

'If it's true.'

'And you're going to find that out. Good job, Robert.'

'Don't sweat it. Any news on the media front?'

'Not really. A few photos of the convoy on the N277 on Twitter, but Volkel often moves large equipment, so no red flags.'

'Lucky devil. That was a real squeaker.'

'Yes,' Delveaux said. 'But we dodged the bullet.'

Transportation had been a logistical nightmare. NOVEMBER-6 had selected Volkel Air Base for relocation, primarily for the availability of a sufficiently sized maintenance hangar, but also because they knew how to hide stuff (even though the storage of American nukes at the facility was apparently a very public secret). After nine days in the Netherlands, Robert Grim had decided it was a small, cramped sleaze-hole of a country, but Volkel was on the other side of that sleazehole, and it had quickly dawned on all of them that even without masts and bowsprit, the *Oracle* was simply too big for overland transport without destroying every overpass, bridge, and road sign along a hundred-mile stretch.

'It's a ship,' Eleanor's confidante and senior agent, Diana Radu, had remarked. 'Why don't we just weigh anchor and set sail?'

Surprisingly, that turned out to be a real possibility. And so it happened that last Sunday, five days after it first appeared, the *Oracle* was boarded up as an entire corps of marines (none of whom knew what they were doing, but who were all just following orders) laid down a half-mile of steel road plates north from the ops area and through the tulip fields. Another mile-and-a-half through town and you reached the boulevard, where a paved exit led to the beach. They closed the entire stretch so yet more marines, disguised as road workers, could remove traffic signs and lampposts. This, of course, caught the eye of a hack writing for the local biweekly. A NOVEMBER-6 agent politely retorted the usual—routine maintenance, yadi yadi yada—and by the time they went to print, the area had long been restored to its original state.

While the public's attention was focused on the memorial services for the Noordwijk cops who had so tragically died a week earlier, a base of concrete slabs was temporarily positioned in the surf, on top of which arose a humongous tower crane. Obviously, *that* was hard to miss, but the weather was too atrocious for beachgoers, and, who really gave a fuck about construction work anyway?

Another crane was erected in the ops area and that night, under the cloak of darkness, they took the roof off the tent and hoisted the neatly wrapped package onto a fourteen-axle lowboy, so the *Oracle* could embark on her secret journey.

All's well that ends well. Noordwijk had been asleep and anyone who wasn't had seen little more than a passing WIDE LOAD. Sure, the lawn on the traffic circle in front of the Palace Hotel would have to be replanted, and a few cars along the boulevard had to be towed, but they managed to reach the pitch-black safety of the beach without any of the expected problems.

Things only derailed when the *Oracle* was loaded onto the cargo ship waiting just beyond the surf, and it jammed into a sandbank.

They had scheduled to match optimal tide conditions, but Grim's worst fear came true. The sea was too shallow at the crane's maximum reach. What followed was a nerve-racking race against the clock before low tide, and worse, dawn. The Defense Department rushed three marine towboats to the scene. This turned out to be a legitimate clusterfuck of red tape, because NOVEMBER-6 was the only division among the Dutch intelligence services that operated under jurisdiction *of*, but due to the highly classified nature of its cases without reporting *to*, the State Department. Eventually, a call to some high-ranking general from the Secretary of State herself (who was familiar with the protocols but hadn't a clue as to what had incentivized the call) saved the day, and the barque was refloated an hour before daybreak.

That's how on Monday, likely for the first time in over three centuries, the *Oracle* was gently bobbing on open seas. By evening, she reached the port of Rotterdam and headed upstream on the river Maas. Just after one o'clock on Tuesday morning, she landed somewhere between the towns of Ravenstein and Grave (no joke, Grim was assured). There, the entire procedure was repeated in reverse and although the air force base was another ten miles away, the N277 cut an almost straight line through cow country and only required a handful of adjustments for the *Oracle* to reach journey's end.

The overhead must have been a nightmare, and Grim was glad he wasn't the one doing the accounting.

'Right,' Delveaux said. 'You done for today?'

'Need to finish up a few things.'

She eyed him suspiciously. 'Are you getting enough rest? You look like you need it.'

'I'm a big boy. I can look after myself.'

'If I'd known you were in The Hague, I would have insisted you take a hotel. You don't report back, Robert. I appreciate initiative, but I hate it when people don't report back.'

He shrugged. 'I thought Glennis would update you.'

'Glennis answers to her superiors in the US. You answer to me.'

So that's what you're afraid of: American interference. And you want me to be your snitch.

'I'm used to fighting my own battles,' he said.

'That's terrific, but that won't fly here. You're fighting my battle, so I expect obedience. It's not open to discussion. Tomorrow you're going to London.'

'Say what?'

'I stumbled onto something of potential interest through an informant at MI5. In 1878 the HMS *Eurydice*, a British Royal Navy ship, capsized in a storm off the Isle of Wight. 317 of the 319 on board drowned, but multiple witnesses report to have seen the ship since. There's an officially documented case in the thirties. A Navy submarine narrowly avoided collision when what looked like the *Eurydice* suddenly appeared out of the mist at the exact place where it supposedly sank. And then there's the case in 1998, when none other than Prince Edward and an ITV crew captured the ship on camera while shooting for a documentary called *Crown and Country*. Radar showed no records of a large ship passing the Isle of Wight that day. Prince Edward passed the footage on to MI5, which still has it on file. And we, my good man, have permission to review it. I told them we have witness accounts of a similar event, which they found rather amusing of course. Nothing that requires high-level clearance, so to speak. So that's what you and Glennis will be doing tomorrow.'

'Fuck a bunch of tomorrows. What does this have to do with our ship?'

'Did you listen to anything I just said? It's the only official documentation in existence of a ghost ship. What *doesn't* it have to do with our ship?'

'They didn't send me to Kansas to investigate the Wicked Witch of the West either. I'm running tests tomorrow.'

'Which R and D can handle. This isn't open to discussion either, Robert. Your flight is booked. We reserved a room with a concierge for you at 45 Park Lane. I suggest you indulge yourself.'

Concierge, or guard? Grim thought but said nothing. So, London. What choice did he have?

Again, he noticed her penetrating gaze, making him want to crawl back into his shell or—and momentarily, he had a vivid image of it— smother her with duct tape. 'We need to jump on any leads we can get, Robert. So eyes and ears open. Ask smart questions. And report back to me. Now go and get some sleep. A car will pick you up at the hotel at six thirty.'

With that she turned and marched across the skybridge, disappearing through the door that had spit her out. As soon as the walls had swallowed the echoes of her footsteps, Grim turned back to the *Oracle*.

The ship's very presence unnerved him. She seemed to be mocking him, and now that he was alone with her, in his mind he heard the bell toll again.

But this time, it wasn't just the bell. The ringing joined the wailing of countless open mouths, and Grim imagined piles of the sick and dying lying on the upper deck.

3

The next evening, as Robert Grim in London dipped into a rosebud-perfumed bath with a beef Wellington on a tray, and as Luca Wolf in Katwijk struggled to wake from a nightmare in which some huge, dark thing dragged him out into the sea, Eleanor Delveaux was waiting on the tarmac of Volkel Air Base for the Gulfstream to land. Behind her was a black Mercedes van, its driver invisible behind tinted glass. The Lieutenant Colonel had escorted her in his jeep, but one phone call to the Commander of the Armed Forces and the man had cleared off, showing obvious contempt for the fact that his base was being comman-deered for purposes he knew little to nothing about. Eleanor's sole response as she watched him go was a curt, 'Yes sir, Loot.'

In the open field it was close to freezing, but that didn't deter Eleanor. She stood proud and she stood alone, as secrets dictated. The wind howled into her face, but her hair was coiled in such a tight knot that not a single strand fluttered. She stood so ramrod straight that she gave the impression of a statue. Even the sleet numbing her face didn't make her squint as she gazed to the east.

Eleanor knew she was hated and didn't care. In the male-dominated world of power, you had to be hard as nails to stand your ground. If that meant that she was perpetuating the stereotype of the unscrupulous battle-axe, then tough. People judged. Fine. In so doing, they inadvert-ently gave her cover to operate freely and bear responsibility for choices no one knew even existed, but nevertheless impacted everybody's daily lives.

Eleanor Delveaux could keep a secret. More than merely giving her satisfaction, it was her *raison d'être*. She didn't crave recognition. She had sacrificed much, if not all, to rise to her position, but her motiva-tion wasn't something as trivial as appreciation. Instead, she saw herself as a servant to a world that must be kept turning at all costs. She, and others like her, was the grease that ensured it did. They kept the world's secrets hidden.

Except now—that damn ship.

A greater secret than she had ever had to carry. A secret equivalent to a black hole. A secret that whispered promises of power in its purest form and could potentially disrupt the world order, because it didn't abide by the rules of the very universe that had spawned it.

Eleanor had finally met her match. No one could keep a secret of this magnitude alone. That burden—the *loneliness*—was simply too great. One couldn't give up all their humanity.

But whom did she trust enough to share it with?

Not Glennis. Getting her involved had been a necessary evil to get Grim. She had taken a risk drawing the attention of the Americans to this extraordinary phenomenon on a close ally's soil, but an *acceptable* risk nonetheless, because she had power over Glennis, who understood that her actual loyalty was to Eleanor first and to her country second.

No, there had been only one option from the get-go. Reckless? Probably, and she despised it. Taking chances went against everything she believed in, but what choice did she have? She had been alienated from her family a long time ago. When Eleanor died, her cremation would be quick, efficient, and undisclosed. There would be no tears shed, except maybe her sister's, though even those would be more from nostalgia than love. Friendships and romances had inevitably been sporadic, brief, and relatively anonymous, and above all, far in the past. Eleanor was at peace with this. Her career was her life and when the sun would set over the former, so it would over the latter.

Until she met Omar Al-Jarrah.

In 2007, Eleanor, not yet with November-6 but with the AIVD's counterterrorism unit, had tracked down a cell of radicalized Saudi Salafists in Rotterdam. The tip came from a very young Glennis Sopamena, who had been assigned to the CIA's Netherlands file due to her dual nationality and bilingualism. Eleanor, Glennis and Diana Radu had traveled to Riyad to exchange intelligence with the Saudi General Intelligence Presidency; a controversial move since the Rotterdam cell was financed via a bank on the Arabian Peninsula. The man who had waited for them in the hotel lobby was incredibly tall, hirsute and wore the desert on his skin. What stood out to her was his casual attire, different to most Islamic government ops, and the way his eyes burned with scarlet flames when he looked at her.

He worshipped *her*. That's how it began. He pressed the right buttons, admired her, saw right through her. Then she worshipped him, too.

They made love, and afterwards Eleanor didn't know what had happened to her. She would never let herself get attached to anyone, but with Omar that seemed impossible. It must be an incantation. The fire in his eyes burned on secrets. On secrets and power and corruption, and when she was with him, it burned on her, too.

For six nights, they shared everything; their bodies, their lives *and* their secrets, and each time the sun rose, she realized she could barely remember anything about him. Nothing about where he came from, his employer, or his convictions. Only that she trusted him through and through.

She knew they didn't have a future, and she told him so the night before she was due to fly home. Omar took her into his massive arms and breathed into her neck, 'There is no future. There's only now.'

Which was enough for both of them.

They rounded up the cell, preventing bloody attacks on Schiphol and the Amsterdam subways. In the ensuing weeks, she felt empty and alone, emotions that until then had never seemed negative to her. Sometimes, she would call him at night, listen to his secrets and think of the desert, a red sandstorm that surged through her mind, and she would imagine she could smell his strange, musky animal scent. But she always remembered who she was in time, and the minute she realized she had allowed herself to become dependent on him, Eleanor nipped her feelings in the bud. There was no incantation, no djinn, no mystery in him. Only neurotransmitters disrupting her functioning.

In 2009, their paths crossed again, and even though they slept together once more, she convinced herself that this time it was different. The secrets they shared, including a few pretty damning photographs of Glennis Sopamena that had come into his possession, were strictly professional. The fire was purely physical.

In the following years, their lives drifted apart. Al-Jarrah climbed high up in the ranks of the House of Saud-controlled GIP*, and Eleanor went on to lead NOVEMBER-6. Still, they became regular confidants, a bond she cherished more than the physical contact. She still desired him, only now she desired his knowledge, his intelligence, his secrets. When the time would come for their biyearly call, she would always feel lighter.

They met again in New York in 2017. He had aged, but the smile, the snow-white teeth, and the flames in his eyes were still the same. They didn't have sex, not because they had grown older, but because they pursued a deeper intimacy. Wrapped in his arms but fully dressed

* General Intelligence Presidency, the primary intelligence agency in Saudi Arabia

on a Jasmin-smelling hotel bed, she told him about the world and her place in it, and he possibly did the same, though when the sun rose, she could barely remember anything ... except that she trusted him through and through.

Omar Al-Jarrah was the only one she could trust with the *Oracle*'s secret, yet now she felt nervous. And that made her queasy. Eleanor never second-guessed her decisions, but this time, she wondered whether she had done the right thing.

Her cell rang. ATC. 'Three minutes,' the controller said.

'Thank you.' She hung up and saw that it was 11:50 p.m. Right on time.

A minute later, the landing lights appeared out of the low clouds east of the base. They seemed to hover for a while, and only at the last moment did the jet materialize and touch down, almost soundlessly compared to the roar of the F-16 fighters you heard throughout the day. The Gulfstream taxied up close to Eleanor and killed its engines.

Her heart pounded in her throat. *Get ahold of yourself. You set off on this course. Now see it through.*

The cabin door opened, and the pilot unfolded the air-stairs less than ten feet from where she was. Then *he* appeared. Better groomed than before, casually dressed. Although his light linnen shirt was too thin for tonight's cold, he didn't even flinch. He simply smiled.

'Eleanor! *Assalamu alaikum!*'

'*Wa alaikumu assalam,*' she said with a smile. 'Welcome to the Netherlands, Omar.'

Omar Al-Jarrah swung down the stairs and approached her with open arms. 'What a wonderful evening you've chosen for our reunion, Eleanor, and how *wonderful* to see you again!'

She caught herself quivering at the heavy Arab accent that coated his otherwise flawless English. She found that she still desired to warm herself against him, and when he embraced her, she staggered. He was so tall that he seemed to dissolve her entirely. His scent reminded her of goats and jackals and the fabled oryxes of the central plains.

She composed herself. 'How was your flight, Omar? You must be cold.'

'We stopped over in London. It doesn't get colder than London.'

'London?'

Grim and Glennis are in London.

'We had to pick up a package. Not important. Oh, I can't *wait* to see your ship, Eleanor. If it really is as you say, you've got nothing less than a miracle on your hands.'

More men emerged from the plane. She had expected a delegation of three or four, but there were nine. That's when her nerves solidified. Most of them wore the traditional thaubs and keffiyehs custom to Saudi officials. One, however, a stocky figure in his late twenties, wore jeans like Omar and a Burberry overcoat. He seemed skittish as he came down the steps, cautiously assessing his surroundings then fixing his gaze on Eleanor. And his face . . .

The color drained from Eleanor's when she recognized him.

'Ah, Abdulaziz, marvelous!' Omar called out. Her initial desire was replaced by confusion, and now she saw the deceit in him, the presence of power and secrets she was now excluded from. 'Come here and introduce yourself to Ms. Delveaux.'

Tentatively, the man came forward. When he held out his hand, she shook it mechanically. 'Hello Ms. Delveaux. My name is Abdulaziz Yamani. I'm a journalist for *The Guardian*.'

She struggled to produce a reply. 'I'm familiar with your work. Why are you here, Mr. Yamani?'

'That's what I want to know!'

But she already understood, she understood it all, and the fact that he was grasping her hand as if begging for help only confirmed it. Yamani wasn't just a correspondent for *The Guardian*. He was also a blogger and a political observer for Al Jazeera. As such, he was a fierce critic of the Saudi regime.

He was the package they picked up in London.

'Naturally,' Omar said, patting Yamani on the back. 'All in due course, yes? Eleanor darling, why don't you show us the way to what we came here for? The weather in this piss-ant country is god-awful.'

She wanted to say something, to convince herself that it wasn't true, but couldn't. She was too shaken up. She had made a terrible miscalculation, but how? All those years, all those nights. Had his devotion been nothing but trickery? A cold calculation to win her trust in anticipation of some hypothetical future opportunity? Or was his deceit more opportunistic in nature, and did he simply deem the ship a more valuable asset than her? Either way, she had gambled and lost. How dire the consequences were, would depend on what she did next.

They need me, she thought. *Don't forget that. This is a demonstration, not an armed robbery. If I play my cards right, not all is lost.*

She opened the van's side door. Planned to ride shotgun—she needed to think, get this back under control—but Omar grabbed her hand and insisted, 'Come sit with me, Eleanor. It's been ages.'

No choice but to comply. One of the men dressed in dark brown *bishts* opened the passenger door and slid next to the driver. Were they armed underneath? No doubt.

Think.

She could signal to the driver in Dutch. Let him know they were in a jam. Give him a different destination, away from the *Oracle*. But where? The Lieutenant Colonel was gone and most of the Joe's in the unit were off duty. Her only option was to head toward the bunkers in the hopes of flagging the attention of Dutch MP's or Yankee guards. But they had been specifically ordered to ignore the Mercedes van and everything that went in and out Hangar 3. Before they even realized something was wrong, these well-trained Saudis would easily take them out.

A confrontation would have incalculable fallout and was to be avoided at all times. So when Omar shut the door and they were all packed in like sardines, she had no choice but to lean forward and tell the driver, 'We're ready to go.'

On the way to the hangar, Omar introduced his delegation to Eleanor with almost childlike glee. One was a forensic expert for the GIP, but most were Mabahith. Eleanor gave them perfunctory nods, but her lips were pressed together and white. The Mabahith were operatives of the Saudi secret police, and to say they had a bad rep was putting it mildly. Their methods were unanimously condemned by the UN, Amnesty International and Human Rights Watch, and as Omar himself had described them to her, years ago during a particularly sultry evening, 'If you like your nails, you don't want to be questioned by that scum. Compared to the Mabahith, the KGB were Mother Theresas.'

She considered surreptitiously slipping her smartphone out of her purse. Discarded the idea immediately.

'Mr. Abdullah bin Saad Al-Mohammadi,' Al-Jarrah said with his perpetual grin, pointing at the man in the passenger seat, 'is a representative of the Royal Guard and a personal confidant of his excellency the crown prince Mohammed bin Salman. Oh, I can't *wait*, Eleanor. I'm so happy you invited us tonight.'

Yamani squirmed and blurted out, 'They have my mother. They showed me a video. She was *begging*, ma'am. They said they want to strike a deal with me and only then, *inshallah*, let my mother go.'

Omar snapped as if stung by a bee. 'You don't deserve to speak God's name, you *rat.*'

So much venom spat from that single word, so incongruous with the smile she had come to know over fifteen years, that a shudder rocked her body.

Yamani started to cry. 'Please, I'm begging you. If there's anything you can do, please do it.'

She understood their game. The dissident had been living in voluntary exile. Perhaps they had lured him to the London embassy, but more likely, just nabbed him at home. Using his mother as bait, they had given him no choice but to come with them. If they wanted to kill him, he must have reasoned, they would have already done it.

Now he didn't seem so sure anymore.

Ahead loomed the dark bulk of Hangar 3. Her mind was racing but couldn't focus. Thoughts whirled like debris in a storm.

The driver stopped before the giant doors. He aimed a clicker. The mullion started to slide, and the dashboard was suddenly bathed in a warm light. Omar crawled up front and beheld the Wonder of Every Man's End for the first time, his face bursting with such ecstasy it seemed to split in two.

'Unbelievable . . . this is magnificent!'

They drove inside. All the Saudis peered out, bristling with excitement. Even Yamani seemed impressed. 'What *is* this ship?' he muttered.

'This is the miracle you're going to make famous, you fuckhead. You'll be a legend. Was that worth all the fuss?'

The hangar was empty. Grim and Glennis were chasing wild geese in England, and Eleanor had sent all her staffers home; a mistake she would pay for dearly.

The driver parked in front of the access to the aluminum footbridge and as instructed, stayed in his seat. There was a queer moment when Eleanor was expected to open the door but didn't budge. In the end, Omar did. They got out and the van drove away, leaving them alone.

The Saudis admired the ship with cautious awe.

'I don't get it,' Yamani said. 'Did you build this?'

'No,' said Eleanor. 'It washed ashore, so to speak.'

Omar burst out laughing. He pointed at the footbridge and asked, 'Can we look up close?'

Now. Do something. Distract them. Drag it out.

But she gestured for them to go ahead.

Yamani, whose fear had given way to curiosity, became skittish again. Sweat was dripping down his jawline. Eleanor followed the company and was last to mount the bridge over the bulwark to the front, supporting herself on the rail.

With nine men and one woman, it was quite crowded. Looking down the length of the ship, what stood out was how narrow its deck was. Without the mast and rigging the forecastle was dominated by the open hatch. Even the Saudis seemed to sense a foreboding and kept a respectful distance.

Maybe she could still convince them to abandon their plan.

Eleanor looked at the three travel carriers she had placed there earlier that evening. As the Saudis admired the *Oracle* like visitors in a museum, she took her chance and opened one of the boxes' wire doors to remove its occupant: a lop-eared rabbit cuffed with an electronic collar. It shuffled in her hands and got comfy.

She pressed a button on the collar and a red LED started to blink. The rabbit tensed up, suddenly alert. She held it up to Omar. 'This rabbit has a tracker linked to my phone. I assume you want a demonstration . . .'

It wasn't the speech she had prepared, and she cursed herself for it. She was supposed to buy herself time.

'Such a cutie!' Omar took the bunny from her and, to her surprise, started to tickle it. 'You cuddly wuddly! You fluffy little cuddly pie! Is that it, Eleanor?'

He nodded toward the hatch. Eleanor nodded too.

'But we wouldn't want you to take out your phone, now would we?' Omar said amiably. He snapped the rabbit's neck and carelessly tossed it into a corner, where it twitched against the bulwark. He said something in Arabic, and two of the Mabahith grabbed Yamani.

Yamani screamed and fought but was no match for his aggressors. He snagged a keffiyeh from one of their heads, then got punched in the face and fell on all fours. When he was dragged to his feet, blood spattered on the deck.

Eleanor gawked in horror at what unfolded before her eyes. From the moment she recognized Yamani, she had known that this was no trade delegation. It was a hit squad. But it was too late to save the poor journalist's life. He was a sacrifice that had to be made. Later she would tell herself that she had been too paralyzed to act, but that wasn't true. It was her sense of self-preservation pure and simple, the only thing in her world that wasn't for sale.

Omar shouted in Arabic, his legs wide at the edge of the hatch, eyes afire and possessed with fury. Bleeding and still struggling, Yamani was hauled toward the opening.

'*What's in the ship?*' he screamed. '*What's in the ship?*'

'*Traitor! I curse you! Be damned!*

'*What's in the ship? What's in the—*'

'Nothing,' Eleanor whispered. 'It's Nothing you should be afraid of.'

And with that, they hurled him in. There was a dull thud when he crashed onto the lower deck, six feet down in the fo'c'sle, forever out of reach.

They all heard the tolling of the bell. So did the two remaining rabbits, going berserk inside their carriers, smashing their bodies against the wiring.

Omar's jaw dropped as he searched her gaze. He looked like a boy in a candy shop. What had she ever seen in him? No djinn, no ifrit, no incantation. He was *human*, and he was a monster.

A few of the Mabahith dropped to their knees and crowded around the hatch. Omar shouted something, and they pulled back, but all were looking inside.

Yamani started to scream.

At first, it came from below. Then, it came from much further to the left.

Then from above.

It was impossible to say whether they were screams of pain or fear, but with such screams, it didn't make much difference.

Eleanor retreated to the bridge, her maxicoat suddenly not enough to keep her warm. For a minute the screaming was everywhere, swelling into an ear-splitting din that filled the static air in Hangar 3. It crawled up from the nerve endings in their fingertips to penetrate their minds, and some of the Mabahith covered their ears and screamed themselves.

Then it died and all became silent.

'*Allahu Akbar,*' Omar whispered.

The men started to cheer and dance. One of them bent over the hatch to gaze inside and almost fell in; another clutched his collar, pulled him back, and flung his arms around him.

Eleanor, pale as a ghost, saw Omar Al-Jarrah come. She cringed as he grabbed her shoulders. The deck was stacked; now, she was his witness. His witness *and* his collateral . . . a power he would possess over her forever. This, their last secret, had brought passion only to him. His eyes sparkled, and she saw no regret, only satisfaction.

'Amazing!' he cheered. 'It's true, it's *true*, the miracle is true! Forever gone, you say?'

'Forever gone,' Eleanor confirmed.

'Name your price. *Any* price. We'll pay it.'

Eleanor smiled.

4

With the short interruption of the holidays (a total washout, because essentially the *Oracle* had cost him not only his dad but also his mom), Luca Wolf tried to get on with his life as well as he could. Didn't work. He couldn't keep up at school and worse, lost his standing with his usual squad. Still, in January, he kissed a girl for the first time, not Emma Reich like he had always imagined, but her best friend Safiya Adan, herself an outsider. Thirteen-year-old passion made hay when the sun shone.

The first time he noticed her like *that* was at Northgo High's Christmas Dance. It was partly her dress, baring her arms and shoulders, but mostly her hair, braided in a spectacular, spiraling pattern of cornrows. A tiny golden leaf hung from the roots high up her forehead. She was the talk of the night, at least on the red carpet where Mrs. Volmer, the school counselor, welcomed all the kids and funneled them toward the school photographer. She clapped her hands when she saw Safiya and declared that she looked *scrumptious*. Ruben Bex, CEO of Fuckupery from junior year, who was just behind them in line, asked if she had caught her hair in a blender. His goons howled, and Mrs. Volmer rebuked him, but she didn't hear the monkey sounds Ruben made in response, or he would likely have been suspended on the spot.

Safiya didn't hear them either, or at least pretended not to. Luca wanted to call out to her that she looked beautiful, like a work of art, but he wasn't the kind of smooth talker who could say something like that without making a total noob of himself.

Truth be told, he didn't want to come to the Dance in the first place, but his friends Elias and Noah convinced him. The event had been up in the air anyway after the paper depot fire, but the school had decided to go ahead with it to brighten everyone's mood. No students or teachers were officially dead, but a senior-year girl's dad was one of the cops lost. And then there were the three missing students.

The official story was that Ibby and Casper had run away to Ibby's family in Morocco. This was apparently confirmed by a cash withdrawal at Marrakesh Airport. Luca found it hard to believe anyone would fall for this, considering Ibby's peers claimed he had never even met his family down there. Besides, why would Casper, the soccer team's top scorer and every girl's heartthrob, give all that up to go with him? ('They had a fling!' 'Really? Some honeymoon . . .') At least in their case, there were breadcrumbs. Luca wondered whether it was Glennis who had laid out the trail.

It was the disappearance of Emma and her dad that got Northgo's rumor mill going full throttle.

'Her parents, didn't they get a divorce six years ago?' Elias asked between classes, a week before the Dance. 'Because I heard someone say her father snapped and *murdered* her. Ibby and Casper too. And that he's hiding out now, until he strikes again.'

'Mr. Reich isn't killer material, cheesecake,' Noah said. 'Laura says he has a Latvian girlfriend and they've gone to Latvistan, and Laura *knows* Emma. She says Emma's mom hired a PI to look into it.'

'But why wouldn't Emma keep in touch?'

'Because she's too busy sucking cock,' a voice behind them said. They turned on cue and stared into Ruben Bex's acne-blasted face. 'Emma's always been a sperm bank and her dad's her pimp. Now, she's reaping the fruits. But I'm sure you already know that, don't you, Fuckface?' Looking at Luca.

Luca should have punched his eye right then and there . . . but he bailed. Not because Ruben had nine inches on him but because of Emma. Because of the contract. And because Van Driel had said, *We have ears everywhere.*

Ruben belched in their faces and walked away. Elias coughed, said it smelled like he had had his mother's shit for breakfast, but only when Ruben was out of earshot.

No one linked the three disappearances with another absence that week: Luca Wolf's. Glennis was right, people got awkward around marital problems. His friends pretended it didn't happen. It was Mrs. Volmer who had summoned him after seventh period on Tuesday and said, 'Hard luck, all you've had to go through. I hope your folks work things out. But whatever happens, you're not the reason he left, don't you forget that. Your father still loves you.'

Luca had been on the verge of tears.

'If you need to talk, I'm here, Luca. Do you need to talk?'

He said he didn't.

'Are you sure? You might to feel better letting it out.'

What he needed more than anything was for this conversation to end, and when it did, he practically dashed out of her office. The next time he saw her was when she ambushed him on the red carpet, arms spread, giving Luca no chance to duck and cover before she hugged him and laid upon him a speech about how happy she was he had decided to come, despite everything.

The Christmas Dance didn't turn out half bad. Halfway through, the DJ played *Stuck with U* and Luca finally mustered enough courage to ask Safiya to dance. She said yes. She was only an inch taller, making it less awkward, and she smelled terrific, like strawberries. He put his lips to her ear and whispered, 'I like your hair.'

'Thanks, Luca. My sister did it. Took her two and a half hours.'

'Wow. Mine took ten seconds.'

A hard lie. In fact, he had spent over fifteen minutes in front of the mirror, but she laughed and that was good. Luca would never forget that Ariana-and-The-Beeb song, nor how her big, dazzling brown eyes kept imploring him, almost as if she was expecting something, though he had no idea what it could be. Maybe he would have figured it out with a little more time . . . but enter Ruben Bex.

'Ah, Fuckface and Chocolate Fudge Brownie. It figures.'

'Call her that again and I'll punch you, you racist piece of cock sauce,' Luca blurted out. Safiya's eyes grew even bigger and more dazzling.

'*What* did you call me?'

'You heard me.'

'Just ignore him,' Safiya said, but then Ruben shoved him, forcing him to let go of her. Luca went ballistic.

'I said don't call her that, *you racist piece of cock sauce.*'

The next shove was much harder and threw him across the dance floor, taking two kids with him like bowling pins. He hit his head and saw stars. When they cleared, he saw all eyes were on them as Safiya turned to Ruben, 'Why don't you pick on someone your own size?'

'Why don't you crawl back to Africa,' Ruben said, only this time he was overheard by Mrs. Volmer, who was pushing her way through the crowd. Ruben was immediately sent home and was suspended for the rest of the week and the first week after the holidays. Northgo High had zero tolerance for racism.

Piece of cock sauce? Safiya texted him later that night with a winking emoji. *The smelliest in the country,* Luca texted back. A winking emoji, too—okay, lame. *Thanks for sticking up for me*—her again, with a pink heart emoji. *He shouldn't have called you that,* he responded, and a heart with arrow emoji. Better. *Welcome to my life,* she wrote—shrugging emoji—and how were you supposed to respond to that?

Over the holidays, as he watched her TikToks on loop (*perved* on her, as the girls at school would say), he realized he had fallen in love. He felt awkward and guilty because of Emma, but Safiya was the distraction he needed, and by New Year's Eve he couldn't stop thinking about her (okay, couldn't stop *perving* on her). It felt like forever before school started and he would see her again.

She had killer moves, she was funny, and she had swag. The fact that she actually talked to him sealed the deal.

Nice GoT shirt, she texted him, to which he responded, *OMG, you like Game of Thrones???* She wrote, *Until they killed off Missandei. I mean, wtf??* and he went, *Yeah.* But then it hit him she was referring to the TikTok he made with Noah and Elias doing this stupid dance, totally childish compared to the stuff she put out, and Luca could have died. But she texted, *You were the cutest! But you sure got some white boy moves.*

The second week of January was midterms. On Thursday, he asked Safiya if she wanted to study at his place. With his mom at work and Jenna at school, they had the place to themselves. Safiya admired the koi pond, and then he showed her his room, a.k.a. the Beachcomber Exhibit. They sat on his bed, math books open between them and a bag of strawberry Rip Roles spreading sugar all over his comforter.

'Do you believe what they say about Emma?' Safiya asked out of the blue.

His cheeks heated up. 'What do you mean?'

'That she's in Latvia? You two were close, right?'

'Weren't you?'

'Yeah, and that's why I don't get it. This isn't like Emma, just going offline like this. I mean, what if she was taken against her will?'

'By her dad?' Luca knew he was dilly-dallying.

'I don't know. I don't think so. I didn't know him well, but he was always real nice.' She put the tip of a Rip Roll in her mouth, stretched it, tore it. 'But who can tell? Nice people do rotten things sometimes. What do *you* think happened to her?'

Luca felt like he couldn't bear it anymore. In the ensuing silence, all the energy in the room seemed to be flowing toward him. The fishing nets on the ceiling seemed to hum, as if the air were charged with electricity. Safiya stopped chewing and looked at him in expectation.

He almost spilled it . . . but lost his nerve. He wasn't ready to face the consequences, so he looked away and said, 'I don't know.'

'I'm sorry about your parents, Luca. I mean, mine are still together, but I believe it sucks.'

'Thanks,' he mumbled.

After making a lame attempt at studying, they found themselves debating *GoT*, which lightened the mood. There was more ogling, and Luca's crush was stronger than ever, when Safiya finally asked, 'Aren't you going to kiss me?'

A million stupid things to say popped into his head, but even Luca Wolf understood that the only unstupid thing was just to do it. So he dropped his marker and kissed her. Her tongue tasted like Rip Rolls and it was delicious, making his skin sizzle. When he pulled back, she gave him a radiant smile.

'I'm glad you waited and didn't do it at the Dance in front of that numbnuts,' she said, then added, 'I always thought you liked Emma.'

'Huh? I, uh . . .'

'Never mind.' She took his face and kissed him again. This time it went on for minutes, until he tasted salt and realized that he was crying.

Startled, she let go. 'Hey, what's up?'

His shoulders shook under her hands. Now that the floodgates were open, he didn't hold back. Everything came out, all the built-up grief and fear that had isolated him from the outside world, yes, even from his mom, who had been wallowing in her own misery. So he cried, as Safiya held him in her arms and whispered comforting words.

When it was over, she asked, 'What's going on, Luca?'

'I guess I miss my dad.' He picked up his marker and wrote on his notebook, *Zip it. They have ears everywhere.*

Safiya frowned. Raised an eyebrow.

He flipped the page and wrote, *Emma isn't in Latvia. And my parents haven't broken up either.*

Safiya suddenly seemed ill at ease. She opened her mouth, but Luca put his finger to her lips. He wasn't sure the house was wired, or if they tracked their phones, but he sure as hell assumed the worst. He wrote, *To the beach. Leave your phone. Trust me.*

She did, at least enough to follow him across the boardwalk to the empty beach, where he told her everything. It was a bleak and windy January afternoon, with the breakers turning into mist as they crashed. Still, Luca felt himself growing lighter with every step. Halfway through, Safiya took his hand, and they walked on like a couple, like they truly belonged together. Now that he had confided in her, maybe they did. Best thing was she asked questions, but never questioned the truth of it. That's where thirteen-year-olds were ahead of grown-ups.

Alone at the waterline, engulfed in wind and spume, they kissed again, and Luca thought, *January isn't half bad.*

But it was also the month he realized the *Oracle* was only the beginning of his problems.

The spyglass showed him that.

5

During the Christmas holiday, Barbara Wolf was in a constant state of limbo. She tried to adjust to her new role as a single mom (impossible without any closure) while at the same time seeking consolation for her despair (impossible without the truth). In the family house in Heemskerk, her sister Loes and her mother tried to comfort her, but after telling so many lies Barbara felt disgusted and kept them at arm's length. Nana took on Jenna for a few days, a load off her back, but Luca didn't want to stay over and locked himself in his room. Each attempt to talk to him only ended in a new cold patch between them. You didn't need to be a psychologist to deduce his inability to fathom what had happened to his father was the cause of his behavior, but she simply didn't know how to cope with it.

Barbara's limbo ended abruptly in January with a visit from Anne Mulder, Emma's mom.

She opened the door with her faux smile on—she was skilled at it by now—but it froze when she saw Anne.

'Anne,' she said, and then, 'Sorry, I was going to call, but I didn't get around to it. I've had a lot on my plate myself, you may have heard. But it's so good to see you . . .'

'Hello, Barbara.' She was clasping a leather folder to her chest. 'Don't sweat it. Do you have a minute? I'd like to talk to you.'

'Please, come in,' she said, and stood aside.

When the children were younger and inseparable, Barbara and Anne had been friends by default, but those years were overshadowed by a bad divorce and serious substance abuse. Now, Emma's mom looked much older and disturbingly more *broken*. But there was something else amiss. Barbara didn't know what it was, but she didn't like it. At all.

'Is Luca home?' Anne asked, as Barbara hung her coat.

'No, he's at school.'

'Thought he might be. Just as well to talk this over between us.'

She knows. I don't know how, but she knows.

It was the leather-cased folder. It didn't fit the bill. Anne Mulder wore cable knit shawls and gloves, bought her groceries at EkoPlaza, and always brought her own cotton shoppers. Not the kind of stiff, leather organizer she was carrying now.

'Would you care for a cup of coffee?' she asked.

'Tea, please.'

The kitchen looked out onto the patio and the glass wall of the raised pond, behind which seven koi lazily flashed their colors in their underwater dream. Like every visitor, Anne stopped to observe them. They swam, their fins swirling like veils, or stared through the glass with almost human contemplation. The pond was Alexander's pride; he had built it himself.

Barbara turned on the water heater, put a teabag in the pot, and dug out the strongest ristretto pod for herself. She needed caffeine asap.

'You seem on edge, Barbara,' Anne said from behind, and Barbara almost yelped. 'Are you alright?'

'Sure.' Avoiding her visitor's eyes, Barbara took a cup from the cabinet, put it in the machine, and pressed the button. 'It hasn't been the same since Alexander left. You know what it's like, after the divorce, like the walls are closing in on you. But listen to me yapping about myself.' She dreaded asking the next question, but she knew it was expected. 'Have you heard anything from Emma?'

'Nada,' Anne said. 'Absolutely nothing. And the police are just sitting on their asses. Interpol believes from his AmEx transactions, she's in Riga with her father. They can't issue an international arrest warrant because Martin has full custody, can you believe it? Meanwhile, they've got nothing on her! No cash withdrawals, no phone activity, no logins, zip! Shouldn't that raise a red flag?'

'Unbelievable.'

'You're at their complete mercy. So I had no other choice than to take matters into my own hands.'

Too late, Barbara realized what she was implying. Anne stopped at the framed picture of Alexander and the children at Lago Maggiore. 'I never would have believed this would happen to you, Barbara. You had such a good marriage.'

'What can I say? I didn't see it coming either.'

'Laura's parents told me you went to the Ardennes to try and patch things up, and that Alexander stayed. So he hasn't come back yet?'

'He hasn't,' Barbara said. 'Honestly, I wonder if he ever will. It's been such a mess. He says he needs more time, but how much time are you supposed to give someone?'

'So you have heard from him?'

That got her keyed up. 'Just through WhatsApp. We haven't spoken.'

'Hm,' Anne said.

The water heater clicked, allowing Barbara to pull herself away from Anne's prying eyes. She poured hot water into the pot as she searched her memory for Glennis' directions. Finally, she led Anne to the dinner table, where she downed her espresso in a single gulp. 'What can I do for you, Anne?'

'I'd like to discuss the morning of December 8. The morning Emma and Martin disappeared. Wasn't that the same morning you left for Belgium?'

'That's right, yes. What an awful day.'

'Don't worry, I get it. You pulled the kids from school to try and save your family. You got to do what you got to do, right? Family's number one.'

'We did what we thought was right. But I'm not so sure about it anymore. God, the last thing I want is for the children to suffer.'

'Oh, they will, mind you. Children always suffer from their parents' rotten behavior, no matter how you try and counsel it away. Tear up the family and you tear up their lives. Emma's father got custody because I was *out of my mind*. Once every three weeks I was allowed to see her, can you fuckin believe it? Pity visits! What a life!' She let out a shriek, an awful, bitter sound that seemed intended to pass for a laugh. 'Anyway, it's quite the coincidence that it all happened on the same day, wouldn't you agree? Emma's and Martin's disappearance and Luca's, shall we say, *family trip* to Belgium?'

Barbara was too stunned to speak.

'It was also the same day those boys ran away. Casper and Ibrahim. And the paper depot fire in Sassenheim. It's a lot. Five dead cops. Four children and two fathers gone. All on the same day in sleepy Noordwijk. And of the four children, only one has checked in. Luca.'

You're forgetting there was another story on the news that morning, Barbara thought. *The viral campaign with the ship exhibit,* Mysteries of the Dutch Seaborne Empire. *You've connected almost all the dots, but you're missing the most important one.*

'I really don't know what to say, Anne.'

'In a minute, Barbara. I think you'll have plenty to say. But first I want to show you something.'

She pulled the folder unto her lap and took out a few sheets of thick paper. She put them face down on the table between them.

'Are you absolutely positive it was Tuesday morning when you left?'

Barbara nodded. 'I don't remember the exact time, but—'

'I mean, I know from the attendance register neither Emma nor Luca showed up to school that morning. But you didn't by any chance leave later in the day, in the afternoon perhaps?'

'I don't understand where you're going with this, Anne.'

But she suddenly did, even before Anne flipped the first two sheets. They were photographs, CCTV grabs by the looks of them. They showed two people riding bikes. Shot through fog, the images were vague and grainy, but she instantly knew who they were, and when the pictures were taken.

'You see, I was suspicious from the outset,' said Anne. 'Emma and Martin aren't in Latvia. Martin would never pull Emma out of school to start a new life, where she doesn't even speak the language. Her education was far too important to him. And Emma would never leave without letting me know her whereabouts. Someone's hiding something. Someone's not telling the truth.' She gazed at Barbara with a rather incongruous, triumphant gleam. 'So, I hired a private eye.'

She slid the prints across the table. The first was from a front door security cam somewhere in town, Barbara assumed. Despite the poor quality and strange angle, she could clearly see Emma, who was sideways facing the camera. Luca, however, was little more than a smudge on the edge of the image.

There was no doubt about the second photo's vantage point. It was taken where the road to Noordwijk crossed the lock in the canal. It showed both cyclists from behind. This time, Luca's parka was clearly visible.

'These were taken on December 8 in Katwijk. My guy searched every possible route they could have taken in Noordwijk, and there are *a lot* more cams there. At the library, the Shell station . . . not a single eye caught them there. Not one. And that can only mean one thing.' She smiled at her, almost regrettably. 'Luca and Emma rode to school together, Barbara, but they never got there.'

'This isn't Luca,' Barbara said. 'Luca was in the back of the car with Jenna that morning, on his way to Belgium. I was there.'

'Except it is Luca. You're lying.'

'Anne, be reasonable.' She planted her finger on the first photo. 'This is clearly Emma, but whoever the other one is, you can't tell. And look at the other picture, all you see is a winter coat with a hood. If these are from that morning, Emma really did bike to school with someone, but it wasn't Luca.'

'They always go together, Barbara, you know that!'

'What do you want me to say? Luca was with us. Whatever it is you're insinuating, these photos prove nothing.'

'See, I was afraid you would say that,' Anne said with clear satisfaction. 'But take a look.'

She flipped the third picture. No CCTV this time. This one was much more focused. Luca, full frontal, riding his bike. In broad daylight. No mist.

'What am I looking at?'

'This was taken yesterday with a zoom lens.'

'You had a PI take photos of Luca? Anne, for heaven's sake . . .'

'What choice did I have? Look, it's obvious! It's the same blue parka. The same bike, a black Cannondale. See how the fender is bent to the left? It's the same in the picture from December 8.'

'This wouldn't fly in a court of law, Anne,' she heard herself say, even though she knew she was bluffing. Probably. She didn't really know.

'*What happened, Barbara?*' Throwing a tantrum now. '*What did he do to my Emma?*'

'Who, Luca?'

Anne slammed the table so hard the teaspoon rattled in her cup. Through her desperation, she was still rolling her eyes. '*Not Luca, knucklehead! Alexander!*'

So there it was. Luca lured Emma into the mist, and Alexander was the predator who made her disappear. Why not.

She doesn't have a story. She's trying to put it all together; coming here was her last shot. But the thing that connected everything that day—that damned ship—was overshadowed by everything else.

Barbara suddenly realized she could give her that story.

'Listen,' she began unsteadily, 'I feel your pain. I really do. But I'm in pain too, you know. That boy in the photo isn't Luca. They all wear the same coats nowadays. Ride the same bikes. Luca was with us. And I get it. Martin has put you through hell and back with the divorce! It's no surprise he took Emma. I'm sorry, I truly am, but that's no excuse for you to come here with all your accusations when I'm going through a difficult time myself, okay?'

Anne Mulder, once her friend, wailed inconsolably, but Barbara didn't have the strength to put her arm around her. Yes, she had the power to give her a story, but the only way through this was if she stuck to the game plan. Awful as it was, there was no other option. So she sat in silence across the table, while outside the koi floated gracefully unaware.

Anne pulled herself together, and then she got downright vicious. Barbara told her it was time to leave.

'I'm not done with you,' Anne sneered as she snatched her coat from the hanger. 'You and Luca are not getting away with this. Let's see what the police say when I show them these photos. Because I will, you can count on that.'

'Do what you have to do, Anne,' she said wearily. 'But leave Luca out of it. I sincerely wish you all the best. And I hope they find Emma.'

'Fuck you. Lyin' bitch.'

She slammed the door, and Barbara closed her eyes.

She was still standing there ten minutes later when her cell phone rang.

'Hi, Glennis,' Barbara said.

'Hello Barbara. You handled that well.'

'So, you are listening. Surprise, surprise.'

'Ears everywhere, remember?' Glennis chuckled. 'We've never made a secret of it. And I'm sure you understand. Soon, when this is all behind us, it won't be necessary anymore. You did yourself a great service.'

In some messed-up way, Barbara felt invigorated that Glennis had her back. The encounter with Anne had drained her more than she would have imagined. Glennis was the lesser of two evils. Maybe it had something to do with keeping your friends close, but your enemies closer. *Or Stockholm syndrome*, she mulled.

'She'll go to the police.'

'As she has on a daily basis for the past weeks. We'll handle Anne Mulder, don't you worry. Luca is safe.'

'I feel awful about it.'

'I understand. You're acing it. For Alexander.'

'Oh, to hell with that. I don't believe you'll find Alexander any more than you do. That was never the purpose of your little operation, was it?'

'I haven't a clue what you're talking about, Barbara.'

'You're losing your hold on us. Maybe you don't even know it yet. Alexander was the carrot you were dangling in front of us. Hush, not a word, or we'll never find Alexander. But lose that, and how long do you think we'll keep our mouths shut, Glennis?'

'Let me remind you there will be dire consequences if—'

'Screw your consequences, you've got *nothing*.' Finally, she blew her top, and it felt good. 'You act like a bunch of children with a secret they understand absolutely *nothing* about. If you seriously think you're in control, you're even more stupid than I thought.'

She hung up. Her hands were trembling, but her phone was dark. And stayed dark.

Barbara knew what she had to do.

Anne Mulder had walked the walk.

6

The morning after he dropped the spyglass during his nocturnal foray on the beach, Luca had returned to look for it. He hadn't expected to find it and probably would have been relieved if the waves had washed it away. But his curiosity trumped his fear, and above all, he had *hope*. What had he had seen was outside the realm of normality and so was what had happened to Emma and his dad. Maybe one could lead him to the other.

All it took was retracing his steps from the previous night, and there it was, half buried in the sand. As if it were waiting for him.

He picked it up, dusted it off. It felt heavy in his hands. Too heavy. Something made Luca look up then. The sky was muted. Seagulls sped overhead. His scalp itched. The itch spread down his neck to his back, causing him to shiver involuntarily.

The way he had heard those footsteps slosh in the surf.

That escalating menace from the sea.

Then look, Chickenshit. Or you'll never know if it was real.

He almost did, but then such a suffocating fear came over him that his vision blurred. He couldn't do it. Instead, he folded the monocular, took it back to the dune house, and hid it between his t-shirts in the roller case. Going through his belongings, Glennis had apparently overlooked it (or deemed it insignificant), because when he got home a few days later, it was still there. He put it away in what his dad used to call his 'Lookah-slocker,' an antique, washed-up coffer they had once lugged home from the beach on a wheelbarrow ("A *real* treasure locker! *Luca's* locker! *Lookah-slocker!*"—dork). In it, Luca kept his most valuable discoveries.

Sometimes he took it out. Usually when he couldn't sleep, and the loss of his dad caved a deep, black hole into his stomach. He would twist its rings until it extended into a tube the length of his forearm. He would feel up the leather and brass fittings with his fingertips, carefully studying their structure. Never did he peek through it, though. He told himself that with that cracked lens and built-up moisture inside, he would see jack shit anyway. The spyglass was clearly broken and always had been.

But often he knew better.

On the Sunday after midterms, he couldn't resist any longer and took it to the dunes on the south end of the boulevard. He wormed his way through barbed wire and climbed the incline amid windswept tufts of marram grass. When the town and beach bars were out of sight, he perched in a depression of silky sand. On the beach below, he saw the occasional beachcomber strolling by, but up here he was alone.

Alone with the sea.

This was where it was supposed to happen, not within the walls of his bedroom.

He took out the spyglass and extended its length. His lips were dry. There was menace in the air, in the screeching gulls swooping overhead and in the grey mass of water slipping into a hazy horizon. But it couldn't hold him back anymore. He aimed the viewer at the sea, squeezed his left eye shut, and looked.

He knew right away he wasn't looking at the North Sea. Not as he knew it, anyway. Gazing through the eyepiece, Luca felt the hair stirring at the nape of his neck. The sea was unusually clear; not blue like the Mediterranean in summer but more like he imagined a Greenland fjord: deep, dark, cold, and furious. The waves boomed on a mad arabesque of rocky outcrops, nothing like the Dutch coastline.

Luca lowered the spyglass and gazed at the Katwijk beach. It was still there. He saw a family with children looking for shells, a leopard dog frolicking around them. But the minute he put the spyglass to his eye, he saw that *other* seascape—the arch of the bay, the white curds of foam jumping off black rocks—and the family was gone.

He opened his left eye and *saw both*.

The sea-breeze blew in his hair, his heart pumped in his chest, and his eyes watered, but a smile pulled at the corners of his mouth. 'It's real,' he whispered.

Unless I'm going crazy.

But he wasn't. As he squinted, transfixed at what the spyglass was showing him, he could smell how incredibly fresh the sea wind was, almost as if there were no such things as super tankers and oil rigs and industrial pollution. Only the promise of open water stretching far beyond the horizon, all the way to . . .

. . . to the Northern icefields.

Where did that come from? Luca didn't know, but it was true nonetheless. He aimed left. The dunes rose far higher in the Spyglass world, into hills covered in tangled beach-grass. And there was a sound too: the beating of a drum and the low monotone chanting of female voices, interwoven in a rhythmic duet.

With his heart in his throat, he lowered the viewer and stared ahead. The sound faded . . . but not entirely. He could still hear it coming from some place *beyond*. It made him queasy, like he was floating.

Hold onto something, he thought. *The grass, the sand. Because I don't know if I'll find my way back. And I'm not sure I want to see this.*

See what? What the hell am I even looking at?

But he understood that the *real* question was: *Through whose eyes am I looking?*

Because he felt the ubiquitous presence of an *other*, a stranger, nearby, like a shadow eclipsing him and taking him by the hand. A guardian? Or an imposter?

He raised the spyglass and in Luca's perception, two worlds slid into one. The singing swelled and became a melodious hum. In it, he recognized the words of a long-dead tongue, singing about the rising seas and the struggle of the lands, all of which he knew because *his other* knew. When Luca aimed the spyglass at the waterline, he saw people wading. They were clad in animal skins and wore buffalo horns and antlers. A hollowed-out tree-trunk canoe was filled to the brim with berries, roots, hazelnuts, and strips of dried meat. In the middle sat a youngster, his head held high, his gaze fixed on the sea. The incoming tide rocked the canoe, spume splashed off its bow. They pushed him off, and the chanting became a high-pitched wailing, backed by the quick, intensifying rhythm of the tom-tom.

I think I'm feeling woozy, Luca thought, and it was true. His vision spiraled. He lowered the spyglass, but it wasn't the Katwijk beach he saw. Instead, the rocky headland stretched into a silvery black sea. It knocked Luca completely out of joint. He rubbed his eyes. Still there. Waves of blind panic washed over him.

'No, no, *no,*' he moaned. Again, he peeked through the eyepiece, *but spyglass or not, he saw the exact same thing.*

The rocky beach was now deserted, and the music gone, but the sea swelled to a roar. A monster wave crashed, sweeping the empty, hollowed-out tree trunk ashore, but there was no trace of the youngster.

Stop it! He had been misled; this had nothing to do with his dad. He desperately tried to hold on to the world that he knew, *his* world, but couldn't. Instead, he sensed a new presence, suddenly very near, and this time it was something altogether different. Something older and more primitive that bore the pungent odor of game. Luca looked around and what he then saw knocked him into pure survival instinct. He leaped forward, stumbled and smacked headfirst onto the sand, dropping the spyglass.

It was looming over him.

Enormous and dark.

He screamed and tumbled down the dune, eating sand, getting it in his clothes, his eyes, his hair. Grabbed onto something, crawled up on all fours. Looked up. Around.

It was gone. He was in Katwijk.

Slowly, very slowly he found his footing. He sank his head between his arms and took a deep breath, afraid he might throw up. When he felt up to it, he started to scramble back up to the depression. The spyglass was still there. Luca approached it as if it were a poisonous snake. Only after he had convinced himself it wouldn't pull any other tricks did he pick it up. He stashed it in his coat and ran.

When he got home, he buried it deep into the Lookah-slocker.

Didn't want to ever touch it again.

But the spyglass wouldn't let go of *him*.

7

After Anne Mulder's visit, Barbara called Rachelle, a seventeen-year-old from down the street, to babysit Jenna and Luca. Then, she drove to Every Man's End.

She idled along the fence. She didn't dare kill the Qashqai's engine, afraid—convinced—there would be patrols, but her headlights revealed the announcement of their charade in a fuck-you-sized font along the length of the enclosure: ALL ABOARD! 'MYSTERIES OF THE DUTCH SEABORNE EMPIRE', EXHIBITION COMING APRIL 2023! Posters of clippers and trade merchants with narrative captions teased a walkaround tour of the premises. They had executed it to perfection.

To the left, there was a dead-end road leading away from the grounds. Farms provided cover, so she turned onto it. On a dirt track beyond a tulip nursery, she stopped and doused the headlights.

Barbara got out and slowly started to walk back down the road. The dunes arched at the end of it, framing a quiet darkness below. It was the first time she had come out here since Alexander's disappearance. Barbara wasn't the kind of woman to believe in fairy tales. Deep in her heart she was convinced that her husband was dead. Still, she had come in hopes of some sort of echo. A whisp of breath, or a familiar scent from ground zero that could vouch for his lingering presence.

She couldn't find it.

She stopped at the last farm before Every Man's End. This must be where the owner lived, the flower farmer who had come to Luca's aid that morning. She could see lights behind the curtains, but she didn't dare knock. His house would be wired too. Luca swore he had seen him in another safehouse in the dunes, which didn't seem at all improbable.

Barbara stood on the margin of the road for twenty minutes, torn between her fear of getting noticed and the prospect of having to return empty-handed. Then she got a lucky break. The front door opened and a man came out, buried in his coat, a German Shepherd on a leash sniffling ahead of him.

Barbara watched them as they went along the street, away from Every Man's End. Heart thumping, she pursued. When she drew near, she cleared her throat and said, 'Excuse me, sir?'

The Shepherd erupted into hysterical yapping and, ears pulled back, went for her. She leaped back as the farmer yanked the leash, cutting off the dog before its teeth could snap. '*Sheep, down!*'

Sheep went down but the leash stayed taut and his barking persisted. 'Brilliant move, sneak up on a sheepdog in the dead of night,' the man said. Another yank and he snarled, '*Enough!*'

Sheep settled down.

'I'm sorry, it was a stupid thing to do.' She glanced around, afraid that the barking had attracted unwanted attention of the neighbors . . . or worse. For now, all seemed quiet. 'Do you own the land where they're putting up the exhibit?'

He squinted. 'What's it to you?'

Check. 'That's where my husband disappeared. I'm Luca's mother. The boy you found at the ship that morning.'

'Oh. I, uh . . .' Suddenly on his toes, he scanned around. When he spoke again, it was subdued. 'Why the hell did you come here?'

'Please, I only need a minute of your time.' She grabbed his sleeve and like him, she muted her voice, but her desperation showed. 'I *know* they're listening. They held us for four days in some house in the dunes, and I know they held you there as well. They've been watching our every move, while they want me to stick to some friggin story about my husband leaving us, and I feel like I'll go crazy if I can't talk to *someone*! You *know* what happened. You *know* that ship wasn't some ordinary thing . . .'

A play of emotions flashed across his face, but his attitude remained defensive. *And scared*, Barbara realized. *He's truly scared.* Not Sheep, who was now curiously sniffing her feet.

'Listen ma'am, you'd better go . . .'

'What if it was your wife who went missing?' she pleaded, her voice pitching to a squeak. 'Or your children, for crissakes! Please!'

'Alright, alright,' he hissed. 'But not here, dammit.'

With that, he marched ahead of her and she followed. 'Thank you. Thank you. Do you really believe they're *here*? It seems so quiet tonight . . .'

'Quiet my ass. They have eyes everywhere. They're watching over their toy day and night. Back and forth traffic all day. Constant hammering and drilling and whatnot.' He was quiet, then said, 'How's your boy?'

'Miserable.'

'Hm. Figures. He was in a right state when I saw him. Wim Hopman, by the way.'

His free hand stayed in his pocket, so she answered with a nod. 'Barbara Wolf.'

The road dead-ended, and they took a trail into the dark fields. There, Hopman relaxed a little and paused. 'You need to let it go.'

'Let it go? Are you kidding me?'

'If you know what's good for you. I'm terribly sorry about your husband, but it's too dangerous. This is far bigger than you and me.'

'But I have no choice! Do you think I *want* this? I didn't ask for any of this!'

'So what is it you're going to do?'

'I'm going to blow their cover! My husband is not coming back, and neither are the others. I don't know where they are, but God, I pray every night that they've found peace. And I don't even *believe* in God!' Her voice broke and she started to cry. 'If Alexander is dead, I will not allow them to brush his death under the rug, like he was trash. This isn't Russia or North Korea! Oh, *dammit*, look at me!' She stamped the ground, wiping her sleeve across her face. So much for her intent to remain calm. Hopman eyed her uneasily. She tried to pull herself together and concluded, 'We need a whistle-blower. If there were enough of us . . .'

'Ma'am, listen to me.' He turned and pointed to the dark rise of a building they had just passed. 'See that old depot over there? That was Bart Dijkstra's tennis club. Real good place. My boys used to play there before they went off to college, and it's where my wife and I would have our coffees on Wednesdays and Saturdays. Bart's fiancée Isa used to run the bar. Care to know why I say *used to*?' He gestured for her to get going and muffled his voice once more. 'Because they're both gone. I saw Bart go into that damn ship myself. I even warned him not to, because whatever was buggin your son had got hold of me as well. I warned him, but he wanted to be a hero and get these cops out. Noble, but stupid.'

'What happened?'

'That damn bell started ringing, that's what.' He wavered and kicked a root ball. Sheep snapped at it. 'Still bothers me, that bell. The sound was coming from everywhere all at once. The first few days after they returned us home, you could hear it tolling all the time. They were running tests, you know? Testing out their ship. Gave me the jitters. But the weird thing is, I never heard it after that. Not since mid-December.' Hopman seemed to linger on the thought, but Barbara didn't want to interrupt him now that he was revved up. 'Anyway, that's when Isa started calling out his name. Screaming, more like it.'

'So she went after him.'

'Oh, no. Isa didn't go in, she was too smart for that. She must have sensed something was wrong. She was a witness that morning, and what have they done with the witnesses?'

'They locked her up in the dunes too!'

'Yep. At least, it figures. They took us both off the grid for four days, so why not her too? For us, it was enough to sign their NDA without a fight. But don't fret, they're paying the big bucks. Many times the worth of that bloody field's yield, that's for sure.'

So they gave you money, Barbara thought. *Alexander was enough to hold sway over us.*

'So Isa, and most likely the cops from the second team. They all saw what happened. Not all up close, but one of them was about to follow her squad inside, when she must have gotten a hunch. She was the one who put a cork in it. You could find her; she could be your whistle-blower. Plus, you'll have your reliable witness. But I wouldn't recommend it, because of what happened to Isa.'

'What happened to Isa?'

'Isa is dead,' Wim Hopman said.

'What?'

'There's a lot coming through the grapevine these days, and most of it is horse piss, but this you better believe. Ineke heard it a couple days after they let us out. The official story is she veered off the N206 northbound and had a head-on with a common ash, about halfway toward Haarlem. Seeing as she was driving one of them Swifts, more biscuit box than car, there wasn't much armor. She didn't stand a chance.'

'That's awful.'

'Yeah, I reckon. It's fishy, too, if you ask me. Nobody knows where Bart is, he's still unaccounted for. And out of the blue, she's dead in a wreck. You could think up a dozen scenarios. So did the newspaper. But none of them mentioned what Heflin Smit saw. He's a mechanic for box harvesters and potting machines and whatnot, and he was coming southbound on the 206 that day. Says an unmarked van, no license plate, cut her off and practically pushed her down the embankment.'

Barbara stopped and covered her mouth.

'It's only two lanes and Heflin had to swerve around, or he would have hit the van himself. Says it then sped away. But there was no camera, and no one else ever saw it. The police filed his report, but there's no mention of the van. So we're down to the grapevine.'

'They wouldn't go that far.'

'Wouldn't they?' Hopman asked. 'The 206 goes right by that dune reserve south of Zandvoort. Close to where they held us, I'd say. And Isa's accident was days after they'd let us go. Now hear me out. What if she refused to be bought? What if she refused to sign the NDA and threatened to talk to the media? Right, so they lock her up a few more days. Tighten the screws a li'l further. But what if that just pisses her off even more? Now she's gettin to be a *real* problem, and there comes a point they want to be shed of it.'

Barbara didn't know what to say. Her head was spinning.

Sheep perked up his ears and gazed into the dark, suddenly alert. Wim Hopman stood and listened. When he turned to her again, he put a brittle hand on her shoulder.

'Please,' he said. 'For your own safety and for your son's, let it go. They'll stop at nothing.'

8

Around the time Hopman's German shepherd jumped on Barbara at Every Man's End, Luca lay in bed brooding, vainly trying to make sense of what the spyglass had shown him. His temples started to throb, his blood seemed to sing, and after a while he realized he wasn't staring at his own fish-net-clad ceiling but at a tent cover made of animal hide.

Luca sat up. It *was* still his bedroom, no doubt about that—same desk, same chair where he had carelessly flung his clothes. On the ground, his sports bag. But at the same time, he saw warm light flickering on caribou skin and smelled the smoky, strangely spiced odor of a moss-kindled fire. It was like one of those colored images in a Magic Eye book where if you stared at it long enough, you suddenly saw a 3D shark or a jumping horseman. Once you saw it, you couldn't *unsee* it.

Again, he got the feeling he was watching through somebody else's eyes.

There were three women with him in the big tent. One was draped in bearskin, another was wearing rags and feathers in her hair and a curved, black beak. The third wore a large feline skull with half-moon fangs. They were preparing their ritual and one of them gave him some dried mushrooms. He could see hands reaching out to take them, but they weren't his hands, they were the wrinkly hands of his guardian.

'Who are you?' whispered Luca.

'*Nunyunnini,*' a voice sang in his head and then it was gone, the women and the tent gone, and Luca was staring at the window of his Katwijk bedroom.

This hadn't been the first time. Last Wednesday, he was daydreaming his way through third period earth science class. One moment, he was trying to survive Ms. Kuypers' never-ending spasms on endogenic and exogenic forces; the next, he was in the bunk of a gloomy captain's cabin, looking through a stranger's eyes at the nauseating roll of the waves outside the porthole. He instantly felt seasick, and tried to grab onto his desk, but it wasn't there. He stared at where his classroom's windows ought to be and saw nothing but weather-beaten, oiled wood—he could even smell it—and a much smaller stern window gallery. In front of it sat a sturdy man bent over a diary, scribbling with a quill dipped in ink. Luca's instincts told him that he knew and trusted this man, but from beyond a thin bulkhead came an anguished wailing that cut him to the marrow. They were many, a chorus of the sick and dying. And above it all, there was the wind, the wind in the rigging and the relentless surge of the sea . . .

'Is something the matter, Luca?'

He practically gawked at Ms. Kuypers. 'N-no,' he muttered, thinking, *That was the* Oracle. *I was on the* Oracle! 'Sorry, I . . . I was out of it for a second.'

Elias was watching him, and worse, so was Safiya. He tried to smile at her, then lowered his gaze to his notebook.

The page screamed with pen slashes in the shape of a woolly mammoth.

'Dude, are you okay?' Safiya had asked after class. 'What's going on? You were shaking.'

'I'm good!' Flashing her the okay sign.

'Don't lie to me, Luca. Not chill.'

'Absolutely not.'

One more time, he had thought. *One more time to prove I'm not crazy, and I'll tell her.*

This was your one more time, Luca now thought and got up.

He pulled on two hoodies. Going downstairs to get his coat wasn't an option, as it led past Rachelle. She was watching TV and texting her Romeo, and Luca had no desire to give her the chance to prove she was worth her four-fifty an hour. He opened the Lookah-slocker, rummaged about, and found his spyglass. He put it in his backpack and threw it over his shoulders.

Every thirteen-year-old boy was aware of the backup exits from their house, and Luca was no different. From his own bedroom window, you couldn't reach the patio without breaking your ankles; the wall was slippery and there were no footholds. From Jenna's room, it was a different story. Theoretically, at least. Luca had never attempted it because he had never felt the need to. Until now.

He snuck into his sister's room and opened the door. Jenna was sound asleep by the glimmer of the nightlight stars projected on the ceiling. He tiptoed to the window and heaved it open, holding it tight to keep it from grating and squeaking. Ignoring the sudden draft, he slid Jenna's My Little Ponies aside, hoisted himself onto the sill, and climbed out.

Across the patio stretched a pergola laced with his mom's Blue Rain that blossomed every April. He tested the wood, then lowered his weight onto the frame. On all fours, he made his way forward hand over hand. Halfway, the crossbeams creaked and bent under his weight. For a second he froze, terrified of the snap that would send him splash-bang into the koi pond. Then he bolted ahead and reached the roof of the shed on the other end unharmed. He lowered himself down the rim, found the door handle with his foot, and jumped onto the patio.

Inside, all remained calm. Luca didn't hesitate and took his Cannondale from the shed. Once he reached the end of the alley and steered down the street, triumph washed over him. It worked; he got out!

Right, so now Safiya. He stopped under a streetlamp, opened Snapchat and sent, *Where U LIVE?!!*

In the town of Voorhout, that much he knew, so he started to head there. Less than three minutes later he got, *Wow, all caps.* An address on the Lavendelweg. *You know it won't be Valentine's till Feb.* And a brain emoji.

ETA was thirty-one minutes according to his maps app. *Make it twenty-one*, he thought and pumped the pedals. Fingers crossed he would make it back home before his mom. If she came home and found his room empty, she would probably call in the army.

Twenty minutes later, he was in Voorhout, and five minutes after that, he reached the Lavendelweg. It was a typical Dutch street in a typical

Dutch community. Safiya's house wedged between her neighbors in a tight row. The problem was it couldn't be accessed from the back as it bordered a canal. There was a brick garage in the front, but if he climbed onto it, he would be fully exposed. Plus, he didn't even know whether Safiya's room was front or back. So much for his romantic climb-through-the-bedroom-window act. No other option but to text her.

Wdym, come outside???? *Stalker! Know what time it is?*

Please, it's important, he texted. Sad face emoji.

My dad will kill me. And u!!!!

Still, a few minutes later, the front door opened, and Safiya snuck outside. She glanced over her shoulder and pulled the door to a crack. Beyond the living room curtains the light from a TV flickered.

She ran to meet him at the end of the front yard, her face all *WTF?* But she quickly broke into a smile. 'Seriously,' she whispered. 'You're crazy! What are you doing here?'

'I need to talk to y—' he started, but she cut him off.

'Keep it down, stupid! Follow me.' She dragged him by his sleeve. A few houses down, they turned a corner and stood on the footbridge crossing the waterway. This week, Safiya's hair was braided in neat rows. In the halo of the streetlamp, she looked mysterious and gorgeous.

'What's so important that you couldn't text it?' she asked. 'You didn't come here to break up with me, did you?'

He was aghast. 'No, of course not!'

'Oh, that's okay, then. Otherwise, I'd really have to let my dad kill you. And they were planning to ask you to dinner this week.'

Luca slid his backpack off and took out the monocular. He extended it full length and held it out to her. 'Here, look through this and tell me what you see.'

She gazed at him with one raised eyebrow, with no intention to take it.

'Please, it's important. I'm not messing with you.'

'This better be good.' She took the spyglass, raised it to her eye and aimed it at the far end of the canal. She then turned it in her hands and brushed the cracked lens with her finger. 'Nothing. That's what I see. This thing is broken.'

'Try again.'

'You're so weird.'

'Come on.'

She sighed theatrically and looked again. 'Nothing, weirdo.' She handed it back to him. 'See for yourself. All you can see is a blur. And it's way too dark anyway.'

She sensed his hesitation and raised her brow again, a gesture that held more power than anything. 'It won't bite you.'

He couldn't show her he was chicken now, so Luca raised the spyglass for the first time since that day in the dunes and peeked through the eyepiece. Dark blots. She was right. He twisted the copper ring, tapped the tube against the bridge's rail, but no change.

'Come on, don't let me down *now* . . .'

But he thought he understood why it did, so he told her everything. He started with how he had found the spyglass on the beach, the night after his dad and Emma disappeared into the *Oracle* and ended with the visions that could jump him whenever he let his guard down. Safiya listened quietly, her lips slightly parted, the cynical eyebrow gone. At least that was something.

'It's like that thing has opened a door in my mind,' Luca said. 'At first, I needed the spyglass to see it, but now the door is wide open, and I can see without it. And sometimes . . . something comes through that door. Or *someone*.'

'That's creepy.'

'You bet it is. I don't *want* to see it. It scares the shit out of me every time, and I hate it. But I *have* to look. I need to know what happened to my dad, you know?'

She took his hand and squeezed it. 'I know.' She said it with so much conviction, this beautiful girl with eyes like nighttime oceans, that Luca got all light in the head. 'Come on, let's head back. If I stay out any longer, my folks will find out. I'm glad you told me, Luca.'

They walked slowly.

'You probably think I'm crazy.'

'Bruh, the Mind Flayer is crazy. So are the Demodogs. You're just . . . challenged.'

He smiled. She smiled back.

'I don't think you're crazy, Luca. When a boy knocks on my door late at night and tells me he hallucinates about people wearing animal skulls, it's my regular Tuesday.'

'You're evil.'

'Aww, love you too.'

'So, uh . . . dinner?'

'If you don't think it's lame. They are my *parents*.'

He said he didn't think it was lame at all, and they rounded the corner. Even though his head was fuller than ever and he had never felt so heavy in his life, it was nice to just be there and hold her hand. That way, he could pretend it all wasn't that important.

'Do you want to know what it all means?' she asked just before they reached her house.

'I . . . I'm not sure.'

'Maybe you should summon it.'

'But I don't know how. I have no control over it.'

She stopped and put her hands on his shoulders. 'Then take control.' She put a kiss on his cheek and was gone.

9

Barbara sat in the dark behind the wheel of the Qashqai. She had attempted to leave but was too upset by Wim Hopman's revelations to drive, so she parked in the shoulder and cupped her hands over her eyes. Only when she looked up, did she see that a sickly orange glow bathed the Nissan's interior.

She got out and saw something she could not at first fathom. Every Man's End was burning.

She made out the outline of a gigantic tent, engulfed in flames. Within seconds it was consumed from all sides. Strips of burning tarpaulin swirled hundreds of feet up in the rising heat, fizzling out or raining down everywhere, still smoldering. Smoke billowed from the inferno, enough to cover the moon, and before long, the only thing left standing was a steel-framed skeleton. Burning within was the shape of a giant ship.

'No, no, no, *no* . . .' she yammered.

Tears were flowing down her cheeks. Even though she had given up hope that Alexander was still alive, seeing the *Oracle* burn to ashes made it final, as if his last remnants were also burning.

She called Glennis, who picked up after the first ring. 'What have you done, you *monsters?*'

'Barbara . . . what are you talking about?'

'The ship! It's burning! You're just letting it burn!'

'How do you know?'

'I'm in Noordwijk, you stupid cow!'

Glennis instantly switched gears. 'No, Barbara. What you see burning isn't the *Oracle*. It's a diversion. Did you really think we were going to organize that exhibition? Of course not. We've been building a replica. The official account will say that unfortunately, there was a short circuit in one of the tent's generators that caused a rapid fire. This spells bankruptcy for the organizers. Nice and tidy. The ship—the *real* ship—has been in a secured location for weeks.'

'But where . . . how . . .'

'I'm not at liberty to say, Barbara. But I assure you it's safe. We could hardly leave it out in an open field, I'm sure you understand.'

She remembered what Hopman had told her about the ship's bell. *In the first days after they returned us home you could hear it tolling all the time. They were running tests, you know? Testing out their ship. Gave me the jitters. But the weird thing is, I never heard it after that. Not since mid-December.*

Sirens wailed in the distance. Barbara felt her legs give way and barely noticed she had sunk to her knees. The acrid smell of burning plastic stung her nostrils even from three hundred yards away, and she listened to the roar of the blaze.

Alexander was gone, really gone. She understood that now. It didn't matter if they were hiding the *Oracle* someplace else or not. Alexander was no longer here, nor would he ever come back. She had kissed him goodbye that morning and left to take Jenna to school. Then Luca's call had come, and Alexander had fallen into darkness.

'. . . hello? Barbara? Are you still there? Hello?'

She ended the call and didn't pick up when it immediately rang again. She wasn't going to tell Glennis what was on her mind.

She was going to take them down.

And when all was said and done, everyone would know her husband's name.

10

By the third week of January, Robert Grim reached the conclusion that the *Oracle* needed to be destroyed. It was an obscenity. It corrupted reality and the people who believed they exercised power over it. He told Eleanor Delvaux, of course, in her office beyond Hangar 3, but she cut him straight off.

'You've got to be kidding,' she said. 'A miracle falls in our lap with powers we haven't even begun to unravel, and your first inclination is to destroy it? What a primitive human impulse.'

'That ship isn't a miracle, it's a supernatural time bomb! Why isn't anybody listening to me when I say these things?'

'Nonsense. If you were to drop a Tesla amid a jungle tribe undefiled by western civilization, they wouldn't understand it either. You can't blame that on the Tesla. Human inferiority doesn't render a superhuman object pernicious.'

'No, but its *nature* does! And as far as your scenario goes, I see three possible outcomes. The first is that these rainforest dwellers would see your Tesla as a miracle, just like you called the *Oracle*. They'll drop to their knees in worship. "Oh, Mighty Thunder God, we thank thee for thy Shining Monster Bean." The second outcome is much more likely, which is that they'll take their axes and chop it to pieces. And good for them, because the third outcome should always be avoided, which is that one of those aboriginals gets behind the wheel, accidentally finds the start button, loses control, and takes out the entire pygmy village!'

'That's not very politically correct, Grim.'

'Because you don't give a flying fuck about political correctness! How the hell can we do scientific research if you're not interested in the results? Why am I even here if you're going to reject every single one of my conclusions?'

She laughed, the sound merry and disdainful at the same time. 'I hired you to lead the investigation, but *I* draw the conclusions. And frankly, you haven't given me much. So, chop chop. Work to do.'

Furious, Grim stormed out of her office. This had confirmed his suspicions: Eleanor was stalling him. Fuck if he knew why. There was zero justification for keeping Glennis and him in the Netherlands after five weeks with nothing to show for it. Glennis was likely getting in hot water with her sups at The Point who, being American, *must* have their own agenda for exploiting the Dutch miracle ship.

How come they hadn't interfered?

Because she doesn't report to them, Grim thought. *It's Eleanor she reports to now.*

That chilled him . . . because of what it meant for *him*.

One thing was clear: there was nothing close to a scientific investigation going on. What was there to investigate? You had the ship, or better, the *hatch*, that made anything dead and alive disappear. No point in racking your brains about the hows and whys. In Grim's experience, supernatural phenomena followed their own unique set of rules, different from the laws of physics as we understood them, but rules nonetheless. You were safe (relatively) as long as you went along and preserved the fragile status quo.

There was just one glitch, and that was the crux of it all. Supernatural phenomena followed their own set of rules . . . *until they didn't*. Because down below, they spread like mycelia, shooting spores in all directions until they surreptitiously infected their entire surroundings and popped up everywhere in fairy rings of poisonous shrooms.

Then, pandemonium. Screams. Destruction.

He could warn them till the cows came home, but they wouldn't listen. Not Glennis, with her evasive answers. Nor Eleanor, with her deviations. London, for instance. Some blurry video of an old ship, a shouting prince, big fucking deal. It had all been a red herring. They were throwing him curveballs.

But why?

Grim knew he was so caught up in their mess that his only option was to play along. He also had enough self-awareness to know that "playing along" was his weakest suit. But his future might well depend on it, so he resigned to be Eleanor's lapdog. Bark when she asked him to bark. Roll over when she asked him to roll over. Maybe the day would come when he could rip her throat out.

So, Robert Grim went back to his research. Back to square one. Which meant, back to where it all started. There was only one person who had seen the whole caboodle. That's why the next evening, he drove to Katwijk aan Zee.

He had the boy's file translated, so he was up to speed. Grim found him where he expected to find him, on the soccer fields of the Quick Boys Sports Park, running after a ball with a whole bunch of other twerps in the drizzling rain. Grim wasn't exactly fond of children, and children *playing* really got his goat, so by the time they finished practice and he was waiting in the floodlights for the little squirt to finally emerge from showering or liquoring up in the canteen or whatever the fuck he was doing in there, Grim was in a rotten mood.

One stroke of luck, the kid was on foot. The five hundred yards separating the Sports Park from the Wolf home gave Grim ample opportunity to accost him. There he came, sports bag slung over his shoulder, but Grim had to let him go by as some boys were loading into a soccer mom's van and he didn't want to draw attention to himself as some kind of perv. After she drove away, he hurried and caught up with him.

'Hey, kid. Speak English?'

'Uh . . . a little bit?'

He held out a bag of Chupa Chups. 'Lollypop?'

Luca stopped and looked at him incredulously. 'Seriously? You're an old dude and you're offering me candy?'

'Whatever.' Grim put the bag away. 'How 'bout this: you're Luca Wolf and in December, you saw your father disappear into a ship called the *Oracle*. You, your mom, and your sister were put under house arrest for a while by a special branch of the secret service. I'm not a hundred percent sure who was on your case, but I bet that bitch Glennis was involved. Hi, Luca, my name is Robert Grim. Better?'

'Whoa,' Luca said. Cautiously backing away though, as his wariness had turned into downright alarm. 'Are you one of them?'

'Me? God, no.' Grim waved his hand. 'I'm just the poor schmuck they hired to investigate their toy. I hate the fuckers.'

He said it because it was true, but also because he knew from the boy's file that *Luca* hated them, and that he had been a bit of a pain in the ass because of it. Good for him.

'So, you're like Dr. Sam Owen.'

'Who?'

'*Stranger Things*. In season two he's hired by the government to hush up what happened in Hawkin's Lab.'

Grim couldn't suppress a smile. 'Haven't seen it. A long time ago, another boy compared me to Fox Mulder from *The X-Files*.'

'The what?'

'You don't know *The X-Files*? Damn, yet another generation. You've probably never heard of *The Twilight Zone* either.'

'Like I said: old dude,' Luca replied not unfriendly.

'Touché. Was I right about Glennis?'

Luca hesitated, then nodded. 'She was the worst. Sneaky. With the others, you knew they were lying and not on your side, but she just smiled all the time.' He was quiet, then burst out laughing. 'You called her a *bitch*?'

Grim winked over his horn-rimmed glasses. 'My job comes with certain perks. Listen, I saw a bench under the trees just up the road. It's probably not too wet. I was wondering if we could talk for a minute.'

'Are you recording me?' Luca asked, surprising Grim. The kid was shrewder than he had expected. He was smart to be suspicious of grown-ups. Also, his English was a whole lot better than just 'a little bit.' That part had been a gamble—but sometimes the dice rolled in your favor.

'Uh, no. All I've got in my pockets are those Chupa Chups, my car keys, and my phone.'

'You can do Voice Memos with a phone.'

He took it out, unlocked it and handed it to Luca, who swiped through his apps, then gave it back. 'Okay.'

'Of course, I *could* have a micro bug hidden in one of my coat buttons. Secret ops like me always do, so I guess you'll just have to take my word for it.'

'You don't,' Luca said. 'But I will have one of those Chupa Chups.'

Grim handed him a red one and they walked away from the Sports Park. On the left were houses, on the right were bushes that separated a nursing home from the dunes.

'Tell me, how come your English is so good? In America, kids your age can barely speak their own language.'

'Games. Apps. Netflix. And school, I guess. Are you an American?'

'Yep.'

'What are you doing here?'

'They didn't have a Dr. Sam Owens in the Netherlands.'

That seemed to make perfect sense to Luca, so he didn't pursue it. Instead, he asked, 'Did you find out anything about my dad?' It was obvious he was taking pains not to sound too hopeful and Grim regretted having to disappoint him.

'Afraid not. Nor any of the others. The feds, the secret service . . . even Interpol couldn't come up with anything.' He saw Luca's puzzled expression and added, 'That's the international police.'

'Duh. They're looking in the wrong place.' The tip of his lollipop was dancing up and down.

'Is that true.'

'If they're looking on the outside, I mean.'

'Then where *should* we be looking?'

'Inside the ship.'

'Huh. Interesting.'

There was something irresistibly logical about it. Childish maybe, as it overlooked a few obvious realities, but still, it revealed Luca's casual willingness to accept the supernatural almost matter-of-factly as an explanation for the disappearance of his father. He reminded Grim of the other boy—the one who, years back, had compared him to Fox Mulder. That boy had had a few years on Luca, but he had possessed the same kind of irrefutable logic mixed with blind idealism. In matters of the ethereal, kids were always more advanced than grown-ups and to this day, Grim regretted that he hadn't listened to him.

They reached the bench by the nursing home and sat. Grim asked Luca to tell him what he had seen on the morning of December 8. Luca did, and after he was done, Grim asked him to tell it again. He tried hard to gain new insights or follow leads others might have missed but got nothing. Nothing he didn't already know. Trying (failing) not to show his disappointment to Luca, he began to suspect he had made this whole damn trip for nothing.

'Let's circle back,' Grim said. 'When you claimed we were looking in the wrong place, what exactly did you mean?'

'The hatch. It leads into the ship, but it also leads someplace else. And I don't think there's a hatch on the other side. Otherwise, they would have come back on day one.'

'Want to hear something? We sent in cameras. Drones. Robocars on vacuum hoses. Search dogs and at least two hundred rabbits. Nothing came back.'

The boy shrugged. 'Like I said. No hatch.'

Delveaux would probably have his scalp if she knew he shared classified information with an outsider. But fuck her and the shark she rode in on. The kid was mourning, he needed a break. 'What do you think is on the other side?'

With obvious hesitation, Luca took out his phone, swiped some, tapped some, and turned the screen to Grim. It was Google Translate. He read the text in the box as Luca said it out loud. 'The cod hold.'

'The cod hold?'

'I heard Casper say it when he was trapped in there. "Ibby sank into the cod hold". And later, when I was waiting for my dad to come out, I thought I saw something. In my head. I thought it was just a daydream, but it wasn't. I . . . don't want to talk about it.'

'Spill it,' Grim said. 'Could be important.'

He sighed. 'Fine. I saw my dad and the others standing on deck, only it was night and there were no stars. They fell overboard one by one. I saw them sink into the dark, slowly, with their mouths open and their arms floating.' He paused to swallow. 'I think the cod hold is a really bad place where you go when you're cursed and your ship sinks.'

'You mean Davy Jones' Locker.'

'Isn't that from *Pirates of the Caribbean*? Emma mentioned it.'

'It goes back a bit further than that; it's an old seafaring legend. But it sounds like the English equivalent of what you're saying. As an expression, it just means the bottom of the sea. In other words, dead. Not to be insensitive.'

Luca shook his head. 'It's not the same thing. My dad's in the cod hold. He isn't dead.'

Grim didn't answer.

'And that's not the only thing I saw.'

'It isn't?'

'No. But you won't believe me anyway.'

'Why not?'

Luca looked at him as if it were obvious. 'Because you're old.'

'That's the third time you've said that. Didn't your mother teach you any manners? I feel almost hurt.' At least that won him a smile.

'A *grown-up* then,' Luca said, infusing the word with so much contempt that Grim burst out laughing.

'Try me. And giddyup, will you? Your mother will be wondering where you are.'

That's when Luca Wolf's story took a turn for the improbable. It wasn't that Grim believed he was deliberately duping him, but whereas the awful image of people falling overboard had almost certainly been a symbol of his father's likely demise, the visions he now claimed he had were clearly the fantasies of a traumatized child. Grim listened with diminishing attention, irritated by the boy's inconsistencies . . . and then raised an eyebrow.

'Wait, come again?'

'So I was inside the *Oracle*'s cabin and heard a sound like a whole bunch of sick and dying people moaning. Maybe hundreds. Like *uuuhhhh . . .*'

An itch bit the back of Grim's skull. In fact, his entire scalp seemed to be crawling. The death ship. The smallpox epidemic of 1716.

There's no way the kid could have known about that.

He and Glennis had dug deep into the almanacs of the Dutch National Archives to find but a single reference to the *Oracle* being used to dump bodies into the sea. They hadn't been able to confirm the story anywhere else.

A lucky shot?

But Grim believed in luck no more than he believed in stubborn denial of the supernatural when facts proved the contrary. The similarities were too eerie.

'Tell me what the cabin looked like on the inside.'

'There were a couple of windows where you could see the sea. At the back of the ship, I think. Everything was wood, and all of it was shiny, like our floor after my dad waxes it. I even remember the smell. Heavy, stuffy like an attic with no windows. I can't remember all the furniture, except this rack of long, old-fashioned rifles. I was in a bunk and in front of the windows, a man sat writing at a table. It felt like I knew him, like he was my father. Only not *my* father, of course. The father of whoever's eyes I was looking through.'

Grim gaped at the boy. He had detailed the captain's cabin beyond the *Oracle*'s poop deck down to the musket rack.

'It's true,' Luca said triumphantly. 'I can see it on your face. It *was* the *Oracle*.'

'Maybe you should tell me about your visions after all.'

He did, and Grim's thoughts were working overtime. This was huge. After weeks of famine, Eleanor Delveaux was hungry for a breakthrough. If he relayed this to her, she would have the boy incarcerated within hours. It was the last thing Grim wanted to put him and his family through. So what *would* he do? Extrasensory perception. Moments of clairvoyance. Grim had seen and ignored such omens in his previous life and was not prepared to do it again.

'I just want to know what it all means,' Luca pondered. 'Safiya says I have to summon it to find out, but I don't know how.'

'Who's Safiya?'

'The girl I'm seeing. We kissed.'

'You *talked* about it? Jesus fuck . . . never let them find out.'

'Think I'm stupid?'

'You have no idea what they're capable of, Luca. Don't involve anyone else. And you and your squeeze, only ever talk about it in person. Never on the phone. Never online. They've got you bugged and hacked. You'll put her in danger too.'

Luca studied him, ill at ease. 'Are *you* going to tell anyone?'

'No,' Grim said. 'But I want you to tell me if anything else happens. And whatever you do, do *not* summon it. These things are dangerous so don't fuck around with them. You need to go now, but walk me to my car. I'll give you my number. Don't put it in your phone, and never *ever* use your own phone to reach me. Put it in your head and flush the note.'

'Will do. It feels nice to talk to a grown-up about it.'

But not the wrong one, Grim thought. *I could have been one of the wrong ones.*

Grim got up, but Luca didn't move. 'What's the matter?'

'If the *Oracle*'s real, do you think the other things I saw are real, too? The *older* things, I mean?'

'I don't know, Luca.'

'I hope not. I think they're from much longer ago, from a time when there were still woolly mammoths. And . . . something else.'

'What?'

Luca shuddered with visceral revulsion; a mere physical reaction that Grim found more foreboding than anything he had said. 'I don't want to find out.'

11

There was a knock on the door of Eleanor's private suite. Before Hangar 3 and its annexes were temporarily requisitioned by NOVEMBER-6, the suite and adjacent office had belonged to an air force officer. It had a sofa, a stately desk, even a faux fireplace. Most of her on-site staff went home after duty or stayed in a nearby hotel, but in the past weeks, Eleanor had made the suite her home.

She invited in Glennis Sopamena and Diana Radu, and Diana handed her a report. 'This just in from Zaky. Take a look at Officer 6.'

Zaky was Zaky Dukakis, one of their best in IT, who was working on the case at the head office in The Hague.

Eleanor skimmed through the file. Logged keystrokes, a cell phone's search history, yada yada. 'Anything I need to worry about?'

'Not yet, we think. But you might want to judge for yourself.'

Officer 6 was Yvonne Schrootman of the Noordwijk police. Officer 6 had gotten the call about Officers 1 and 2 not having returned from the *Oracle* and had witnessed Officers 3, 4 and 5 disappearing into the ship. She was police, in other words a damn nuisance.

They had convinced most of the police witnesses that their coworkers had participated in the '*Mysteries of the Dutch Seaborne Empire*' campaign as a practical joke, to add to its mystery. They simply walked out on the other side, the fog providing the perfect cover. Tragically, they were also the ones who died in the fire later that day. But Schrootman had seen it from up close and because she was a cop herself, they hadn't locked her up but sent her on vacation instead. A mandatory, all-paid three-month vacation, imposed by the chief of police. She was currently in Southeast Asia with her fiancée, me-timing her survivor guilt away. A gamble, but it had seemed safer than holding her or letting her stew in her own misgivings at home. Apparently, such misgivings had now whipped up after all.

'The past few days, she's been searching "*Oracle* Noordwijk", "strange appearance of Noordwijk ship", "maritime exhibition Noordwijk", and here's the winner: "Sassenheim fire hoax". All including the names of the missing cops and the odd search into Dutch coverup scandals.'

Glennis flashed her toothy smile. 'She's not stupid. She knows what she saw.'

'We anticipated that. Where is she?'

'The Royal Pita Maha on Bali,' Diana said. 'They're pushing the boat out, so to say.'

'Is she talking?'

'Not by phone or email. What she discusses with her partner, we don't know.'

'All of it, probably. That's just textbook survivor's behavior.' Eleanor shut the folder and pushed it back over her desk. 'Her story is a fantasy. As long as we keep it watertight, she won't pose any problems. Have Dukakis bug her place up before she gets home. For now, we'll play it by ear.'

'Agreed,' Diana said.

And hopefully, that would be the end of it. Eleanor loathed to be forced into stronger measures. But sometimes it proved impossible to avoid, like with that snitch Isa Stam. It was easy. You profiled them, and if the profile showed that sooner or later they were bound to talk, you intervened. In the case of Stam, who hadn't just doubted the events like Schrootman, but had been seriously vexed, intervention unfortunately was needed sooner than later.

'Anything else?'

'That's it. Have a good evening, Ms. Delveaux.'

As Diana prepared to leave, Glennis held back. 'One more thing, about our American puppet.'

'Good luck with *him*,' Diana said, smiling. She didn't need Glennis to assert it was a private conversation. 'I'll leave you to it.' She exited the suite and shut the door behind her.

'So what's up with Grim?'

'He's eccentric, but he's no fool. I can't spin our presence here much longer.'

'Do you have to? You're attributing him authority he doesn't have. He does as we say.'

'He doesn't trust us. He's a tinderbox, and he's seriously afraid of the ship. Surely you've noticed?'

Eleanor thought about their recent conversation and had to agree. The man was a flake. He was also a nutcase and a boozer, not nearly the specialist they had hoped for.

'What if he escalates? Best-case scenario, he'll singlehandedly set the *Oracle* on fire. Worst-case, he calls West Point to cast doubt on my actions. Admin will take that call, and he'll be able to tell them a few things that will immediately jolt some higher-ups into action. The highest, I believe.'

'He won't,' Eleanor snapped. 'He despises authority.'

'He despises us. He thinks we minimize the danger. I don't *think* he'll go that far, but if he does, I'll lose control of the narrative, and you better believe the Americans stationed here at Volkel will be doing more than watching over a bunch of nukes.'

Eleanor burst from her chair. 'Then it's your job to rule the roost, Glennis. You are the sole source of what West Point knows and doesn't know. This is non-negotiable.'

But Glennis didn't lower her eyes. 'Is he right, Ms. Delveaux? Are we minimizing the danger?'

'Nonsense. You were there for the entire investigation. You know the ship is harmless if you stay away from the hatch. As for the hatch itself, we understand little more about it now than we did on day one. Grim's probably right about one thing: such things cannot be understood. All we can do is keep them from the public eye to preserve the status quo. How's that different from what you're doing in your New York woods?'

'If that's so, Grim has a valid point. What good are we doing here?'

Eleanor didn't want to answer her question. It annoyed her. Glennis' *fastidiousness* annoyed her. And the woman just wouldn't stop *looking* at her.

'It would be a disaster if the ship were to fall into the wrong hands, Ms. Delveaux.'

'This conversation is over.'

'I didn't mean to—'

With a bang, Eleanor jerked open the left drawer of her desk and took out a white envelope. 'Let me be very clear, Glennis. Because you seem to be getting your wires crossed.'

She took a stack of photographs from the envelope and put the first one face-up on her desk. Glennis had seen it before, but turned pale nonetheless.

'The only thing that matters is *you* keep control over the narrative to your superiors. How you do that, I frankly don't give a rat's ass.'

The photo showed several US Army soldiers wearing desert combats. On the grubby, concrete floor between them lay an Afghani man. The Afghani was naked and chained. The soldiers were laughing.

'This is your narrative now: interesting case study, low priority, more time required. Nothing more, nothing less.'

She turned up the second photograph. It was a close-up of the first, and now you could clearly recognize the GI Jane smiling at the camera as Glennis Sopamena. Sixteen years younger, but the smile was the same.

'Put your photos away,' Glennis said hoarsely.

'You might want to take a good look, because it's been a while. Sometimes it's good to be reminded of certain things, even when the optics don't look good.'

But Glennis didn't want to be reminded. Photos 3 and 4 showed the soldiers forcing the Afghani to kiss the American flag, ass up with the barrel of an M16 between his butt cheeks. Glennis wasn't the one with the gun, nor the one with the flag, but neither was she stopping her companions in the act.

In photo 5 the Afghani was dead, his face dunked in a pool of his own blood.

Eleanor got the photos in 2009 from Omar Al-Jarrah. How *he* had gotten them, she didn't know, nor did she care (although she now understood it had been key to winning her trust). Eleanor had confronted Glennis almost immediately. According to Glennis, the Afghani was a Taliban fighter who had placed a roadside IED near the Mazar-i-Sharif airport, killing three US armed forces. Three of her *friends*, she added. What her battalion had done to the man was dirty, and she wished she could undo it, but war was a dirty business. Eleanor said she understood. She also understood—they both did—that Eleanor now had leverage over Glennis to acquire intel from her that would otherwise remain classified. Perhaps this pressure had eventually pushed Glennis to leave the CIA in 2014 and join the US Military Academy in West Point. Rising through the ranks, her background in intelligence eventually put her in charge of the Black Spring file . . . and of all the cases she had leaked to Eleanor, this was by far the most remarkable.

'I just want to make sure we're on the same page here,' Eleanor said, as she collected the photos and put them back into the envelope. 'It was a long time ago. We know you're not like that anymore. It would be a pity for this to stain your record.'

Something unexpected occurred. Glennis' big smile reappeared, as if nothing had happened. 'Of course we're on the same page, Ms. Delveaux. Will that be all?'

Perhaps it was a defense mechanism or a mask she used to gain composure. But it was also a power-grab, and that unsettled Eleanor. 'Wait. If . . .' She hesitated. 'If I had reached a different conclusion about Officer 6. If I had asked you to take stronger action. You would have complied, right Glennis?'

Her smile didn't waver. 'Of course, Ms. Delveaux. Whatever you say.'

'And if you thought my judgement were wrong, you'd tell me, wouldn't you?'

'But you're never wrong.'

She folded her hands. 'Very well. Good night, Glennis.'

'Good night, Ms. Delveaux.'

Glennis left, and the second she had closed the door, Eleanor clenched her bottom lip with her thumb and index finger and pulled it so hard it bled. With a cramped face she let go and leaned back.

What had gotten into her? For a moment, she had shown *weakness*, and Eleanor Delveaux was never *weak*. The idea alone revolted her.

The pain cleared her head, but it wasn't enough. She dug her nails into her cheeks and yanked them down, fast and efficient. This wasn't for clarity; this was *punishment*. Her cheeks immediately started to burn. She felt wetness trickling down her jaw.

Eleanor exhaled and closed her eyes. Over the past few weeks, she had teetered between self-loathing and acceptance of her new reality, always aware that she mustn't let her guard down. That would be a sign of *weakness* and elicited the kind of impulsive decision-making that had landed her in this hot mess to begin with.

She had had a moment of *weakness* when she had brought Omar Al-Jarrah aboard. The appearance of the *Oracle* had been curbed with a simple fake news story in the local media, but with the disappearance of Abdulaziz Yamani, Eleanor had been sucked into a political scandal that dominated the global news. Everyone had seen the CCTV footage of the Saudi hit squad in the exiled journalist's London apartment complex. Even a month later it was on the news almost daily, although by now, no one expected a body to be found. World leaders condemned the regime in the strongest terms but, lo and behold, failed to impose serious repercussions.

Who had *not* been implicated in Yamani's disappearance was Eleanor Delveaux, and if she wished to keep it that way, she had no other option than to cave in. Al-Jarrah had her by the short and curlies the same way she had Glennis. Come to think of it, it was kind of ironic.

Just another step up in the food chain, she thought, tasting metal in her mouth.

Outcome: the *Oracle* was going to Saudi Arabia, without ever spilling her secrets. Al-Jarrah had given her a February 14 deadline to make arrangements. On that day, transport would be ready.

A Valentine's surprise.

Blood pooled in her mouth. She stirred her tongue and swallowed. Eleanor had never felt devoted to anyone and so never felt hatred for anyone. But right now, she *hated* Omar Al-Jarrah with a deep, black, poisonous hate that festered within her like a fungus.

Grim would think he had gotten his way. With the ship supposedly destroyed, he could take his pension, go home, and rot, unaware that the object of his superstitious fear was being weaponized by a rogue state. Did Glennis suspect anything? Possibly, but it didn't matter anymore. On Eleanor's order, Diana Radu would assist with the logistics without asking questions. Van Driel would; his former military rank had gotten him used to giving orders instead of following them, and he was a tough dog. Well, he could question all he wanted. She was still in charge.

The evidence would be destroyed, and without a paper trail it wouldn't matter if a couple civilians on whichever side of the Atlantic had ghost stories to tell.

As for her own future, the fact that NOVEMBER-6 operated under the radar of Dutch law ensured that despite her failure, she could stay on unscathed. Eleanor reported to only one superintendent—speed-dial 9 if she was ever in need—but even he knew only what she chose to tell him. That's what justified NOVEMBER-6's existence in the first place.

But Eleanor wouldn't stay on.

Because *she* knew.

Besides, she hadn't sold out cheap. Half of her payment was already secured on a untraceable account in Turks and Caicos.

Nice and tidy.

Eleanor got up and stood in front of the mirror above the mantelpiece. Red gashes tiger-striped her hollow cheeks underneath sunken eyes. When she bared her teeth, a gruesome bloody smile stared back at her.

You're still in control, she told herself. *Nothing is lost yet. You aren't lost yet. That's paramount.*

She took a roll of cotton rounds from her purse and dabbed the blood off her face, using water first, then disinfectant. She didn't twitch a muscle. Next, she applied moisturizer. Concealer. Foundation.

It took her a full half-hour, but when she was done, she looked as good as new.

12

The night before everything changed dramatically was Saturday, January 31.

Seven weeks had passed since the appearance of the *Oracle* and Luca Wolf was exhausted. His life had evolved too fast. He felt like he was being swept away by a wild tide that had wrecked his body and drained his mind. Lying in bed, he could feel the tension in his muscles slowly ebb away, as his thoughts drifted into a fantasy where Safiya, dressed all in white, was showing off her moves at the Christmas Dance. He recognized her style from her TikTok videos: sensuous, but with a fuck-you attitude built on a bedrock of self-esteem. Several boys challenged her to battle, including Ruben Bex (and for some weird reason, Mrs. Volmer too), but Luca saw himself elbow his way in, exclaim 'Move over', and destroy *everybody* with moves he could only dream to possess in real life. But Luca had eyes only for Safiya, who, clearly impressed, smiled at him. With that smile in mind, he fell asleep.

Luca slept as at Volkel Air Base, hidden in the captain's cabin of the *Oracle*, Robert Grim stared at axed-up crates and barrels thinking, *If I were the captain, where would I keep that damn log?* He slept as sitting at the antique table, Grim dozed off too and dreamed of mighty wing-beats, of a dead mouse in the talons of a horned owl, of eyes that should have stayed shut but were now staring at him, *accusing* him. He slept as Grim woke up screaming like a baby, so gut-wrenchingly loud that Glennis, the last one still on duty at this hour, rushed over to see who was dying.

Luca slept as far out at sea, mighty waves crashed against Mammoth III's legs and the cracks in the steel grew wider, while at the bottom of a dark, smoke-stained stairwell, the wind whispered through the blind eye sockets of a prehistoric skull. He slept as Eleanor Delveaux answered a phone call in her suite and got the confirmation that a cargo vessel had left Jeddah, heading for the Suez Canal.

And he slept as his mom messaged one Denise Post, fiancée of Yvonne Schrootman, a.k.a. Officer 6. She used an old phone she had found in a storage box in the attic, a prepaid sim, and an anonymous Facebook account created especially for the occasion. The message read: *I need to talk to Yvonne about the ship. It could be a matter of life or death. You have no idea how hard it's been to track you down, but I can't reach out to Yvonne directly. It's not safe. I don't even know if your account is safe, but that's a gamble I'll have to take.*

Luca slept through all this, only to wake up shortly after two-thirty and find Emma Reich standing in his bedroom. No longer a little boy and fearing the invasion of his privacy more than the monsters under his bed, Luca kept his bedroom door closed, but it was wide open now. Emma painted a motionless silhouette in the doorway, but he still knew it was her. He recognized the shape of the long, beige coat she had worn on the day she had disappeared. The knitted cap and her hair that once had flowed so beautifully, but now hung in wet, lifeless strings. He could even see her gloved fingers hanging by her sides.

They were trembling. Barely noticeable.

Then reality struck—*Emma was in his room*—and Luca's heart skipped a few beats before it started pumping again, painfully and much faster now.

He sat up and whispered, 'Emma? Emma, is that really you?'

She started to move. Her feet seemed nailed to the floor, but her upper body started to wobble very fast, just an inch or so left and right, reminding Luca of one of those solar powered dashboard dolls. He could hear her coat rustle.

She wouldn't stop.

Luca slipped out of bed and tiptoed across the room in his boxer briefs. Only from right up close could he discern her face in the dark. It really was her. Luca felt sick to his stomach. Tears stung in his eyes.

'Emma, you're here, oh Jesus Emma, I missed you so much . . .'

Then he saw her grin and realized he must be dreaming after all. She was grinning ear to ear. Literally. Her grin bared more teeth than humanly possible. There were so *many*. The entire bottom half of her face raptured into that grin. Above it, her eyes were black and watery sparkles. They fixed on him.

Now, he could also hear how fast she was breathing, almost hyper-ventilating, to the back-and-forth of her wobbling. It didn't sound like lungs breathing in any natural way. It sounded like lungs that had *forgotten* how to breathe, deprived of oxygen for too long. With every breath, she exuded the mysterious, briny odor of the sea.

'Emma?' Wavering. 'Are you okay?'

He cautiously lifted her left hand. The wobbling stopped. So did the breathing.

In perfect quietude, she grinned.

Stared.

Something tingled high up his back and sent a shiver down his spine. Luca was aware he should be scared, *terrified* in fact, but he wasn't because he knew he was dreaming. And in dreams, wasn't he free to do as he wished? As he had always wanted to? You didn't have to answer for what you did in dreams, did you?

He took off her glove and dropped it. Her hand was cold and fish-belly white. The skin felt like a rotting prune. He had to warm her up.

'Emma, I missed you so much . . .' he whispered. '*I love you, Emma. I've always loved you, you know that, right?*'

Only why did she keep grinning like that?

He came forward, closing the gap between them, raising his face. She tilted her head as if to welcome him. Her lips curled even further back from her grin, like a predator about to attack. Luca became vaguely aware of the repulsiveness of her breath, smelling not only the sea, but algae and decay and the horrible living things that infested the spume, and far away, the voice of reason screamed, *Oh Jesus what am I doing, what the fuck am I doing, knock it off this isn't Emma this could never be Emma Emma is dead think about Safiya wake up wake up WAKE UP . . .*

But then the Emma-thing grabbed his naked shoulders. Her gloved hand brutally forced his head closer and her cold, wet fingers caressed his cheek. *And she kissed him.* Luca's body shook and his eyes bulged. His sexual tension now climaxed in fear and disgust. He tried to pull away but couldn't. It was as if his face had melted into that horrid grin. Greedy black eyes locked onto his. Cold seawater poured from her sockets and splashed onto his face and shoulders. It gushed from her mouth into his, saline and rancid, and he thought, *I can't breathe!* His mouth overflowed and his throat immediately contorted, gagged, and gave in as large gulps of seawater surged down his windpipe, flooding his lungs.

As Luca started to drown, he realized it hadn't been a dream after all. There was no awakening from death. He saw himself sinking into a bottomless depth. All around him floated the drowned: young men and old women with slow hair and lifeless limbs. Children with swollen bellies, their faces marbled with death patterns. All of them bore an expression of profound terror, spawned not from their submission to death, but from a single glance at what was waiting down below.

Supreme, unnamable, utterly insane . . .

. . . and alive.

When Luca came to, he was lying in bed, in his shadow-filled room. He sat up and slapped his hands all over his chest and shoulders. Clammy. With sweat, not seawater.

He glanced at his phone and saw it was four-thirty. A *vision*, he thought, laying back down and numbing out.

Still, he wasn't free of it yet, because when he rolled over to face the doorway, he saw the hunched shape of Emma still there. She was wobbling again, fast but ever so slightly. Luca watched her with mesmerized obsession until he decided it was better to shut his eyes, allowing the mercy of sleep to expel the image.

INTERMEZZO

FISH

1

Peter Slikke first saw the unusually large herring gull when it dropped a gurnard on the skipper's head. They were on the stern of the *Albatross* working the tackle when it happened. Captain Jorg Eelman was wearing his yellow oilskins but not his hood, so the fish smacked his skull with the sound of someone slapping him in the face, slathering a trail of slime on the little hair he had left. Jorg staggered and looked up, touching his head. The gull screamed and came in for a landing on the outrigger, where it folded its wings and regarded them expectantly.

Deckhands Hendrik, Johan and Koen had witnessed it from amidships and roared with laughter. Hendrik slapped his knees and bellowed, 'In your *face!*'

'Bull's-eye, cap'n! Kapow!

Jorg wiped his hand on his waterproof and scratched his neck. 'I'll be damned. Did that whopper over yonder drop this?'

'Sure did,' Peter said. 'He's huge.'

'Look at Quirky over there!' Koen laughed, and so its nickname was born. 'Looks like he wants you to eat it. Just like me ma's cat. Always puts dead mice and rats on her doormat. As a present, like.'

Peter didn't believe gulls were capable of such social behavior, but the way the bird was eyeing Jorg from up on the boom was striking. It turned and jerked its head, as if to say, *Go ahead, slimy and raw.*

Hogwash, of course. The fish had slipped from its beak, accidentally hitting the skipper. Gulls were like precision missiles, flocking the trawler in large numbers hoping to snatch some of the catch, but even they sometimes dropped the occasional prize. It was probably waiting for the inconvenient humans to leave the stern so it could get down to its snack.

But that wasn't so. An hour later, when Peter returned to the stern, he found the gurnard untouched on the deck and the gull still perched on the rigger, now stretched almost horizontally over the water. He recognized the bird by its sheer size and the prominent blood-red teardrop stain below its yellow beak.

'What do you want?' he softly asked.

The gull glimpsed at him with grey-yellow eyes, and its beak opened into a grin. Peter Slikke, who like his father and grandfather before him had always been a fisherman, couldn't shake the sense that the bird was watching over him.

Quirky, Peter thought. And he smiled.

2

By the end of the second day, Quirky had brought them three gurnards, a common dab, a horse mackerel, and an octopus. The gull's company obviously amused the six-man crew of the *Albatross*, who dubbed it their unofficial mascot. But inevitably, its behavior was subject to debate.

'My ole' man always said the comin of a gull at sea means good fortune,' Hendrik Barhorst said that night in the galley, while they ate from deep steel bowls. 'Money, good catch, so on. But I've never heard of a bird bringin gifts.'

'I heard you ain't s'pose to kill a bird on the mast and always keep 'em in your prayers,' said Jan Kikkert.

'I don't pray,' Koen retorted.

Jorg Eelman glanced at each of them, mulling it over in silence.

During the day, they had worked the North Sea's fishing grounds approximately seventy nautical miles from the port of Oudeschild. Quirky would drop its fish at their feet then alight on the boom or the crane. Never did it eat them. It just perched there, watching them, showing that strange anticipation and those weird jerks of the head. One time Koen tried tossing a gurnard back to it, but the bird just hopped aside, and the fish fell back into the sea.

Another peculiar thing was that all the fish Quirky brought were dead. Gulls usually struck when the crew was hauling in nets ballooning with live, squirming catch. Whatever they snatched, they expertly killed with their hooked beaks a yardarm away, wary of preying buddies. But Quirky's fish were never mauled. They were just dead. The only explanation Peter could think of was that it must have stolen them from the sorting boxes, but no one ever saw it do that.

On the third day, Quirky stopped bringing them fish. Instead, it threw a brass maritime compass at their feet. It crashed onto the deck with such a loud clatter that they all jumped.

'Bloody 'ell, 'es gone off 'is head now,' Johan said as he turned the compass in his hands. 'Look at it! This fuckin thing looks like it's been around for ages!'

It was the most magnificent piece of navigational equipment Peter had ever seen, the kind that went out of use generations ago. It was broken, though. The glass was cracked, and whichever way you turned it, the needle always pointed northwest.

Quirky shrieked discordantly and they all upped their heads. It fluttered its wings and stamped on the rigger with webbed feet, fixing its yellow eyes on them in a tense glare.

No one was laughing now.

'Where in God's name did he find that thing? asked Hendrik.

'Beats me,' Jorg said. 'But it's a keeper. Gotta be worth somethin.'

Shortly after dark, Koen and Hendrik came to the bridge, particularly upset. At the time, Peter was at the helm and Jorg was keeping him company. It was the skipper who urged everybody for calm. Hendrik said the gull had thrown a golden wedding ring at his feet that exactly matched his wife's.

'Don't play me for a fool now,' Jorg warned.

'I swear to God he ain't,' Koen came to Hendrik's defense. 'I was right there. The gull dropped it right in front of us!'

Hendrik took his own wedding ring off and held them both out. The twisting curves, the small gem—yeah, they were identical.

'Jenny and I didn't get 'em engraved, we saw no need for anything fancy like that. So I get it, this proves nothin. But what's goin on here, Jorg? I don't like it one bit.'

Jorg looked from one to the other. 'Did anyone else see it?'

'I *swear* we ain't foolin around!' Koen protested. 'Where's Hendrik gonna get a ring like that out here? From his wife or sumthin? He didn't know that damn bird was going to keep pesterin us, did he?'

Peter saw they were telling the truth, and so did Jorg. Hendrik and Koen were simple men, too sturdy to scare easy and certainly incapable of faking such dismay. Hendrik was truly out of sorts and remained so until they used the satellite phone to call home. Hearing his wife's voice reassured him, until she said she wasn't wearing her ring and couldn't find it anywhere. With that, the mood on the *Albatross* turned permanently.

The men ate in silence, each deep in thought. It was Johan who finally spoke up. 'I didn't want to say anything yesterday, because I thought you were all full of hot crap. But my grandpa used to say a seagull hangin around a ship wasn't a good omen at all. He said it spelled disaster.'

That night, when it was Peter's turn for a few hours' rack-time, he lay awake in his bunk, eyes wide open in the dark. He thought he heard a sound then, but after listening for a while longer, he reckoned he must have imagined it. He never mentioned it to his mates.

They didn't need to know that it had sounded like a bird urgently tapping the door with its beak, as if it had critical business inside.

3

The following day—the day before they were to return to port for the fish auction—dawned somber and quiet. The skies were leaden and the *Albatross* was afloat on a sea as dark and slick as oil. The crew was demoralized and conversation limited to an absolute minimum. No one whistled or hummed. Peter caught his men searching the sky time and again, like sailors of yesteryear anticipating some ominous fate . . . and then felt his own gaze drawn to it as well.

As they were casting out the nets for the third time that day, a shadow glided over them, and something fell amidships with a wet thud. Peter instinctively flinched, but some of the others had already seen it and gasped. Koen cried out in horror.

On the deck lay a human heart.

Peter looked up just in time to see the bloated gull land on the boom and screech at them. Its beak stayed open as if threatening them, revealing its filthy red gullet. No longer did it show just a single tear-drop bloodstain; it was *dripping* with blood.

'Sweet Jesus!' Koen wailed. 'It's a heart! It's a fuckin heart!'

He poked the organ with the tip of his boot. Blood leaked from the severed aorta, mixing with accumulated seawater. Koen pressed the back of his hand to his mouth and smothered a gag.

'Where the hell did he find that thing?' Jan asked. 'Shoo! Get the fuck outta here!'

He lunged at the gull, but it was far beyond his reach and didn't even flinch. Peter would never forget what he saw then: the bird spread its wings like a prophet spreading his arms, summoning unholy powers from ancient constellations . . . and *hissed* at Jan.

'Holy mother of God,' Jorg whispered.

Peter wanted to tear his eyes away but couldn't. A primitive fear choked his throat like a gulp of hot brine. Maybe these ancient mariner's superstitions about omens good and bad weren't so far-fetched after all.

'Hendrik, don't!' someone yelled.

Too late, Peter saw Hendrik going up to the rail, his face determined, his mouth clinched so tight it was almost invisible. He had the orange flare gun in his hand. 'Enough,' he said. 'I don't know what you are, but your days of bothering us are over.'

Hendrik's hand trembled as he aimed, but the gull was a large target and when he pulled the trigger, the flare hit the bird square in its center. Bright pink fire sputtered, and the gull was blown off the boom in a spray of feathers. It rained down into the sea, where the flare fizzled out.

Everything went quiet. They were too stunned to speak. Even the sea was quiet—*unnaturally* quiet, Peter would later attest.

Where the gull had sunk, a bubble of air rose to the surface. No, not air. Peter caught a whiff of rotten eggs.

Suddenly, the *Albatross* dipped dangerously starboard. The men screamed and flailed their arms. Water splashed all around the bow and the air was immediately filled with a penetrating stench. For a moment, it looked like the stern would take water, but the trawler tilted back, rocking heavily.

'What was that?'

'Yugggh, that smell!'

Jorg's eyes searched for Peter's, and Peter wished he hadn't seen his expression. 'Methane,' the skipper grunted.

Peter nodded, licking his lips. Methane was an odorless gas, but the sulfur compounds of rotting organisms from the seabed betrayed its presence. Methane bubbles escaping cracks in the earth's crust and rising to the surface lowered the relative density of water to such an extent that it could cause entire ships to sink. Peter had heard the tales, especially from the west Atlantic, but here? In the North Sea?

'Oh Jesus, Hendrik, now you've done it!' Jan moaned. 'What did I tell you? You've killed the gull and now we're all toast!'

All around the *Albatross*, the water bubbled like it was boiling. Peter could see white columns rising under the surface.

The ship staggered, but they weren't toast. Instead, dead fish started to surface. They were in various stages of decay and gave off a stench that was worse than the gas.

There were hundreds.

No, thousands.

3

PANDEMONIUM

1

Alexander came back on Sunday morning, February 1.

The three of them were having breakfast, and Jenna, facing the parlor, was the first to see him. Later, Barbara wouldn't be able to say how long he had been there. She hadn't yet drawn the front curtains that morning, so hadn't looked in that area yet. And then, everything unfolded so *fast*.

'Daddy!' Jenna cried. She jumped from her chair so suddenly that it tipped over and lunged across the room on stubby legs.

'Jenna, what—' Barbara began, but then the word sank in, and she felt a terrible visceral reaction. Her insides went limp, a heat rose behind her cheeks, and her brain seemed to be pressing against her skull. That single word opened a floodgate, and through it avalanched all the emotions and rottenness of the past weeks. *Daddy*.

She whirled around in her chair, the butter knife still in her hand. At the same time—time crawled like molasses at this critical moment, giving her brain the opportunity to observe in absolute clarity—she saw Luca also turning to face the parlor.

It was him.

The knife clattered down on her plate.

'Oh God, Alexander . . .' she muttered. Then she yelled, '*Alexander!*'

She went after Jenna. She didn't think. Not about how he could have gotten in with the doors still latched; not about why he was suddenly back, or why after all this time he had chosen to just stand in front of the sofa instead of coming to hug them. It was pure instinct that drove her.

Jenna flung herself around her daddy's legs. Only when he didn't catch her and throw her up in the air, like he used to when he greeted his li'l girl, did Barbara realize that something was wrong.

'Daddy, daddy, daddy, daddy!'

With the curtains closed, the front room was dark, but still the second shock came, followed by a general paralysis that stopped her dead in her tracks. A single glance was enough to recognize Alexander's AC Milan cap and duffle coat. The horn buttons gleamed in the half-light. One of his shoulders was much higher than the other, like a tipped scale. In fact, his entire body seemed smacked out of true. The fingers jutting out of his sleeves were doughy and wrinkly, like after a hot bath. They were bent like crab legs, knuckles tight, tendons taut but absolutely still. And his face . . .

The muscles in Alexander's neck were hulkier than ever before, supporting a hideous grin that split his once so affable face ear to ear. His eyes glared with bleak insanity. They showed no joy, no life, only intense, deranged concentration.

That posture. That grin. Those eyes.

Not Alexander.

'Jenna, let go of him . . .'

But Jenna had buried her face in his coat and cried with a muffled voice, '*I missed you so much daddy, I missed you so much . . .*'

'*Jenna, get away from daddy, right now!*'

Jenna seemed to realize that something was wrong but didn't let go. A terrible thought came to Barbara, unformed, hard to put into words. It was as if something was using Alexander's body to mimic life, something that didn't know how to be human and only managed to replicate this crude mockery of a person.

One of those crab hands snapped up and strained to caress Jenna's forehead. Barbara's paralysis broke at once, and she lunged forward.

Jenna got quiet and peered up. 'Daddy?'

Barbara yanked her back by her collar. She was *very* close to him now, closer than she wanted to be. She looked away and never touched him, suddenly convinced it was a matter of life or death to avoid his touch. Jenna yelped and flew backward. Barbara caught her before she slammed into the coffee table and dragged her away from him. Alexander's shoes stood amid a puddle of dirty water, and Barbara could smell the sea and something else, the revolting stench of decomposition. She hurled Jenna onto her arm and went for the back room. Initially, Jenna struggled but then saw him over her mom's shoulder, saw what her father had become, and screamed in sheer horror.

'Luca, watch your sister.'

But Luca didn't budge. His face was ashen, rigid, blank. Still at the breakfast table, a half-eaten croissant forgotten in his hand, he stared helplessly at the thing in the parlor.

'*Luca, for God's sake!*'

He jerked awake as if from a trance, blinked and dropped his roll. 'S-sure, Mom, yeah . . .'

He slid from his chair, knelt in front of bawling Jenna, and held her in his arms. It gave Barbara the chance to look back.

The shadow in the front room now moved, wobbling out of control like one of those chicken-shaped spring rockers in the playground across the street. Only *this* didn't remind Barbara of a chicken but rather a starved wolf, stiff-legged and panting. Her heart pounded in her chest. She couldn't think, couldn't decide what to do. Dozens of scenarios for Alexander's return had played out in her head, all ending in an emotional reunion, he grabbing her face and kissing her over and over. But not this. She didn't even know what *this* was.

She took a wary step toward the parlor, but stopped dead in her tracks when Luca cried, 'Mom, don't!' Trying in vain to console his sister, his eyes fixed onto her. 'Emma was in my room last night. I thought I'd dreamt it, because when I woke up this morning she wasn't there anymore.' He stared over Jenna's shoulder into the front room. 'Her eyes were black, and she was grinning at me. I wish she hadn't done that.'

Suddenly Jenna bellowed, *'What's wrong with Daddy? Why is he showing me these horrible things?'*

'Things?' A painful jolt of alarm shot through Barbara's gut. 'What horrible things, Jenna?'

She yanked her daughter away from Luca's arms and knelt before her. Jenna looked back with bleary eyes, drawing a blank. She seemed to have sunk into a state of shock.

'Luca, what's she talking about? Did Emma do anything last night? *Did Emma say anything?*'

She was aware she was shrieking, pushing Luca back into his shell. Couldn't help it; her brain was tumbling in rapid circles.

Alexander. She had to see Alexander. See if she could wake him up from that weird state he was in. See if her mind wasn't playing tricks.

Her eyes were black, and she was grinning at me. I wish she hadn't done that.

'Stay here, both of you.'

'I want to get out of here, Mom. Get out of the house. Right now.'

She ignored him and slipped back to the front room where everything was dominated by the shadow looming before her. *Unnatural*, she thought. The way he was rocking. The way he was breathing.

'Alexander? Sweetheart, can you hear me?'

He just stood there, those abnormally piercing eyes pinning her to the ground.

That grin.

Teeth and molars alternated in a ridiculous imitation of a smile. *Alexander's* teeth and molars. What on earth could grin like that and think it looked human?

She jumped at the sound of a camera shutter and spun on her heels. Luca stood between the sliders dividing the front and back rooms, phone up.

'Else, no one's going to believe us,' he said and snapped another.

Of course. Photos. Evidence. Luca was more on the ball than she was, dammit. She dug her iPhone out of her pocket and wanted to swipe the screen to camera when she saw twelve missed calls.

All from Glennis.

Fuck. Her phone was in silent mode.

Did Glennis know what was going on? Had to, why else would she have called so often? Call Glennis. That was her recourse. No police— the contract. Friend or foe, Glennis would know what to do.

Glennis picked up on the first ring. 'Barbara, get away from him immediately!'

Bewildered, she stammered, 'Alexander is back . . .'

'We know. He's not the only one. We're on our way.'

'How . . .'

'Doesn't matter. We'll be there in five.'

'There's something wrong with him!' she burst out. *'There's something all wrong with him, what should I do?'*

'Listen, Barbara, stay away from him! Whatever you do, do not touch him! You hear me? Do not touch him!'

Her head was spinning. Jenna had touched him. She peered around. Where was Jenna? No longer at the kitchen table.

Oh God, where's Jenna?

She disconnected and looked at Luca with horrified eyes. *'Where's your sister?'*

'She's right . . .'

But she had passed him already and both saw the back room was empty.

'Jenna? Jenna! Jenna, where are you!'

Driven by sickening waves of panic, she ran down the hall, trying to look everywhere at once.

'Mom, wait, don't leave me alone with him!'

'Jenna!'

The kitchen was empty. Barbara flung open doors, the restroom, the hall-way, the cellar. No, the cellar always gave Jenna the blue funk. Too dark.

'Mom!'

'Jenna! Oh God, where are you!'

Up the stairs. Five leaps and she was on the landing, calling out her daughter's name. Within seconds, she looked through all the bedrooms.

One instant, she thought. *I was gone for one instant. Luca was with her, goddammit . . .*

But the horror stories went spinning through her head; stories of parents who lost sight of their children for a single second. *All it takes is one instant. One instant and a freak turn of fate. Had you gone the other way, you would have seen her walking out the mall hand-in-hand with a stranger. But you went the other way, as if something had deliberately sent you in the wrong direction. And me? I went upstairs.*

'Mom? Mom, get back here!' Downstairs, sheer panic in Luca's voice now.

A new thought struck her like a bucket of ice, as she went down on all fours to peek under the big bed. *We'll be there in five*, Glennis had said. They were going to take Alexander away. Them too, and no one would ever know the truth. Five minutes. How much time had already passed?

She thought feverishly as she hit the storeroom, the last door behind which Jenna could be hiding. Five minutes to publicly expose what was going on. To save themselves from getting buried in the cover-up. But what could she do? And what about the contract?

Oh, fuck their stupid contract! You think this is gonna get any more desperate than it already is?

But it did.

Footsteps running down the hall. Luca shouting, 'Mom! Dad's doin' something!'

She hurtled down the stairs, almost crashing into him at the bottom.

'Look . . .' He hid behind her as they trudged back into the living room.

She cupped her mouth.

Something was leaking from Alexander's right hand onto the rug. Blood, she thought, but on second glance, she saw it was sludgy and inky black.

'Alexander . . .'

Grinning, he showed her the palm of his hand, dripping like a stigmata. Barbara instinctively grabbed her son. Then, Alexander turned and scrambled onto the couch. His moves were quick and jerky. If it had been a movie, you would think they had cut out a bunch of tween frames.

'Mom, what's he doing?'

Alexander raised his hand and started to write on the wall. The letters seemed to grow from beneath his palm, crooked and crude, but with merciless clarity she still recognized Alexander's handwriting. That was the worst.

'Give . . . and . . . give . . .' Luca stammered, reading out what he wrote.

Barbara didn't speak. Her legs went weak, and it was all she could do to stand and watch. When he was done, he turned and stood frozen on the couch. Black foulness sprouted from his palm and spattered the leather.

GIVE AND GIVE IN ABUNDANCE

'What does it mean?' Luca asked.

Barbara didn't think they would get an answer, but then Alexander pointed past them toward the back room. Their eyes followed his finger. Luca saw it. She saw it.

Beyond the dinner table, beyond the window, beyond the patio and the rock garden, rose the glass wall of the carp pond. Beyond it, Jenna was floating like a ghost, halfway toward the bottom, her hair fanning about her head. Her eyes were open and staring blindly through the glass. Her mouth hung open too, but no air bubbles were coming out.

Whirling around her were the koi, dreaming of other worlds. The largest nibbled indifferently on Jenna's pinkie.

Barbara began to scream.

2

For Eleanor Delveaux, February 1 started at 5.59 a.m. when she woke from a restless sleep, one minute before her alarm. She started her morning routine with a double ristretto (no sugar) and sucking the juice out of half a lemon. Then she opened her laptop and read her email, mostly status updates on other ongoing NOVEMBER-6 cases. The *Oracle* had tested the organization's capacities and resources to the limit these past few weeks (the fact that she had moved her office from The Hague to this small air force officer's suite at Volkel was testament to it), but there was always more on her plate. Assisting the AIVD with the infiltration of a returned jihadis cabal. Shadowing a morbidly obese man in Amsterdam with a penchant for Russian snuff sites who got very young, very attractive women to do his bidding with a little bit too much ease for it to coincidence. An unusual fish kill in the North Sea. She perfunctorily worked through the files.

What she *didn't* do this Sunday morning was go to the ship. She was detaching herself from it. Soon, the whole affair would be settled, and if you couldn't change things, you might as well accept them. Still, it would never occur to her to forsake her duty. Until the time came when she would use speed-dial 9 to announce her departure and take her new passport from the safe in The Hague (which showed her photo, but not the name Eleanor Delveaux), she would conscientiously deal with day-to-day business.

A knock on the door and Glennis entered without waiting to be admitted. It was 7:36 and Eleanor, who would later that day fear not only for the survival of NOVEMBER-6, but also for her life, suddenly had a terrible premonition.

'Glennis, I hope you have a good reason to— Christ, you look like you've seen a ghost.'

She had.

Eleanor thought all hell had broken loose when she had involved Al-Jarrah. She was wrong. This was hell.

3

Later, Luca wouldn't be able to recall at what point his mind had switched to survival mode. Maybe it was when he first saw his dad in the corner of the parlor and thought, *So Emma was real too. Oh God, and I kissed her!* Or maybe it was when his mom couldn't stop screaming Jenna's name, or when the black vans came screeching to a halt in front of the house. Whatever the case, his reality had turned into a freak sideshow to which he was a terrified spectator, incapable of anything but mechanical reaction.

No, it was the fish mouths. The fish mouths opening and releasing air that bubbled up between Jenna's fingers.

He couldn't shake the images. His mom leaning in and fishing his sister's miserable, limp body from the pond. How she hurled Jenna onto her shoulder and shook her, forcing gulps of water from Jenna's mouth with each jolt. How in a flash, he saw her pale and lifeless face. Oh, if only he could stop watching. These images would haunt his nightmares.

'*Oh please, Jenna, baby, please wake up!*'

Tears stung his eyes in the cold morning air. 'Mom, is she . . . is she alive? Is she *alive?*'

With Jenna in her arms, his mom burst through the kitchen door and yelled, '*Call 112!*'

Luca rushed after her, wriggling his phone from his pocket with fingers that refused to obey. Of course, call 112. That's what you were supposed to do in a situation like this. But reason came back and formed a surprisingly coherent thought.

'But what about Dad?'

In the hallway, Barbara put Jenna on her back and started pumping her chest. Another image he would never forget: with each pump, Jenna's body shook like a doll in a growing puddle of water. All reason went out the window again, and Luca stood paralyzed. But his question finally got through to his mom, who looked up, hollow-eyed. '*Who cares? She's not breathing! Hurry!*'

She pinched Jenna's nostrils and blew air into her mouth.

'Mom, is she *alive?*'

'*Luca, for crying out loud!*' Between breaths.

He had to act. He couldn't. He was frozen.

Someone banged on the door. Luca jumped and saw a blurred figure behind the frosted glass. Someone had come to their aid. As his mom rolled Jenna onto her side to let the water out, he slipped past her and was at the door in seconds. He tried tugging it open. It wouldn't budge. Of course, the latch. He flipped it and opened the door.

It was Roger Teunis, their next-door neighbor. A master griller at backyard BBQs in better times. 'Bloody hell, Luca, what's going on?' he said but then saw for himself. 'Oh Jesus.'

Roger pushed Luca aside and knelt by Jenna and Barbara. 'Does she have a pulse?'

'I don't know,' Barbara wailed. 'Please help her, help my baby . . .'

Roger took Jenna's wrist as Barbara resumed CPR. He looked up and, collected and determined, said, 'Luca, go get me some towels, and make it fast.'

The calm in his voice propelled Luca into action. But he wasn't halfway up the stairs before Roger screamed. Luca saw him stagger back, lose his footing and stumble over Barbara, toppling her like a domino.

'*Jesus what the fuck is that? What the fuck is that!*'

Luca's white-knuckled hands grasped the banister. The thing pretending to be his father appeared in the parlor doorway. It looked down on the jumble of people on the ground, Jenna, Roger, his mom. Daylight poured through the open front door on its left, illuminating the horrid grin and the branched, black-and-blue trail of death patterns on its temples and neck. Luca would have screamed but for his empty lungs.

His mom apparently had air for two, because she bellowed, '*Oh God, Roger, keep him away from us, he did this, keep him away from us!*'

With all the strength she could muster, she pushed Roger off her and tended to Jenna. Roger remained frozen on his ass a little longer, staring at the thing in the doorway, then scrambled to his feet. Bewildered, he looked around for a weapon, something to swing or stab or throw.

'Luca, get outta here!' he yelled.

Towels. His brain resurfaced it from a jumbled remix of the past several minutes. He needed towels. Towels for his sister.

Two things occurred to him simultaneously: Roger was off to the kitchen, and the squealing of brakes from at least three cars outside. Then his legs carried him upstairs.

Let her be alive. Let her be alive. Let her . . .

He became vaguely aware of a stifled whining and realized it came from him. He tried to cut it but couldn't. He had one goal only. Towels for his sister.

Found them in the bathroom, neatly rolled, like his mom always stored them. He snatched three or four and dashed back toward the stairs. Two steps down and through the open front door he caught a glimpse of people running up the yard. From the other side of the hallway, Roger returned, leaping over Barbara and Jenna, wielding a kitchen knife.

Luca had never heard the sound in real life—*pshew!*—but instantly knew from a thousand TV shows what it was. A gun with a silencer. Roger went down with a dull thud and the knife crashed to the floor.

This isn't happening, Luca thought, frozen atop the stairs. *Not really, not really.*

Somewhere, far away, he heard his mom scream. Men rushed inside wielding guns. No cop attire, and Luca immediately knew who they were.

'Who the fuck was that?'

'He was coming right at me!'

'Ma'am, get up with your hands behind your head!'

Luca saw it all. The small, round hole on Roger's left brow and the growing pool of blood reaching Jenna's soaked shoes. His mom never stopping the compressions and growling like a wild dog. The N6 agents taking stock of the situation until their eyes landed on the thing in the front room. Number 1 staggering back and raising his gun before being curbed by Number 2. 'Do not damage him!'

'Ma'am! On your feet I said!'

More came in, including the giant Luca recognized as Uncle Jim, whose nose Jenna had once pinched, crowing with delight, but who now cast an indifferent glance at her lifeless body and turned to face his dad. The giant produced a taser. There was a dry click and his dad went rigid, falling backward into the parlor. Luca could only see his shoes, kicking and twitching on the threshold.

'*For the last time, ma'am, up! Right now!*'

'*Can't you see I'm trying to save her life!*'

Suddenly, a familiar voice. 'Barbara, do as he says. Let us help her, we know CPR.'

Glennis. Almost instinctively, Luca shrank back into the corner of the staircase, but he was still fully in view. No one had yet looked up with the chaos unfolding downstairs, but that would happen soon enough. Still, he stayed put, slave to his own apathetic body, and watched his mom continue to give Jenna mouth-to-mouth.

Glennis, her usual smile nowhere in sight, glanced over at Roger and snarled, 'Dammit, Roy. Why did you do that?'

'He was coming at me with a knife! What else was I supposed to do?'

'We need to be quick. Get her off the girl.'

Roy and a crony grabbed his mom by the shoulders and hauled her to her feet. She started a fit. '*No! Help my baby! Help my baby!*

But none of the intruders helped Jenna; their priority was restraining Barbara. A third agent came to their aid, but Barbara's foot caught him in crotch and he doubled over. Roy hooked his arm around her head. Growling, she bit it, forcing him to let go. Now she had only one assailant on her, and it almost looked like she was going to squirm herself free, but then Roy punched her hard in her side. She gurgled and coughed and collapsed into their arms.

'Mom!'

It came out before he knew it. Faces shot up. Glennis and Jim saw him simultaneously.

'Get him,' said Glennis.

His mom's frantic eyes found his and with a gut-wrenching howl he would never forget, she yelled, '*Luca, run!*'

Jim was already halfway up the stairs, and Luca knew that if he turned now, he wouldn't stand a chance. With a last-ditch effort, he snapped out of his paralysis, let go of the towels, gripped both banisters and launched himself into the air. Luca wasn't incredibly strong but strong enough to keep himself afloat and with clenched abs and a strength born from agony, he kicked his feet forward. The heels of his sneakers hit Jim square in the face. Although the man seemed made of stone, he wheezed a bloody '*uck!*' and, arms flailing, fell backward.

Even before the crash—the sound of bone crunching—Luca turned and ran. You didn't need to tell Luca which way to go because he had done it before. There was screaming from downstairs, but by the sound of it, someone had already taken Jim's place and was thundering up the stairs, two at a time. Luca didn't bother to look who it was. Instead, he lunged across Jenna's room and flung open the window. Behind him, the door slammed against the opposite wall. He threw his legs up and over the sill, certain he was going to get caught, already bracing for his hoodie to be yanked back and choke him. It didn't happen. In a flash, he saw a man, a snatching hand, but then his feet found wood and Luca performed a feat that, if he had had time to think about it, he wouldn't have even considered. He *ran* across the frame of his mom's pergola, bridging the backyard, bridging the koi pond, balancing his arms like a tightrope walker. Three quarters of the way, he knew he was going to fall, or the frame would snap, but one last leap and he managed to reach the roof of the shed.

His lungs sucked in gulps of cold air. Now, he *did* look back, to gauge his chances. His pursuer leaned out of Jenna's window, assessed the frame, and decided against it. Like a cuckoo in a clock, he bounced back inside and brayed in a voice not nearly as pure as a cuckoo's, '*The backyard!*'

Luca didn't hesitate. The roof's far-edge bordered on a back alley. He ran to it, lowered himself and let go. He did it too hastily and landed with an '*oof*' on his ass, grazing his hands. From the other side of the wooden fence came the sound of running footsteps.

Please Mom, tell me you didn't forget to lock the gate, you always do, let it be so this time . . .

It was locked. It started rattling. Luca jumped to his feet and ran. Someone smash-banged into the gate in an evident attempt to break it down. Boots kicking against wood. Luca dashed through the alley and out into the street, turned left without thinking and reached the corner of Park Lane right as the man Glennis had called Roy came running at him from ahead.

'There you are, you little shit.'

Roy was much faster than him, but Luca swerved and ran onto the road with his pursuer on his heels. That's why he only caught a glimpse of flashing chrome, only heard the roar of the engine and the blare of the horn at the last second, so close he could taste oil and feel its wind. The car missed Luca by a hair's breadth but hit Roy head-on. The crash of splintering glass, metal and bones shattered the morning light into a thousand rays. Next, the screeching of brakes, the stench of smoking rubber, and the dull, wet thud like of a bag of potatoes smacking on asphalt.

That was the last Luca heard. Now across the street, he reached the trail leading into the woodlands and, beyond it, the dunes.

Luca did as his mother had told him to.

Luca ran.

4

Eleanor feverishly studied the laptop screens in her makeshift comms room. She was alone in the suite behind Hangar 3 but wouldn't be for much longer. Last night, she had sent Grim on forced R&R to a hotel in The Hague, after Glennis had found him sleeping (and probably drunk) in the great cabin of the *Oracle*. He was an obsessive brain-fart, but his idiosyncratic nature sometimes spawned good ideas and *this*, this was his fucking expertise. Right now, he was being airlifted to Volkel with the same Cougar transport bird that had sent Glennis and the six other NOVEMBER-6 agents stationed at the base to the west of the country, immediately following the initial report. But Eleanor wasn't going to wait for Grim's arrival to cook up a protocol. NOVEMBER-6 consisted of twenty-seven well-trained operatives who not only excelled in data analytics but could also engage on the ground. Three of them were on leave; the others she had divided into extraction teams that were currently en route to the various hot zones. The teams were boosted, as emergencies authorized Eleanor to do, by marines and local police, none of who knew exactly who had deployed them and for what objective.

This was an emergency all right.

Or better, a flaming clusterfuck.

Zaky Dukakis, their IT guy in The Hague, had uncovered it during a routine check on the *Oracle* families. The frequency of the checks had been scaled down, but thankfully, Dukakis had come in early that Sunday.

'Look at this,' Glennis had said barging into her office and pushing her laptop next to Eleanor's, only an hour ago. No formalities, none of her usual histrionics, an order. That was bad business.

'What am I looking at, Glennis?' But she had figured it out before Glennis told her, and her stomach turned.

'This is the Wolf family's living room in Katwijk. The Wolfs are—'

'I know who the Wolfs are. And is that . . .'

'Alexander Wolf, yes, seems to be.'

Eleanor rolled her chair in and pressed her nose almost to the screen. The picture was a perfect high-def from one of their spy cams, probably enclosed into a TV LED or the sound system. The Wolfs' parlor was dusky, but there was no mistaking the figure looming motionless in front of the couch. 'That's impossible.' She produced barely more than a whisper. 'He was gone . . .'

'I know, ma'am.'

'Where the hell did he come from? I mean, how long has he been there?' Eleanor realized she was jabbering but couldn't help it. Her head was spinning.

'Unclear. Zaky just called. There's a glitch at 2:03am. When the image kicks back in again at 3:17, he's there.'

'What do you mean, a glitch?'

'There's over an hour of video missing, from all the cams in the house. But from 3:17 on, you can see him in the image.' She sounded cautious. 'It's a little creepy, actually.'

'But how's that possible?'

'Could be static. An electrical surge. We don't know yet.'

Eleanor noticed she was cutting her nails into her palms and forced herself to stop. Half-moons were imprinted deeply into the skin. She couldn't tear her eyes away from the silhouette in the dusky parlor. A *little creepy.*

'Are these live images?'

'Yes, you can see the time at the bottom of the screen,' Glennis said.

'And is the family up yet?'

'Only the little girl. Zaky says she's upstairs in bed, playing with her ponies.'

'That will buy us some time. Hopefully.'

'Should I warn Barbara? Mrs. Wolf, I mean?'

'Not if we can avoid it. You and the big guns are going there stat to nip this in the bud. We don't want her to realize her husband is back and make a bad situation worse.' She looked at her watch. 'It's still early, let's hope she sleeps in on Sundays.'

Something occurred to her then. Something terrible.

'What other families are we watching?'

'Um . . . Alaoui, Molhuizen . . . The Hopmans, though none of them disappeared.'

Call Dukakis, she wanted to say, but at that moment Dukakis called Glennis. Glennis answered and even before she had put him on speaker, Eleanor could hear the sheer panic in his voice. '*Glennis, he's not the only one!*'

She snatched the phone from her hand. 'Dukakis, what's happening?'

'I've got a picture here of the Molhuizens in Katwijk. It's seriously bad . . .'

'Send it.'

'Oh Jesus, his face. What's the matter with his face?'

'Dukakis, snap out of it!'

With a *ploink*, a link popped up on Glennis' desktop. 'Open it, ladies.' His voice sounded hoarse. 'I think you better start making calls.'

A vein throbbed behind her temple, so hard it hurt. She put the phone down between the two laptops as Glennis clicked the link.

It showed a living room accessorized with kitschy deco and mica framed photos. Apparently a pipe had burst because the room was flooded with gray water. Standing knee-deep was Casper Molhuizen, the second to disappear through the *Oracle's* hatch on December 8, now revisiting his parental home like a melted wax version of himself. There was no other way Eleanor could put it. In no way did his face reflect the merry portrait on the wall behind him. Something had violently knocked it askew. The bone structure was shattered. His mouth was agape in a frozen bellow, glowing with torment, insanity, hunger.

Three bodies floated face-down in the water. Eleanor didn't need confirmation to know they were Mr. and Mrs. Molhuizen and Casper's younger sister Faye. Faye was still in her PJs, and Eleanor could see a friendship bracelet around the pale bare skin of her ankle, just below the water surface.

Glennis put both hands over her mouth.

'And take a look at this,' Dukakis said. The image flipped to a fisheye view on the other side of the room. 'You watchin?'

Eleanor was. GIVE AND GIVE IN ABUNDANCE it said in screaming, drooping letters rooted into the plasterwork of the ceiling and wall like pitch-black vines of seaweed. Looking at them, Eleanor felt herself go giddy. She had the vague realization that something was happening to her, like someone about to faint experiencing a precognitive flash. There was a buzzing of static, and she brought her fingers to her temples. The black veins on the wall were *alive*. Suddenly, they clamped onto her mind like the tentacles of a jellyfish, and the inscription slithered into her head, twisting and crawling and twining itself around her brain: GIVE AND GIVE IN ABUNDANCE, GIVE AND GIVE IN ABUNDANCE.

Eleanor staggered. She was still watching the screen, where the Casper-thing had started to wobble, but she was also looking at the words in her head. She could see both. It was a terrible sensation, because through the words, *something was staring back at her.*

Not Casper. Something else.

Glennis snapped the laptop shut and broke the spell. Eleanor gaped at her in bewilderment. Glennis' eyes were sunk too deep in black sockets, yet they were bulging, if such a contradiction was at all possible.

'What was that? God, are you alright?'

'I think so. You?'

'Yeah . . . Zaky?'

No word from the other end of the line.

'Zaky! Answer me!'

'I think I'm feeling woozy . . .' a dreamy voice came.

'Turn off your screen!'

Apparently that got through to him because next, he sounded more like himself. 'Holy fuck, what was that?'

Glennis ignored him and turned to Eleanor with shock in her eyes. 'It got into my head. Did you feel that? It got into my head, how's that possible?'

'Beats me, Glennis. Put your head between your knees.'

'Wh-what?'

'Your head. Put it between your knees. You look like you need it.'

'I'm okay, I think.'

Glennis was, and ten minutes later she was on her way to the heliport. But not after she had arranged for a live communication with Grim ('Long-distance telepathic manipulation,' he had spouted, as if he *knew* this shit, 'your sole protection is a buddy system where one constantly watches the other. And whatever you do, do not touch them! Don't even *look* at them, you hear me?'). Radu and Van Driel were brought up to speed. Protocol stated that both the returned and the witnesses had to be secured at Volkel before more people died or the story leaked to the media. Otherwise, this shipwreck would flame into a catastrophe.

Now, alone in her suite with constant intel from Glennis and Van Driel in her ear and the three-screen, cumulative data of an unfolding tragedy before her eyes, her thoughts drifted back to the words that had taken root in her brain, words that had briefly opened the gate to an immense darkness.

GIVE AND GIVE IN ABUNDANCE.

They came back.

They *all* came back.

5

Initially, Luca's flight was impromptu, with a single train of thought whipping him on: *Outta here, GTFO, doesn't matter where, just get out.* He blindly crossed the strip of woodland. It was no more than half a mile wide, but the trail zigzagged steeply and before long, he was out of breath and in pain with side stitches.

That crash. That car slammed straight into him. Dude is fucking dead! It's my fault he's dead!

No, it's not. It's their fault and a stroke of luck for you. But Uncle Jim's something else. He may have broken his neck with that smack he made, and they'll definitely pin that on you . . .

Good, he thought insensitively. Fuckers shot Roger. Murdered him in cold blood. What *he* had done was self-defense. And his sister . . .

He cut that thought short. Better to assume Jim and Roy *weren't* dead. Hurt, yes, and the collision had certainly slowed them down, but there were so many of them, and they were undoubtedly on his heels. So, Luca ran.

It didn't take long before he emerged from the woods at the make-shift dirt pitch where he played five-a-side on Sundays with his friends. Here, he finally turned to look. Nothing. Trees were blocking his view. Beyond the pitch was a nature reserve and when he reached the gate he bolted straight ahead into the dunes. SANCTUARY—QUIET, the sign read, but on this crisp Sunday morning it was probably teeming with hikers and joggers. Best to leave the trail asap.

High up on the first dune he veered left, climbed a bank overgrown with burnet rose and hoisted himself onto a crooked wooden post supporting a wire fence. He looked back and went cold. *They were there.* Three of them. On the other side of the dirt pitch, less than three hundred yards behind. The bushes provided some cover, but . . .

Luca jumped into the thickets on the other side of the fence. Branches smacked his face and tore at his sweater as he plowed his way through. This was his chance; the dune's expanse alternated between grasslands and brush. If he could lie low there, maybe he could remain invisible.

But not here. They were close. Too close.

He tripped and went sprawling. Luca moaned as thorns bit his hands. He waited to catch his breath and for the stitches to subside, but then he saw the image of his mom before him: *Luca, run!* He had never heard her scream like that before. Where had they taken her? And Jenna? Was Jenna even alive?

They probably don't even give a shit, he thought, and that got him to his feet. He worked his way through a tangle of brush, turned slightly, and reached a clearing of drift sand. He stopped to look around. Here, he was hidden from any trails but found that not being able to see his pursuers was more unsettling than the actual risk of being seen. What if he ran straight into an ambush? He had to assume there were more than the three he had spotted. For all he knew, they had surrounded the reserve and were closing in on him at this very moment.

Before him rose the highest dune in the area, crowned with a graffiti-clad observation post, a concrete remnant of an old German bunker. They would never guess he would go there; it was too conspicuous. So up the slope he went. The last part, Luca belly-crawled like a commando through dense underbrush to stay out of sight. It slowed him down a bunch and he lost precious time. When he finally peeped out of the bushes at the top, he half-expected them to be waiting for him there.

They weren't.

As far as the eye could see, the reserve was deserted. Which was strange. Where were they? Carefully, Luca got up to his knees, hiding behind the concrete bulwark. Wind whipped at his hair. He had a clear overview of the trail, all the way from the woodlands to the dunes. Had they already pushed onwards, below and beyond?

Suits me. Let them think I'm still running. Let them think I'm halfway down to fucking Antarctica.

To the north, Luca could see the orange roofs of Katwijk, the Quick Boys Sports Park, and the lighthouse. Out west, ships aligned the horizon to be cleared for the port of Rotterdam. South was the skyline of The Hague.

Something was off. They weren't stupid. What were they plotting? He had wasted too much time crawling.

He took out his phone to check the time . . . and stopped breathing. His phone. Fucking hell. If they could hack it, they could track it.

They know where I am.

Luca looked up to see his nightmare come true. On the trail into the reserve, a man was coming, and coming in *fast*. In fact, he was sprinting. There was only one trail up the observation dune, and he had almost reached it. Luca looked further to the right and saw a woman trudging up the same slope he had used. She wasn't running, but close to it, and she was already halfway up the hill.

They were storming the bunker.

For some seconds, Luca was overwhelmed with panic. Then he sprang to his feet. A heavy, concrete slab capped the bunker, leaving a twelve-inch observation opening, just enough room for a kid to worm through. Luca had no such intentions, but instead placed his phone on the edge and shoved it in. There was a hollow crash when it hit the ground. Ouch. Parting with your phone would pierce any teen's heart, but it would give them something to work on.

One peek around the bunker and he saw the sprinting operative had cut the distance between them by half. Without further delay, Luca jumped down the south side and began his descent with the pale February sun in his face. Marram grass snared to catch his ankles. He ran until he felt like he was flying. Dry sand flowed into his footprints, erasing his tracks, leaving only vague hollows. If only he could reach the trail before . . .

Duck. Or they'll see you.

He instinctively knew the voice was right. To the left, the slope descended into a steep embankment, eroded by wind. Underneath it was a natural cavity laced with roots. Luca jumped in, rolled, and began digging himself into the wall, writhing and grinding his body. He pulled his hood over his head just in time before the wall collapsed on top of him. Dry sand muffled his screams. It bit into his eyes and filled his mouth. It got dark. Luca felt like he was being smothered by the heaviest, coldest blanket in the world.

He wanted to thrash but held himself back. He lay in a fetal position on his stomach. He could breathe. His body had created a cavity and there was oxygen. He wouldn't suffocate, not right away, at least.

This was good.

He spat and blinked until tears washed away the sand. The stinging subsided. So did the pounding of his heart. Slowly, very slowly, he wriggled his hand up along his body, and started to dig a hole in front of him, the way you dug a tunnel through a sandcastle. He didn't need to get far before he could see light. Dry sand kept closing the hole around his fingers, but that was okay. He wasn't deep. He could peek if he wanted to. Get out if necessary.

So what now?

Waiting was worse than running.

For what felt like an eternity, Luca lay shivering in the dark. Before, he had barely sensed the cold. It was a mild winter morning but without a coat and in the quiet embrace of the earth, it started to get to him. His fear and misery had exhausted him. He could hardly believe that only an hour ago, he was eating breakfast with Jenna and his mom. How could the world have changed so rapidly?

Not the world. My world. The world out there is still spinning like nothing happened, and no one knows what has turned Luca Wolf's insignificant little life upside down.

But was that true? If his dad was back, if Emma was back, didn't that mean that they were *all* back? And if so, their cover had blown up in their stupid faces.

They would pull out all the stops to bury this. The fact that they killed Roger was proof. Even if it was an accidental reflex with tragic consequences, Luca still remembered how coolly Glennis had reacted when she had seen their dead neighbor in the hallway. They weren't pulling any punches. And they sure as hell wouldn't hesitate to lock up any witnesses. Not for a few days, this time. Maybe forever.

He closed his eyes only to snap them open again when he heard muffled voices. Luca couldn't quash the impulse to dig another peep-hole. As soon as he saw light, he pushed his hand up and peeked underneath it.

Holy f . . .

There was a sneaker right in front of him. Less than three feet away. A hem of denim. He immediately jerked his hand back and all got dark again. Stupid! Did they see him? His body started to convulse, so fiercely that Luca feared it was impossible to miss from aboveground. He bit his lip until it bled and forced himself to get a grip. He succeeded only somewhat.

'No, he came down this way,' he heard a man's voice say. 'Up there, you can clearly see his tracks.'

A woman's voice replied, but Luca couldn't make out what she was saying. Dammit, so he left tracks after all. He hoped—prayed—the collapsed embankment looked natural from outside.

'Come on. He's scared, he's alone, and he's fucking thirteen. Little shit can't hide much longer.'

Now he could hear what the woman was saying. 'What he did with the phone was pretty damn clever. Gave him the chance to get a lead on us.'

Yeah, three feet's worth, Luca thought, and he suddenly got the irresistible urge to start giggling. He bit his lip again, but soon the tears were streaming down his face. He was vaguely aware it must be hysteria or madness because he had never been so scared in his life. Still, he laughed, soundlessly and with a puffed-up face. What's more, he was proud. She was a mole and she called him clever.

That may be, Miss, but I'm also a mole here. That got him going again. *Oh, cut it out or I'll explode, and then I'm toast!*

'There's a jogger,' the guy announced. 'Maybe he saw something.'

It got quiet, and underground Luca laughed so hard his stomach ached. His whole body ached, from his scratched hands to his bleeding lip to his stinging eyes, but he laughed, and he laughed away all his anxieties.

What was that thing that pretended to be Dad?

That instantly killed his laughter. Luca tried to push the thought away but couldn't, and suddenly became aware of where he was: in a cold, dark grave under the ground, buried alive among all things supposed to be dead.

That wasn't his dad in the parlor. And it wasn't Emma either, last night. They were shells that *looked* like the people he loved, but were puppeted by something else, something not even human.

He shivered. Why had they come back?

Because they had a message.

Give and give in abundance.

Luca thought of his little sister and began to cry.

6

With an increasing sense of defeat, Eleanor listened to the news from the west. Extraction teams were on the move throughout Flower Country. In The Hague, Hyacinth Team was first to arrive after the Forensic Institute received an alarming call from Inge Grootstal. She was the better half of their own poor Peter, who had been stupid enough to lean out and back into the *Oracle*'s hatch on day one of the investigation. An NFI employee herself, Inge knew only that a chemical accident had killed her husband. Except now she claimed he was standing at the side of her bed. At least she had had the presence of mind to call her superior and not the police, afraid she wouldn't be believed, but by the time Hyacinth Team arrived, they found her in the bathroom. She had clogged the toilet bowl with a towel, flushed, and drowned herself in it.

'Christ, how does someone even do that?' Grim asked pale with shock. Ever since his arrival at Volkel, he had behaved like a sore muscle and hadn't stopped pacing up and down her suite, which wasn't exactly helping her focus. Eleanor had to refrain from pulling the Glock from her purse and forcing him to sit at gunpoint.

'Willpower, Grim,' she said. 'A whole lot of willpower.'

But she knew it was them. The Returned. If there had been any doubts, they were quashed when Van Driel forwarded them an intercepted 112 call from Rijnsoever, just north of Katwijk, where beach strollers had witnessed an entire Moroccan family disappear into the waves. 'And the youngest was just a toddler!' the woman calling cried. 'The mother held him under till he didn't come up again and then she just walked into the waves herself. We were too far away to stop her, but when we got there, *we saw her headscarf wash ashore!*'

They had been the Alaouis. That was clear the minute they checked the CCTV images from their apartment, where the likely suspect was waiting with a lugubrious grin and a message etched into the wall.

'Turn it off,' Grim snarled. Eleanor was glad to.

'Kill them if the situation demands it,' she commanded Glennis, Van Driel, and the other team leaders. She spoke English to avoid having to translate for Grim. But Grim protested. He wanted them alive. Some of them, at least. Otherwise, he predicted something much worse might happen.

'Listen, Robert, if they can get in people's heads so easily and just snap them, all my people are at their mercy.'

'They already are, and so are we,' Grim said. 'But they won't harm them. Not all of them, at least.'

'What do you mean?'

'Think about it. All these folks disappeared inexplicably and now they're back. All of them, almost two months later. Just as inexplicably, and with a glaringly clear message. To emphasize this, they're claiming victims, and it isn't random. *All their victims drown.* They're trying to make a point here, whatever it may be. And here's the thing: you don't kill off your audience if you've got something to say.'

Eleanor gazed at him in disbelief. 'I'm not going to negotiate with them if that's what you're asking.'

'You have no choice, Eleanor! You have no clue what power you're up against. And I'm sorry, but this is exactly why you brought me here, so please *listen* to me, will you? *Evil for evil's sake doesn't exist.* What we call "evil" has its reasons. Its motivation. Things spun out of control in Black Spring because people got carried away by fear and ignored what Katherine really wanted. I implore you to not make the same mistake here.'

She sighed. 'Alright. What do you suggest?'

'I suggest we listen to what they have to say.'

Eleanor thought of the message weaving itself into her brain that morning and wondered how close she had been to her own demise. And that was just from watching images on a screen. Long-distance telepathic manipulation, Grim had called it. On 5G fucking speed dial, she might add.

'Fine. But how in the hell do you transport something like that?'

'If I'm right, they'll *let* themselves be transported,' Grim said. He saw her expression and quickly added, 'Well, uhm, avoid physical contact. Seems better. Maybe use those animal control poles dog catchers use. I'm just spitballing here . . .'

'If this ends in a massacre, Grim, I'm holding you responsible.'

It already was, of course.

In Katwijk, Glennis' Wild Rose Team had decided to bypass the Molhuizen residence (the entire family was dead, and no one would discover them for a while) and rush to the Wolfs' instead, to salvage what they could. They were too late. The little girl had drowned in the carp pond. The mother, hysterical, was drugged and retained, but not before the whole situation had gone wayward. A neighbor was shot. And the kid who found the ship back in December had escaped.

'He did *what* now?' Eleanor asked very softly into her phone.

'Ran into the dunes,' Glennis reported. 'Don't worry, we expect to find him. But I'm not sure how to say this. He kicked Jim down the stairs and—'

'Jim is five times his size. How did the little fuck even do that?'

'He was above him, ma'am. Happened really fast. Jim broke his arm and a collarbone. But there's something else. When the kid ran into the street, Roy took off after him. Roy Beernink. A Volkswagen van hit him full-on. He's in the hospital with a possible basilar skull fracture. They don't know if he's going to make it.'

Eleanor closed her eyes. When she opened them, she saw Grim staring at her with an expression that could either be shock or hysterical pleasure, and she almost executed him on the spot.

Think, she implored herself. *Think, think, think.*

'Were there any witnesses?'

'Half the neighborhood, but the good news is none of them saw Alexander, and we took care of the dead neighbor before the cops and the EMS showed up. But we need an explanation for why he won't be coming home. It was Roy, he was a little too trigger-happy when he entered the house. It's kind of ironic that he's the one who—'

'Clean up the mess and get the hell out of there. Call up Daisy Team to help you look for the boy. He hates our guts, and I don't want him spilling his story to the papers.'

'Daisy Team is on its way to the former Reich home to look for Martin and Emma. The house is on the market.'

'So call them back, as long as it's not an open house today! And Glennis?'

'Yes, ma'am?'

'Next time you call me, it better be to tell me you got that little worm, understood? I want him. He took out two of our best men.'

Grim had been right about one thing: the Returned let themselves be captured without a fight. In The Hague, Hyacinth Team neutralized Peter with a taser, a blanket, and enough ketamine to knock out a horse. Like his wife, they zipped him in a body bag, except his was leather-strapped to a gurney. The body bags were Grim's idea and highly effective. In Katwijk, Wild Rose Team applied the same tactic to Alexander Wolf as did Purple Lily Team to Ibby Alaoui. At Every Man's End, Daffodil Team put a bullet through Bart Dijkstra's head because they found the missing coach making 'suspicious movements' under the stands of his indoor tennis court. Eleanor guessed in that dark setting, the monstrous sight alone was cause enough for someone to pull the trigger, but she didn't mention it, as no one got hurt. They bagged and tagged the corpse . . . and good riddance, because only then the reports started to filter through that *none* of the Returned was technically breathing.

At least, not all the time.

When he heard that, Grim snatched the phone from her fingers and ordered them to strap Dijkstra's body bag as well.

In Noordwijk, they were out on a limb. There had been memorial services for all five missing police officers, and they had been national news. If *they* were to be seen by their families, then the shit really would hit the fan. Endless, nerve-wracking minutes ticked by between Van Driel's updates.

'Told you,' Grim gloated. 'The fire was a mistake . . .'

'*Now*, Grim? *Now?*'

Officer 1 lived alone in the center of town, and Violet Team quickly and efficiently neutralized him—no casualties. Officer 2 lived with her husband in Noordwijk aan Zee, and Dandelion Team picked her up. They found her husband with his eyes rolled back into his skull on the backyard terrace, where he had jammed a garden hose down his throat, taped his nose and mouth shut and turned on the tap. As if that weren't enough, Van Driel reported that the puddle they found him in was salt water and full of algae and seaweed. Two marines and a NOVEMBER-6 op had started to hallucinate during the extraction, but their comrades dragged them off before anything fatal could happen.

Officer 3, a rookie, had been living alone as well, but when they raided his former appartement in Voorhout they found only the sleepy and startled new owners. At 10:37am, while Casper Molhuizen was

retained in Katwijk without further incident and Eleanor was still waiting for good news about that fugitive little squirt Wolf, Van Driel
called.

'Open Twitter.'

'What?'

'Open Twitter, I said! Hashtag *zombiecop*.'

She did.

The hashtag led her to the account of one Bertram van Eijk, @
bveijk73, and worse, a retweet from the *Leidsch Dagblad*, the local newspaper. The tweet showed cell phone footage of the rookie. He was
standing in front of a house in a residential neighborhood. Bystanders
carefully approached him, but then stopped, put off by his face. The
caption read, *Voorhout this morning, #zombiecop looks just like police
officer Joshua Bol who died in #Sassenheim paper depot fire. Sickening
joke!!!*

'Eleanor, do you see it?' Van Driel demanded. Yeah, she saw it alright.
She also saw several other bystanders with their phones up. And this
wasn't @bveijk73's only tweet. Three pictures. Three videos. All rant-
ing about the 'joke' (in one tweet he called the mask a *disgusting, fake
prosthetic*), but some onlookers looked like they weren't so sure it really
was a joke. *'Eleanor!'*

This isn't happening, she thought. *I didn't deserve this.*

'Yes, I see it,' she mumbled. 'Where is this?'

'Up in Voorhout.' He switched from Dunglish to Dutch. 'We were
able to trace and will be there in a couple minutes. It's the cop's parent's
house. Can Dukakis hack his account?'

'Dukakis is in the field.'

'Someone else, then?'

'Everyone's in the field today . . .'

'So call the AIVD and get one of their cybers! That jerk has tagged
everybody, NOS, RTL, *AD*, *Telegraaf* . . .'

'Embrace it,' Grim said, who had gotten the gist. 'Seriously. Film
the operation with a couple of phones. And do it casually. Smiles on
faces. It's better to go with the flow of a tasteless joke pulled by some
friends than having people think it's real. Even if he killed someone,
make it look like that's part of it. With a little luck, you just might
pull it off.'

It was quiet on the other end, so Eleanor asked, 'Did you get that?'

'Yes,' Van Driel said. 'It's nuts, but I don't have anything better to
offer.'

'Do it. Pull out all the stops.'

Van Driel was hardly gone before Eleanor had the AIVD on the line. When her phone rang again several minutes later, she expected to hear Van Driel again, but it was Glennis.

'This better be good news, Glennis.'

'It's Daisy Team,' Glennis said, and Eleanor didn't need her flustered tone to know it *wasn't* good news. 'We couldn't reach them, so we went to the Reich home ourselves to check on them. It's really bad . . .'

She pinched her eyes with her thumb and index finger. 'How many are dead?'

'Three. Jasper, Yip-Huen and one of the marines who was with them.'

With pursed lips, she listened to what had happened. A tropical aquarium, this time. There was debate as to whether all three had drowned, because the faces and necks of Yip-Huen and the marine were sliced up so badly when Jasper's dying weight had toppled the entire thing over on them, that hemorrhage could have been the leading cause of death. They found Emma and Martin Reich towering over the bodies in a giant pool of blood, shards as sharp as guillotines and a whole bunch of dead cardinal tetras. The Wild Rose Team decided to shoot *père* first before daring to capture *fille* alive. Sort of alive, at least.

'Where's Diana?' Eleanor asked sharply. 'Wasn't she with Daisy Team?'

'She's in her car. We don't know where the other marines who were with them are, but . . . her hair has turned white, Ms. Delveaux. She's in total shock. She wrote the same message that's on all these walls with lipstick on her windscreen and she keeps mumbling—'

'"Give and give in abundance."'

'Yes.'

For some reason, this detail shocked her more than everything that had come before. Diana Radu was an ex-commander and one of her longest serving operatives. Cooked an amazing lasagne ai funghi, which she sometimes brought for staff meetings. No chance of that any time soon.

It was this triviality that finally made Eleanor grasp the full scope of the situation. NOVEMBER-6 had suffered a wound that would fester for months if not years, and any sense of control was now at the mercy of some supernatural force only Robert Grim seemed to begin to understand.

It was madness. And it wasn't over yet.

By eleven, a full-blown manhunt for Luca Wolf was under way. Van Driel called at 11:06am, cautiously optimistic about Officer 3. Grim's strategy seemed to pay off. Their numerical superiority had driven back the looky-loos, Zombie Cop had been neutralized in the ensuing chaos, and they were now offering their heartfelt apologies to the neighbors. A guerrilla film gag by some friends, they claimed. Maybe a tad morbid, but the guy had been a fan of cheap horror flicks and would have appreciated the joke. No, they hadn't anticipated it blowing up on social media, and would everybody please delete the footage out of respect for the relatives?

Risky, but with a little luck . . .

@bveijk73's Twitter account went dark for a while, and when it was reactivated, the incriminating tweets had been deleted. Van Eijk himself was sufficiently intimidated to prevent him from mentioning it again. The *Leidsch Dagblad*'s coverage died a silent death. And all the while, Officer 3's single mother lay in bed, peacefully waiting for it all to blow over, so she could be zipped in a bag. She looked like she had slept through the commotion, but in fact her lungs were full of water.

Officer 4 in Noordwijkerhout was extracted before his family, still asleep, had even been aware that he had returned. But with Officer 5, things went sideways after all.

Her name was Sandra Koch, and the good news was that her husband and children were alive. The bad news was that they had fled their house in terror and sounded the alarm before NOVEMBER-6 could intervene. Pictures shared with family members were spreading on Facebook, half of Noordwijk had gathered around the house, police (including members of Sandra's own unit) were on the scene, and as if that wasn't bad enough, a TV West van drove up the same time Violet Team arrived. It was a clusterfuck of unprecedented magnitude. Only when their chief ordered them to stand down would the cops allow Van Driel and his team to handle the situation, which in this case meant that they preemptively shot Sandra. She hadn't yet killed or imprinted a message on anyone, and it was imperative she didn't try that in public. Meanwhile, the police tried to keep the media at bay, which only fueled their interest further. Violet Team had no other choice than to get the hell out with Sandra's body and lie low. With a bit of luck—after all of this, Eleanor felt *entitled* to a bit of luck—the situation was so bizarre it had to be explained as fake news.

Only at 11:45am, when all teams had gathered in the compound in the dunes, did Eleanor dare to take inventory. Eleven civilian deaths, four of them children. Three of their own dead, Roy Beernink a vegetable, Diana Radu not much better. One fugitive child who knew too much. And nine returned monstrosities with a message for everyone.

Still, that wasn't rock bottom. That came when Grim left her suite to take a leak and shouted her name. The urgency in his voice was enough to make her jump in her seat and hurry out onto the skybridge.

She smelled it before she saw it. Rot, not dry but *damp*, a stench so overwhelming it sucked all the oxygen from the hangar. It stank like an old sewer where dead leaves and filth putrefied in still water.

The *Oracle* was decomposing.

Like all living things, the once imposing ship seemed to have shrunk in death. Tears and cracks had ripped open her skin. Paint was flaking off and mold emerged from underneath, dark, spongy smudges interspersed with twisted vines of inky-black weed curling through the woodwork like tentacles. One glance and Eleanor knew where she had seen them before.

'Dear God . . .' she whispered. The repulsive air punched through her lungs and made her gag.

Grim stood on the forecastle, his shirtsleeves rolled up, his glasses sparkling under the floodlights. 'Mission accomplished. She's done, Eleanor. Watch.'

He sat on the edge of the open hatch and dangled his legs inside. 'Grim, *don't!*' she yelled, but was already lowering himself inside. Next, he disappeared.

She stood petrified, her hands clutching the gallery's rail. Then she realized no bell was tolling.

Grim's head popped up.

'Done and dusted,' he said.

And Eleanor didn't know *what* to say.

Before she could think of something, her phone buzzed. In all the commotion, the ramifications had completely escaped her, but now they all came back. Eleanor saw her life spinning away in a web of consequences, and all could be traced back to her own hubris.

The screen said, *Omar Al-Jarrah*.

7

Luca didn't know how long he had been in his burrow in the dunes. He didn't sleep but hovered in a state not far from it, and he needed a brief, clear moment to get back on the move. He emerged like a crab crawling from its hole in the sand. He looked around, eyes blinking against the brilliant sunlight.

He saw nobody. Nobody saw him.

Escaping the clutches of November-6 that afternoon was probably more luck than anything. His next hiding place was beneath a tarpaulin on the stands of the Quick Boys Sports Park, assuming again that his assailants would never guess that he would seek shelter so close to home. That's where he finally dozed off to the sound of choppers circling the dunes further south, imagining they were the roar of fans during a Saturday match. What brought him around was a different sound, an alarming sound and all too real.

Disoriented, he lifted the tarp and peeked out from between the blue-and-white seats. The sun had crept to the west. The soccer field slumbered in silence. Luca had almost convinced himself that he had dreamt it after all, but then it came again.

The barking of a dog.

Across the field, a German shepherd was sniffing the fence at the exact spot where he had climbed over it. The dog barked and started pawing the ground, like it was trying to dig underneath. Its master was harder to make out behind billboards, but when the guy peered through the gap between them, Luca could see him talking through a wire.

Search dog. I'm fucked.

Further away, near the main entrance, another dog was barking, and that got Luca going. Marking the spot his dog had tagged, the wire guy turned his back against the fence, and Luca could faintly hear him speak. Waiting for his pal to pick up the scent on his side of the fence, most likely. As quickly as he could, Luca tiptoed down the concrete stand, painfully aware that if the man turned around or the dog noticed him, he would be finished.

Down boy, Safiya's voice said in his head. God, Safiya! How he wanted to be by her side. She would know what to do.

Her answer came immediately, in her usual snark. *That's nice, but right now you're gonna keep your eyes open because this was just a fluke, and you sure as hell ain't gonna get this lucky twice. Geez!*

Luca wasn't a kid who normally believed in psychic flashes and was pretty sure the voice was a just product of his overheated mind, but fact was the dog didn't see him. As soon as he reached the perimeter trench, he ran to the far corner of the field, ducking behind sponsor signs. Here a set of fully exposed stairs led up to the outer promenade and a fence lined with bushes. Always bushes . . . if only he could reach them.

Luca peered across the pitch and saw the dog nervously pacing behind the fence. His handler was waving toward the clubhouse. From that direction, the second handler was approaching across the patio. *They were inside.*

Luca ran. He flew up the stairs, his sneakers kicking up sand. Before he reached the top, the dogs went berserk. Luca didn't stop, didn't even look back. The barking wiped out all his happy thoughts. He lunged for the fence and that got him halfway up, rattling it so violently they probably heard it in England. Up and over it, he just let himself drop. He crashed into the dirt, rolled over, grazing a knee and elbow before scrambling up and away.

Fucking dog saw him. The dude too? Didn't matter. They were on him, and his scent would lead the way.

What popped through Luca's mind then was *Jurassic World*. The way Owen tricked the Indominus rex after it escaped from its paddock. The movies could teach you stuff.

But where could he find—

He cut his thought short as the bushes opened to a car park. He knew this place. It was the access road to the beach. During summer, it was jam-packed with cars. Now there were just a few. Scanning their fuel caps, Luca blanked. How would you even get in to them? Owen was clever. Luca wasn't. Luca was thirteen.

No longer did he hear barking or voices coming from the sports park, but that was no incentive to linger. He left the cars aside . . . then saw the scooters parked at the fence. Three of them. The first turned out to be electric, but the other two had fuel caps. Locked, dammit. Frustrated, he shook them and looked around.

He found what he was looking for by the exit to the road. Paving stones. He jerked and wrenched and pried one free. Back to the scooters. Luca had never been a hooligan and was restrained by conscience. It was a shitty thing to do to the owner, and if anyone—

Just do it, wimp!

Safiya again. Wow, she was bad news. Luca looked one last time to make sure he was alone, then kicked over the creakiest of the two bikes and with all his strength, slammed the tile onto the fuel tank. After the third blow, the metal tore, and a transparent liquid spattered onto the ground.

He tossed the tile aside, heaved the bike up, dropped it onto its other side. Now the gasoline gushed out. Luca washed his hands in it and dabbed his neck, dabbed his cheeks, screaming almost when it stung his cuts. He gritted his teeth and carried on. The flow had stopped, so he pushed the scooter aside and stepped into the puddle of fuel on the ground. He stamped his feet in it, rubbed it all over his sneakers and the hems of his jeans, and ran the last drops through his hair. That should do the trick. Now onwards.

A car turned into the lot. The driver and Luca flashed glances, but there was no recognition. So Luca crossed the road and charged into more bushes with dogs now barking from a distance.

The very idea of going back into the dunes exhausted him, so he chose the summer campsite instead. Luca spent fifteen minutes reeking of gasoline in a steel dumpster behind the reception building, when a thought crossed his mind: *What if the dogs follow the gasoline trail? They aren't just hungry dinosaurs lured by a tasty snack, they are trained K9s!*

That got him moving again. He abandoned his soaked shoes and socks in the dumpster and took off barefoot, too tired and confused at this point to consider the smartest strategy. The seashell trail toward the beach was hell, the soft sand when he got there felt like pillows under his shredded soles.

The last hours of daylight, Luca spent in another burrow in the sand, this time under an empty beach bungalow's porch. It was dark by the time he crawled out. By then, the sound of the surf had settled into his brain like a constant whisper, predicting not just ruin but impending death.

Under the cloak of darkness, he snuck back into town, starving, shivering, his throat screaming for water. But there was always someone who hadn't locked the gate. Always someone with an outdoor tap or boots left out or an unlocked bike.

More offences on Luca's record.

8

Robert Grim hadn't anticipated having moral qualms at sixty-seven, but here he was. Sometime between his discovery that the *Oracle* lost her magic trick and the arrival of the Returned at Volkel, he decided he couldn't work for Eleanor Delveaux anymore.

It was her hunt for the boy. The witch was obsessed with it.

Grim had seen before how unscrupulously Delveaux ripped people of their basic freedoms under the pretext of homeland security. Up to a point he was able to turn a blind eye because he had once filled her shoes. It was an ethical wasp's nest where you got stung serving the greater good. But the look on her face when he climbed out of the Oracle's hatch hadn't been just shock . . . it was the first sign of madness. Grim had seen madness before and knew where it led. He could hardly predict her intentions, but Luca Wolf was just a kid, dammit. He lost his sister. Saw his dad return a monster and his house raided. Now they were hunting him like a wild animal.

Still, common sense dictated that he should curry favor with her for the time being. Grim's survival instinct was clearly not as strong as it was ten years ago, and he realized for the first time (and with a good amount of shock), *Christ, I'm really gettin older.* Amply compensating for this, however, was his fascination. There would come a time when Delveaux would deem him, too, a danger for what he knew, but as long as he kept feeding her his pseudo-science and makeshift ploys, he could postpone the inevitable. And enjoy a front row seat for what was possibly the most important discovery of the century.

Not bad.

The convoy carrying the Returned arrived at Volkel just after 3pm. For obvious reasons Grim had advised against flying them in with the Cougar, even when they were knocked out with a shitload of ketamine. Instead, they were escorted down various highways in an inconspicuous U-Haul. The driver was wired to Van Driel in a support vehicle for the entire distance to make sure his shipment wouldn't suddenly start playing mind games and force him off a bridge and into a river.

Eleanor commandeered an underground ammo bunker and a reluctant colonel showcasing his fruit salad on his uniform led the inspection. Grim assumed he was some hotshot post commander grudgingly following the ministry's orders. The bunker was perfect, though. The piss-poor state of the Dutch army meant it was nearly empty, and it had enough steel-door storage lockers and gun vaults to detain each of the Returned separately.

Two armed MPs guarded the entrance when the convoy arrived. Grim and Eleanor bookended the hotshot.

'What in the world is *happening* here?' he asked, as nine gurneys with body bags were unloaded and placed side-by-side on the platform. Before Eleanor could answer, the MPs gasped. Grim saw them reach for their Glocks.

Reason: one of the body bags sat up.

Something moved inside.

Turned its head.

'*Kalm!*' ordered Van Driel, a word that sounded exactly the same in Dutch as it did in English, followed by a command that almost certainly meant '*weapons down.*' But the MPs saw the NOVEMBER-6 personnel reaching for their stun guns and had no such plans.

Then all the bags sat up. Grim heard the rustling of plastic and the stretching of leather, as the belts strapping their waists to the gurneys tightened.

'Fucking hell . . .' the hotshot whispered, pale despite his ribbons.

And Eleanor said, 'The less you know, the better.'

'Know what?' He stood at attention, possibly more out of habit than respect. 'I've had it. It's always the same with you people. Fucking freakshow.' And with that, he turned to his patrol jeep and drove off.

Stun guns and syringes ready, Van Driel and the others gently pushed the body bags back down flat before they dared carrying them down the stairs. None looked too happy to be assigned this job. Everyone was on edge, including the MPs, who still had their hands on their Glocks but knew better than to speak.

'Are they still . . .' Delveaux hesitated. 'Telepathically active?'

'Not since we tranqed the shit out of them,' Van Driel said. He pointed to another three gurneys that were being unloaded from the van. 'Those are the ones we shot. Where do you want them?'

'Locked up as well, separate rooms,' Grim said. 'When we're positive it's safe, I'll have forensics take a look at them. Get some cooling beds from a local morgue.'

They got to work, and Delveaux turned to Grim. 'Right, you can handle this on your own. I've got another mess to clean up.'

'Aren't you even the least bit curious about them?'

That got him little more than an icy grin. 'Didn't you tell me that this is what I hired you for, and that I'd better start listening to you? I'm listening.'

Bullshit, thought Grim. At this very moment, everyone at HQ was busy putting up smokescreens and spreading online conspiracy theories. The faster you muddied the waters, the less damage in the long run. It was SOP for NOVEMBER-6, and they didn't need Eleanor for that.

So what's your deal here? It's not like you're scared; you don't have the emotional capacity for that. You got something else up your sleeve, and I'm not liking it one bit . . .

But this was a pissing contest he wasn't going to win, so he cheerfully cooed, 'Viva fake news. Back in my day we didn't even have a name for it.'

'Just make sure there won't be any more families I have to bring it to. Report back every hour.'

It's almost like you care, he thought, but then he remembered the transport that had arrived at Volkel just before. The Transport of the Living. Its passengers included Barbara Wolf (out cold), Officer 5's family (scared shitless), the Hopmans (dumbfounded), and a woman he didn't know (snow-white hair and dead eyes). No underground bunker for them, but no luxury bungalow in the dunes either, not this time. They were held in vacant plain service barracks that had all the charm of a bunk in Auschwitz.

Downstairs, Grim watched from the doorway as the last gurney was rolled into its vault between empty gun racks. Van Driel unzipped the pouch a few inches then turned. 'Awright, good luck, boss.'

His mouth dry, Grim stared at the human shape on the gurney. EMMA REICH, read the tag on the zipper. Grim had prepared himself for this moment, but it shocked him all the same. Emma had once been pretty. A child. She wasn't pretty anymore. And you couldn't call something that repulsive a child either.

He cleared his throat. 'Aren't you going to take them out of the bags?'

'Nope,' Van Driel said, slipping past him. 'I unzipped 'em, and that's as far as I'll go. They're all yours now, boss.'

'Wait, where you going?'

'Listen.' A vein throbbed in his temple, the scribble of ink on his forearms suddenly seemed out of place, and his accent grew thicker. 'Those things creep me the fuck out. I've seen enough. This isn't what I signed up for. If this was my call, I'd light up this whole place and turn it into a crematorium. You say the word, and I'll bring the gas. But until then, you got plenty of worker bees at your disposal who are lower on the payroll than me.'

Before Grim could respond, the thing that had once been Emma Reich sat up. One of her hands slid out of the body bag and crawled across the dark plastic like a spider. The veins under her translucent skin were black. Her eyes, just as black, settled first on Van Driel and then on Grim. The rupture that was her mouth grew even wider, gaping like a crocodile into a grotesque grin.

Grim practically tripped over Van Driel as both fled the gun vault. Grim slammed the door shut and jammed the bolt lock in place. The bang echoed throughout the depot.

'Right.' Panting. 'I see your point.' Taking a moment to catch his breath. The central area with its cold glow suddenly seemed too crypt-like for his taste. 'I'll call you if I, uh . . . need anything.'

'Gas, Grim. Nothing else.'

Ja, Herr Kampfkommandant.

But burning them was not an option. Behind their monstrous appearance, they were still people with names and families. Besides, they had returned with a message. And by the time it got dark, they had wholly captivated Robert Grim's curiosity. By then, the central area looked less crypt-like and more autopsy room. Erica Kramer, a coroner at the Netherlands Forensic Institute, eventually pulled him away from the three carved up bodies and suggested a break.

'You smoke?' Kramer asked in the cold evening air aboveground, proffering a half-empty pack.

'No, but after tonight, I might start.'

'I hear ya.' She cupped her hands around the cigarette pressed between her lips and lit it. When the lighter flashed, Grim saw her hands tremble.

'Not your typical Sunday night, huh?'

'No, it's not exactly *The Great Dutch Bake Off*.' She inhaled deeply, bringing a little color back to her face. Only then did she notice his puzzled face. 'It's a TV show. A cake baking contest. On Sundays, the entire country tunes in.'

'Figures. On our side of the pond, it's MMA Fighting and *Cops*. Different strokes, I guess.'

She chuckled but said no more.

'So what do you think?'

'Yikes. You've got to give me *something*, Robert. I mean, where did these things even come from?'

'You signed the NDA, right?' He didn't wait for her answer because he had seen to it himself. 'So the message is, "Shut up and do your job." Don't look at me, I didn't write the damn thing. But believe me, it's for your own good to know as little as possible.' She gave him a look that made it abundantly clear she wasn't going to settle for this. Grim could appreciate that. 'All you need to know right now is they went missing for a while and this is how they came back.'

Kramer inhaled again and kept the smoke in for a long time before blowing it out. 'Flowers,' she said.

'Come again?'

'Flowers and seedpods. That's what I think. The only way to make sense of what I've seen tonight is comparing it to biological processes we know and understand. I don't know if it can explain everything, but it's all I've got.'

Grim respected that. He also respected how well she was coping under the circumstances. At least they hadn't come back to life. The bullets that blew Bart Dijkstra's, Sandra Kocken's, and Martin Reich's brains out were fatal. Whatever they had been, they were dead now. Thank goodness, because if any of them had sat up during the autopsy and grasped the coroner's arm, she probably would have had a stroke on the spot.

'In nature, we see that everything serves one and the same purpose,' Erica Kramer said. 'Reproduction. A plant grows many flowers in the hope that some will be successful and become pollinated, but once their function has been fulfilled, they wither away. Nature doesn't care about beauty. It cares about the purpose. The same goes for the flower's seedpods. As soon as they've released their seeds, they dry up and are dispersed.'

Just like the ship, Grim thought.

'I've never seen anything like what's infected these people. It looks like algae, but it's difficult to be conclusive before I've put the samples under a microscope. This whole thing needs extensive research. It would help if we could do an ex-lap on one of the living but . . . God, is that even ethical?'

'We can look into all that later. Right now, I need answers.'

'That's not how scientific research works, Robert. You know that.'

'And you know these aren't normal circumstances. Give me your best theory.'

She sighed. 'Algae vary from single-cell microorganisms to the most diverse kelp and seaweeds. We know cases of algae surviving inside the human body and attacking the central nervous system. The symptoms look like poisoning. Vestibular dysfunction, neural anomalies, paralysis, things like that. But this is different. Here, the intruder appears to have mutated into a single parasitic organism. Either that, or it's a swarm with what seems like a shared consciousness, like schools of fish. But here's the thing. It's intelligent. The way it entangles itself with their organs and arteries . . . Robert, no human being should be able to survive that kind of internal damage. Maybe it kept festering after they died, but if you look at the people you're holding in those cells . . .'

'Finish that thought.'

'They don't breathe, they *imitate* breathing. Like the intruder is pretending to be human. I'm not even sure if their bodies are still alive.'

Oh, they are, Grim thought. *And that makes it worse. How else did they remember where they lived? Or who their loved ones were, whom they were supposed to kill?*

The horror of this thought easily rivaled what he had seen in the autopsy room. Once the bodies had been opened up, he told himself they were no longer people. Just anatomy class projects. Mannequins from a twisted mind. Kramer had urged him to look, and he had managed not to gag, despite the putrid stench no surgical mask could block. It was the stench of something from the sea that had crawled into their bodies and died there. Death had broken them. No other way around it. Their frozen, cramped fingers. Their glazed eyes, black like camera lenses. But most of all, their gaping mouths. Mouths so big you could put your entire fist in.

The worst of it was that their organs were still human, in some sick, ravaged sense. Dark, jellied tendrils had wrapped possessively around organs, sunk into tissue and penetrated arteries. They seemed to be made up of the same biological material found in the messages on the walls of all those houses in Noordwijk and Katwijk.

With something resembling kitchen tongs, Kramer had tried to pull a piece from Martin Reich's lung. It made a slurping sound and Grim knew he would never eat squid again.

'I still don't see your flower analogy,' he continued. In the dense woods sheltering the bunkers, an owl hooted.

'If we assume this thing is intelligent, we need to look at what its purpose is. And that brings us to their message. Not only the one they wrote on the walls, but projected telepathically, if I may paraphrase you.'

'Yep.'

'I didn't pick up anything. And I was pretty close to them.'

'I wasn't kidding.'

'I'm not suggesting you were. I've seen enough to curb my skepticism for tonight. But don't you agree they're rather . . . apathetic? I'm not stupid, Robert. I don't know *what* they've done, but you don't put us underground in an army base guarded by secret service agents, if all they did was scribble a message on a few walls. Don't give me that guilty look. I knew this wasn't going to be a bubble wrap party. But this? A bunch of pallid, mangled bodies on gurneys. Am I right to assume I haven't seen a fraction of what they're capable of?'

'I think I know where you're heading with this.'

'If they had anything to say, they've said it. They've fulfilled their purpose. And now they're wilting like flowers. The way they look now, I'm guessing half of them will be dead by midnight. The rest by daylight.'

Grim stared at her while that sank in. Eventually he said, 'So it's up to me to decipher their message, so I'll know what they want.'

'Not *they*, Robert. *It*. If my theory is correct, they're flowers of the same plant. I think your objective is to discover what kind of plant this is. And you'd better hurry up, because I think it's fucking pissed.'

9

This time, Luca didn't have a phone when he reached Safiya's house in Voorhout, and ringing the doorbell was not an option. Mr. and Mrs. Adan were good people, but at this point, he didn't trust anyone. No other option but to wade through the canal behind the house to reach their backyard. The water looked dark, dirty and cold. Any other night Luca might have hesitated, but he was famished and bone-tired, and craving a hug.

He left the stolen bike on the bank and eased himself into the water. It wasn't cold, it was freezing, and Luca gasped. The water came up to his armpits, much deeper than he had expected. His lungs seemed to shrivel and his heart skip a few beats, immobilizing him with his arms held high. Then he rebooted.

Get going.

He counted the houses. Most gardens had a waterside deck where he imagined fun, lazy summer vibes. One had a small rowboat tethered to a support he had to wade around, making the water come up to his neck. At what he counted was Safiya's house, he put his hands on the edge and hoisted himself onto the deck. The cold bit into him as stinking ditch water gushed from his clothes, and his whole body shivered. *Oh Jesus. Move.*

Teeth chattering, he staggered across the backyard. The Adans had drawn the curtains, but lights shone behind them. Also in Safiya's room upstairs. Getting there wasn't a problem: the green bin, the board-to-board fencing and the rail of the awning would get any easy-moving thirteen-year-old where they needed to be. Except his limbs were rigid, his worn-out sneaks (snagged from the same shed as the bike) slid off the fence, and he hit the awning's casing so hard that somebody *had* to have heard it. He had to muster the last of his strength to grab the windowsill and knock.

Didn't take long before the blinds rolled up and Safiya's startled face appeared. Seeing him, she nervously glanced over her shoulder then opened the window cautiously to avoid knocking him off the sill.

'Seriously, again?' she whispered. 'If you're going to make a habit of dropping by after dark, why don't I ask my dad to give you a key?'

'H-h-help me,' Luca pleaded.

Then she saw his wet clothes and the expression on his face, and her eyes grew wide. 'Omigod, Luca. What happened to you?' She grabbed hold of him. 'Jesus, you're all . . . yuck, did you crawl through the canal?'

'C-c-c-c-cold,' was all Luca could say.

'Come here. No, put your foot there. Like that. Wait, I'll get a towel, before you'll ruin the carpet.'

She snatched a towel from the hanger under the sink and spread it under the sill. Luca rolled inside and almost collapsed, but she helped him onto his feet, sizing him up head-to-toe.

'Let me guess, this is about what happened at the beach today.' Luca looked at her puzzled. 'Ibby's family. They say they all drowned themselves in the sea. The parents supposedly held the kids under, it's awful. Class app is blowing up. I didn't tell anyone, but Ibby went into that ship too, didn't he?'

Luca was dumbstruck.

'Never mind, we'll deal with that later. Let's get you out of those wet clothes. I'll steal some of my dad's. He's XXL, but at least they're dry.'

Safiya tried to go, but Luca grabbed her shoulders. He wanted to say something but burst into tears instead.

10

There was still a chance she could get out of this mess unscathed. Not all was lost. That's what Eleanor told herself when she slipped out of Hangar 3 that evening and headed toward Ward C.

The base was quiet. Flight operations had ended for the day, and she had sent her entire staff to the hotel, except for the team assisting Grim. He was currently in the ammo bunker playing with his new toys. Eleanor couldn't care less what he was up to, as long as they didn't stir up new troubles. Meanwhile, Glennis and her team were paying house visits to Luca Wolf's peers in Katwijk. He was now the subject of a nationwide missing person alert, wanted on suspicion of involvement in his family's disappearance. The little worm had had the devil's luck, but he couldn't hide in the dunes forever. With all the resources they brought to bear on him, Eleanor hoped he would get his foot caught in an animal trap.

As for her, she hadn't been able to focus at all on the aftermath of the raids in the west. Her thoughts kept going back to that day's phone calls. The phone calls and the *Oracle*.

As soon as she had discovered what was happening to the ship, she had it sprayed with a chemical sealant to prevent further decay. But it was hopeless. The *Oracle* was rotting. Invasive algae nestled in every crack in the wood, like fungus in a cellar. The process was fast, and Eleanor doubted if anything could stop it. At this rate, it would crumble into a pile of driftwood in mere days.

But whatever curse possessed the ship ultimately was of little importance. The only thing that mattered was the hatch, and that was now closed for good. Poof. Magic gone.

But not all was lost.

She only realized she had a lifeboat right in front of her when she heard herself say it out loud. It was incredible how the subconscious could extricate us from the most impossible predicaments when fear was near.

Omar Al-Jarrah wasn't just angry, he was freaking out. In his voice, which used to have the power to enchant and captivate her, she heard a man scared out of his mind and acting purely on impulse. She was glad he wasn't there, or he would surely have killed her. *And if I screw this up, that could still be in the cards.*

'You've betrayed me!'

'Omar, what—'

'"Forever gone", my ass! It's all over the fucking news!'

Time. She needed time to think. She hadn't followed the news, but she could pretty much guess. 'I don't know what you're talking about, Omar. I've been dealing with a situation all morning.'

'Well, here's a situation you're going to deal with. I just sent you an email with a bunch of pictures and an audio file. Open it. I'm calling you back in five minutes, that's plenty of time to get you up to speed.'

'What kind of—'

'*Five minutes, Eleanor!*' He ended the call.

She ignored Grim whose head still poked out of the *Oracle's* hatch ('Sure, I'll wait,' he whined), and rushed back to her suite. On her way, she opened *The Guardian* on her iPhone. She didn't need to search; it was front page news. Abdulaziz Yamani had been one of their own, after all, dominating the headlines since his disappearance. This morning, he had reappeared in King's Cross Station across the road from *The Guardian's* HQ, killing three in "a possible terrorist attack". The disturbing pictures from witnesses suggested something completely different, Eleanor thought, but she didn't have time to read the entire article. What she did read was that authorities killed him when he had apparently "assaulted" them.

She swiped *The Guardian* away, sat behind her desk and opened her email. No courtesies, no cutie-pie or honeybun. Just three pics and a MP4 file. The first two showed her and Yamani shaking hands on the tarmac in Volkel. The third showed her and Yamani looking at the *Oracle*. The photos were timestamped. She played the audio file and heard him say, 'Hello Ms. Delveaux. My name is Abdulaziz Yamani. I am a journalist for *The Guardian*.' Then she heard herself answer, '*Wa alaikumu assalam*. Welcome to the Netherlands, Mr. Yamani.'

She hadn't said that. The audio had been tampered with, but they had done a good job. What did she expect? She should have seen it coming from a mile away. Incriminating photos had been Al-Jarrah's MO fourteen years ago. It was so blatant it was almost funny. Except it wasn't, of course. It wouldn't hold up in a court of law, but it was more than enough to drag her name through the mire and threaten the future of NOVEMBER-6.

She had a full minute left before her phone lit up. 'Don't think this is all I have on you, Eleanor. I'm going to crush you. And if I think you haven't paid enough, I'll come for you and crush your body. I won't send a death squad to do it. I'll come for you myself. Nobody fucks me over. Nobody.'

She believed him. 'Are you done?'

'Be very careful with your words, bitch.'

'You need to calm down, Omar. I didn't fuck you over, you know that. You've had a shock, I get it. It caught us off-guard, too. But think about it. Isn't this exactly what you wanted?'

'What I *paid* for is a black hole. Something that would make them disappear forever.'

'Sure. And what happened? The whole world suspects the Saudis. Your crown prince can smile in front of the cameras all he wants, but he isn't fooling anyone.'

Silence from the other end. She felt her pulse ramped up to an alarming rate. Her life depended on what she said next.

'Let's be frank. You didn't buy the ship for *supporters* of the House of Saud. If the *Oracle* made your enemies disappear forever, you'd be the prime suspect, and there'd be nothing you could do about it. But no, here's a ship that presents you with the opportunity to wash your hands in innocence! Here's a man, a treacherous man, a dissident. You went to London to question him, but you never kidnapped him. You didn't saw him to pieces with a bone saw, like everyone says. And here's your evidence: today, he shows up in London and kills a bunch of people in a terrorist attack. The way *I* see it, you were right to question him, as he apparently *was* dangerous. *That's* your narrative.'

'But it's completely unpredictable,' Al-Jarrah said. The anger had temporarily subsided from his voice, leaving only cool calculation. That was good. It made him malleable.

'It isn't, there's a pattern. Sure, it begs further investigation, and I imagine you can build on our findings. But Omar, this is a blessing. Here's the perfect way for you to make certain problems go away . . .

because they don't actually disappear. They go missing for a while before they turn up half-conscious, unable to speak. They snap and wreak havoc. All existing suspicions around *you* turn out to be false. You're not associated with any of it. The local authorities clean up the mess, just like they did with Yamani. Everything wraps up nice and tidy.'

Nothing from Al-Jarrah. Just his breathing. Had he taken the bait? She knew she had one more thing to say to seal the deal.

'Surely you must have realized that an unconventional purchase likes this comes with an element of unpredictability. This is not some high-tech weapon from a lab.' She made sure that the smile curling her lips came through in her voice. 'You yourself called it a miracle.'

He gave her twelve days.

Transport was planned for the 14th. On the 13th, Al-Jarrah would come to the Netherlands, giving her twelve days to demonstrate things would turn out as she had deluded him into believing they would. More details were guaranteed to leak, which she would have to answer for. How the media and public were going to interpret Yamani's distorted face, for instance. Whether they would link it to the images from Noordwijk. And then there were the details that wouldn't be made public but would certainly raise tensions between MI6 and the GIP, such as the message Yamani almost certainly had left on the wall at King's Cross or in his apartment. Perhaps in English? Or Arabic?

Give and give in abundance.

بوفرة أ عط ثم عط.

Nothing she couldn't handle. They were just more smokescreens. When he had calmed down, Omar Al-Jarrah hadn't believed that Eleanor deliberately fucked him over.

Except she had.

Because there was no ship anymore.

With that bluff, she had signed her death sentence . . . and bought herself enough time to arrange her own vanishing act.

Twelve days, she said to herself, as she paced through the cold evening toward Ward C. *Twelve days to clean up this mess.*

Ward C was a dark, low barracks hidden between the trees. It housed classrooms, a canteen, and bunk rooms for cadets. The present occupants were on combat training in Norway, leaving the facility vacant for those who were officially their incarcerated civilian witnesses, but whom Eleanor regarded as snoops who knew too much for their own good. Snoops and fallen angels.

She went in through the main entrance using the key on her ring and followed Van Driel's instructions. The stairwell, the corridors; even with everything Eleanor Delveaux knew about the ways of the world, the eeriness of an empty building didn't daunt her. Her footsteps were resolute, piercing through the smell of chlorine and floor polish. These were the footsteps of a woman who knew exactly where she was and what she had come to do.

She stopped at door T23. She put the key with the corresponding label into the lock and the door opened.

A shadow was waiting in the dark.

'Hello, Eleanor,' a voice said.

The voice was flat and monotonous, but still she recognized it, and that *was* daunting. She flipped the light switch and even though she braced herself, she still got a shock.

Diana Radu had once been a strong woman. Now she was a wreck. Whatever she had seen at the Reichs' residence had robbed her of her sanity. Glennis hadn't exaggerated when she said that her hair had turned white. Once dark and voluminous, it had now lost all its pigment, leaving only a faded, pale, lifeless hue. Eleanor was familiar with the phenomenon from parapsychology but had never seen any scientific evidence to support it, until now.

Radu's face was frozen and hollow. She was slumped in a wooden chair between two bunkbeds. Her clothes were rumpled, her blouse untucked.

'Hello, Diana,' Eleanor said. 'I'm sorry it's taken me this long to come and see you. And I'm sorry we had to hold you in such deplorable conditions. Glennis gave you a sedative. Van Driel said you couldn't be reasoned with when you woke up and that you showed little control over your impulses. Can I reason with you now, Diana?'

Radu began to laugh in quiet madness. There was no pleasure in that laughter, only a desperate plea. Bulging with terror, her eyes began to leak.

No more lasagne ai funghi, Eleanor thought. 'You're clearly out of it, but you must be aware that our operations require resilience. And in that regard, exercising due diligence with the information we have been trusted with is paramount. So, what do you need to show due diligence?'

'Due diligence?' she said, her voice choked because she was inhaling instead of exhaling as she spoke, and Eleanor's blood dropped ten degrees. 'There is no due diligence. Only destruction and death in silvery water. And you know who's waiting . . .'

'Who, Diana?' Eleanor snapped. 'Who's waiting?'

She giggled. 'The water will rise. You will see it as I did. Everyone will. So much for your due diligence, *Eleanor.*'

It was the way she pronounced her name. Emphasized it. Not a statement, but a provocation. A threat.

Radu's face gorgonized into a silent scream. Warily, Eleanor stepped up and stood behind her, putting her hands on her shoulders. It was sad to see what had become of her once so reliable asset. Sad to see what it had come to.

'I got a call today,' Eleanor said, gently massaging Radu's shoulders. 'King, Diana. Remember how often we told each other how much we hated the prospect of having to call him? Well, *he* called *us*. Of his own accord. That hasn't happened in six years.'

King (certainly not his real name) was the man on speed-dial 9. He was the intermediary who made it possible for November-6 to operate outside the prying eyes of the government bureaucracy. He was the one who liaised between her and the ministry to get approval on necessary grants and requests, no questions asked. Eleanor had never met him and could only picture him based on his voice. The instinctive aversion she felt toward him wasn't a reaction to his oily secrecy but rather to his utter lack of it. In a book or a film, such a shadowy figure would lisp or stutter, or at least have a strong German brogue. In reality, he sounded run-of-the-mill boring. But that was exactly what unnerved her. This voice would use the same inflection to report an administrative delay as to inform her she would be facing a firing squad at dawn.

'He said that a nosey reporter from *de Volkskrant* has been digging around in the wrong places.' She continued rubbing Radu's shoulders. She didn't react. 'Linking what happened this morning with December 8. King asked what in the hell we were up to. Can you imagine?'

Eleanor let out a high-pitched laugh. Up went her hands, into Radu's hair. It felt like straw. She started to rub her scalp. 'He threatened to sever all ties. All the way up to the highest level. To cut us off. If anything leaks, they'll pull the plug. No one's going to have our backs.'

That wasn't news to her. November-6's privilege was also its Achilles heel: if the shit hit the fan, they were on their own. You just didn't think it would ever come to that when you signed up. Now that the threat was real, Eleanor realized she wasn't the only one in this boat. They *all* were.

The only solution was that it would all disappear.

The snoops and the fallen angels.

'I had a moment of weakness,' she whispered. 'But not anymore. I see very clearly now. It's a pity you've broken under the pressure, Diana. Van Driel didn't, and neither did Glennis.' She leaned close and whispered in her ear, '*But you're weak.*'

Her fingers clutched Radu's ravaged hair by the roots as she put her other hand underneath her chin. With a jerk, she wrenched her head back. It hit the back of the wooden chair with a crack that sounded like a dead branch snapping. Only it wasn't the wood that had snapped. Radu's body went limp. Eleanor let go of her head.

When she walked away, her footsteps echoed through the corridors just as resolutely as before, but Eleanor Delveaux felt better now than she had in a very long time.

11

Safiya made him shower first, because he hadn't been able to utter a word. There, Luca began to drink. He licked the hot water from his lips, unable to stop, slowly ousting the cold from his body. Afterwards, when he sat on Safiya's bed in Mr. Adan's oversize boxers and tees and Safiya's pink bathrobe, she gave him half a cereal loaf, a tub of curried chicken spread and a pack of chocolate chip cookies. Luca snatched the cookies from her hand, tore the packaging open, and stuffed two in his mouth. Before he had properly swallowed, he started on a third.

'When's the last time you ate?' Safiya asked.

'This morning,' he said, spraying crumbs all over her comforter. He tapped them up with his finger and put them back into his mouth. Then his face darkened. This morning was when everything had gone wrong. He wondered if his half-eaten croissant would still be on the breakfast table.

Safiya opened the lid of the tub, and spooning up the curried chicken with the bread, Luca finished them both. He drank the tea she had made for him, which was nice and hot. 'Aren't you getting in trouble for this?' he asked, pointing at the small buffet he had just devoured.

'Nah. My mom probably thinks my dad ate it. Else I'll say I got hungry for a snack. I'm not even sure they'll notice. Soccer's on, and then it's time for *The Great Dutch Bake Off*. Which means you can snatch the TV from their cold dead hands. They watch all that white people shit. Don't ask me why.'

'What time is it?'

'Quarter to eight.'

'For real?' He would have believed her if she had said ten.

'Time for you to start spilling the beans, Luca.'

So he did. The only thing he left out was the part about kissing Emma. That would be like telling the girl you loved about your sex fantasies. It was just weird. Besides, he wasn't even sure if it had actually happened. It was all a bit fuzzy.

'I'm so sorry about your sister, Luca,' Safiya said softly when he was done. 'Do you think she's . . .?'

She stopped mid-sentence as Luca gazed at his hands. 'I don't know.'

'Where you think they took your mom? And your dad?'

'Don't know. I only know they're after me. And they won't stop until they find me.'

'Because they're afraid you'll talk.'

Luca nodded.

'So why don't you? My sister's friend knows this vlogger who's got over three hundred thousand followers. If you do what they're trying to stop you from doing, you'll take away their power. Maybe then they'll leave you alone.'

'But who's going to believe me?'

'I'll get my dad to help us. He'll believe us.'

'No!' Alarmed, he grabbed her arm. 'He won't. And there's no way I can prove it. You don't know what they're capable of, Safiya. They'd convince him I've done some bad shit. Like I killed Jenna and my folks. And even if he would, they'd come after him, too. I don't want to put your folks in danger.'

She considered this and made a decision. 'Last week, when you told me about your visions, I said you should try and summon it. I think it's time.' She got up.

'What, now?'

'Yes, now! Wanna go to Disneyland first? You were the one who said the spyglass opened a door especially for you and shows you all kinds of shit. So now your dad and Emma are back, and from what I understand so is Ibby, and a whole bunch of people *died*. Don't you want to know what you got to do to keep more people from dying?'

'But why me? Why am *I* supposed to be the chosen one?'

'Fuck if I know,' Safiya hissed, muting her voice. 'Why did Frodo have to bring the ring to Mordor? It's always the cuties who have to restore balance.'

'The cuties.'

'You look pretty cute in that robe, boy.'

Luca went red.

She waved it away. 'Don't be a wimp. What you did today was fire. Listen, I think you're the chosen one because you found the ship.'

'Okay,' Luca sighed. 'But I wish I knew how.'

'That's where I come in.' She went to her desk and opened a small jewelry box. Out came a zipper bag. Back on the bed, she handed it to him.

'What's this?' Luca asked.

Safiya looked at him, eyes twinkling. 'What you told me last week got me thinking. Didn't you say the lady in your vision gave you magic mushrooms? The shaman lady? Last night, my folks went out, and I heard my sister and her friends having these weird, hysterical laughing fits. I snuck downstairs and found a half-eaten, homemade cake in the kitchen. First, I thought gross, it's all moldy, but then I smelled it and knew what it was.'

'What?'

'Space cake, stupid.'

'Oh.' And again, 'Oh.' He got it now.

'I snagged a piece for you. It gave my sis and her friends mostly the giggles, by the sound of it, but online it says you can trip pretty hard on it.' She shot him a meaningful look. 'Maybe it can help you summon it.'

With nervous awe, he tossed the bag in his hands. 'I've never done drugs before.'

'My sister let me have a drag of her joint one time. On the condition I wouldn't tell my folks, of course. Gave me a killer headache. But this is different. This isn't *recreational use*.'

'I dunno . . .'

'Listen, this is what we're going to do. You're gonna stop being a wuss and eat that cake. The website said it takes at least an hour for the effects to kick in and that's good, because if I don't watch at least part of *The Great Dutch Bake Off* with my folks, they'll think I'm dead or something.' To which she rolled her eyes. 'Meanwhile, you'll be in my bed with your head under the covers and if you hear anyone come upstairs, put a sock in it till I let you know it's me, okay? If my folks find a boy in my bed, they'll burn us both at the stake. And if the boy is stoned as well, they'll add gasoline. Now, *eat your cake*.'

What convinced him was the prospect of lying in Safiya's bed for an entire hour. He would have walked across hot coals for that.

'Okay, here goes,' he mumbled. He broke off a chunk. The sickly-sweet smell went straight to his lungs, and he flapped his hand in front of his face. 'Yegggh, it stinks.'

'It probably tastes better than it smells.'

It didn't. It was disgusting. He stuffed the whole piece into his mouth, too nervous to give it more thought. It didn't taste like anything he had ever tasted before. It made him think of moldy bread, almost causing him to gag. As quickly as he could, he washed it down with Safiya's tea.

No turning back now.

'Good boy,' Safiya said. 'You're brave, Luca. Let's summon up a couple of weird old witches in an hour or so. I'll be there. I won't leave you on your own. Now move it, under the covers.'

Luca gazed at her with a look usually reserved for religious fanatics worshipping their idols. Right now, the way she had taken charge, risked everything, and known exactly what to do, he thought his girl was pretty fire, too.

12

Eleven-fifteen.

Robert Grim sat in Alexander Wolf's vault, his chest against the back of a chair, elbows on knees, arms folded. His shirtsleeves were rolled-up and stained with autopsy blood, but that didn't bother him. The heavy steel door was open. Wolf stood in front of his gurney, arms dangling. The body bag behind him was zipped open. At times, he took a breath, sounding as if his throat was full of jelly. But most of the time he didn't breathe at all.

One consciousness. One intelligence.

A hivemind.

These words had been stuck in Grim's head the whole evening.

He saw it now. The ship wasn't the Oracle, the Returned were the Oracles. The ship had brought them back and fulfilled its purpose. The Oracles spread their message and fulfilled *their* purpose. But what was next?

Give and give in abundance.

A sacrifice. The drowned, the dead. *They* had been the message.

What Grim saw before him was a procession of people walking out of the hills one cold winter night and into a river. He shivered involuntarily. Some things were better left buried.

'What are you?' he asked softly. Still, his voice sounded too loud in the bunker's subterranean silence, so he lowered it even more. '*Who* are you?'

Wolf didn't reply. He stared out from deep within his ravaged face. The right corner of his mouth drooped like dough and distorted the grotesque parody of a grin into a primitive mask of pain and horror.

He's wilting, Grim thought. *Kramer was right.*

But not altogether. Sub-skin, something seemed to slither. The grin recovered somewhat.

'You're not done yet, are you?' Grim said. 'Kramer was close, but she missed the mark. She said you'd all be dead by midnight. Dawn at the latest. But you're waiting for something, aren't you?'

The Wolf-thing remained quiet. Stared.

'Not for me, or I'd be dead by now.'

Nothing.

'You're waiting for someone else.'

Robert Grim pushed his chair aside and stood before the ruined husk that according to his file had once been a passionate administrative lawyer, a loving husband, and a fun dad. Up close, he could smell its repulsive stench, reminiscent of the cadavers on the autopsy table. Sea. Death. Still, Grim put his hand on Wolf's shoulder. It felt cold and cataleptic, but he didn't pull away.

'Alexander . . . I really hope you're gone in there. But if not, I think we're waiting for the same thing.' He gently squeezed the rigid flesh. 'He's the answer. Let's just hope he's aware of it.'

As if to confirm, Alexander Wolf began to speak.

13

Dozing off under Safiya's comforter, Luca lost track of time. She had left Spotify on, and Beyoncé and Dua Lipa were playing softly through a Bluetooth speaker. Not really his vibe, so he soon drifted off. After everything he had been through, it felt great to surrender himself to the soft embrace of Safiya's bed, deliciously suffused with Safiya's scent, a strawberry-chewing gum combo mixed with laundry detergent and her mom's perfume that she sometimes wore. Lying there, he felt more inti-mate with her than ever before. Knowing that she was downstairs watching TV with her folks and probably hella stressed about his pres-ence, he couldn't help but chuckle. But when he suddenly heard muffled voices on the landing, he started.

They were close. Too close.

'How many times do I have to tell you to turn off the lights before you come downstairs, Safiya?' It was Mr. Adan. 'You say you wanna save the planet. Hell, you can't even save our house.'

Luca cautiously probed to make sure his hair wasn't jutting out anywhere and tried pressing himself flat into the mattress. Next thing, the door opened, and the voices were no longer muffled.

'Dad! Leave me alone, I forgot . . .'

'Forgot? What do you think that Polar Bear is gonna tell her cubs when the last sheet of ice she was standing on melted away? "I forgot?"'

Luca's eyes practically popped, and his face bloated. For a second, he feared he would burst out coughing and give himself away, but he managed to suck it up and instead, got the most intense fit of the muffled giggles he had ever had.

Polar bears? *Polar bears?*

'Alright already! I'll remember next time. I'm done watching TV anyway. Imma stay up here and chill.'

Did they take his wet clothes off the floor? Luca couldn't remember. His brain was a sieve.

'You alright, Fee?'

'Yeah, tired is all. Go on, you and Mom watch your show.'

No, we're gonna to have ourselves a nice long talk about global warming, Luca thought. Mr. Adan was a big, friendly man, and the thought of him sitting on the bed with that giant ass of his crushing him during a rant about polar bears made him go limp. Luca was laughing himself silly; it was all too funny.

He wasn't aware that Mr. Adan had already left the room, so when the comforter was suddenly pulled back, he braced himself. But it was Safiya.

'Dude! That was close!'

He wanted to say something. Couldn't.

'O . . . kay.' She looked at him with her trademark raised eyebrow and a face that was all *WTF*, which only made his giggles worse. 'I was gonna ask if you're feeling anything, but I'd say that's pretty obvious.'

Feel anything? Luca felt amazing.

'I really need you to zip it, or they'll hear you.'

'Whoa.' Suddenly enthralled with the shape of her face, he sat up. He had always found her beautiful, but now, now she seemed to be radiating in an aura of light. He grabbed her shoulders and said, 'Safiya, I love you.'

He had never told her that before, but he was seeing everything so much clearer now.

'You crazy. Tell me again when you're not tripping and maybe I'll believe you.'

But she did let him kiss her, and it was their best kiss ever. He was wrong. *This* was the most intimate they had been.

'Chop chop, Luca,' she said as she pulled away. 'Any ideas on how to summon it?'

He smiled. That was clear to him too.

They started to prep. Safiya went downstairs to tell her folks she was taking a bath and turning in after, so nighty-night. Mr. and Mrs. Adan were too absorbed in *The Great Dutch Bake Off* to remark that she had taken a shower an hour ago, or notice that she snagged a bag of tea lights from the kitchen cupboard, a box of matches from the counter, and a can of coke from the fridge. Back upstairs, she and Luca tiptoed to the bathroom and locked themselves in.

Safiya ran the bath. One by one, they lit the tea lights around the sink and the tub. For a while, Luca stared spellbound at the flame burning between his fingers. It sparkled so beautifully! It shrank, smaller and smaller, until just before it singed his fingertips, it turned blue and vanished into spirals of smoke. Thrilled, Luca watched them swirl. Then he was distracted by the gurgling of the water flowing into the tub, and he listened to that. So intense, the way a sound could overwhelm a room!

Safiya elbowed him out of his trance. Apparently, she had left him alone for a while because now she put a chair next to the hamper and a pair of swimmer's goggles on the edge of the bath. Then she locked the door again.

'My mom always says that with a man like my dad in the house, it's critical to have these. Calls 'em dump thumpers.' She showed him the incense cones, and Luca burst out laughing. She lit them, and soon, the wintery fragrance of pinewood filled the room. The R&B from Safiya's speaker was replaced with a dreamy soundscape of something called *Tribal Spirit* that, along with the flickering candlelight, created a rather enchanting atmosphere.

For ritual rookies they slayed, Luca thought.

'You alright?'

He had the time to think he was *more* than alright, and that there wasn't a trace left of his earlier distress, though he could feel hers. To think, *Is* this *what all the fuss is about? Drugs being dangerous and all that crap?* It didn't feel dangerous. Quite the contrary. His senses were alive, his brain crackling. He was flowing through a four-dimensional, heavenly plane of consciousness where he had complete control of himself and his surroundings.

'M'yeah,' he said.

'Okay, so, uh . . . go ahead, I guess.'

She sat on the chair, and Luca dropped the robe off his shoulders. He pulled Mr. Adan's T-shirt over his head and dropped that too. The next part, he should have given more thought to. The boxer shorts were too big for him and he had to hold them up to prevent exposing himself. Safiya glossed over him in disbelief.

'Prude! You're not seriously getting in with your undies on? That is so American.'

'Better American than Swedish.'

'I think you should be naked,' she said, her face dead serious. 'That's the only way to become one with the water.'

Like any thirteen-year-old, Luca was ashamed of his body. Taking showers with the boys after soccer, sure, but this was different. This was a girl. Worse, the girl he liked. What if she laughed? Or worse still, what if something started stirring down there? Still, his hypersensitive state dissolved his resistance, and deep down he knew she was right. This was no game. It was a ritual. So he took a deep breath, and with all the nonchalance he could muster, he dropped his boxers.

He stood in front of her.

She didn't speak.

Then she did. 'Okay, that crap about becoming one with the water, I was yankin your chain.' She smiled a brilliant smile. 'I just wanted to see you naked. Sorry, I shouldn't take advantage of you while you're high as a kite.'

'Bitch,' he hissed, turning crimson and quickly covering his crotch.

'Shush.' The mocking faded from her smile, and now it was just warm. 'You got nothing to be ashamed of, Luca. I think you're beautiful.'

Okay, that didn't necessarily make things easier. His hands firmly in place, he turned around and clumsily got into the tub, thinking about mashed potatoes, their counselor Mrs. Volmer, or anything that could X the sex out of a situation. The hot water was nice and made his skin tingle. He quickly lowered himself in. Okay, it *was* kind of funny. She really had him going.

'No more teasing, pinky-swear,' she said. 'I'll be here to make sure nothing goes wrong, okay?'

'Okay. Wish me luck.'

'Luck. And Luca?'

He looked at her.

'Be careful.'

He lay back with his ears submerged and listened for what seemed like an eternity to the flow of the water and the strange, hollowed-out sounds of *Tribal Spirit*. The water dulled the music, making it seem deeper and somehow more tangible. If he listened closely, he could hear other sounds beyond it, coming from within the house. The TV downstairs. The neighbors' voices. And intermingled with it all, his own breathing and heartbeat. Staring at the hot steam under the ceiling and with the scent of Scandinavian forest in his nose, he quickly fell into a zen which he wished would last forever.

But there was work to do.

He sat up and strapped the goggles around his head.

One last time he looked at Safiya, watching over him from across the twilight bathroom.

'Nunyunnini,' he whispered. 'If you're there, I'm here. I'm ready. Show yourself.'

He pinched his nose, lay back and put his head underwater. He managed to count to twenty-seven, then came up again, dripping and gasping for air.

Nothing happened.

Sure, his pulse had increased. Before everything had gone south this morning, for days Luca had been trying to summon a vision. He read online that oxygen starvation could kick the brain into a heightened state of consciousness. But only just now, dozing off on Safiya's bed, had the idea come to him. All those drowned people Emma showed him. The awful thing that happened to Jenna. That, and how Eleven in *Stranger Things* used an isolation tank to get to the Upside Down . . . and the idea for Luca's ritual was born. The New Age crap was just window dressing. Safiya's space cake the igniter.

He had to submit to the water. He went under again, not pinching his nose this time and immediately sat bolt upright, sputtering and coughing. Gulps of hot water stung his throat. Safiya would surely be worried, but before she could break his focus, he tried again, this time face-down, only slowly rotating his body underwater to keep his nose from filling up quickly. By the third try he was used to it.

He stayed under for forty-one seconds, completely relaxed. When he emerged, the bathroom looked hazy. An altered state of consciousness? Or did his goggles just fog up? He yanked them off and got a shock. The colors! The *shining!* Golden halos shimmered around the tealight flames. Luca marveled at the layers of depth hidden in this ordinary bathroom, but now revealing themselves to him. It was absolutely magnificent!

He flung the goggles aside and down he went, barefaced this time. *That's the only way to become one with the water*, Safiya had said. He opened his eyes, staring at the rippling oval of the ceiling. It stung a bit, but that passed. Everything was blurry. He felt nice, as if he were float-ing into his own head instead of the real world. The running of the waterflow and the tom-tom from Safiya's phone seemed to be moving along with him; sounds floating like multi-colored planets in an illumi-nated universe. Entranced, he reached out to give them a whirl, and to his surprise, the music changed.

He reached fifty-four before he resurfaced. He hyperventilated and went down again. This time, he lost count after forty, but that didn't matter anymore. *Something's about to happen*, he thought. *I can feel it. There's a forest in the bathroom, can you see it? There are fireflies between the trees. Shit if I know how the Adans planted this, but it's fucking brilliant! Watch out though because any forest can get you lost . . . or maybe I'm lost already. Jeez, am I trippin! I hope you can at least breathe where I'm headed because how long have I been deprived of oxygen?*

The worry drifted away. He didn't need air. His lungs had adapted and devolved to their original state in the womb. Better, it felt great to forget about the counting and lose his sense of time altogether. It was so much easier to submit to the sensations of the amniotic water and the wooziness in his head.

Part of him was still aware that he surfaced and gasped for air after all, and vaguely alarmed, he realized that there really *was* a forest in the bathroom. Moths fluttered between slender trunks and Luca smelled moss and bark and pine sap. From somewhere far away, he still sensed Safiya watching over him. He filled his lungs and sank back underwater, down and down, deeper than ever before. He had a sensation of someone pulling him by the wrists, deeper still, of being purposefully guided by old, wise hands. Hands that knew how to guide and could offer comfort if they wanted to, but wouldn't always.

When he opened his eyes, he knew it had begun.

The woman looking back at him through the surface was neither young nor old, but she had been of age when the world was still new. Her face had the texture of rotten bark, and her eyes were clear as stars. She was the tribal elder, Luca knew, the Oracle. Like the women in his earlier vision, she wore the yellowed skull of a totem animal on her head. It was the mammoth. But by a quirk of perspective, Luca couldn't tell whether she was standing in front of it, if the skull was actually very small, or if her head was exceptionally large. Only that the mighty tusks curled toward him on either side of her cheeks.

Hello, Luca said. *Can you see me? Can you really see me?*

The woman began to speak. She told him that her ancestors had been roaming the Northern Plains since the ice had retreated and that they lived off the reindeer that herded the land and the silvery fish that populated the sea. Their god was Nunyunnini, the mammoth, but the mammoths had moved on long ago and were never seen anymore, only Nunyunnini the god, and only on the coldest nights of winter, when the sky was alive with colors. So they worshipped his spirit instead, which dwelled in his skull. They kept it in the holy tent where he shared secrets and spoke prophecies through the Oracle's mouth.

But there was yet another god; a god of the sea, who was ancient and nameless, who protected none but demanded sacrifice. Every year when the sun was at its lowest and the water at its highest, the tribe would place one of their youths in a hollowed-out pine trunk and push it off into the sea. For twelve days, the tribe would mourn on the shore, until the waves ungratefully flung the empty and cracked canoe back onto the beach. For the sea was greedy and demanded more. Already had it flooded the Southern Plains and cut them off from the old world, so they doubled the sacrifice: not one, but two half-growns were placed in the canoe.

But the sea kept rising, and the land kept shrinking. And one night, the sea spoke to the Oracle in a dream. It demanded a greater sacrifice still. A tribal sacrifice. That alone would appease the god. She called her advisors together and told them of her vision, but their leader, who wore the antlers of the caribou, said, 'We cannot do that, it's too much. It will ruin us.'

Instead, she suggested the Oracle ask Nunyunnini for his wisdom, which she did. In the holy tent, she inhaled the fumes of smoldering dried moss and mushrooms and spoke to the skull, while outside, in darkness, the hungry sea whispered.

Nunyunnini declared that such an offering should not be made, for Nunyunnini was an indomitable god. The tribe lauded his wisdom and obeyed, taking a stand against the sea. But deep in her heart, where secrets stirred, the Oracle doubted Nunyunnini, for he was wise, but also old, and stubborn.

A strange silence reigned in the north. The tribespeople gathered on the beach. The sea had retreated. As far as the eye could see, there were only black rocks and shallows, and on the exposed seabed, silvery fish thrashed and gulped for air.

'Our stand worked!' cried many. 'Our prayers have been answered!'

And they rushed forward to fill their baskets with fish before they died and rotted in the sun.

But the Oracle knew something was amiss before the others. She read it in the wind. 'It's a trick,' she whispered, staring at the horizon, which was rapidly rolling toward them. 'It's a trick!'

And so the sea punished them. The flood shook the land in an explosion of violence, shattering the sunlight and blinding them all before wiping away the entire civilization. In the last seconds before her death, the Oracle saw Nunyunnini, the old, sluggish mammoth, trudging through the doomed land before the waves swept him away. She balled her fist and cursed him for abandoning them. And since that was her final act, this curse would forever burden her spirit. For in death, she realized the flood wasn't Nunyunnini's fault.

And now, as her spirit tumbled through churning water, Luca tumbled with her. *'What should I do?'* he cried. *'Tell me what I should do!'*

But her hands were no longer holding him, and no longer could he see her. His mouth filled with water, and the water was *alive*, flowing into his lungs as a white-hot flash of panic swept over him. So this was what it was like to drown. It wasn't painless. It was a deep, dark, burning hole that ripped open his chest, into which he fell headlong and disappeared, first his body, then his mind, then his essence.

Hands in his armpits. Pressure on his chest. He coughed and chucked up gulps of water. His mind swung back and forth between the unrelenting, stormy darkness pulling him down and the real world above. The steamy twilight. The bathtub. Safiya. The hands pulled him up.

'Luca! Oh God, Luca, you're here! I thought I'd lost you! I really thought I'd lost you . . .'

She had hauled him onto the edge of the tub. Between his dripping hair, his eyes searched for hers, which were big and scared and filled with tears. 'Course I'm here,' he panted, trying to smile. 'Thanks for saving me.'

'You were gone! You stayed under way too long, and I wanted to get you up, but the water was all fucked up and you weren't there. You weren't there!'

Safiya slapped a towel around him and Luca sat shivering, waiting for normalcy. He was vaguely aware of the sound of a doorbell. Popping the can of coke, Safiya looked up startled.

'Drink this,' she whispered, handing him the can. 'Sugar stops the trip.'

She listened at the bathroom door. With a stomach full of water, Luca didn't think he could manage a single sip, but the sweet taste gave him a nice kick. The can was half empty before he put it down. 'What did you mean, the water was all fucked up? What did you see?'

'It was foaming all over. Swear to God. And when I put my hand in, it was fucking cold! And salty! Can't you taste it?'

She licked the back of her hand, then held it out to Luca. He put his lips to her skin but didn't need to; the aftertaste was still in his mouth.

'That's seawater,' she said.

Or it had been. Now it was bathwater again, venting whisps of steam.

Voices from below. Footsteps on the stairs. They exchanged frightened looks, and Safiya slunk toward the bath just in time before there was a knock on the door. 'Safiya?'

'Dad, I'm taking a bath! What up?'

Luca sloshed his foot around in the water. Ten points for SFX.

'The police are here. They want to know if you've talked to Luca today.'

The temperature seemed to drop ten degrees. The silence lasted two, maybe three seconds, but it felt longer. Much longer.

'I didn't!'

'No texts either?'

'Nope! Last night, though. Want me to send him a message or something?'

'Come downstairs for a sec, will ya. They really want to talk to you.'

Oh fuck. Oh fuck oh fuck oh fuck oh fuck. They found him. And they were trapped in here.

'But I'm taking my bath!' Safiya yelled.

'Well, get out then, dammit!' Mr. Adan lowered his voice. Maybe they were listening from downstairs. 'Saf, they're not looking very pleased. Seems like serious shit. I'm not going to ask you again.'

'Alright, alright! Just give me a sec to dry and get dressed!'

'I'll tell them you'll be down in five. Don't make me look like a liar.'

Safiya reached into the water and pulled the plug. They heard Mr. Adan's footsteps go down the stairs. Luca couldn't think. Maybe the space cake hadn't worn off yet, or maybe it was his utter physical and mental exhaustion, but his head felt literally empty.

'You got a towel, use it,' Safiya hissed. When he didn't react, she shoved him. 'Now, Luca.'

He began to dry himself off while she flipped the hamper. She snagged some jeans and a sweater. The jeans were hers, the sweater her dad's. Luca got out of the tub. Staggered. 'You got to keep them talking,' he muttered. 'Buy me time to get away . . .'

'Like hell I will,' Safiya said, handing him the clothes. 'They'll see straight through me, after all this shit. And I'm not going to leave you alone. Put these on.'

He started to get dressed. Staggered again. She helped him regain his balance then tiptoed to the door and opened it a crack. More voices from downstairs.

'They're in the TV room. Come on, hurry up.'

She led him by the arm onto the landing but instead of going to her room, she pushed him into her parents' bedroom. Confused, Luca waited in the half-light as Safiya disappeared into a closet. When she reappeared, she was wearing her mom's coat and holding out a pair of rundowns to him. LeBron James size, but better than barefoot. Luca sat down and put them on as Safiya ran to the window.

'What's the plan?'

'Shhh. I have an idea. But you got to be quick. There's a black car outside, but I don't think anyone's in it.'

The hinges creaked and Safiya flinched. The thought that they might have heard it downstairs didn't fill Luca with fear so much as profound fatigue. Safiya, however, was scared enough for the both of them. She urged him to hurry.

'Safiya, you comin?' Mr. Adan called out from downstairs. The earlier warmth in his voice was now gone. It sounded threatening. Scared, perhaps.

'Almost ready!' Safiya yelled. At the same time, she practically pushed Luca from the windowsill. The attached shed stretched alongside the short, paved front yard, and in no time, they were looking down onto the street.

'Can you climb down?' Safiya asked.

'Think so. What are you going to do?'

'My dad's always bitchin about the lights,' she said, 'but *he* always leaves the key in his scooter.'

With that, she lowered herself and smoothly jumped from the shed. Luca followed, much slower, and the minute he hung by his arms, they gave way. He fell and landed on his ass. Before he had the chance to recover, Safiya hauled him to his feet and pushed a helmet into his hands. Its weight surprised him. Behind her, shining in the streetlight, was her dad's scooter.

'Did you ever ride it before?' he asked.

'Do you care?'

He didn't. Safiya disappeared into the shed and when she reemerged, she was wearing her own helmet and holding a claw hammer.

'What's that for?'

'Don't be so dewy.' She walked onto the sidewalk, stooped at the black car, and without hesitation, smacked the claw into the front tire. It burst with a dull bang and the car tilted forward to the right. Leaving the hammer stuck in the rubber, she ran back to the scooter. 'Okay, hurry up now. They're not going to like that.'

She yanked the bike off its stand and pushed it onto the street. Luca ran after her, clumsily pulling the helmet over his head. A couple of houses down, she jumped onto the seat. 'Saddle up, baby.'

Luca did. Safiya turned the key. The scooter roared to life.

'Hold on tight.'

Safiya turned the throttle, and they shot forward.

Luca closed his eyes and held on tight.

14

In the dead of night, Robert Grim snuck into the hangar. By the light of his flashlight, he climbed the scaffolding onto the *Oracle*'s deck. The stench of rot was overwhelming, and he pressed a handkerchief to his nose so as not to gag. It was a daredevil feat to get there, but he knew exactly where he would find it: in the hidden room beyond the captain's cabin, exposed when one of the supporting beams collapsed and tore off a chunk of wall.

Just like Alexander had told him.

No, not Alexander. The hivemind.

It was a weathered chest with rusted locks. Grim had to use a crowbar on it, but then the *Oracle* finally gave up its treasure. He scanned the handwriting with the translation app on his phone. It wasn't perfect due to the Old Dutch but close enough.

> *Journal of t'Oostvaerders fluyt ship "The Oracle"*
> *Under 't rule of Hendrik Jan Hopman*
> *Shipmaster of Noortwyck 1715–1716*

INTERMEZZO

LOG

Journey to Saint Petersburgh & Danzig

September 23rd, 1716—Sailed at noon with favourable west wind from Delfshaven. Peculier cargo: a formidable elephant and her calf, brought from the East by Petrofsky, commissioner to Peter the Great of Russia. No expense spared for the tsar and his family in St. Petersburgh! Gangway too narrow to pass, elephants therefor chained on main deck.

Crew counting a dozen hands, all experienced and steady seamen of Noortwyck, no strangers to turbulent seas. Two boys, cook, chirurgeon, Revd Bongersz who led us in prayer to the Almighty for a safe voyage, and five guests; among which the French botanist Monsieur Bougainville and my daughter Jacoba who looks after the animals.

At sunset, steady nor'-nor'-east, calm sea. Elephants greatly rejoice the men, in particular when the mother drinks: she drains the water butt with her long, snake-like nose. The calf follows its mother, a most endearing sight. Yet Jacoba was worried, says the calf is anxious and chuses not to eat.

27 September 1716—Good passage. Favourable wind, men of good cheer. But Elephants restless. Awoken last night by boatswain returning from watch. Reported that the mother was well-nigh mad. Sought to pull the chains out of the deadeye. Shortly after, all startled by a tremendous trumpeting—a frightening sound indeed! One of the boys made to calm the beasts; he helps Jacoba with the feeding as she is unwell from the rigours of the sea. The behemoth became solemn, contemplated the horizon all through the night, though there was aught to be seen in the dark.

September 29th, 1716—Through Skagerrak. Nearing the Sound. Jacoba faring better; the chirurgeon administered a medicament of oils and herbs, yet I presume the contribution of the brandy should not be ignored!

September 30th, 1716—Passed the Sound. Disembarked at Elsinore. Negotiated dues with Danish treasurers, there being no precedent on taxing elephants. Agreed perforce to adopt English duty for sheep—as if the two can be compared! Otherwise, all correct. Weighed anchor at dark, and with the wind abaft, set sail on the Baltic Sea.

October 4th, 1716—Passing Visby with strong nor'-west wind. Turbulent sea agitates all on board. Elephant calf unwell too. Neither eats nor drinks and is emaciated. Jacoba deeply worried. Requested chirurgeon and Monsieur Bougainville to examine the calf; the mother, however, allows no one to see her young. One hopes it will live 'til St. Petersburgh, where its care shall be entrusted to the commissioner.

October 7th, 1716—*Approaching Narva. Bolted the portholes, terrific skies from the north. At midday, the waves rose like blind walls before the low-lying sun.*

Found Jacoba wailing in her cabin, saying that the mother hadn't eaten either. Spare your vain tears, I said; for it is folly to grieve over animals. To which she replied that she had dreamt seeing both elephants die; both exceedingly large and covered with thick, woolly fur to protect them from the northern cold.

First mate who listened through the door, rushed in and crossed himself, saying 'twas a bad omen to dream of dead fellow wayfarers, whether human or animal; and that they will perish before long, as will a member of the crew. Lost temper with mate, for I shan't tolerate superstitions aboard my ship.

Thereupon, went to see the elephants myself, a sorry scene to the wide expanse of the open sea. A thick fur over their leathery skin would have benefited them against the fierce weather in these unforgiving environs! The mother's eye fixt on me. Her gaze appeared to harbour a wisdom found only in magnificence, in age, albeit from a beast. It filled me with melancholy, for it seemed the elephant knew of her fate, yet bearing not a trace of rancour.

Not many more leagues to go. Shall make land on the morrow, which is bound to raise men's spirits.

October 8th, 1716—*Arrived at Saint Petersburgh. Petrofsky beside himself with delight, declaring that his Master the Tsar would be more than pleased. Paid abundantly. Spoke none of the weakened calf, despite it now being all but skin and bones. The commissioner however should be none the wiser, for he has never laid eyes on an elephant ere now! Jacoba inconsolable; prayed the entire day to the Almighty God for their wellbeing. I count my blessings that Jacoba did not see the Russian employ the whip when the mother elephant became uncontrollable!*

October 11th, 1716—*Set off to light rain from St. Petersburgh. Men regained strength. Favourable weather henceforth, calm sea, wind shifted to nor'-east. Making good passage.*

October 18th, 1716—*Arrival in Danzig. Two crew unwell, complaining of fever. And one of the boys. Chirurgeon provides them with medicaments, in the hope they shall recover enough for taking in the crates.*

October 21st, 1716—*Sailed from Danzig with fine cargo of grains, seeds, talc and saltpetre. All correct. Men's health not improved; third hand also ill and delirious. 'Tis all hands on deck. Growing unrest among crew. Although the Revd Minister attempts to allay fears and to instill faith in Almighty God, whisper abounds among the men that our misfortune hails from our having brought the sick elephants aboard.*

Later—*Tragedy is upon us! Chirurgeon came to my cabin at dark, unseen by men, so not to aggravate tensions further. Confided to me that the boy and two hands appear to have malignant aberrations of the skin. Asked whether these might be fleabites, but alas—fears 'tis smallpox! Asked what he could do and he said that if indeed it is, there is no remedy for it. Neither the good doctor nor I have memory of previous cases of smallpox in our parts, for our villages have always been sheltered with our remote location. Which means that none of the men has had it yet! Wherever 't was we allowed this miserable stowaway aboard, our very lives are now in danger.*

Moved the sick to the orlop, hoping to preserve the rest from these inflammations. Forbade Jacoba to leave her cabin, for children ordinarily are the first to contract the pox.

October 23rd, 1716—*No doubt now: smallpox. Heading for Elsinore to have sick attended to.*

October 24th, 1716—*Banished like rabid dogs! Danish in mortal fear of us; fired a warning shot with their canon. Situation on board visibly deteriorating. Second boy ill as well. Penetrating stench emanating from orlop. Sick barely conscious and a harrowing sight; entire body covered in festering boils. Chirurgeon says 'tis pointless to shave them off; all one can do is rub them with vinegar and wait for it to peter away. Yet there is little hope it will. He has never seen such abscesses before. Thank God Jacoba is yet well.*

Men demoralized. Say they saw bright light in the sky at evenfall. Passed the Sound; running before bitter north wind towards North Sea. To which perilous fate are we coursing?

October 26th, 1716—*Mutiny! Murder! Crew rebelled and have thrown sick companions overboard! It falls heavy to describe. Alack, the expression in that poor boy's eyes! Yes, 'tis true that the three hands and the other youth were nigh on dying, but the Catwyck boy only suffered from delirium! Five lives wasted, lost to wind and waves!*

Am lost for what to do next. Bring the culprits to justice? All know the severe punishment for mutiny and murder. How is "The Oracle" to sail further if justice does not prevail? Chirurgeon attempted to assuage the Minister and myself, saying 'twas an act of desperation, yes, unprecedently cruel, yet unavoidable if we are all to remain in good health. But is that not equivalent to glorifying the unforgivable?

Men show neither malice nor vengefulness, rather a grisly resignation; they bear the burden of guilt with perseverance. 'Tis nigh on impossible not to understand what they did. On land, the officers of the maritime court shall have to decide upon their fate. Or . . . no, I cannot write this down. What hellish torment have I been dealt!

Alas, let us pray for the souls we have lost:

Aarnout van Slabbert of Noortwyck (†)

Carel Visser of Noortwyck op Zee (†)

Godefridus Diederickse of Noortwyck op Zee (†)

Symon Teelinck of Noortwyck (†)

Willem Visser of Catwyck op Zee (†)

May God in His mercy keep them under His wings!

October 27th, 1716—*Reached a decision. We shall take it to our graves and not breathe a word of it. Few are chosen to have a beatific life and I shall have to bear the burden of knowing that my soul be stained forevermore, despite the penance the Minister urges me to do. Lord, forgive me!*

Strong nor'-west wind, course set to sou'-sou'-west. Not much farther now.

October 29th, 1716—*Anchored in Delfshaven. Nightmare is over; we wend homewards on land with revived spirits. One hand presently unwell, appears thus far to be no more than a mild fever.*

To the honourable H.J. Hopman
Shipmaster of "The Oracle" of Noortwyck
Every Man's End

Leyden, November 22nd, 1716
My dearest and greatly esteemed brother Hendrik Jan,

Upon reading your latest epistle I promptly and with great concern put pen to paper. Had the circumstances allowed for it, I would have taken my horse and hastened to you to personally bring reason to this madness, but in light of the prevalent epidemic, Leyden has severed all ties with the coastal district and by order of the Portreeve and the Mayor it is forbidden to travel thither. Upon nightfall I shall send a messenger, in the hopes that this missive will reach you under the cloak of darkness and the current downpour. I shall have him take the old road through the Brelofte, lest he be seen.

Dear brother, have I not implored you to breathe nary a word about what you set in motion with that last, accursed journey at sea? Have I not fore-warned you not to bring upon our kin the stain of spite and slander? And now, this blasphemy! This superstition! I forbid you to even think of such heathen things. Has your family not suffered enough? Four of your five children have it, and hundreds more in the entire region. The dreaded pox—the most terrific Nemesis of all. Even here in Leyden, where this Angel of Doom has passed the gates by, we hear the tolling of distant funeral bells throughout the day. Are its death and destruction not torment enough? Nay, you must speak of prophecies whispered by your beloved Jacoba in Saint Jerome's Chapel, of a "horror at sea", aye, even of the poor wench supposedly levitat-ing as if she were possessed by the Devil!

What madness has come upon you? Our late father would turn in his grave had this come to his ears!

You write that Jacoba has not caught it, yet do not the deliriums and fits of senseless aggression that you speak off indicate that the child is unwell? Her mother ought to lay her by her sick sisters, to have it over with. In the city we look upon smallpox as an inevitable rite on the passage to maturity. As long as quackery nor medicine shall hinder it, the sick have no choice but to let it fester and recover or pass away.

My dearly beloved Hendrik, in the face of this ordeal, I beg you to turn to God. You write there are things one cannot speak of, and that you dost believe what is done out of love and common sense is sometimes cruelly judged by law. Yet you cannot escape the Last Judgement. For is it not God's will to bestow upon us such a fierce plague, by which He shall chasten us, and judge us fairly? Is it not through penance the Lord incites His flock to repent? Is adversity not a fair Judgement? Let us turn to Him, He in whose hands our fate resides; and let Him freely take from us without us smiting His hand and ask, "God, what dost Thou?" And is it not in God's hand to ease our pains, and deliver us from Evil? Dear brother, renounce these illusions, for one cannot assist in one's own grace!

Let Johanna do all in her powers to preserve the children's lives, let her give them buttermilk and rub their boils with currant juice, for it may bring them relief. But above all: have faith in God's will.

'Tis truly deplorable outside, a fierce wind rattles the shutters against the windows. I hope with all my might that this letter reaches you. Nay, do not see it as prophetical. I know that Jacoba has spoken of a storm breaking on the Third Day, but such matters belong to the realm of coincidence and no more.

I wish you all the heavenly blessings and remain faithfully and sincerely yours,

Your brother Theodorus Hopman

A nightly journey

November 26th, 1716—*Judgement has been passed. Back aboard "The Oracle". Unfathomable! No man with his wits about him would go to sea in such conditions. Crew and I compelled to participate in this blasphemy, 'tis that or be brought to trial before the admiralty court for murder of hands and boy. So it shall come to pass—and if God is listening in the darkness of this nightmare, then please have mercy!*

The Fifth Day. As foretold, the storm grew to become the worst tempest I have ever seen. Terrible spring tide from nor'-west smote the coast this midday; word goes that it was driven to monstrous heights and left nothing of the doggers on the beach. Similar word from Catwyck. The dunes are yet holding out, but we know it now, do we not? On the Seventh Day they shall fail. We shall all perish . . . unless we complete this abominable task that is bestowed upon us. Thus were the words of Jacoba's prophecy in the chapel: "Only a sacrifice shall forestall thy ruin, and it must be a sacrifice of many. Go forth and give; go forth and give in abundance."

Scarcely had the news spread before the Mayor and his men came to arrest me. Had just enough time to beseech Johanna, "Flee, my darling! Take the carriage, have the maid harness the horses and flee with the sick children, far from here, as swiftly as they can carry you!"

I can only pray that they succeeded.

Arrived at Delfshaven by nightfall. Readied "The Oracle" with the men. Pleaded with the Portreeve that it was madness to sail and well-nigh impossible to escape the malestrom with all sails set. Yet he showed no mercy. Claimed that the worst had already passed; and had Jacoba not spoken of a curious calm on the Sixth Day? Weighed anchor with that ill-boding prospect in mind and embarked toward the unknown.

"The Oracle" has withstood many a storm and ne'er succumbed, yet the trials awaiting her in the mouth of the Maes were the gravest to date. By what miracle did we escape our destruction? Knocked about by terrific sea. Swells swept the deck from stem to stern. Yet could not reef the sails; rigging heavily battered. Ship moaned as she fought her way. Praised crew; worked without hope of salvation should we overturn, staring death in the face all the while. Eve was long and all are worn out. Yet the storm finally on the wane and "The Oracle" rose proudly from the sea, ribs sighing, and sailed forth through steadier waters.

Midnight. First mate took the helm; will steer nor'-nor'-west with the wind lest we stand off the coast in the darkness. Finally retired and brought log up to date. Yet the calm seems deceptive. My gaze keeps returning to the sea beyond the porthole, where a shard of moonlight shines upon the spume, creating the impression it is infused with haunting life. The task before us weighs bitterly upon my soul. The night is heavy with premonition. Yet nothing presses more than the knowledge that we shall set course toward that dreaded place, where that other thing lies dormant—that unholy monster of the Deep.

November 27th, 1716—*The Sixth Day. Course steady nor'-west, wind calm. Fog upsets navigation; appears to drift along with ship. Puts all in sombre light. Mind made up to worst: 'tis the calm predicted by Jacoba. The calm that heralds the end.*

Arrived at Noortwyck before dawn. Could see nothing in fog, but bell proved to be of help. Signal was noticed and we heard the reply, faint and otherworldly from the mist. Anchored and waited whilst the chirurgeon prepared the dress. All, mates and officers alike, were given breeches, fastened to high boots, and gloves made of goatskin. On top, a thick cloak which the doctor rubbed with aromatic wax. Yet the jewel was the mask: spectacles with a long bird-like beak through which we breathed; filled with a purifying substance of cinnamon, myrrh, honey, and dried adder. Such was worn by the plague doctors; the chirurgeon says they offer protection from the miasmas and malignant fumes.

What sinister a sight we must have offered for those on the first barks to appear out of the fog! Fifteen beaked spectres in the dim silence, waiting on "The Oracle's" deck, as the boatswain persistently rang the bell. A thin wailing reached us first, before the sails appeared. I would lie if I were to deny that it made my blood curdle. Then, the difficult task commenced of taking in the sick. Because the storm destroyed the better part of Noortwyck's fleet, the few remaining seaworthy doggers had to go to and fro. Ah, the misery we witnessed! Men, women, children. Blistering with innumerable boils, well-nigh covered in it, their skin alike the bark of a tree. The disfigurements of this pest are inhumane. Those who were able to walk, we drove ahead with sticks to keep them at distance. Yet many required help, and those who were too far gone needed to be borne. Laid them in the orlop for shelter. The stench, despite the mask's fumes, is horrible.

All the sick of Noortwyck. All the sick of Catwyck. Three hundred and fifty souls to the chirurgeon's estimate. What did they think as they were hauled from their bed in the deep of night? What did their loved ones think?

Aye, they were told they be going to the Great Infirmary in Leyden, for care and protection of the community. Their loved ones were asked to pray and submit to the will of God.

'Tis the only way. For cannot an inflammation heal only after the thorn has been removed from the wound? Do we not thus kill two birds with one stone?

And yet, the sounds raising from the hold are driving us mad. They wail, they scream, they are not of sound mind and roll around in their excrement, pounding themselves with their fists. The fluids leaking from their bodies saturate "The Oracle's" cracks with their pestilent contamination—she is cursed! Cursed! Cursed!

November 28th, 1716—For the love of God, 'tis done. Cannot write, cannot, I

December 2nd, 1716—Myself again. Not certain about the date, but almanac and morning light indicate that it tallies. Four days of drifting about in this abominable fog. It clings so tightly to the ship that none can see fifty feet away. Men are broken. Chirurgeon and two hands threw themselves o'er the bulwark on the night of the sacrifice, seeking the oblivion that is the only way out of this existence. The others, as I, dozed in and out of delirium, our reason given way. Till this morning the fog finally dispersed.

But myself again—nay. Shall ne'er be myself again. The hellish deed keeps weighing on my conscience. The burden is too great. The sounds are engraved in my memory. The moaning when we bore them the one after t'other through the hatch on the fo'c'sle, to spare them the sight of the fate of those who preceded, for the same fate awaited them. The endless tolling of the bell, like a funeral carillon. Then the excruciating cry. And then the splash. Time and again, the splash. And all the while I could see only the mother elephant's eye before me—crying. Even now mine hands are trembling when I think about it. Spilling ink over the entire paper. Yet I must take heart, for my trials are not yet over.

I, Hendrik Jan Hopman, Shipmaster of Noortwyck, captain of "The Oracle"; I am responsible for my crew and ship. 'Tis my duty to guide them back to port.

North Sea calm. Heading sou'-west to favourable wind. Was it enough? Did we lay it to rest? We shall soon know. But aye or nay; the mainland shall never be the same as when we first set out.

Postscript

December 6th?, 1716—*These are the last words I shall confide to the log of "The Oracle". At sea again, after all. Last journey for I shall not be able to face alone the storm that is now being unleashed. 'Tis true; I am the only living soul aboard. Don't know crew's whereabouts. Or do I? Among the crabs among the crabs, aye! No one shall ever read this log for it shall perish along with myself and the ship. We too shall be among the crabs*

Latr—*I now know the true meaning of the word "cursed". God is no more. God is dead. There is only Judgement. How else can a man head homewards after all we had endured, convinced that the sacrifice was effective, only to find his wife alone and mad at Every Man's End? How have the sick children fared, well, my dearest; they were taken to the Great Infirmary in Leyden to be cared for, she spake. I said nay, this cannot be true; yet it was; the wretch had turned a deaf ear to my plea to get far away with the children and stayed. Cursed the woman, cursed myself, cursed God. No God could be so cruel as to let a man drown his own children! Where then, I asked, where was Jacoba, to which Mother replied that our oldest had been fetched by the Portreeve two days thereafter and that she knew not of her present whereabouts. Am afraid I lost my temper then. Grabbed her by the neck and wrung it . . .*

Afterwards went to see the Portreeve. Ye must becalm yourself, Hendrik, he pleaded; please, ye must compose yourself. Only under threat of my musket did he admit that Jacoba had been taken to sea in one of the doggers and thrown overboard in a casket weighted with coals to exorcise the Devil.

Jacoba, sweet Jacoba, my dearest Jacoba.

The end is nigh. All are dead. All sunk to the Deep. The sea is the sea the sea the sea is full of bodies they are among the crabs sinking down to the Deep

Farewell

4

ORACLE

1

Luca woke up in a bed filled to the brim with tobacco-scented burgundy pillows. He wasn't sure if it was early or late. A pale, diffuse light fell through the blinds. His head hurt just looking at it, but he remembered where he was: in a high-rise in Amsterdam Bijlmermeer. Pretty random, but Safiya had it all figured out. The flat belonged to a friend of her cousin Aisha. Rahini. Rohinya. Ravindra, something like that. Drove a pink *deux chevaux*, that much he did remember. Safiya was like, *Dude . . .*, when he showed up in it, especially after Aisha had made him out to be some badass mofo, but hey, *style*, man.

Luca listened for voices but could only hear the bustle of rain and wind outside. Where was everyone? Safiya wasn't with him. Go figure, after all the running they had ended up in bed together. Awkward AF, as by then he had entered the last, introspective stage of his trip and felt only partially present on this plain of existence. He had no idea what was expected of him. As a boy. Wanting not to be a total vegetable, he had snuggled up to her; apparently the signal for his body to say, *g'nite, Don Juan*, because he had gone out like a light.

Oh well, she would hardly blame him. Luca was exactly where he needed to be, a safe house where nobody could find him, sinking into the lazy embrace of pillows smelling like adulthood and freedom; concepts he was yet to fully understand but that, alone and unaware of his parents' whereabouts, felt like they belonged to him anyway.

As he drifted off again, he was back on Safiya's scooter. He clung on to her as the cold whooshed past, drawing horizontal tears across his temples. Next thing he knew, Safiya dumped the scooter in a ditch and dragged him onto a desolate railroad platform beside a highway. Suddenly, they were in a train, and whaddaya know, there was Amsterdam and Safiya's older cousin, with whom she was supposed to be super close, saying, 'Jesus Christ, girl, is that boy shitfaced or something?' And Safiya didn't know *what* to say, but Aisha theatrically raised a hand. 'Say no more. If you need a place to crash, I've got you covered.' To which Safiya replied, 'It's worse than that. We need somewhere we can't be found. So do you.'

Enter Ra-something.

Luca fell asleep and woke up only after dark to the sound of muffled voices and Latin music. A heavenly barbecue aroma drifted through

the room luring him to his feet. God, he was starving. Safiya's chocolate chips and curried chicken spread had done little to alleviate that,
and that was almost twenty-four hours ago. Incredible.

He walked barefoot to the door. It opened into a pleasantly warm
living room decorated with such a mad jumble of Christmas lights,
scented candles, palm plants, framed *Vogue* covers, silk-covered furniture, and an XXL wall poster of a greasy pink lipstick that it almost
gave Luca brain-freeze. Safiya was leaning over the bar into a kitchen,
where Aisha and the dude—tall, skinny, twenty-something, wearing
an apron—kept time to the music.

Aisha saw him first and called out, 'Good morning, Wonder Boy!'

'Hi,' Luca said.

'You're up!' Safiya walked over. 'You slept for ages.'

He felt self-conscious as they all gathered around him, sizing him up
from head to toe. The dude in the apron waved a wooden spoon and
offered a friendly smile.

'Yo. You look a lot better than yesterday. Not so corpsy anymore.
Remember where you are?'

Luca surveyed the room. 'In a game of Candy Crush Saga?'

That had them all howling. Aisha crowed, 'Oh my god, did he just
say that? Ravinder, dude is *killing* you!'

Ravinder was his name. Luca produced a faint smile.

'Okay, that's the best compliment I got in a long time. Luca,
right?'

'Yep. And you're Ravinder.'

'Yep. And you're a celebrity. TV says just about every cop west of
Utrecht is looking for you. Hey, whatever it is you did, I don't fuckin
care, man. You're a friend of Aisha's, and if you're a friend of Aisha's, *mi
casa es su casa.*'

'He's *my* friend,' Safiya said. 'And he didn't do anything.'

'Don't care. As long as he likes moksi meti.' He practically stabbed
Luca in the chest with the spoon. 'You like moksi meti?'

'I don't know what that is,' said Luca, who was still processing the
idea that he had been on TV.

'Shame! Shame on you!'

'But if it's what I'm smelling, I can't wait because I'm starving. Hey,
anybody got any, um, boy clothes?'

Aisha clapped her hands, threw her head back and yelped. Safiya
awkwardly tried to signal to him, *Sorry, can't help it, this is just what
they're like*, but Luca smiled and squeezed her hand. They could have
done worse. Much worse.

'Aisha, babe, show him my wardrobe. You can take anything you like, Luca, as long as I get it back. Except the Versaces. Versaces are strictly NA.'

Luca selected an outfit that was a better fit than the Safiya-Mr. Adan combo, and then they ate. Moksi meti turned out to be a blend of roasted chicken, pork and bacon and it was delicious. There was also fried rice and chili shrimp with long beans and curried eggs and pickles. Chinese, Luca inquired, and Ravinder said, Surinamese, dickwad. After a second and third helping, he started to feel at ease. It felt good not to be on the run and just go with the flow, no questions asked. Only after he finished his fourth serving and felt like he was about to explode did Ravinder light a roll-your-own and prompt, 'That's some serious shit you've been through, Luca. Safiya brought us up to speed while you were sleeping.'

'Is that okay?' Safiya asked. 'I had no choice after it aired on TV.'

Luca shrugged. 'I can hardly say no to friends who're helping us lie low. Do they know . . . *everything?*'

Safiya nodded.

'Then you probably think I'm crazy.'

'No, man, shut up,' Aisha said. 'We believe you.'

Luca eyed her incredulously, but Ravinder got his phone out, tapped and slid it toward Luca. It was a *Volkskrant* long read, headlined CONSPIRACY THEORIES IN FLOWER COUNTRY: HOW NOORDWIJK TRAGEDY WAS LINKED TO YAMANI SCANDAL.

'Wow,' Luca marveled. 'Did it leak?'

'Not all of it,' Safiya said. 'There's no mention of the ship. Or the supernatural shizzle. It's about the online conspiracy theories after yesterday's footage.'

'And the tone is obviously cynical,' Aisha added. 'Otherwise, they never would have published it. Don't want to jeopardize their *journalistic integrity.*' Exuberantly rolling her eyes.

'What footage?'

'Show him, Ravinder.' Safiya pushed the phone back.

'Did that say *Yamani?* Wasn't he . . .'

'Yep, the journalist the Saudis chopped into pieces,' Aisha said.

'Still in one piece,' Safiya corrected her. 'Now he's the one doing the chopping.'

Luca's head was spinning. 'I don't follow. What's that got to do with us?'

'Here.' Ravinder handed him the phone again.

This time it was a YouTube video. As soon as it played, Luca practically pressed his nose to the screen and yelled, 'That's them! That's exactly what my dad and Emma looked like!'

First it showed grainy footage of what was apparently Yamani in a London tube station. It jumped to handheld video of a man in a typical Dutch neighborhood. VOORHOUT, a graphic read. Then a picture appeared of a NOORDWIJK WOMAN.

'She was one of the cops! I saw her go into the ship. No doubt, I recognize the perm.'

Their disfigured faces made Luca shiver. A rather suggestive text ended the video: DOES THIS LOOK LIKE NOVICHOK POISONING TO YOU?

'Novi what?'

'It's a Russian nerve gas,' Ravinder explained. 'That's one of their theories. To explain the faces.'

'The other theory is zombies,' Aisha said.

'But I don't get it. What's that journalist got to do with it? Wasn't that in London?'

'Fuck if I know,' Safiya said. 'Maybe it's a bunch of BS. But the point is that the article suggests yesterday's mess and the disappearances are connected. So yeah, it's leaking. And you and me are wanted in connection with all of it. If they find us, I bet we'll disappear, too.'

Luca averted her gaze. 'Anything in it about my family? My mom?'

'No, sorry.'

He nodded. He hadn't expected it to, but he still felt his heart suddenly throbbing in his temples.

'You're the missing link, honey,' Aisha said. 'Safiya told me about the ritual you guys did. Said you really disappeared from the tub. That's fucking creepy!'

Aisha's shivering wasn't an act. Apparently, she was the kind of person who believed that kind of stuff. Luca could appreciate the irony because *he* wasn't. At least, not until recently. Ravinder saw his struggle and regarded him with sympathetic eyes. 'My nana back in Suriname used to do rituals and shit too, man. Called it "winti." Contact with dead ancestors and whatnot. All that shit is real.'

'Winti?'

'Yeah, man. She'd get in a trance from a wind that took over her body and soul. That's what it felt like when a spirit was near, she'd say, like the wind.'

Luca listened to the wind howling between the buildings. 'With me it wasn't like the wind. It was the sea.'

'Nana used to summon it, just like you did. She had this makeshift altar in front of her house where she offered flowers and oranges. And when she wanted to talk to her ancestors, she used a drum to go into a trance. Sometimes she got . . . connected.'

'Safiya told us you got a warning,' Aisha said. 'Like a prophecy or something.'

'I don't know if it was a prophecy,' Luca sighed. 'There was a woman. She showed me something. I really don't want to talk about it. But something terrible happened, and I'm afraid it's going to happen again. Something that will spell doom for all of us.'

They all looked at him. Aisha was the first to speak. '*Hell* no. You gotta end this. I'm not ready to die. Not before I've had hot yoga with Idris Elba.'

Ravinder threw his hands up in the air. 'Bitch, seriously!'

'I mean, wouldn't you?'

'I'm not saying I wouldn't. I'm saying that's not the point here.'

'There's no situation in the world where Idris Elba isn't the point. But if Luca here is some sort of messiah and got a prophecy from some God and shit, he's got to act. Am I wrong?'

Luca's eyes grew wide. 'I know who I can talk to.'

'Who?' they all asked at once.

'The people who are after me are not just secret service, they're a *special branch* of secret service. That's what the man who came to see me last week after soccer practice told me. He's American. He said he was here to investigate the ship. Asked about a million questions. I told him about my visions.'

'American?' Aisha spit it out like it were phlegm. 'They meddle with just about everything, huh? How do you know you can trust him?'

'Oh, he hated the fuckers as much as I do. He was a bit of a fruitcake, but that was obvious.'

'Could have been faking it,' Ravinder said. 'People like that are sneaky.'

But Luca was determined. 'That's a chance I'll have to take. He's my only way in. And he might know what they did to my mom.'

'Remember his name?'

'I don't. But I got his number. He urged me to learn it by heart, so they couldn't trace him. I did.'

'Go for it!' Ravinder said. He handed his phone back to Luca. His heart beating faster, Luca entered the number and tapped ADD CONTACT. The phone asked for a name but no matter how deep Luca tried to dig, he had been too focused on the number to remember. *Bald Eagle*, he registered, paying tribute to *Stranger Things*.

He hesitated, then texted in English, *Is this line secure?* He waited, drumming his fingers on the table, restlessly bouncing his legs. Six minutes later, the phone lit up. *Who's asking?* Bald Eagle wrote.

Give me a Chupa Chup and I'll tell you, Luca sent, and this time he didn't need to wait six minutes.

The phone rang almost immediately.

2

The kid picked up before the first ring. 'Hello?'

'Luca, is that you?'

'Yes.'

'Christ on a bike!' Robert Grim cried out. 'You sure took your sweet time, didn't you? I was starting to believe you lost my number.'

'Sorry. The monster you work for sent an army after me. I had bigger fish to fry.'

'Where are you? Sounds like Carnival in Rio.'

'With friends,' Luca said. 'That's all you need to know.'

Friends, plural. Grim didn't like that. A manic voice was yelling support in the background, which Grim liked even less. How many people—worse, *children*—had he involved?

'Would you mind turning that racket down? I can't hear myself think.'

Luca said something away from the phone and a muffled male voice, clearly *not* a child, replied. The music died. Grim shut his eyes and listened to the rain on the roof of his rental, which was exactly why it had taken him a beat to respond. NOVEMBER-6 was pleasantly unaware of the existence of his private phone, and with everyone on red alert, he couldn't risk using it inside. Today, as a precaution following the media firestorm, Eleanor had ordered the base in lockdown. But since her lap dog Van Driel and his patrols—special agents Jerome, Sita, and Paul—were the only ones left, it had started to dawn on Grim that *he* was the one in lockdown. He was as much a prisoner as the poor sods in Ward C. They made it look like he was free to come and go, but even now, in the dark and pouring rain, he could see the glow of Jerome's Benson & Hedges under the entrance canopy. Fucker was just standing there. Out in the open. If Grim started the engine, he would be doing a whole lot more than that.

This development was more than a little worrying, but his fascination still got the upper hand. After deciphering the *Oracle*'s log last night, Grim knew the truth was right in front of him. The translation app was no good for this, so he had enlisted the help of a nervous student working the graveyard shift at the hotel, offering him a thousand euros cash and the night of his life on the condition he would

keep his mouth shut. They puzzled for hours, back and forth with inter-
pretation and lucky guesses, but the result was stunning.

And Luca Wolf was at the center of it all.

'Listen,' Grim said in a gentler tone. 'Kudos for escaping their
clutches. I'd love to hear how you pulled it off one day. You've probably
been through hell and back.'

'They shot Roger. He was our neighbor. My sister was dying, and
they did nothing to help her.'

'I'm sorry you had to witness that. And you're right, they have a
whole army hunting for you. You've really pissed them off when you
sent two of their best men to the hospital. One of whom is in critical
condition.'

'Good,' Luca said coldly.

'What I'm trying to say is you've got to be careful. Are you safe?'

'Yes.'

'And the people you're with, are you positive you can trust them?'

'Yes.'

'I mean, who are they? Do you even know them?'

The manic voice was back and Grim heard it echo, *'Do you even
know us? Bitch, do we know him, why don't you ask him that!'*

Grim lifted his glasses and pinched the bridge of his nose with his
thumb and index finger. More voices, then Luca again. 'I trust them,
and that's all you need to know. Is this line secure?'

'It's the best I can offer right now. It'll have to do.'

'They took my mom. Do you know where she is?' Suddenly his attitude was gone, and Luca's voice revealed who he really was, a scared
and traumatized child.

Grim felt sorry for him. 'Yes. And I can understand your suspicion
toward me. Pretty healthy, under the circumstances. So I'm going to lay
my cards out on the table, Luca. I want us to trust each other, because
it's our only chance to free your mother and get out of this mess.'

'Where is she?'

'Volkel Air Base. She and a few other witnesses. They're being sheltered for the same reasons you were held before: protection. At least,
that's the cover story. I'm afraid the real reason is they know too much.
Just like I do.'

'How's she doing?'

'Not too well would be my guess, after what she's been through. So
let's not waste any time.'

'I had a vision,' Luca spilled. 'And I think I know what it means.'

'Tell me.'

'Not on the phone. And I want proof that my mom's safe.'

'Luca, I've discovered a few things myself, and if I'm right, the consequences will be dire. There's no time to lose. It would really help if you opened up.'

'Hell no,' Grim heard the voice in the background again. '*Those bitches Guantanamoed your mom, you ain't gonna give him shit!*'

'Not without my mom,' Luca said.

'We're on the same team here! Can you *please* ask your manic friend to shut up for a second?'

That was met with outcry. The male voice said something in Dutch, followed by Luca: 'Can you get my mom off the base?'

Grim sighed. 'What part of the phrase 'air base' don't you people understand? This is *literally* the most secure location in your country. They're hiding the *Oracle* here. Even with most of them out there looking for you, I wouldn't be able to sneak your mom out.'

'But that's not the plan, huh?' Luca suddenly said. 'Lemme guess. My dad's there too. Emma and all the others . . .'

'Yep.'

'You want me to come *there*.'

'The ship's here. The Returned are here, though I prefer to call them Messengers. You're their medium. You're their voice. Yes, I think you need to be here, Luca.'

That got them all quiet, until Luca broke the silence. 'Isn't that dangerous?'

'I can't say it isn't. But what choice do we have? And there's something else. Are you familiar with the term 'hiding in plain sight'? Where I'm from . . . sometimes we needed to hide something too. Often the best way to do that is out in the open. The last place Eleanor expects you to be right now is in her lair. Most of her staff are in the west of the country and I'll have to think of something to get rid of the rest of them, but yes, if you can get to Volkel unseen, I think I can get you *in*.' He hesitated. 'These friends of yours. Is it too much to hope that one of them has a driver's license and an inconspicuous car?'

'Suppose they do,' Luca said. 'What's your plan?'

'The plan is for you to catch up on your sleep tonight. You must be bone tired. It'll give me the opportunity to take care of things here. Tomorrow AM, I'll send you the details for our rendezvous. In the meantime, lie low. That's the most important. Understood?'

'What do you think I'm stupid?'

Grim cleared his throat. 'Right. Sorry.'

'Can I ask you something?'

'Go ahead.'

'If it works. If I get in. Then what?'

'We'll find out what this all means and hopefully put an end to it. But that's just for starters. What would you say to bringing these fuckers down? The two of us. We free your mother and the other innocent people, and then we destroy them.'

'I'm in,' Luca said.

That ended the call. Grim carefully slid his phone into his pocket and put his hands on the wheel. They were trembling. He was nervous, yes, but excited too. He wiped a spot on the fogged windshield and saw Jerome still smoking by the entrance.

Let's give him something to do. He adjusted his seat back and made himself comfy. The darkness and the rain soothed him. Before long, Robert Grim was deep in thought, considering strategies to subvert probably the best-trained guards in the highest secured facility in the country . . . and how to smuggle a kid inside.

It was only when an extremely nasty gust of wind rocked the Subaru, that Grim looked up.

On the Third Day, the storm comes, he thought.

And suddenly, he was scared. Very scared.

3

Eleanor Delveaux spent the night at the Crowne Plaza on the Amsterdam bypass, but sleep she did not. She lay dressed on the bed with her hands folded over her bony ribs, ready to be on the scene quickly in case they had eyes on Luca Wolf and the girl. The BBC reported the evacuation of several North Sea rigs due to an approaching Nor'wester. It was apparently a bad one.

At 5:15am, there was a knock on the door. Eleanor turned off the TV, got up, straightened her blouse, and answered. It was Glennis, her makeup pristine as ever but failing to mask her fatigue.

'You got him?'

'No. We're in the dark on Aisha Said. She didn't come home last night. But she's supposed to be at work at ten, so we'll be waiting.'

'Nothing on the APB?'

'Negative. Dukakis tracked them on CCTV footage from the railway station at Amsterdam Lelylaan, and again when they emerged from the pedestrian underpass. After that, we lost them. We assume they're sheltering somewhere in the city. We've got boots on the ground in all the train and subway stations, but right now Said is our best lead.'

'They can't hide forever. So if that's not it, what's so urgent it couldn't wait until breakfast, Glennis?'

'Open your laptop.' She looked uneasy.

Eleanor sat on the edge of her queen-size and flipped open her MacBook. Glennis rolled the desk chair closer to view the screen.

'Go to Bellingcat.'

'Bellingcat?' Eleanor felt the color drain from her face. What the hell did Bellingcat . . . but she didn't even need to finish the thought. The website popped up, and the first headline read, FROM THE NETHERLANDS: EVIDENCE OF BUSINESS PARK FIRE FRAUD; CONTINUOUS STRING OF MISINFORMATION SURROUNDING DECEMBER 8 EVENT THAT LED TO DISAPPEARANCE OR DEATH OF ELEVEN FAMILIES. It was so astonishing that Eleanor briefly had the urge to drop everything there and then and implement her exit strategy. What kept her rooted was a hunch that there was still time. Perhaps not twelve days . . . but there *was* time.

'Why Bellingcat?' she asked, scrolling through the article. 'Don't they focus on war crimes?'

'They also do fact-checking and human rights abuses. The case has attracted a lot of attention because people have been linking it to the Yamani disappearance. Bellingcat hasn't, but they succeeded where *de Volkskrant* failed in linking the ship to the disappearances and the raids on Sunday. It's all out there.'

Eleanor saw it. THE MYSTERIES OF THE DUTCH SEABORNE EMPIRE. The paper depot fire. The transport. The second fire, burning the exhibit to the ground. Chronicled, exposed, and discredited, all through open-source intelligence. A deleted Facebook post from the Noordwijk councilor for culture, admitting to having no knowledge of the exhibit. Tweeted photos of the nightly convoy on the Maas and through the Brabant countryside. The missing and dead civilians. It wasn't Bellingcat's style to speculate about rumors they couldn't corroborate, so they hadn't yet linked Yamani to the case. But Eleanor remembered Al-Jarrah's photos in her email. He could corroborate it, alright.

'What's their theory?' she heard herself ask, her voice faint over the pulsing of the blood in her head.

'That the fire was a smokescreen. They conclude that the victims, as well as the missing children, their fathers, and the tennis coach, got involved in an unknown event just outside of Noordwijk on December 8 and haven't been seen since. They have pretty incriminating records from a police scanner. They know a ship was found at Every Man's End, they know a fake news story was spread, and they know the ship was boarded up and transported in a military convoy to Noord-Brabant.

The last photo they published was on the N277, which goes right by Volkel.'

'Unbelievable,' Eleanor mumbled. All their efforts. All the precautions. All for nothing.

'And then there are last Sunday's raids. The missing families that can all be linked to December 8. The Alaoui family tragedy. And yes, the Joshua Bol and Sandra Kocken footage on Twitter. Officer 3 and Officer 5. They haven't drawn any conclusions from their disfigured faces, but they do show them.'

A thought crossed Eleanor's mind. 'Bellingcat is all open source, right?'

'Entirely.'

'It doesn't add up. I know their methodology. They present evidence in cases that thousands are already speculating about online. But until today, *nobody* has linked any of it to the ship. Not a single tweet, says Dukakis. Not even after Sunday. Why is that? *Because we know how to do our jobs*, that's why. We've eliminated all causality. So how is it possible that Bellingcat suddenly cuts through to the ship?'

Glennis gasped. 'A whistleblower.'

'Exactly. Someone planted the seeds.'

'The boy?'

She shook her head. 'Unlikely. A thirteen-year-old with a story to tell turns to *De Telegraaf* or NOS, not Bellingcat. This is someone who's familiar with the mechanisms of international media. Someone who's thought this out.'

Now Glennis' jaw dropped. 'Yvonne Schrootman.'

'Again, dead on. Officer 6. Seems like we made a mistake letting that bird fly.'

'Christ almighty.'

'She still in Bali?'

'As far as I recall, yes. I'll put Zaky on it right away.'

'Have her arrested the second customs check her at the airport.'

Glennis rolled her chair back. 'Should we really? If she's their rat and she disappears . . .'

'Oh, she's their rat alright. If she disappears, there'll be no one to vouch for their story. Without a source or evidence, it's just speculation.'

Glennis wasn't convinced . . . and Eleanor suddenly understood the look on her face. She thought Eleanor was losing her grip. Loyal Glennis, whom she had put in executive charge of the entire operation. She hadn't been the same since Sunday, when she found Diana

Radu and her dead Daisy Team in the Reich's home. Understandable perhaps, but this wasn't the time to show *weakness*.

'Glennis, are you questioning my judgment?'

'No ma'am.'

'Because I've asked you to speak up if you think I'm in the wrong.'

'That's not it. But with this leaked to the media, I'm going to have to give something to West Point. They'll know I haven't been straight with them. That's bound to have consequences.'

'So we'll just have to spin it some more, won't we?' Eleanor snarked.

'I was wondering . . .'

'What, Glennis?'

She sighed. 'Yamani. I've seen his face. Is there something I need to know? Your career isn't the only one on the line here.'

Eleanor broke into a genuine smile, the kind that could melt granite. 'Of course not. The conspiracy nutjobs have been pumping out nothing but crap about him, and I hope you're not falling for it. If a similar event was happening in London, don't you think we'd know? We've had constant dialogue with the SIS and Scotland Yard. I've seen the footage and the likeness is notable, but nothing more. Whatever mess they've gotten themselves into, it's not our problem. Our hands are full enough as it is, wouldn't you agree?'

'True that.'

Her smile widened. It didn't matter whether Glennis believed her or not. If she valued her future, she would get creative and spin it.

'Thank you for bringing me up to speed. Find that snitch, Glennis. And find that Wolf kid before he can corroborate her story. Have Dukakis put every eye we have on it. I want him yesterday.'

'Yes, Ms. Delveaux.'

'And Glennis?' Halfway to the door, Glennis paused and turned. 'Rest for a few hours. You've been through a lot.'

'Thank you. It was hard to see Diana like that. I hope she recovers.'

'Don't worry, she's getting the best possible care. Van Driel is seeing to it personally.' At least, the last part was true. 'See you at breakfast. And remember. Rest.'

They said goodbye. Eleanor locked the door and closed her eyes.

4

By 9am, pacing up and down his office at the rear of Hangar 3, Robert Grim was a bundle of nerves. He had spent the better part of the night in the Subaru, for which his back was paying dearly, but that wasn't his biggest worry. Neither was getting the kid onto the base; he had his key card. His biggest worries were Van Driel, Jerome, Sita and Paul. Grim had no idea how to neutralize them.

The fact that it was Eleanor's pit bull himself who eventually sparked the idea and fanned the flames, was ironic. Maybe even poetic justice.

'Boss,' Van Driel prompted as he entered his office. 'I need your help with our nine quiet tenants.'

'What's up?'

'We're gonna sweep up the mess.'

'Say what now?'

'Boss's orders. The *real* boss.' Van Driel chuckled.

'What do you mean, sweep up the mess?'

'Light it up. The whole shebang: the ship, the zombies, everything.'

'You can't do that! They're people!'

'They're monsters. I told you I wouldn't come near them unless it was to bring the gas. Chill out, it may not come to that, but we need to be ready if we get the word. It's all gone down the drain, thanks to Bellingcat.'

'But what about my investigation? I'm this close to a major break-through!' Grim feigned indignation. In fact, his brain was working overtime.

'Until we get the call, they're all yours, David Attenborough. But we're moving your pets to the hangar. And you're coming with me.'

This could potentially work in his favor. The Returned and the *Oracle*, brought together. Van Driel focused on the relocation. And the guards . . .

'Where are Sita, Paul and Jerome?' Grim inquired.

'I want to send Paul and Jerome ahead to fuel up a truck. Can you, me and Sita transport these things with the three of us? I don't want them to start fucking with our heads.'

'I don't think they will.' Grim spoke slowly, stalling to think. 'The coroner described what's happening to them as "wilting," and she was spot-on. I expect them all to die soon. The same algae that ravaged the ship are eating them up from the inside. I bet we'll find three or four of them dead in their cells right now.' Grim didn't expect that at all, but Van Driel didn't need to know. He nodded slowly, as if he reached a decision. 'I think the three of us will be safe with those zap-guns you have.'

'Your responsibility. Ten minutes, front gate,' Van Driel said and dismissed.

As soon as the door shut behind him, Grim took out his phone and sent Luca instructions. The boy confirmed. He closed his eyes and tried to steady his heartbeat, praying it would work. You could hardly call it a plan and it would require a lot of improv, but it was all he had. It *had* to work.

Grim got up and listened at the door, then crossed the hall toward Delveaux's office. Over the past few weeks, Grim discovered he had a reputation among the NOVEMBER-6 crew for being an eccentric. An *American* eccentric at that. He hadn't necessarily sought such a reputation, but once aware of it, he had actively cultivated it. Eccentrics had their perks, but they weren't trouble. He felt comfortable in his role as their mad scientist with a penchant for the supernatural. He could act like a wayward spirit, haunting the corridors of the facility at night. His keyring accessed all the annexes, and Hangar 3 and its offices weren't exactly fortresses.

He opened the door to Eleanor's office, slipped inside, and hurried to the adjacent officers' suite. The blinds were down and light was dim, but he knew where to look. He opened the right desk drawer and sifted through the stationery. It was still there. Maybe it wasn't even Eleanor's.

A small, yellow aerosol can that looked very much like body spray but wasn't.

5

As Grim sat wedged in between Sita and Van Driel, heading for the ammo bunker in the same U-Haul that had transported the Returned to Volkel, Luca and Safiya were in the rear of Ravinder's pink deux-chevaux, hitting the highway with Amsterdam in the rearview mirror. Turned out Ravinder was a freelance photographer for fashion glossies, his next shoot scheduled only later that afternoon, and Aisha said her boss was a dick and anyway, fuck him. Luca took that to mean both were up for a little adventure. The car sucked, but at least it gave them wheels. Ravinder jammed two mesh sunshades in front of the rear side windows to help conceal his contraband. The downpour blasting across the A2 did the rest. The storm was picking up. The trees on the embankment were nothing more than blurred smudges. They couldn't go north of fifty, and often a gust would pound the side of their hunk-a-junk pushing it dangerously close to the guardrail.

'What's the word, Fi?' Aisha called.

Safiya was working Streetview on Aisha's phone with Luca peeking over her shoulder. Grim's instructions had been brief: *Google Maps. "Pieperz & zo—Rechtstreeks van de boer!"* * 11 *on the dot.*

_____

* *Taters & Stuff—Straight from the Farm!*

'I think it's a farmers' market.'

'What a bummer,' Ravinder said. 'In the movies that shit always sounds rad. *Rendezvous with Bald Eagle at the Omega Waypoint at eleven hundred hours.* Nu uh. See you at Taters & Stuff.'

'Dude doesn't speak a word of Dutch, he probably doesn't even know what he wrote,' Safiya said. 'In any case, it'll be hard to miss.'

She went back to satellite view. Luca pointed to the wooded area a couple of miles north. 'Wouldn't it have been safer to meet there? The countryside seems exposed.'

'My guess is that Bald Eagle strategically chose his spot. It's a rural area away from the main road, but it's only two miles off-base. That tells me every second counts. He probably can't stay away for long.'

'Yeah, and what does that tell you?' Aisha asked. 'That it's teeming with bad guys. I really don't think it's a good idea to go with him. He's taking you straight into the lion's den.'

A sudden squall yanked at the deux-chevaux, and it swerved to the left. 'Whoa . . .' Ravinder uttered, steering back and slowing down some more.

Luca licked his lips and said, 'It's our only chance.'

6

'Holy crap,' Van Driel grunted with suppressed disgust, as he descended the stairs of the bunker. He padded his hand to his nose and mouth, muffling his words. 'What the hell happened here?'

The stench hit Grim the moment he opened the entrance door, but down here it was overwhelming. He bent over against the wall, wheezed, and pulled the rain-soaked collar of his jacket over his nose. On the staircase behind him, Sita was gagging. The depot smelled like Grim imagined the remains of a beached whale would smell after a buildup of gases exploded it.

Grim peered past Van Driel into the central area. The fluorescent ceiling panels left nothing to the imagination. It looked like a surreal crime scene. After the autopsies on Sunday night, Kramer had stitched Bart Dijkstra's and Sandra Kocken's bodies back up, but at Grim's request, left Martin Reich exposed on the makeshift cutting table. He had wanted to ascertain whether the intruder had died along with the body or mutated post-mortem.

The latter was the case.

The shape on the gurney was barely recognizable as human. Two flaccid, liver-purple flaps of skin hung from either side of a giant cavity.

Inside it, some nasty thing had wreaked havoc. The glazed, spongy black mass Kramer had identified as a predatory species of algae had festered and flourished and finally spread even outside the body.

It must have fed on his blood, Grim thought. *His blood and his soft tissue.*

It now covered the bunker's entire central area. Stygian veins wound down the gurney's frame like tentacles. Large masses of it shrouded the tiles, the steel cell doors, even the walls. Everywhere it clung to surfaces, fungus-like organisms seemed to sprout, some murky, some gooey, some with unnatural, anemonian polyps that slowly throbbed like living hearts.

With obvious difficulty, Van Driel forced himself to enter the room, and Grim and Sita followed.

'What even *is* that?' Sita stammered. 'Is the air safe to breathe?'

That was anyone's guess. Grim supposed it wouldn't harm them, since it hadn't jumped during the autopsies. But there was so *much* of it now. And what did he know? This was way beyond him. An image arose unbidden behind his eyes, making the hairs in the nape of his neck bristle: microscopic spores of this venom fixing themselves onto the damp surfaces of his eyes and tongue . . . *growing.*

'It was nothing like this on Sunday,' he said with a hoarse voice. 'Whatever is it, it's alive. It's self-sustaining . . .'

'Time to exterminate it then.' Van Driel kicked his boot into a glob on the floor. It squelched like he had stepped on a jellyfish. 'Boss, you have the key to the vaults. Let's see if they're still alive.'

His legs numb, Grim crossed the room, trying to avoid stepping in the filth. He aimed for the steel door with the yellow Post-it note reading ALEXANDER WOLF and scrabbled for the right key.

'Pops,' Van Driel called out. Grim turned just in time to catch something tossed in his direction. A stun gun. 'Don't zap yourself, because this thing will put you on the floor, and that's not where you want to be right now.'

The stun gun turned out to be an excessive precaution. Halfway down the dim vault, Alexander Wolf stood next to his gurney. His posture seemed frozen since last night, but his left hand was juddering, his black eyes oozed with thick discharge caking his lids, and the lips framing his gaping mouth were cleft. He looked like a gravely sick dog, waiting for its owner to come home before it could die. It evoked pity rather than revulsion or fear.

'Let's get one thing clear,' Van Driel said. 'The second any of you feels even a hint of their mindfuckery, speak up, capisce? Speak up and get the hell out of Dodge.'

Sita and Grim affirmed, and they got to it. One by one, they went through the gun vaults. Grim assumed it would be easy, in their catatonic state, to usher the Returned onto their gurneys, but Van Driel insisted on jabbing his stun gun to the side of their necks each time and pulling the trigger. Grim found it hard to watch. If Sita did, she didn't show it.

With gaffer tape they secured the body bags to the gurneys, then rolled all nine of them into the central area.

'How are we getting them up the stairs?' Grim asked. He tentatively regarded Sita. 'I mean, I have a bad back . . .'

'Give me a break.'

It was a gross underestimation; Sita and Van Driel were perfectly fine on their own with Van Driel as a brake weight from behind and Sita controlling them from above. Grim only assisted with collapsing the undercarriages. Squeezing himself past the guard dog in the staircase, Grim saw the hem of his uniform jacket slip up. A service gun was tucked under his belt. Right hip, no holster. And he noticed something else too: no walkie-talkie. Grim had watched all of them carefully for the past thirty-six hours. Nobody at Volkel used radio. All comms went strictly through smartphones.

Van Driel came back down and shoved a roll of gaffer tape and a wrench from the U-Haul's toolkit into his hands.

'There. Make yourself useful and wrap the dead one.'

Grim stared at the wrench. 'What's this for?'

'If you want to scoop it up with your bare hands, be my guest.'

Robert Grim cursed Van Driel and all the landmines he evaded in Afghanistan, but he took to work. Starting at the foot, he wrapped the gurney, gradually overlapping his way up to create an airtight cocoon containing the remains of Mr. Reich. He used the wrench to tear off the growth bulking over the edges. It ripped, it squealed, it shrunk, and the air in Grim's lungs felt too heavy. His stomach convulsed, and it was all he could do to not throw up. Gasping, he turned away, dropped his tools, and smothered a cry of frustration.

By the time it was done and the cargo was loaded, Sita and Van Driel were soaking wet and Grim suspected he would have to throw away a good pair of shoes. He checked his watch. Almost an hour gone. It all came down to what happened next in the hangar.

On their way over, Grim listened to the swishing of the wipers before he chose the right moment to break the silence. 'Listen, that bunker needs to be decontaminated, or it will just keep festering. But I want to be clear, I'm not going back there. Eleanor made me responsible for the Returned, so I'm staying with them.'

'Take a chill pill, pops,' Van Driel said. 'Jerome and Paul just confirmed they're back with the fuel. Sita, you guys can go down there and Clorox the shit out of that dump.'

Sita didn't seem pleased about the prospect but nodded anyway.

The hangar's sliding doors were open in the wake of the fuel truck. Van Driel pulled in and parked the U-Haul as close as possible to the *Oracle*'s hull. A hose meant for refueling F-16s was fixed to the tanker, the nozzle at the other end ready for use on the concrete floor. The rigging and sails, stored to rot on pallets in the corner of the facility, were now placed along with the masts against the remnants of the ship. Jerome emerged from a forklift, saluting Van Driel.

'Beauty, eh?' he glared. 'Twelve thousand gallons. Enough to keep six F-16s in the air for two hours. Or one ship for ten seconds.' He roared.

Here too, the smell of decay was oppressive, but moldering wood was like Febreze after rotting corpses. Despite the still lingering, briny tang of the sea, the air was much more breathable. Surface treatment hadn't stopped the ship's degradation. The once proud *fluyt* was now a wreck that looked as if it had been salvaged after centuries on the seabed, exposed to not only the current, temperature fluctuations and salinity, but also to that same species of predatory algae they had seen in the bunker. It emerged in thick veins from the gaps and cracks, reminding Grim of an old seaman's sketch of a clipper caught in the arms of a colossal octopus. Despite his aversion to the *Oracle*, seeing her like this made him oddly melancholic.

Van Driel ordered Sita, Paul and Jerome to cleanse the gun vaults, and they departed in Jerome's car. He went to the front, pressed a button, and the electric doors rolled in their tracks, shutting out the torrent.

'You and me, we're going to unload them,' he said when he returned. 'They're not heavy. Bear with me, pops, you can change into something dry in a jiffy.'

'Let's get to it then,' Grim muttered.

Van Driel climbed into the truck's cargo hold and pushed the first gurney to the ramp. Grim took out his stun gun, crammed it within reach between the frame and the foam pad, then took hold of the handles. One by one, they unloaded the Returned. Mid-way through, Grim opened his mouth. 'Can I ask you something?'

Van Driel raised an eyebrow but didn't say a word.

'Why the sudden hurry? No matter what got leaked out there, in here you're hermetically sealed. The media can't access the ship.' He paused, then added, 'Or the people you locked up.' It seemed to hit the mark, and Grim took the win. 'If Eleanor wants to get rid of the ship, she could dispose of it without a million-dollar insurance claim from your DoD. Chop-chop, through the woodchipper. There's not much left of it anyway. But no, she wants to torch the entire place. What does that tell you?'

'I thought you were hired to investigate the spooky stuff, not comment on policy.'

'It tells *me* she's panicking,' Grim continued unperturbed. 'And that begs the question: why? Why's your boss getting the willies?'

'I have a hunch you've got a theory.'

Grim stopped and opened his palms on the body bag. 'Come on, you're not stupid. You saw the videos.' He smiled, seeing it provoked Van Driel. 'That guy Yamani. The day he disappeared I suddenly had to go to London. Eleanor conveniently sent Glennis and me on a wild goose chase. Want to know what I think?'

'That you should quit yappin and start doing your job?'

'That Glennis was the last person she wanted around. Because this was something even her most loyal confidants weren't allowed to see. Where were *you* that day?'

'Even if I did remember, it's none of your fucking business.'

'But you don't, huh? That's the thing. Eleanor sidelined all of us. Even you, her loyal lap dog. I bet you and Diana were sent on leave that day.'

Van Driel forcefully pushed the last gurney against Grim's chest. It hurt, but he didn't want to give the man the satisfaction of showing it. 'On with it, pops.'

Grim assisted him, but he was steamed up now and continued, 'What's it like to know your boss betrayed you all? Heck, what's it like to know she betrayed your country? You're ex-military, that must strike a chord. Because it's true. She sided with a rogue state. And she would've gotten away with it, except the *Oracle* had different plans. She didn't anticipate these people coming back. It all went south after that.' His smile widened into a grin. 'Now, who knows who's after her, and the consequences are beyond my imagination. It's funny if you think about it. I warned her about this from the outset.'

'Why don't you stow the chatter and save your whining for her?'

'Because you're complicit if you take part in it. You know I'm right. Your boss is ruthless, and you're her Mr. Fixit. Do you *want* to be?'

Van Driel didn't answer, which was an answer in itself.

'Tell me. Your *live* prisoners. The witnesses. Are we throwing them onto your bonfire, or were you ordered to make them disappear in some other way?'

'Mister, you're senile,' Van Driel snarled and turned away.

'Am I?' Grim asked, watching him roll the first gurney under the *Oracle's* hull. He trailed him like a shadow, ever the aggravating eccentric. 'It's hardly a stretch. Eleanor isn't exactly a stickler for human rights. And what about me? Are you getting rid of me too? Surely I know too much?'

'Keep this up and you'll find out.'

That's when Grim snuck up from behind so close that the ex-military's instincts kicked in and he started to turn. Grim didn't hesitate, put the stun gun to the back of his neck and pushed the button. There was a sizzle, a crackle, and Van Driel screamed. He flailed his arms, and his knees buckled, launching the gurney on a roll. Grim kept the zapper pressed against his neck as he moved with him. With his free hand he reached for the yellow aerosol can in his coat pocket and triggered a cloud of pepper spray into Van Driel's face, three, four, five seconds.

'Thanks, but I won't be sticking around for that, Moonshine,' he confided.

Van Driel bellowed and writhed on the concrete floor. He raised his hands to his face, and Grim took advantage of the moment to go for his gun. Even in pain, Van Driel appeared to anticipate his move, because he kicked his legs at him. But blinded by the spray, he missed. Grim managed to get hold of the grip and yanked. The gun spun across the floor. He kicked it out of Van Driel's reach and ran after it, escaping his reaching arms. He picked it up and aimed at Van Driel.

'Fuck!' the latter roared. *'That was pepper spray! What did you do that for?'*

'Never tell an old man he's senile,' Grim panted.

He needed a moment to catch his breath. His heart throbbed in the back of his throat. He studied the gun. GLOCK 17 GEN 4, the barrel read. In Black Spring they had a service weapon in the locker, but Grim had never had to use it, and his gun skills were basic at best. The Glock didn't appear to have a safety lever, but Grim couldn't imagine Van Driel walking around with a cocked gun. He fiddled with the slide, pulled it back—

The weapon clicked. Ah, cocked now.

'Fuck!' Van Driel yelled again, wheezing in air. Tears were streaming down his face. The skin around his eyes was crimson.

'Up,' Grim said. 'And in case you can't see it, I have your gun pointed at you.'

'*I'm in pain, motherfucker!*'

Admittedly, it looked excruciatingly painful. 'Give me your phone then. Slowly.'

'Fuck you.' He tried to open his eyes but couldn't. He had no intentions of following Grim's orders. 'I need water, or I'll go blind.'

'You'll get some as soon as I have your phone. I mean it.'

'Or what? You'll shoot me? You don't have the guts.'

'Do you really want to do this dance? It's such a goddam cliché. Alright, I'm going to count to three.'

'Fuck you.'

'One.'

'Fuck you!'

'Two . . .'

'*Fuck you!*'

'Three!'

Grim aimed up and fired. A low bang discharged through the hangar, and the bullet buried itself in the *Oracle*'s cutwater. Van Driel screamed and flinched. Grim too, but he found his bearings. He hoped the cloudburst had drowned out the gunshot elsewhere on the base.

'Your phone, *right* now! The next one's for your knee!'

'*Alright, alright, alright!*' Perhaps Van Driel had gambled on the likelihood that Grim didn't know how to lock and load, because now he didn't hesitate to take his phone out and shoved it over to Grim.

'Good man.' Grim picked it up. It was a regular iPhone. 'Got Face ID?'

'I need water. You promised me water!'

Right. Even if he had it, his face was pretty much fucked at this point.

Grim looked around. Underneath the skybridge was the workshop, an array of chairs and tables with toolboxes and electronics where earlier on, they had prepared the experiments. There was also a cooler with a pack of bottled waters. Never taking his eyes off Van Driel, he ran over, snatched two 8 oz bottles from the cooler and dragged a red plastic stacking chair along on the way back.

'This is yours if you give me your passcode,' Grim said. 'The second is yours if you sit in this chair like a good boy. Think you can do that for me, Moonshine?'

'Give me that.'

Grim sighed and aimed the Glock again. 'You still don't get it. Honestly, I don't give a flying fuck about your eyes. Right now I'm on a mission, and you're in my way. So listen carefully. There are two ways we can go about this. Either, you do as I say, in which case it'll be unpleasant for a while, but I'll do what I need to do and leave, and you walk away unharmed. Or I put two holes in you, then *still* do what I need to do and *still* leave. The first hole will be in your knee. The second in your head. I *really* don't want to do that, but I suggest you don't test a senile old man a second time.'

Van Driel stared at him with twitching red eyes before he squeezed them shut again. He believed his bluff. Grim hadn't been so sure himself, but he was glad it wasn't called.

'The code, please.'

'8-8-4-8-0-0.'

Grim entered it and got to the Home Screen. He rolled a bottle toward Van Driel, who grabbed it, uncapped it, and poured it over his face.

Topping his messages, Grim found a group chat labeled as TEAM BELLADONNA. The members were SITA, JEROME, and PAUL. He scrolled back to observe Van Driel's texting habits. Brief sentences, no hoo-ha, no punctuation . . . and in fucking Dutch.

He thought for the space of two seconds, then took out his own phone, opened Luca's chat and wrote, *Urgent request for help: Imagine you're a sourpuss commando on a really bad day. Now imagine you're texting orders that leave no room for doubt. Please translate the following into Dutch. AND LET YOUR GROWN-UP FRIENDS HELP YOU.* He sent it, then wrote, *E wants base evacuated due to supervision* and sent that. Then, *Lock depot asap and standby in hotel till further notice* and sent that too.

He didn't need to wait long before three dancing dots appeared . . . dancing for what seemed like the longest ninety seconds of his life. Then two messages popped up. They were in Dutch, and besides a few matching words—*depot, standby, hotel*—it was all Greek to him. Careful not to misspell anything, he began to copy them into the TEAM BELLA-DONNA chat. Doubt hit before he sent them, and he returned to Luca. *Are you absolutely sure I can send this behind enemy lines? Your mom's life may depend on it.*

This time the answer came immediately: *Send it.*

Grim did.

What followed less than twenty seconds later was the twenty-first century's middle finger to any lyricist, ballad-monger, or literary aficionado; Jerome's epistolary tour de force: OK.

Grim let the air escape between his teeth, put the phone away, and gestured with the Glock. 'Sit.'

Van Driel scrambled up, heaved himself onto the chair and hung his head between his knees. 'I need more water.'

'And you'll get it, as soon as you sit nice and tight.' He went to the U-Haul's cargo hold and reached inside for the storage box. 'I can assure you this gun is aimed at you at all times, so no monkey business.'

He came back with a roll of gaffer tape, the same tape they had used on the Returned, eliciting immediate protest. 'Aw, come on. Is that necessary?'

'Yes indeed. And here's the plan. I'm going to throw you this roll, and you're going to tape your ankles to the chair's legs.'

'I can barely see! How you want me to—'

'You don't need your eyes to know where your ankles are. Get cracking.' He threw the roll. It landed with a thud at Van Driel's feet. Grudgingly, he bent over to pick it up and do what he was told.

'Good, now keep going. Tighter.'

When it was done, Grim forced him to wind the tape around his waist and the back of his chair, passing the roll from one hand to the other. Round and round it went.

'Very good. Now, reach down and grab the chair's legs behind you.' He did as was instructed. 'Good. I'm going to come up very close behind you now. You might feel the urge to try something funny, but I want you to know I have your Glock aimed at the base of your spine and I'll be trigger-happy at even the slightest hint of movement.'

Van Driel shook his head and made a sound of disbelief at how he had allowed this whackjob to outsmart him. Grim didn't care. What he did care about was that Van Driel would sit still, which he did. Grim tied both his wrists and when it was done, he went on to wrap gaffer tape around his entire upper body and the chair's back, now including the arms. Only then did he dare to put the Glock away, to have both hands available to pull his package tight. But he didn't stop wrapping. He only stopped when he had almost reached the end of the roll and Van Driel sat in his chair like a caterpillar in a cocoon.

'*Now* can I get some water?' he moaned. His face looked like it had fallen flat into a giant hogweed. Grim took the second bottle and emptied it onto the man's eyes. 'More,' he panted. 'More, more.'

Grim went to fetch the pack but when he came back, he was appalled to see Van Driel and his chair had moved at least five feet toward the hangar doors. 'Are you fucking kidding me?' Grim asked. 'Where you think you're going?'

'Fucker,' Van Driel grumbled at him. The chair was apparently light enough to waggle his way to cloud cuckoo land, and not without the risk of toppling over. Grim admired the man's dogged determination.

'You should be thankful that I'm still helping you.' He started to squirt water onto his face but quit after the fifth bottle and ignored Van Driel's pleas for more. 'You'll get more, but first I want you to tell me where Ward C is.'

Van Driel shook his head again. 'What's the plan, Grim? You wanna be a hero? Eleanor *will* find you, you know that. November-6 gave you a life. We own you. You have nowhere to go.'

'My plan is none of your business. Tell me what I need to know, or I'll get the stun gun again. And this time I won't help you up.'

Van Driel gave him directions where he could find the detainees. When Grim asked for the keys, he started to laugh. He couldn't stop.

'What's so funny?'

'They're in my pants,' Van Driel hiccupped, going lobster more than he already was. Grim looked at the cocoon he had created, and his thought was both simple and weary: *No god is ever on my side*.

He ran over to the workshop and returned with a box cutter. 'We can do this with or without pain,' he snarled. Van Driel screamed as Grim patted his hip and made a smooth cut through the rubber. It took some wriggling and fiddling, but then he located the keyring and yanked it out.

'Right, I gotta go. But it hurts my feelings there's no trust between us.'

Without no hesitation, he approached Van Driel with the last stretch of tape. Van Driel saw him coming and cocked his head like a turkey, but Grim pulled the tape over his mouth and wound it around the back of his head. Muffled exclamations of protest. Grim ignored them and looked at his watch. He had dallied for too long. Luca must already be close to the point of rendezvous, and he still had an errand to run at the base. Grim wavered. Could he risk leaving Van Driel alone? If he locked the hangar, the man couldn't effectively go anywhere, but the ease with which he had just managed to waggle his chair bothered him, and he could still make plenty of noise.

Robert Grim scanned the room.

Saw the forklift.

Got an idea.

7

Eleven twenty.

Ravinder passed Taters & Stuff for the third time, but the few bare oaks haunting the countryside offered little cover, and there was still no sign of Grim. Luca started to worry that maybe he wouldn't show up. If something had gone sideways, if they botched that cryptic translation assignment and the plan had fallen short, they were doomed.

Your mom's life may depend on it, he had sent.

They pulled in before a gate that accessed farmland and debated whether they should drop him a message or leave him to it, when finally, the phone lit up. 'Bald Eagle checking in,' Ravinder announced. '*Multiple delays. Don't ask. On my way.* Awright, let's roll . . .'

He reversed and took the deux-chevaux back to the farmer's market, where he parked on the shoulder. A few minutes later, headlights approached from the direction of the main road. An inconspicuously grey rental car snailed by, but the downpour made it impossible to distinguish the driver. It seemed to momentarily accelerate, then the taillights flashed.

Luca prepared to get out, but Safiya grabbed his arm. 'Wait. It could be a trick. You need to be sure it's him.'

They peered intently out the rear window. The other car's door swung open and out popped an umbrella. The wind flipped it immediately, ravaging the ribs. Ravinder had his eyes pinned on the rear-view, his left hand clutching the wheel and his right the stick. That was almost cute, Luca thought. Like the deux-chevaux could outrace a secret service car.

The driver approached, stooping, struggling with his umbrella. He tapped the side window. Luca recognized him.

'It's him!'

He opened the door. Grim and his umbrella sheltered him somewhat from the rain but not the wind, which blasted water in his face. The American pointed at the deux-chevaux. 'Are you kidding me?'

'It was all we had,' Luca confessed, switching to English.

'Figures.' He put his head inside, sized up Aisha, Ravinder, and Safiya over his fogged-up specs and said, 'That looks very nice, and I'd like to thank you all for your care, but if you don't mind, I'm going to take Luca now. We have no time to lose.'

'On one condition,' Luca said. Initially he had had trouble with the language, especially last night on the phone, but he was surprised at how quickly he picked it up. Long live Netflix.

'What's that?'

He grabbed Safiya's hand. 'Safiya joins us.'

'Absolutely not.'

'Then I'm not coming.'

'Luca . . . smuggling one child onto the base is insane as it is. You don't seriously think I'd get a *second* child involved?'

'The APB was for the both of us. That means they're after her as much as me. I'm not going anywhere without her.' He squeezed her hand. 'It's because of her that I'm here at all.'

'You're out of your mind. She's a hundred times safer if she just lies low with Grover and Abby over there. Your little thing for her is very romantic, but you don't want to put your cuddle bug in danger, do you?'

Safiya leaned in and coaxed, 'I don't care, Mr. Grim. I'm coming with Luca.'

Grim gazed at Ravinder and Aisha for support. He didn't get it. 'I'd do what they say, sir,' said Aisha. 'If this one gets an idea stuck in her head, you can preach till the cows come home, but she gets it her way. *Belieeeve* me.'

Grim gave her an eyeroll that could turn daisies into dust and nodded toward his car. 'I'm telling you, you're out of your mind. Come on, get a move on.'

'Yes!' Luca cheered, as if they just won a trip to Disneyland. He stumbled out, soon followed by the others, as Grim opened the trunk of his rental.

'It'll be tight, but it's your party.'

Luca climbed in, followed by Safiya. It really was tight, but if you bent your knees, it wasn't too bad. They had to spoon to make it work for the both of them, and that actually wasn't bad at all.

'I've seen twin fetuses in a womb less ugly than the two of you,' Grim repudiated. 'Guys, not a sound. It's only a short drive. We might hit some lights, and we'll have to pass the gate. Volkel security won't search the car, but sometimes they ask questions. I'd rather not have to explain why there are two kids in my trunk.'

He lowered the lid halfway to shut out the rain and turned to Aisha and Ravinder. 'Thanks for your help. Just in case, the number I have is one of yours, right?'

Aisha nodded. Ravinder stood to attention and saluted. 'Bald Eagle, dismissed!'

Grim stared at him. 'As of twenty minutes ago, the last knucklehead who called me unflattering names got nerve-gassed and bound to a chair with gaffer tape. I'd advise you not to test me.'

Safiya called out goodbyes to Aisha. 'You go girl!' Aisha hailed to her, flashing a big, fat wink.

'Hey, Luca?' Ravinder said.

'Yeah?'

'Good luck saving the world.'

8

It was when they had cleared the gate and followed the main road at a steady thirty-five an hour that Grim got the jitters. His hands began to shake. He jerked at the wheel. The sentry had waved them through, coming and going, but didn't his swift return raise suspicion? And did Jerome, Sita and Paul really fall for his ploy? What if they didn't believe his fakery and returned to the hangar to verify? Improbable, but it was dangerous to bet on assumptions. The one thing he knew for sure was that he had left three frightened, wide-eyes citizens in the hangar along with a bewitched ship, nine withering zombies, and a gagged and extremely pissed ex-commando.

Initially, his intention had been to bring only Barbara Wolf from Ward C, but when he saw the state she was in, he opened the Hopmans' cell as well. There were more, but they were safer there than in the hangar. He decided to come back for them later.

What he found shocked him. These people had been held since Sunday without sanitary facilities or anything to eat or drink. It confirmed Grim's worst assumption that they had been detained with no intention of being released.

Hopman stared at him from his bunk as if he saw a ghost. He uttered something in Dutch, and judging by his tone, the tulip grower was at the end of his tether.

'I apologize, but we Americans are worse with languages than we are with our cholesterol.'

'Are you an American?' he asked in a heavy accent.

'Reporting to the beaches of Normandy. Wim Hopman, I presume?' Grim gave him a puzzled yet bemused look. 'I read your great-great-grandfather's diary. Nice guy. Strangled his wife.' He winked at Ineke.

'Pardon me?'

'No time. I've come to recruit you. We have one chance to get you out of here, and if you feel like testifying against the people who did this to you, I suggest you join us.'

They didn't need to be told twice. Barbara Wolf was waiting down the corridor and as it turned out, she and Wim Hopman had met before.

Seeing a familiar face at least gave her some desperately needed footing, because earlier she had barely been able to form a single coherent
sentence.

As Grim led them toward the exit, he briefly explained who he was,
where they were, and what day it was. Barbara grasped his arm and
pleaded, 'Can you get us out of here?'

'That's step two. Step one is a reunion.'

'A reunion? With whom? Luca? Oh, God, is Luca here too?'

'Not yet. I'll go fetch him in a minute.'

'You want to bring him in *here*? Are you crazy?'

'If you could just calm—'

'Why would you do that? And how do you know my son?'

'Please, Mrs. Wolf.' He stood in front of her and grasped her shoulders. 'Barbara. Listen to me. I know what happened to your little girl.
It's awful. But a whole lot of other awful things are about to happen,
and don't ask me how, but your son may be the only one who can stop
it. He *must* come to the ship and to your husband. So if you please—'

'Alexander's here too?'

'Yes. But you don't need to be afraid of—'

'I won't allow it! I'm his mother and I won't allow it!'

Robert Grim could sympathize with her, but what he couldn't do was
waste any more time. It was Ineke Hopman who eventually got them
going. 'Ma'am, I don't know what this is about, but this man just set us
free. If we want to get out, we better do as he says.'

Barbara protested all the way to the hangar and froze only when she
finally beheld the ship. She glared at it with a mixture of revulsion,
fear, and awe. Grim realized she took the *Oracle* as the cause of her
anguish and the destruction of her family. She didn't yet understand
that it had only been the means to an end.

Wim Hopman joined them. 'Sweet Jesus! What happened to it?
And what's that smell?'

'Natural decay,' Grim said. 'This is pretty much what it would have
looked like if it had remained at the bottom of the sea, wouldn't you
say?'

'If you call this natural, I'll eat my clump.'

'Come again?'

'He means his wooden shoe,' Ineke clarified. 'It's a Dutch expression.
But this, Mr. Grim, is a work of hell.'

Grim pulled out the Glock. 'Any of you know how to use this?'

'We live on a farm. My husband does a fare amount of skeet
shooting.'

'With a pistol?'

'No, but—'

'Europe and your sane gun laws. Never mind.' Grim handed him the gun and nodded to Van Driel. Hopman's eyes widened. Van Driel was still taped to his chair, elevated at least nine feet in the air on the fork-lift, looking like a somewhat oversized veal steak skewered on a carving fork. He regarded them with blazing red eyes. 'Moonshine there isn't going anywhere, but he is our collateral in case their people come back. Do you understand what I'm saying?'

'Christ, they're not going to thank you for this.'

'That monster forced me to take a dump in a corner,' Ineke scoffed. 'If I had my way with him, he wouldn't have gotten off so easy.'

Barbara noticed the gurneys with the body bags below the hull of the ship and cautiously approached them. After he immobilized Van Driel, Grim had unzipped the pouches to the extent that the tape allowed. Now, most were at rest but even from afar, he could hear one or two rustling as their contents stirred.

Barbara's voice seemed devoid of oxygen. 'Which one of them is Alexander?'

'Oh God, what are those?' Ineke gasped. Wim's eyes nearly popped at the sight of them. For seconds, it seemed like both would make a run for it, but Grim's primary concern was Barbara. He couldn't begin to fathom how awful this moment must be for her. That's why he checked the tags and pointed at Alexander's. 'This is him. But you need to understand that thing is no longer your husband.'

'I know,' she said. 'Alexander would never have done to Jenna what that thing did to her.'

She gingerly stepped closer. Once in reach, she suddenly screamed and brought her fists down on the body bag, again and again. Her tantrum came unexpected, but it shouldn't have, of course.

'Whoa, careful with him! We still need him, Barbara . . .'

But she let out all her despair, and the defenseless thing in the body bag shook like a rag doll. Grim managed to pull her away only when she had had enough and raised her arms in surrender.

'Sorry, sorry, sorry. I'm done. If you need to get my son, you idiot, do it now. I want him by my side.'

That had been earlier. Now, Grim peered at the road through the pouring rain with not one, but two kids in the trunk and a growing conviction that things in the hangar had completely derailed. He had Hopman bolt the access doors from the inside, putting them effectively in lockdown, but that did little to allay his sense of foreboding. Barbara

Wolf could have snapped. He had made a terrible misjudgment; the Returned weren't done setting examples. Worst case, the Grand High Bitch was back.

A patrol jeep sped down the road. Grim held his breath, as it passed without decelerating.

Right then. On to Hangar 3. After? Expose the truth. Pass it on to the authorities. Good authorities, here or stateside, which weren't rotten to the core. Hope, no, *pray* that they would listen.

Please let me be right. Let the kid be what I think he is.

9

Eleanor was in the rear of the Jag with Glennis driving when the call came. They just left Bijlmermeer after following up on a lead from an Antillean tipster. The boy had caught her attention, she said, because he was a white kid in a crowd of colored folk and that reminded her of the kids from the police alert. The girl was there too. The other two were adults not old enough to be their parents, and they departed in a rather jazzy car.

Dukakis spun around in the passenger seat. 'We have a pink Citroën deux-chevaux registered in the Bijlmer to a Ravinder Sylvester.' He tapped the screen of his iPhone. 'And let's see . . . bingo. He's friends with Aisha Said on Insta.'

'Finally,' Eleanor said. 'Have all units look out for that car. And run a background on Sylvester.'

Dukakis' phone buzzed. He answered, then handed it to Eleanor. 'Steven. Says it's urgent.'

Eleanor took it and put it on speaker. 'What? This better be important, we're tied-up.'

'Believe me, you'll want to hear this. So I'm on patrol outside the main gate and I first see Jerome, Sita and Paul leave the base. I reckon I give them a call, and they relay that on your order, Van Driel has put them on standby at the hotel.'

Eleanor squinted. 'I don't get it. I never gave such an order.'

'Yeah well, I don't know anything about that, but I figured if Van Driel said it, it's legit. Except twenty minutes later, I'll be damned if I don't see the old fella's car exit as well.'

'Who, Van Driel?'

'No, the nutty professor. Robert Grim.'

'Grim? But . . .'

'See, I thought it was suspicious after what Van Driel had said and all. So I trail him, and I keep my distance so he doesn't notice me, and a couple of miles up the road he turns into cow country. Turns out he had a package ready for pickup. Three guesses what it was.'

'I'm in no mood for games, Steven.'

'The kids you're looking for.'

'*What?*'

Up front, Dukakis' jaw dropped.

'Seriously, I'm not pulling your leg.'

'Are you *absolutely* positive?'

'Totally.' Steven sounded like he was smiling. 'I was watching from across the field, but I had my binos. They hitched a ride with a bunch of idiots in a pink hippy car, would you believe it, and pops just stashed them in the trunk and passed security like it was nothing. You've got to hand it to him, dude's got balls.'

'Just now?'

'Just now! They went through the gate a minute ago! I called Van Driel first, but he didn't pick up. You haven't lost a second.'

'And yet you managed to yap on about it for two full minutes, Steven. Precious minutes. We'll have to discuss that in your next PA.'

'I—I'm sorry, ma'am, I . . .'

'Do not lose sight of the gate for a second,' Eleanor snapped. 'Not even to blink your eyes. If Grim or any other suspicious vehicle exits, you follow it and call me stat, understood?'

'Sure, I . . .'

She ended the call, as Glennis pulled in behind a gas station. Rarely in her career had Eleanor Delveaux been at a loss for words, but now she looked at Glennis dumbfounded. The latter seemed just as perplexed. 'If Grim was able to leave the base . . .'

'. . . then he's neutralized Van Driel,' Eleanor finished for her. 'I don't understand how that's possible.'

'It's the only explanation for that weird order to Sita, Jerome and Paul. But *why?* Has *he* been in cahoots with Wolf? If so, it's impossible this is the first time they connected.'

'It appears our investigator has been playing his own game, Glennis.'

Dukakis jumped in. 'You want me to try and call Van Driel?'

'Don't. If Grim has his phone, I don't want him to know we're on to him.'

Dear God, how could she have been so blind? The joke was on her. She couldn't comprehend Grim's motives, let alone his reasons for bringing the boy to the base. But in Eleanor's nihilistic ideology, abstract concepts as reasons or meaning didn't matter. All that mattered now was saving face and containing a public scandal. If Grim brought those kids to Volkel, all the better. Different roads lead to Rome. The Bellingcat story was bad, but once she showed accountability to King, she could tell him things could have been worse. Much worse.

'Should we head out there?' Glennis asked. 'We can be there in ninety minutes.'

Eleanor slowly shook her head. 'No. Send Jerome, Paul and Sita, but tell them to keep a low profile. I want to surprise them, and I want to be there when we do. We're heading to The Hague and will carry on from there in the Cougar, so we won't lose any time.'

'What's in The Hague?'

She smiled a delighted smile, the smile of a grandmother at Christmas anticipating the joys of seeing her grandson. 'Jim is. That little dweeb broke his arm. I'm sure he'd love to teach him a lesson.'

10

Barbara Wolf had spent the last forty-eight hours in a dark place she would rather not emerge from, if it meant facing what happened to Jenna. It was a prospect she wasn't ready for.

The arrival of the tall, bespectacled American, the presence of the Hopmans, and the promise of her son forced her anyway, whether she wanted or not. At first, she barely realized where she was or what had happened. Her head ached. Her body was stiff and her eyes were swollen and crusted from constant crying. Worse, she was famished. There was a bruise on her cheek, and her mind flashed a memory of her fighting

(*No! Help my baby! Help my baby!*)

because suddenly they had been all over the hallway, they shot Roger and they downed Alexander, but what they didn't do was help Jenna, Jenna who

(*She's not breathing! Hurry!*)

was lying on the ground, left to her fate, and she had known right then that she was dead. Amid the chaos of Alexander's return, she had let her little girl slip her attention, and Barbara could only hope that it happened quick, that Jenna didn't realize what was happening when it forced her to the backyard and into the pond, and when it restricted her natural impulse to lift her head above the water when she was running out of air. And she, her mother, she had gone the other way, only to find . . .

Stop it, don't think about it, don't you dare think about it.

But she had to. The way Jenna floated languidly behind the carp pond's raised window. Her hair fanning in a halo around her head. The koi nibbling at her little finger . . .

Barbara abruptly cut her thoughts off and took in her surroundings. She found herself in a maintenance hangar of some sorts. The rain was hammering on the roof. Rising before her was the ship, the origin of all her misery. It was huge, but it was also on the verge of ruin. She felt Ineke Hopman's arm around her shoulders. Wim was at a respectable distance, peering with revulsion at the squirming shapes on the gurneys. The Hopmans had shared their story with her, and she hers with them, including Alexander's return and the death of her baby

(*Oh please, Jenna, baby, please wake up!*)

and only now did she remember telling them all this.

'Wim, get away from them. I don't want you to be there.'

His voice sounded hoarse, as if something were stuck in his throat. 'I wanted to see if I could find Bart. He must be in one of those zipped bags.' He came back, pale as a ghost. 'Their faces—'

He didn't get a chance to finish as a sudden urgent banging came from elsewhere in the facility. Gun raised, Hopman hurried to the stairs accessing the skywalk and the adjacent rooms.

'Be careful!' Ineke called out after him. 'Don't show yourself unless it's him!'

'I've got this boy,' he said, waving the Glock. 'No one else is coming in here.'

They heard his footsteps die away, and Ineke, still with her arm around Barbara's shoulders, guided her toward the cluster of tables and chairs by the wall. 'Come on, let's sit down for a minute.'

Her consolation had the heartfelt, almost professional sincerity of a trained caregiver, but it was still a stranger's consolation. Even after she drank the water Ineke gave her, Barbara still felt trapped, her mind numb inside a disjointed body, and the only thing in the world that could possibly ground her was—

'*Mom!*'

'Luca? *Oh God, Luca!*'

Barbara jumped up so quickly that her chair launched into the wall. Luca came running down the stairs, and she crossed the distance with her arms spread wide. They burst into simultaneous tears as they flew into an embrace, each knocking the other off balance. But boy, was balance restored.

'Sweetheart, oh sweetheart, I was so terribly afraid they'd caught you and hurt you. Oh, I'm so happy to see you.'

She touched him everywhere all at once, his messy hair, his ears, his strange clothes. Luca pressed his face into her shoulder and cried harder. 'Sh-sh-she's dead, isn't sh-sh-she? J-J-J-Jenna I mean . . .'

'Yes, sweetheart. She's gone.'

He tried to say more, but his words were lost in hysterical sobs. She stroked his back and repeated that Jenna was gone, again and again, finally making it real. But *he* was alive, and she told him that she was damn proud of him, that he had done a great job, and that she would never let him go. She meant all those things even when it was difficult at this dark hour to say it with conviction, but she owed it to Luca. He was all she had left of her family, and they had to stick it out together. It was up to her to lead them both back into the light.

But who would lead *her* if she lost her way?

11

Grim wasn't left untouched by the emotional reunion between mother and son, but he also noticed what it did to the Returned. Before, they had wilted into their catatonic, near-dead slumber, but as soon as the boy ran down the stairs, they started to thrash about and tear at their gaffer tape straps. Most of the gurney's wheels weren't locked and as a result started to swivel. Van Driel witnessed the clamor from his elevated position amid all of them. Seeing Luca, at first, he snorted a single bark of disbelief. Now, there was obvious fear in his bloodshot eyes.

'Christ, what's wrong with them?' Wim Hopman raised the Glock, but Grim gently pushed it down.

'They're reacting to the boy, just like I hoped they would.'

'But why?'

'In a minute. Help me lock the casters.'

'I really hope you know what you're doing.'

Grim crouched at the nearest frame. 'They won't harm you. Just don't touch them.'

Hopman squeaked a nervous, high-pitched laugh. 'I had no such intentions.' But he kneeled anyway and began flipping the brakes into place.

With the job done, they joined the others. Barbara noticed the girl with the teared-up eyes keeping her distance. 'Safiya?' she called, followed by something that almost certainly meant *What are* you *doing here?*

Still crying, Luca explained, prompting Barbara to gesture the girl to come over. She drew her into a tender but rather wobbly group hug.

Ineke beheld them with a look exclusively reserved for mothers who had seen their own children fly and reminisced on the fact with both endearment and melancholy. Grim, who hated children, thought these two weren't too bad. They had chutzpah.

'Sorry to be the party pooper,' he said, 'but we have no time to lose. Most of their thugs are out west looking for Luca, but besides Moonshine over there, three more are only fifteen minutes away. I tricked them off base and my guess is we're okay for now, but we have a lot of ground to cover, and I want to get out of here sooner rather than later.'

Luca untangled himself from his mother's embrace and took a few wavering steps toward the Returned, who were still trashing in their stubborn, soulless perseverance. Grim grabbed his arm, and he looked back. 'Is one of those my dad?'

Grim nodded. 'Not yet, Luca. Let's talk.'

Luca understood.

There were enough chairs in the workshop for the six of them. Barbara moved hers close to Luca and put her hand on his neck. This would probably have embarrassed the boy under normal circumstances, but today he let her. He in turn didn't want to let go of Safiya's hand, who didn't seem to mind at all. The Hopmans sat across them. Grim put his seat in between them, closing a sort-of circle. He stowed the leather briefcase from his office beneath the chair, sat, and scouted the room. With Van Driel balancing on the forklift a stone's throw away, they formed an unlikely bunch.

'Tell us what you have to say,' Ineke said. 'The sooner we get out of here, the better. I'm starving.'

'Me too,' Barbara said. 'Why did you bring my son here? And why are those people after him?'

'Because he's their star witness,' Grim said. 'He's the last one out there who can derail their coverup. And believe me, that doesn't sit well with Eleanor.'

'Who's Eleanor?' Wim asked.

Luca shivered theatrically. 'A creepy bitch.'

'Not exactly politically correct,' Grim admitted, 'but that pretty much covers it. Eleanor Delveaux. She's in charge.'

'What kind of organization is this anyway?' Ineke asked. 'They kidnapped my husband and me and locked us up without a trial. They *murdered* a neighbor who was a witness. How's that possible, in this country?'

Grim glanced over each of them, a tad uneasy. 'I assume we've all seen enough not have to beat around the bush about the supernatural aspect of all this.'

Luca and Safiya nodded passionately. Barbara lowered her eyes and turned her entire body away from the principle but nodded regardless. His gaze fixed on the Hopmans. They had seen less of it first-hand and from them, Grim expected the most skepticism. But Ineke crossed herself and said, 'I don't see what else can explain that,' nodding towards the squirming body bags. 'Wim?'

'I knew it the minute I heard the bell toll that morning,' he grunted. He folded his arms and that was all he had to say about it.

'Good, because that makes this conversation a lot easier. They're called NOVEMBER-6 and are officially an extension of your secret services AIVD and MIVD, but an extension you never heard of. That's their premise. I was brought here by a similar authority in America, and you've all met the woman who's affiliated with them, Glennis.'

'Is Glennis American?' Luca asked. 'But she speaks . . .'

'Fluent Dutch, I know. She's half-American. And it's no coincidence that when the Oracle appeared, they asked me to lead their investigation. In my former life, my work included observing and obscuring a similar supernatural phenomenon in the States. What that phenomenon was is irrelevant right now, but take it from me that for decades, it constituted an immediate threat to the people living within its reach.'

'Omigod,' Safiya said. 'You're a ghostbuster.' Luca's eyes beamed with admiration.

'Nice, but no. The truth is much less glamorous. We couldn't exorcise anything; we could only contain it. To do so, we needed funds as well as secrecy. The public cannot deal with the supernatural. Not in a world where science has taken the place of religion and superstition. It derails society. Which is why long ago, before Glennis' time, before my time even, West Point Military Academy in New York founded the American authority. They helped us keep it secret and gave us government support. In 2012, that situation came to, shall we say, a natural conclusion. But the framework continued to exist, to monitor its aftereffects.'

'And then the ship appeared,' Luca said.

'Yes. Now, how a foreign spook like Eleanor came to know of my existence beats me, because secrecy was top priority. She must have had something on Glennis to wheedle it out of her. That's the Achilles heel of organizations like that. Power corrupts. If there are rotten apples at the helm, other interests come into play, and institutions with so much jurisdictional leeway are a just hop, skip, and jump from the Gestapo.'

'Christ,' Wim said. 'They're halfway there already.'

'How far will they go?' Barbara asked. 'Is Ineke right? Do they really want to kill us?'

Grim shot her a candid look. 'In old spy novels, the CIA sent people who needed to disappear to a Maui retreat. Ludlum, Le Carré, Forsyth, the bunch. The idea had a certain romantic appeal, but I think there are much cheaper ways to silence people.' He pulled an imaginary trigger. 'No muss, no fuss, and above all, no leaks. I think Eleanor may even have intended the ship itself to serve that purpose.'

'Weaponize the supernatural,' Ineke scoffed. 'Now I've seen it all.'

'Except they had no control. None! They were so busy sweeping it under the rug, that they completely lost sight of the implications. And last Sunday, it recoiled right in their fucking faces. Pardon my French.'

Barbara shrugged. 'But what's Luca got to do with this? Why did you want to bring him here?'

'Early last week my investigation hit a brick wall, so I paid Luca a visit.'

'You met with my son without my permission? I'm not too happy about that.'

Luca looked from his mom to Grim with a pained expression.

'I understand your concern, but this is more important than any of us. Luca found the *Oracle*. He saw it all go down. I was hoping to pry some information out of him that would set me on a different track.'

Effectively sidelining Grim, Barbara asked her son something in Dutch. Luca, a teenager despite everything, sulked, and Grim intervened. 'I advised him to zip it up, assuming that's what you asked. Luca told me something important had happened to him. I didn't want to expose either of you to the risk of the wrong people getting wind of it. I also urged Luca to remember my number and call me if it happened again. Last night he did. Luca, do you want to tell her what you told me?'

'Okay,' the boy said.

'The abridged version please. *Tempus fugit* and I'm dying to hear all the stuff you *haven't* told me.'

12

Luca gave them the entire story, starting with the spyglass and the woolly mammoth, whose shadow he had felt looming over him for the past few weeks. It was strangely invigorating to be released of his burden. Safiya helped him whenever he stumbled, then took over and told them about the ritual in the bathtub. Luca concluded with his vision of the sunken land. When he was done, his mom asked, 'Sweetheart . . . why didn't you say something?'

'You wouldn't have believed me. You were so hung up on dad.'

'Luca . . .' She pulled him practically inside her. 'I am so terribly sorry I gave you that impression. I should never have let that happen. Never.'

With an awkward smile, Luca tried to wiggle out of her clutch. During the telling of his story, he had mostly stared at his hands, but now he scanned the room. On the Hopmans' faces he saw sympathetic disbelief: he was a child, he was traumatized, so duh, would he spew hooey. But Robert Grim was staring at him with the fascinated perplexity of a scientist who had put all his hypotheses to the test and seen them confirmed.

'So you saw a tribe who offered people to the sea every year,' he said.

'Yes. They pushed them off in hollowed-out tree trunks that would wash ashore empty. The spyglass showed me.'

'And then one day, it wasn't enough. The sea spoke to the Oracle and demanded a greater sacrifice.'

'Yes.'

'A *tribal sacrifice*, as you called it. A sacrifice of many.'

'Yes.'

'And they didn't heed it, so they were punished.'

'Yeah. She predicted it would happen, but no one would listen to her, and then a flood came.'

Grim leaned back and whistled between his teeth. 'Incredible.'

'Wait,' said Wim, glaring at Grim in helpless wonder. 'You believe his fairy tales?'

'The kid knew things he couldn't have known. He literally detailed the interior of the *Oracle's* cabin to me, and what he said about the sick and dying was also true. During the smallpox epidemic of 1716, the *Oracle* was deployed in Noordwijk to dump hundreds of the sick at sea. Believe me, this wasn't anything like the *Diamond Princess* during COVID. They just threw them overboard.'

'That's terrible!' Ineke exclaimed.

Luca nodded. 'But true. Emma showed it to me. All those people, all those children, I saw them sinking. Down and down. I could see their faces. They looked like they were rotting.'

Wim peered up at the ship with dazed eyes and stroked his chin.

'And there's something else,' said Grim. 'But I'll get to that in a minute. What's important right now is that if what Luca saw is true, we should at least be able to put it in historical context. And frankly, I don't recall an entire European civilization getting swept away by a tsunami.'

'Oh, but I do,' said Ineke.

Wim looked at her, dumbfounded.

'Doggerland.'

'Doggerland?'

Ineke shrugged, almost apologetically. 'I watch National Geographic a lot. A documentary came up recently, and when you said the word "tsunami", I remembered. Not all the details, but after the last ice age, sea levels were much lower and there was a vast stretch of tundra connecting Britain with mainland Europe. For decades, trawlers have been dredging up mammoth tusks and reindeer horns, even arrowheads from some primitive civilization, but they only started mapping it out in the nineties. Called it Doggerland.' She turned to Luca. 'Is it possible you heard about it on TV or at school? Because what you said is exactly what happened. When the glaciers melted, the land gradually became submerged, but it was a tsunami that supposedly gave it the final push.'

'That's what she told me!' Luca slid to the edge of his seat and in an absentminded, instinctive reaction, his mom grabbed the backrest. 'I swear to God, I didn't see it on TV. The old woman showed it to me. She said the sea kept taking more and more of her land, because the sea was . . . what's the word . . .'

'Greedy,' Safiya filled in.

'Yeah, because the sea was greedy. So they offered more, but it was never enough.'

Grim stared at him feverishly, trying to fathom what this implied. Safiya tapped his arm. 'Sir, can I have your phone?'

'What do you need my phone for?'

'I don't have mine. And well . . . you're a smart man, but right now you look like you couldn't even find your own glasses on your nose. I'm seventy years younger than you, and these are the fastest thumbs in the country. Need more?'

'How old do you think I am?' Grim moaned, but he handed her his phone anyway. 'Find out what you can.'

Luca snuggled up to her so he could watch. First hit was Wikipedia.

'Here, Doggerland. Exactly where you said it was, by the looks of it.' A bit awkwardly, Safiya began to read aloud. '"*It was probably a rich habitat with human life in the Meso . . . li . . . thic period, although rising sea levels gradually reduced it to low-lying islands before its final sub . . . mergence, following a tsunami caused by the Sto . . . regga Slide.*"'

'Whoa . . . 8,200 years ago,' Luca said. 'Click on that.'

Safiya's eyes flew across the screen. 'That Storegga-thing was a submarine landslide off the coast of Norway. About . . .'

'Whoa, megatsunami!'

'Zip it, doofus. About 180 miles of conti . . . nental shelf broke off, whatever the hell that is, and caused a . . . okay, a megatsunami in the North Atlantic and the North Sea. Here. *"This event would have had a catastrophic impact on the con . . . temporary Mesolithic population on what had remained of Doggerland."'*

'Maybe they should have listened to her after all,' Grim commented, and the skin on Luca's arms and neck started to crawl, as if all sorts of things were shifting around underneath.

He believes me. He's a grown man, an investigator, and he believes me. That's fucking scary.

Wim Hopman, reverting to Dutch, didn't and Luca couldn't blame him. 'Sorry, kid, but this is all gibberish to me. Even if all what you're saying is true, whoopie doo. What's it got to do with the ship?'

'Wim, English please,' Ineke said, then confided to Grim, 'My husband is wondering how this is connected to the ship.'

'I'll tell you how. Because in 1716 the *exact* same thing happened. Except then, the call for a sacrifice was heeded with the dumping of the sick, and the prophesied flood was averted.' Grim produced the briefcase from under his chair, took an antiquated, leatherbound book out and handed it to Hopman. 'Before, I thought your presence here was merely coincidental. I needed backup to hold the fort, and you and your wife were available. But I was wrong. You're here for a reason.'

'What's this?' Wim asked, with the book clumsily in his lap.

'It's the *Oracle*'s log.'

'I knew it!' Luca called out, glancing from Safiya to his mom. 'I knew there was a log! I told you so, I saw the man in the cabin writing . . .'

'Jesus Christus.' Wim opened the book and read out loud, '*Journal of t'Oostvaerders fluyt ship "The Oracle," Under 't rule of Hendrik Jan Hopman, Shipmaster of Noortwyck 1715-1716.*'

Ineke gaped at her husband, now forgetting to speak English herself. 'Did you know this?'

'No. Well, I knew my ancestors were merchant seamen but never the details.'

'You're probably descended from his brother's line,' Grim said. 'All of Hendrik Jan Hopman's offspring died in 1716, rather tragically I might add. But before the *Oracle*'s last, fateful journey, the captain and his family lived at Every Man's End. Had a habit of bringing the ship's bell ashore with him. That may explain why it appeared in your backyard.'

Luca noticed Wim's hands were trembling now. So was the skin under his right eye. 'I've racked my brain about that bell. Sixty years ago, my folks used to have a bell like that on the farm. They always rang it to call in the farmhands, or us kids when we were out getting into trouble. But after they died, the bell was gone too. I always reckoned they must have taken it to some thrift shop. But the morning that damn ship appeared, I heard it again. Only it didn't stir up any good memories. The sound was *wrong*, you know?'

Luca, who had heard it too, nodded, *Gotcha.*

Grim turned to him again. 'Remember what you told me about the captain writing in the cabin? How there was something familiar about him, like you were watching your father?'

'Sure.'

'During the last official voyage of the *Oracle*, the captain brought his daughter along. You were looking through her eyes. And here's the kicker. She had visions too.'

Grim showed them his stack of scribbled notes shoved between the pages of the book and told them about what he and his translator had managed to decipher, drawing perfect parallels with Luca's story. When he described the captain's daughter's dream about an elephant with thick, woolly fur, Luca jumped so suddenly that he startled everyone.

'That's him! That's Nunyunnini!'

Grim said, 'It's literally how you would describe a mammoth . . .'

'. . . if you didn't know what it was,' Ineke finished his sentence. She regarded the log with a superstitious fear, as if it were a bewitched grimoire that could bite her at any moment. 'Paleontology was nonexistent in the early eighteenth century. National Geographic, right? I'm pretty sure mammoths hadn't been discovered yet. Dear God, what's going on here?'

'If you think *that's* an eerie similarity, wait 'til you hear this one.' He turned a few pages and pointed to a section. 'When the girl made her prophecy in the chapel, she said, "*Only a sacrifice shall forestall thy ruin, and it must be a sacrifice of many. Go forth and give; go forth and give in abundance.*"'

A shudder went through his mom. She put her hands to her mouth and her eyes grew wide with horror. She had read the Dutch excerpt. Now she turned to Luca, excruciatingly slow, and muttered between her fingers, 'Give and give in abundance . . .'

'Excuse me, what's this about?' Wim asked.

'Just before Jenna ...' She swallowed her tears away. 'When Alexander returned on Sunday, he wrote those words on the wall. *Give and give in abundance*. I don't know how he did it, it looked like the ink was flowing from his hand.'

'Not ink,' Grim said. 'Algae. Those words appeared on walls everywhere, Barbara. Everywhere the people who disappeared into the *Oracle* returned. Mostly where they used to live. With their families, or in their parental homes.'

'How many are dead?' his mom asked.

Luca braced himself but still wasn't prepared for what Grim said. 'Fourteen.'

'No!' Ineke gasped.

'Three were NOVEMBER-6, but the others were family members and children. All drowned.'

It finally sank in. Mouth open, Luca stared from Safiya to Grim, who nodded even before he spoke. 'They're setting examples ...'

His voice choked. Something strange happened then. His senses seemed to turn inward. Sounds became dull. Luca listened to the thrumming of the rain on the hangar's roof and the sounds he seemed to hear *beyond* it, not with his ears but with his soul. It resembled the throbbing of giant machinery, perhaps the turning of the wheels of the universe itself, threatening, *imminent*, and a powerful premonition overwhelmed him.

They didn't need to hurry.

They were already too late.

'So it's true,' Safiya said. 'It's all happening again.'

13

Robert Grim had a hunch that time was running out when Luca raised the alarm. For Grim, this didn't come in the form of a prophetic whim but with a disturbing realization that a simple but terribly dangerous mechanism was already in motion, the components of which he couldn't begin to fathom. One had to do with their presence in the hangar. Another was the necessity for a timely solution to the threat they had exposed.

I need more time. Time to be absolutely sure.

But he knew there was none, and when Luca suddenly whirled out of his chair, it hardly came as a surprise.

'Do you guys hear that?'

The boy tilted then raised his head, like a deer first smelling a forest fire. Grim listened and heard only the sound of the rain.

'What do you mean?' Barbara asked.

'*Shhh.*' Luca raised his hand. The way he stood there, his young face fully focused and aglow from the hangar's panel lights, Grim felt there was something almost saintly about him. A strange energy seemed to fill the air. Grim wasn't sure if the others noticed it, but he certainly did. All stared at Luca. All acutely alarmed. But beyond Safiya's fear glimmered an adoration that exceeded mere infatuation. Beyond Barbara's motherly worry dawned an awe resembling religious devotion. Even Ineke and Wim regarded the boy with an air of submission, in anticipation of what he had to say.

They know, Grim thought. *They can feel it. This is what it looks like when disciples start to gather around their messiah.*

'We have to go,' Luca said. His voice sounded shrill, and his complexion was beyond pale. He no longer resembled a deer that smelled a whiff of danger. He resembled a deer that realized it was trapped by wildfire.

'But sweetheart, what's wrong?'

'I don't *know* . . . Can't you feel it?'

Safiya peered around and said, 'Okay, you're seriously freaking me out now.'

'What are we supposed to feel, Luca?' Ineke asked, trying but failing to sound composed. The boy attempted to speak but couldn't and didn't need to. Because Grim felt it. The sudden burst of electricity in the air shot through the fillings in his teeth and made the hairs on his arms ripple like seaweed in a shifting current. The Returned responded to the change as well. Their gurneys rattled under the fury with which they tried to tear themselves free from the body bags. Terrified, Van Driel vented muffled screams.

'She wanted to warn you,' Grim said. The gooseflesh had spread over his entire body. 'Safiya was right. It's happening again. The Oracle wanted to show you that if we don't listen, something terrible will happen.'

Luca nodded, his eyes glassy with panic. 'I know, but *please*, we have to go . . .'

Barbara stood behind her son and clasped his shoulders. 'Robert, for god's sake, let's get the hell out of here. I don't know what's going on, but I believe him.'

'Agreed,' Hopman said. They all got up. 'Those things are giving me the jitters. What the boy says, too. I think we better listen.'

Grim made a decision. 'Luca. To your father. Right now.'

'What?' Yanking Luca back, Barbara looked aghast. 'No! What are you talking about?'

'Don't you get it? He's been waiting for Luca.'

'What do you mean?'

'Alexander, the others, the ship, they're all manifestations of the same hivemind. They're all infected by the same algae, giving them life when in fact they should be dead, and letting the ship rot now that it's fulfilled its purpose. They're all wilting like shredded flowers. But Alexander can't be shredded yet. He can't be at peace, because he hasn't fulfilled his purpose.'

'What purpose?'

'Me, mom,' Luca said. 'He needs to talk to me. I'm the one with the visions this time.'

'I won't allow it,' Barbara said, tightening her grip. 'This is insane.'

'Mom . . .'

'I won't have it! He murdered Jenna! I don't want him to hurt you too!'

'Barbara,' Grim said, his voice calm. 'Whatever happens, Luca is the messenger. It's not going to hurt him.'

'How do you know? You don't know that! I want to get out of here. You're all so hung up on what Luca says; he said we have to leave . . .'

'She's right,' Wim agreed. 'Can't we put the damn gurney in that truck over yonder and get the hell out? I don't want to stay here another minute.'

'It *has* to happen here,' Luca said. 'Because of the ship.' He turned and grabbed his mother's hands. 'Mom, I have to do this. Mr. Grim is right. If I don't, it's all been for nothing.'

Barbara started to cry. Grim saw it was torture for the boy, but still he had the strength to put his arms around her. If there had been any doubt left about who Luca Wolf really was, it was now obliterated.

He allowed them ten seconds. Then he said, 'Come on, let's go.' The boy looked back. 'Do we still have time, Luca?'

'I . . . I don't think so. How would I know?'

'But you do,' said Grim. 'You're the Oracle.'

14

'What do I have to do?' Luca Wolf asked softly.

The Returned reacted to his proximity like predators to prey. No longer were they squirming, they were *panting*. It was an awful sound, hungry yet diseased, like the rattling of vocal cords thick with the metastases of an aggressive cancer. Luca saw his dad. Not his face, not yet; his mom's hand on his neck held him back. He sensed her fear.

Luca was afraid too, but it would have been so much easier if he didn't have to bear her emotions as well.

I am the Oracle.

He accepted his fate with a peculiar, detached sense of loss. He was mourning his childhood, which had quietly but irreversibly slipped away over the past few days. Part of him wanted to turn and cling on to his mom, who smelled so soothingly of her usual detergent, of his parents' bedroom and, underneath it, of *mom*, because it would be so much easier than the task ahead: not the task of a boy, but of a man. But he couldn't look away.

His dad was waiting for him.

Grim handed him the box cutter from the workshop. 'For starters, you cut the tape and free your father. He'll show you what's next.'

His mom was torn. 'Do you realize how crazy this is? I should put an end to it.'

'It's also the most important thing I've ever done.'

'I don't want you to. I really don't.'

He answered in Dutch this time. 'It'll be alright, trust me. It won't hurt me, but I couldn't bear it if it hurt you. So please, step back with Safiya and the others.'

She clasped his fingers, shook them, but then Safiya tapped her arm and she let go. 'Please be careful,' she moaned. 'I love you so much, Luca . . .'

'I love you too, Mom.'

She turned and joined Safiya and the Hopmans. Safiya blew him a kiss, which Luca caught and pressed to his mouth. Then he turned to Grim.

'If I do this, what will happen to my dad?'

But he already knew. *Wilting flowers.*

'You'll set him free,' Grim said gently. 'I don't even know for sure if your dad is still in there, but if so, you'll give him the peace he deserves.'

'Alright.'

Grim squeezed his shoulder and turned around, directing the others to step back. Luca was thankful. Maybe the old man was a little cray cray, but he sure as hell knew what he was doing, and he had been a beacon of calm throughout this madness. Luca started to like him.

He carefully approached the gurney with his dad's partially unzipped pouch. He saw the thing living inside it at the same time it saw him. Tears sprang into his eyes. Grim hadn't exaggerated: his dad's face was literally wasting away, and not by any organic process of decomposition. The intruder had ravaged it. Soggy flaps of skin and broken bone structures etched only barely recognizable shapes. Underneath them, death patterns reigned: a sub-skin craquelure of purple-black, split veins penetrating from the neck. The choked gurgles it produced were amplified by the huge cavity of its mouth, releasing gassy fumes that carried the unmistakable odor of the sea. The quivering black eyes were fixed on Luca.

Worst of all . . . it was still his dad's face.

With a bitter growl, Luca swept the box cutter through the air. It sliced through the tape, snapping his dad's shoulder strap. Immediately, the thing in the body bag bounced up. Luca shrunk back. His mom wailed at a distance.

Its waist and legs were still shackled, but it managed to free an arm from the pouch and reached for him. Luca was appalled to see it was still wearing the duffle coat with the horn buttons, the same coat his dad was wearing the morning he vanished. It was a sudden and unpleasant reminder of something Luca had tried his best to forget. *Now you can find your way back*, he had said, as he wound the rope around his dad's waist. Dad had tapped him on the forehead, saying, *Aye aye, captain.*

Those had been his last words.

'Show it to me, dad,' he spoke softly. 'But don't be too rough on me, will you?'

For the last time, he came closer. He turned to its legs, ignoring his instincts that begged him to run. He reached with the knife . . .

. . . and a thunderous bang interrupted him. Light flowed into the hangar from the left, followed by a fierce draft. Startled, Luca dropped the knife and looked where it was coming from.

The access door to the tarmac, adjacent to the much larger airplane doors, had bounced wide open. Two, three, four figures came through it. The man up front was large, his face wet with rain. He had an iron ram in his hand, which he carelessly dropped to the floor. Second in line was Eleanor Delveaux, holding an umbrella in one gloved hand and a gun in the other.

'Well, hello,' Eleanor said. She looked from Luca to the others with an expression predominated by greed. 'There you are. There you all are. I've got bad news for you. There's a new captain on this ship.'

Luca was too dumbfounded to say anything. His dad snatched at him but missed.

Someone screamed.

And then, in rapid succession, three gunshots.

15

Barbara's adrenaline launched her senses into such hypersensitivity that she witnessed the raid from start to finish with uncensored lucidity.

She saw the unknown man with the battering ram enter, followed by Eleanor Delveaux in her signature red maxicoat with a gun in her hand. In her wake was Glennis, also armed, then the giant named Jim. In the Super Hi-Vision slo-mo mode of her brain, Barbara had the time to hear her little girl's voice crow, *Uncle Jim is so funny!* and see Jenna pinch his nose. Now, Jim's left arm hung in a cast and a sling, mementos of his rendezvous with Luca. She couldn't believe they had brought him along.

Luca. Oh God, Luca, caught in the middle of that American's insane plan. Summoning a bloody vision, here at Volkel Air Base, aided by a monster that had once been Alexander. To save the country from impending doom. It was madness, madness, madness.

She saw Luca drop the utility knife. She wanted to yell for him to get here but the words stuck in her throat. The distance between her and her son spanned twenty feet max. In her head, she saw herself bridging it in seconds, but that didn't happen either. Her legs simply refused to obey. She saw Safiya and Grim to her left and Ineke to her right looking in shock at Delveaux and her goons. Wim was the only one to react. He reached for the Glock in his coat pocket and aimed it at Van Driel, who was still balancing on the forklift, taped to his chair. This went unnoticed by Van Driel, as behind his tape, he was frantically moaning to attract Eleanor's attention, clearly avoiding any wiggling and a nasty fall. That's why Delveaux and the others initially didn't notice Wim either.

'Well, hello,' she heard Delveaux say. 'There you are. There you all are. I've got bad news for you. There's a new captain on this ship.'

Footsteps drew Barbara's attention up to the skywalk overhead, where she spotted the three armed operatives before everyone else did. They must have forced their way in through the hangar's back entrance. Their bird's-eye view of the situation included Wim, who took a reluctant step toward Van Driel, Glock in hand. What was his plan? Hold him at gunpoint and force all the others to lower their weapons? Reckless and stupid, but alas, the man was a tulip grower, not a strategist. And suddenly Barbara knew what was about to unfold.

'Wim, drop the gun!' she yelled.

Startled, Wim looked at her, no longer aiming the Glock at Van Driel. When the first shot came, Barbara initially thought it was Wim who had fired, because the bullet plowed into *Oracle*'s hull, spraying woodchips everywhere. But the second bullet tore into Wim's shoulder below his raised arm, and he dropped the Glock with a surprised '*Ungh!*' The third hit him in the chest.

'Ineke . . .' he stammered.

Bewildered, Wim sought out his wife as he clutched his chest and sank to his knees. Ineke caught him and for a moment, they seemed locked in an awkward dance. Then he folded to the ground, and she started to scream his name over and over.

Luca, Barbara thought. *Oh God, Luca.*

She saw, she heard, she felt everything. Luca, incredulously staring at the Hopmans, unable to fathom what had just happened. Safiya cupping her mouth and smothering a squeal. Robert Grim, raising his hands and crying, '*Don't shoot! Don't shoot!*' while Delveaux, Glennis, and Mr. Battering Ram closed in on them from the front, and two other intruders, a man and a woman she had never seen before, came at them from the flight of stairs. She even saw Wim's Glock on the ground, a few feet away and within reach, but also saw the gunman on the skywalk. She knew the very second she would lunge for it, Luca would become an orphan.

'Don't shoot, don't shoot!' Grim cried again. 'Why did you do that? That man was innocent!'

'He was going to shoot Van Driel!' the gunman shouted. 'Hands where I can see them, all of you, and step away from the gun! Right now!'

Barbara put her hands in the air and saw the children do the same. Only Ineke took no notice. She was fixated on her husband, screaming, trying to stanch the bleeding with her bare hands. 'Somebody help him,' she wailed, 'oh Wim, stay awake, please stay awake, oh God, *somebody help him!*'

Even Delveaux was visibly unsettled by the violent turn of events. Barbara saw her tentatively glance from her own people to Luca and the Returned, then to Grim and finally to Wim and Ineke. Collecting herself, she gave a stern nod and said, 'Sita, Dukakis . . .'

The two operatives who had descended the stairs pushed forward. The second Ineke looked up and Barbara caught a glimpse of Wim, whose face was frighteningly white with blood sputtering from his gasping mouth, she knew that any help would be in vain. Still, the woman named Sita snatched Wim's Glock from the floor and pulled Ineke away from her husband, as the man named Dukakis sank to his knee and began to fold a makeshift compress from his jacket.

'Why did you shoot him?' Grim shouted again. 'That man didn't hurt a fly!'

'You're responsible for that,' Eleanor fumed. She edged closer, carelessly dropping her umbrella prompting Glennis to trip over it. 'What were you thinking, bringing these people here? This has escalated way beyond.'

'I was trying to save your country! I was trying to make sense of this, which you've been sabotaging from day one!'

'Give me a break. You deceived us. I don't look kindly on deceivers.'

Behind her, Jim had worked his way between the gurneys and shoved Alexander's aside. It teetered but didn't topple. Alexander was still upright in the body bag groping for Luca, but he was now out of reach. Luca had no eye for his father; a bigger horror was now towering over him.

'Hey, kiddo,' Jim said with a compassionate smile. 'Remember me?' At which his good hand grabbed Luca by the neck and flung him to the floor. Luca's chin hit the concrete with a smack that resonated through Barbara's bones, and both she and Safiya screamed his name. Barbara saw her son *bleeding*. She leaped forward but was immediately yanked back. She turned and saw Glennis, who had put her gun away and now held her right arm by the wrist and tightly grabbed her left shoulder.

'Barbara,' Glennis said. 'Calm down, and nothing bad will happen.'

Barbara spat in her face. Glennis didn't bat an eye. She simply held her, like it was no effort whatsoever. Struggling, Barbara yelled, 'Keep your hands off him, you monster! Keep your hands off my son!'

Dazed, Luca felt his bleeding chin and rolled onto his side, bumping against the frame of Alexander's gurney. The thing above again tried to reach for him. The rain-soaked man who had bashed in the door ignored this and mounted the forklift, started its engine, pulled a lever, and lowered Van Driel. This sent his chair into a wobble and Van Driel into a fit, but he didn't fall—*Pity*, Barbara thought. To her right, Wim Hopman was stretched in an ever-growing pool of his own blood, with Dukakis putting his full weight onto the compress an taking his pulse. Ineke washysterical in Sita's clutches. The last operative—the man who shot Wim—had gone down the stairs and now grabbed Safiya, who fought him but screamed in pain when he twisted her arm behind her back. Over at the gurneys, Jim snatched Luca's box cutter from the ground and slipped it into his sling. With his good hand, he reached for

Van Driel's descending chair and steadied him until touchdown. Then, he ripped the tape off Van Driel's mouth, triggering an unharmonious '*Goddammit!*' from the ex-commando. Next, the giant slashed his cocoon top to bottom.

Now Eleanor had the only gun, and she was aiming it at Grim.

'Get that gun out of my face!' he shouted, frothing with anger. 'I'm unarmed!'

'Robert . . .' She sounded solemn, almost sorrowful. 'Did you really think you could outfox us?'

'I said, get that gun out of my face!'

She lowered it a little, but her attitude didn't waver. 'And why? Please help me understand.'

'Because you've lost your sense of humanity! How is this serving your country, Eleanor? How?'

'That's none of your business!'

'You lock people up. You kill people. And not for a second did you stop and consider what the ship actually *wants*. You left me no choice!'

'You work for *me*, Grim. You're on a mission, and you have no authority to make such decisions. What you've done is desertion.'

'Says who!' Grim marveled in contempt. 'You dabbled with the Saudis! How much did they offer you?'

She wavered only for a second, but she *did* waver. 'Shut up, you moron.'

'We all know it, even your goons here. And yet they keep dancing to your tune. Fuckin braindeads. So tell me. How much was it?'

Barbara saw hate, rage, and madness fester behind Eleanor Delveaux's thin film of composure, and for a minute, she was afraid she would execute Grim on the spot. And then kill the rest of them. Barbara simply couldn't imagine how this spiraling tragedy could lead to any other outcome, and suddenly she was terribly afraid.

But instead, Delveaux twitched her lips and put the gun in her purse. 'It doesn't matter what you think. In fact, you've plowed the ground for me. You dug up the little worm. I should be thanking you. As for you, Mr. Wolf,' she continued in Dutch, turning around to face Luca. 'You've put us to great expense. And you've put Roy, one of our best men, into a coma.'

'*Bitch*. He was after *me*. I wish that car had killed him.'

'Do you? Tell that to Jim. Roy was a buddy of yours, wasn't he, Jim? And as a matter of fact, I think Jim has an ax to grind with you as well.'

'Yes I do, Ms. Delveaux,' Jim said, smiling at Luca again. 'A hefty medical bill is what I would call it.'

And suddenly Barbara understood things could get direr after all.

'And you, Grim,' Eleanor continued, 'Get your miserable face out of my sight. Marco, if I'm not mistaken, you have a score to settle as well.'

'Zip-a-dee-doo-dah,' Van Driel said, stepping forward. Looking bedraggled in his glue-stained uniform and bloodshot eyes, his grin revealed differently, and now Grim understood it too.

'Wait,' he protested, going pale. 'Eleanor, listen. I brought the boy here because he knew—*hey!*'

Van Driel had snatched him by the collar. Grim was half a head taller, but Van Driel had at least a hundred pounds on him. The ex-commando regarded him with narrow eyes then lunged, headbutting Grim in the face. Barbara heard a dull thud, and with a scream, Grim went sprawling, clutching at his face. Safiya shrieked, but Barbara's focus moved to Jim, who took Luca by his hood and threw him to his knees. Jim knelt to pin him down, but Luca was faster, rolled over, and kicked his plaster cast arm. The giant roared. He charged, and the blunt force of his good arm alone was enough to keep Luca's flailing limbs at bay. Still, his impairment hindered him enough that Luca would have managed to slip away . . . if the coward hadn't growled 'Jerome,' triggering Mr. Battering Ram to rush to his aid.

'*Keep your hands off him!*' Barbara yelled again. '*He's just a child!*'

But they didn't. Using the gaffer tape, they bound his wrists behind his back. In turn, Van Driel dragged Grim to his feet and toward the open area facing the gurneys. Blood trickled down the American's face. He was struggling but realized he didn't stand a chance, so he appealed to Eleanor instead.

'Eleanor, listen to me, we found it! We discovered what it means! The ship, the Returned, the whole shebang!'

But Van Driel yanked him to his knees, and Grim yelled again. Jerome started to bind his hands as well.

'*Ow*, fucker, you're hurting me! Eleanor, please, this is a matter of life and death . . . let me explain. This could end in disaster if we don't act quickly . . .'

Eleanor regarded Grim like a piece of trash, and with an absolute cynicism that dashed all hope, said, 'I don't care.'

That's when Dukakis let go of Wim's compress and stood up shaking his head.

He's dead, Barbara thought. *They murdered Wim.*

Ineke leaped from Sita's grasp and plunged onto her husband's body, crying. As if on cue, Jim and Van Driel struck almost in sync. Van Driel bashed his fist it into Grim's ribs, doubling him over with a choked gurgle. Jim poised like a football player and punted Luca in the stomach. Her son folded too, lurching sideways to the floor.

All became a red haze. Later, Barbara would remember that she had screamed. She would remember Glennis' grip weakening. She would even remember the look of shock on her face.

'Jim, that's enough! There's no need for that!'

'Shut your face, Glennis,' Jim snapped.

Glennis didn't intervene. This was sheer sadism, this was the culmination of a prolonged degeneration within a rogue institution . . . and she didn't stand up to it. Because she felt it wasn't in her place to do so? Or because she was already too deeply involved?

With a knee in his back, Van Driel pinned Grim to ground, pressing his bleeding face into the concrete. Barbara could hear his glasses snap. And she could hear him say, 'I ought to zapp and pepper spray you. But I'll do it the other way round. First, I'll spray you full of chemicals. Then I'll use the zapper on you. I'll stick it in your mouth, until you catch fucking fire.'

Meanwhile, Luca had curled up like a fetus beneath Alexander's gurney. But now, Jim worked him onto his stomach and twisted his arms behind his back, forcing a scream out of him.

'You broke my arm, you little shit,' Jim said. 'It's my turn now.'

He put his weight on Luca's arms, bending them further. But then Alexander reached for his son again, his hand grazing the back of Jim's head. Jim flinched and let go of Luca. Annoyed, he reached for the gun in his belt. For a single frozen second, Barbara's choked *no* hovered in the air between them, as Alexander's black, lidless eyes fixed on him. Then Jim pulled the trigger.

The bullet hit the thing that was once her husband between the eyes. Its head burst open and flew back. What splattered out wasn't blood or brains but a black mist of dusty particles, as if a dirt cup in a vacuum cleaner had exploded. Eleanor and Jim, closest to it, turned away and shielded their faces. The mist lingered like the afterimage of a fireworks display, then swirled and disappeared.

Spores. Algae. It's alive.

Alexander's body hit the gurney and started to shake. Barbara thought of an old song her father used to play: *For goodness sakes, I got the hippy-hippy shakes!* She had the urge to laugh, but then two black veins emerged from the bullet hole and slithered across Alexander's face like greedy tentacles, killing all desire to laugh. They seemed viscous, liquid almost, but organic at the same time. Slurping sounds filled the air as they sucked their way into his face, concealing it for the very last time. But that wasn't the end of it. More of the veins emerged, crawling down his body, infesting it, devouring it.

I'm not seeing this, Barbara thought, but she was, and so was Jim, stepping backward as in a spongy dream. Glennis, Safiya and Wim's killer who held her watched in equal bewilderment, and so did Jerome, Dukakis, Sita, and Van Driel, who had completely forgotten about Grim. The only one not watching was Eleanor. She staggered back, cupping her hands over her face as she hunched and sneezed.

The Alexander-thing was now a shapeless black mass, pulsing in the body bag like a nightmarish anemone. It had lost all resemblance to anything human. Veins bulged and stretched over the edge of the gurney, reaching down. Reaching for Luca, Barbara understood.

It wants the Oracle. Even now that the carrier is dead, it's still alive, and it wants Luca. Because it's been waiting for him.

Out of nowhere, Safiya flashed by. Apparently, she managed to tear herself loose from her capturer, who grabbed for her but missed. She launched herself forward, hurdling over Grim, and seized the far end of Alexander's gurney with both hands.

'I'm sorry, Luca!' she yelled.

With a mighty yank, she upended the thing and sent it crashing.

The giant glob of algae that had once been Alexander smacked from the pouch onto the floor at equal distance from Jim and Luca. It found them both at the same time.

With a completely different effect on each.

Oozy veins slithered onto Jim's shoes and disappeared into the legs of his jeans. His body rocked, his head whipped back, and the gun fell from his hand. Within seconds, the veins reemerged from his sleeves and from underneath his collar *subcutaneously*, as if on their way up, they had eaten their way in. A web of twisting dark spider veins spread across his clenched hands, neck, and face. By now, they had likely burrowed through to his heart and Jim was either dead or dying, but his mouth still gasped in soundless denial before he crumpled and sprawled across the toppled gurney.

Luca, however . . .

Luca was still on the floor. It penetrated his body through his mouth. Finally, the scream was born, the scream that had been building inside Barbara all this time, now escaping her lips and filling the air. It was a primordial scream, a scream of madness, a scream that could only end with the popping of the vocal cords.

Luca opened his eyes. They were as black as Alexander's had been. Her son got up to his feet, his head flung back.

Then he started to float.

16

Luca was no longer in the hangar. He was in his own little room, a.k.a. his Beachcomber Exhibit.

Except he wasn't, not really, because it was knocked out of true, as dreams often did. He recognized his bed, his desk, the fishing nets on the ceiling and orange crates on the walls with his collection of urchins, mermaids' purses, and unmessaged bottles. And of course, his Lookah-slocker. But this exhibit was bigger than his actual room and it had 360-degree windows like the top floor in a lighthouse.

He brushed his chin with his fingertips, then his chest and stomach. No pain. It would come back for sure, but right now, he considered himself lucky with the *actuality* of his vision.

You know what you gotta do, captain, an all too familiar voice said.

Something was handed to him over his shoulder. Luca wasn't surprised to see the spyglass. He took it, not bothering to look back. He knew whom he would see there. After all, hadn't they collected these treasures together, hauling them across the boulevard and to his house in his wheelbarrow?

He understood now that his finding the spyglass had been no accident, that late December night on the beach.

He hadn't been alone. His dad had been there.

Propelled by a love greater than whatever loss awaited him, Luca gazed out the window that normally overlooked the backyard carp pond and the houses beyond it, but now provided a view of the dunes and the sea. He raised the spyglass and beheld what the sea wanted to show him . . .

. . . but the sea wasn't the only thing that put on a show.

17

Robert Grim realized the vision had started only after it was well under way. Before, he had been writhing in pain. Van Driel's first punch had bruised or broken a rib or two and fostered a breathing sounding like a whistle, but the kick to his left thigh had been the real killer. It shot through his leg like hot acid and instantaneously turned his muscles into stone. Ah, the pain! Moonshine, now more akin to a deadly comet, *sat* on him, bulldozing his face into the concrete and breaking one of the lenses of his glasses. Tiny splinters sliced the bridge of his nose. He was lucky they hadn't pierced his eye.

His injuries were one thing, but the fucker broke his glasses. Without them, he could barely see. It infuriated him.

Then, just like that, he was gone. Grim rolled over, wheezing, instinctively crossing his arms before his face for protection, but there were no further assaults. Even before he carefully pushed his glasses back in place (at which the frame painfully grazed a splinter jotting from his brow) he saw the ceiling panels flicker. There was a loud shriek of electricity, and several tubes exploded in a shower of glass and sparks. Grim looked up and saw through his remaining lens Luca Wolf levitating in the air right in front of him . . . just as a captain's daughter named Jacoba Hopman was said to have done in 1716.

He did it, he thought, ecstatic despite everything. *The kid fucking did it.*

It got darker. A storm was coming. Outside, where the rain still lashed the roof, but inside as well. Everyone saw it, everyone watched. Safiya, bracing herself at his feet, her mouth agape. Barbara, screaming her son's name over and over. Ineke, looking up from her husband's body, her hair fluttering in the growing wind. Even the November-6 ops stared up at Luca and the *Oracle* as if bewitched—and perhaps they were. No longer did they bother with their captives. Van Driel retreated, lurking at Eleanor's side. Everyone shrank back, step by careful step, in a choreography of fear.

Luca, or whatever possessed him, rose above the *Oracle*'s bow and behind him, the ship came to life. The forecastle creaked and bulged. Waves of seawater crashed through the gunwales and cascaded down the ship's flank. Even when it was impossible to see it, Grim knew the waves were erupting from the hatch. After all, the hatch had been a portal to the sea from the beginning.

Was the water real? Or did it just spawn from Luca's vision? Probably, but it sure *seemed* real, because as it reached him, it soaked his clothes, and the cold took his breath away. The briny smell was overwhelming.

Then the Oracle began to speak. Not in English, not in Dutch, but in an older tongue that he understood regardless.

'A *storm shall come,*' it said, and there *was* a storm. Grim saw flashes of swelling clouds over a desolate coastal landscape with flattened marram grass, of whirling planks torn from a boardwalk and the roof of a seaside bar tumbling over a beach hazy with a barrage of rain.

'*And the storm,*' the Oracle spoke, '*shall bring the sea.*'

The sea spoke through the Oracle's mouth, but its voice wasn't Luca's, or even remotely human. And yes, Grim saw the sea. He saw it rise, an endless, swelling surge of raging crests and splashing spume under an ink-black sky. *And it kept rising.* It evoked such atavistic fear that Grim could do nothing but scream. The sea was a living thing. The *Oracle* rose on its swell and started to lean on the verge of crashing down on top of him. Grim tried to scramble back but couldn't.

Then Safiya was there, yelling, 'Come on, Mr. Grim, on your feet! Can you stand?'

That shattered the illusion. Dazed, still sprawled on the hangar floor, he tried to get up. But the sea was there, too. He could see it reflected in Safiya's dark eyes.

'Help me up, will you?' He reached, and Safiya pulled his arm. 'Wait, *ow-ow*, not so fast . . .'

But then he saw the horror that had befallen Luca's tormentor right next to him—the algae were still eating him from the inside out—and Grim got to his feet alright. His left leg hurt like mad and buckled immediately, but Safiya supported him before he could keel over.

'*Your flood barriers shall fail,*' the Oracle spoke, and leaning on the girl, Grim saw how it would unfold. No seaquake, no tsunami, but a disaster of human error. He saw the sea surge into nocturnal rivers, he saw the floodgates of the Delta Works wide open. He saw container ships capsize, he saw ports flooded, he saw levees breaking.

'*There shall be ruin, it shall be sudden, and thousands upon thousands shall perish.*'

He saw it. They all saw it. Flooded polders and towns as far as the eye could see. The skyline of a dark city. And the drowned. Countless drowned, greedily slouched back to the open waters.

A horrific grin spread across Luca's face. '*Unless . . .*' it said with clear contempt, '*unless you give. Give and give in abundance. Give an offer of many.*'

A new flash, and now Grim saw the image that Luca had chronicled to him before: bodies sinking into deep, black water, descending in frozen horror toward whatever lived down there. *And Grim saw it.* Only a split-second, but it was enough to leave a lasting imprint on his soul. In that flash, Grim saw the cod hold, and it brought him to the edge of insanity.

The Oracle raised Luca's fingers in a V, and he grinned, '*Two days.*'

Black, veiny polyps emerged from Luca's mouth and crawled all over him. Luca's levitating body began to shake like a puppet. His eyes rolled back as he produced a stifled moan, and finally Grim recognized the boy's voice again. His face flushed as it dawned on him: *Seed pods. Oh no. Luca's purpose has been fulfilled. The message has been delivered. Now it will dispose of him, as well.*

'*Luca, no-no-no!*' Barbara wailed, but the Luca-thing convulsed in the air, already barely recognizable.

A roaring thunder. Grim's head turned. Everyone's head turned. It came from outside, from the tarmac beyond the airplane doors, as if some enormous thing was fast approaching across the rain-swept field. Grim heard Safiya gasp. Heard the tendons in Eleanor's neck crack. As for himself, he could only watch. Robert Grim had been trained his entire life to act, but he was past that now. Long past.

A metallic bang, and the airplane doors rattled. Yet another, radical atmospheric shift darkened the hangar. A shadow fell across the floor. A ripple shimmered through the steel walls. *Something was here.* Something huge. He couldn't see it yet, but he could feel it. The thickening air. The crackling on his cerebral cortex. The swarming darkness. The roaring, the snorting. And yes, the smell. A feral musk, the way an old travelling circus used to smell, but heavier. Older.

'Over there!' Safiya yelled.

She pointed at the opposite wall. The ripple had etched into a shape. Vague at first, but in a blink of the eye its edges materialized, larger now, as if a quirk of perception not only brought it closer but launched it into reality. Charcoaled outlines, red and ochre coloring—dawning on Hangar 3's partition wall was unmistakably a cave painting of a woolly mammoth.

The animal was drawn in a life-size full frontal. Grim observed its raised shoulders, its fatty hump, its long, curved tusks. He felt the urge to cling to Safiya and run to the best of his ability, because the painting was *charged*, the *air* was charged, ready for the birth of . . .

A titanic crash shook the hangar. From the cave painting exploded the shape of the mammoth's head, suddenly 3D, suddenly *real*, as if the wall were made from latex instead of steel and the animal charged right through it. A shockwave knocked the entire group in disarray. Grim crumpled onto his side. Eleanor tripped into Van Driel. Safiya screamed. Dukakis screamed. Had Grim had the strength, he would have screamed as well. And Luca . . .

The sea was smashed out of him. So were the algae. The boy was now wearing a mammoth skull, his head completely enveloped.

Nunyunnini did not speak to them the way the sea had done, perhaps because his language was beyond their comprehension. But he did sculpt an image into their heads. Robert Grim saw a woolly mammoth—not a cave painting or an imprint or a skull—rising from a stormy sea, magnificent, indomitable, supreme. Mighty waves crashed into its furry legs, but the animal stood unyielding, even when it seemed old and hurt. As they were looking at it, the living, breathing creature passed into a steel, four-legged oil rig. They were one and the same. Grim saw a gaping hole in the industrial complex where an explosion had—

Oh, fuck.

'It's the Mammoth III!' Safiya yelled.

The girl's words struck like lightning.

'It was constantly on the news here!'

Of course. The accident on the rig, last October. The US media had covered the story too, albeit briefly, because . . . well, Europe. But Grim remembered it had been an ecological headache, because, weakened by the explosion, the platform was in danger of collapse before it could be decommissioned.

More importantly: four dead at sea.

Why didn't I see that earlier? In both timelines there was a chain of events triggered by a smaller event on the North Sea. At Doggerland, it was the annual sacrifice they pushed off in a canoe. In the eighteenth century, it was the five sick hands they threw overboard to drown.

'It's been awakened,' Grim uttered. 'That thing from below. Its *hunger* was aroused, and now it's demanding more . . .'

But seeing the Mammoth III, Grim got the intrinsic, incontrovertible conviction that a different answer was possible.

Then the vision was over. Light seeped into view and brought back the real world. The pain returned, hitting Grim's battered body like a rockslide: his thigh, his abdomen, his chest, his head. He coughed and folded. The others were scattered across the floor below the skybridge, forced back against the wall. They all shared the same expression of survivors after a disaster. Van Driel, sickly pale and revenge apparently no longer front of mind, gaped at the barely recognizable blob that once was Jim. Barbara scrambled up from under Glennis, stumbled forward, and kneeled with Safiya by her son, crying.

The sea had let go of Luca, but now that the *Oracle* and the Returned had fulfilled their purpose, their disposal accelerated. Algae infested ship and bodies. The forecastle collapsed. The aluminum footbridge was launched, spraying grates and beams, then crashed onto concrete. Last to go was the stern and its decorated emblem with the now illegible inscription *ORACLE*. It turned gracefully toward them, as if taking a final bow, then slumped into a thick, black mass that stank of sea, sludge, and decay. Barbara dragged Luca away from it, the same time he opened his eyes and gave her a bedazzled look.

The *Oracle* was gone.

Robert Grim turned to Eleanor, who seemed utterly speechless, and said, 'Now will you listen to me?'

18

Eleanor Delveaux heard Glennis call for her but didn't look back as she marched across the skybridge. Her stride was hasty but controlled, but the minute she hit the door to the adjacent offices, she did something neither Glennis nor her staff had ever seen her do. Eleanor ran, as fast as her heels permitted.

She had inhaled it.

The cloud of mold from Alexander's exploded head. The spores of algae. She had *inhaled* it and could still smell it now, as if it had settled inside her windpipe.

Eleanor knew such a thing was possible. She was familiar with *Conidiobolus* infections in West Africa, a fungus found in salamander guts which infiltrated the human body through the nose, dissolved bone, collapsed cheeks, and jellied the face from the inside. With the thermophilic, brain-infecting yeast *Exophilia dermatitidis*, which in East Asia had given twenty healthy youths a sudden headache, after which they all died with a skull full of black goo. She knew that diabetics (and really, everyone taking iron supplements) risked a contagion of *Zygomycetes*; a fungus related to regular bread mold that once trapped inside your bodily iron surplus, necrotized the eye sockets, causing blindness first and death second. And she herself had handled a case of a woman in Amsterdam who had literally gone mad when bathroom mold from her old, damp house had penetrated her prefrontal cortex.

Fungi had the ability to change the human body into broiling vessels of misery. And *this* spore had not only ravaged the bodies of the Returned but possessed them as well.

She slammed open the door to the officer's suite, ran to the sink, clenched it and started to cough up her lungs. With furious, strained abdominal spasms, she expelled the air. Eventually she gave up, not because she thought she had had enough, but because her chest was burning and her throat was raw. She snatched the bottle of Stolichnaya from the mantel, put it to her lips, gargled, spit, gargled some more, and drank. That burned too, but this was a fire she could swallow.

She steadied herself to see a hollow, damp face staring back from the mirror. She tugged her eyelids and rolled her eyes to inspect the white and bloodshot red. Nothing. She examined her mouth, her palate, her throat. Soft tissue the color of liver. Nothing out of the ordinary.

She was herself.

Nothing but herself.

And yet she didn't *feel* like herself.

Countless microorganisms had likely already saturated the mucous membrane of her trachea and embedded themselves deeper down into her alveoli, entering the blood system and spreading all over her body to weave a web of—

Her hand shot up and slapped her face hard. Cut it out. Such thoughts made her *weak*, and she was supposed to stand up against *weakness*. Now more than ever.

You can't change it, said a voice of reason. *Focus on what you can control. That little worm, for instance. He was flying. And that thing that came through the wall. Let's focus on that.*

So the ship had had a purpose after all. She would have to deal with that now. She had misjudged the situation.

Again, the voice nagged.

Another slap and her ears rang. Her cheek burned. Standing up against weakness was one thing; silencing that pesky voice was a win-win.

Her first impulse was still to destroy the entire file, but she now knew that that wouldn't cut it. Amid the chaos following the vision, Grim had explained it to her, but she had barely been able to listen. Besides, the vision had told her all she needed to know. The boy—the Oracle— had channeled it, but it was the sea that made it abundantly clear what was needed.

A sacrifice.

An offer of many, to prevent a greater disaster.

The destroyed city she had seen . . . *that was Rotterdam*.

Eleanor Delveaux had always regarded the supernatural aspects of the *Oracle* with pragmatic detachment, but she had never had a super-natural experience herself. Now that she had, she saw no reason to change her MO. Her escape into anonymity was inevitable because of the Saudi riyals that were certain to be put on her head, but that didn't mean she would allow widespread devastation in the Netherlands. Grim may have accused her of desertion, but he was a fool who didn't understand Al-Jarrah set her up. *She did not desert*. The case was hers, and now that she knew the crux of the matter, it was her responsibility to act. She would disappear, but not without leaving an unblemished record.

So she had to look at what the sea asked of her.

Luca Wolf, for instance. The sea had been about to finish him off, but then that *other* had appeared. The mammoth. An opposite, something clearly *not* sent by the sea, had stood in its way.

That implied that the mammoth was an orchestrating force as well, and that the boy had power. Eleanor didn't understand why this filled her with such tremendous, instinctive fear.

Then, Grim had claimed there might be another way to avert disaster, other than sacrificing innocent people on the North Sea. It had to do with the rig. The doomed Aurora Offshore facility, where the explosion had occurred last year. The Mammoth III.

Something loomed there. Something waited in the heart of that blackened jumble of decks and pumps and pipelines. That, too, filled her with revulsion and the same, inexplicable fear.

If lives could be spared, it was a good thing. So why didn't it *feel* good?

Eleanor listened to the rain. Listened to her heartbeat. The suite had a distant and hostile quality to it, as if she were looking at it through a lens. Her revulsion spread. *Like a fungus*, she thought. Everything felt askew: the desk, the sofa, the faux fireplace, and she at its center. Almost as if, just beyond the cracks of visible reality, it was rocking to the rhythm of . . .

She squeezed her eyes shut. Shook her head. Saw spots when she looked again, but the suite had reestablished itself. She wouldn't allow herself to go wonky. She wouldn't show *weakness*.

At least, there was one silver lining. An hour ago, she got confirmation that Denpasar customs had detained Yvonne Schrootman. Everyone was accounted for. That meant she was pulling the strings again.

The buzzing of her phone shook Eleanor out of her thoughts. A sudden, piercing stab flashed through her head and forced her to shut her eyes again. When she opened them, the pain was gone, and she had the phone in her hand. An internal number. She considered not answering but saw her finger mechanically swipe the touchscreen.

'Hello?'

'Is this Ms. Delveaux of NOVEMBER-6?'

'Speaking.'

'Ah, Volkel Tower here. Listen, RAPCON South just sent a jet with a civilian call sign into our frequency. He's got engine problems and is requesting an emergency landing on 24 right. We wanted to pass him through to Eindhoven, but he says he's unable.'

Eleanor's index finger fidgeted against her phone. 'Why call me?'

'Because he has the same call sign as the jet that came here for you in December. The Saudi Gulfstream. I was wondering if you knew anything about it.'

For two endless seconds, the world turned ashen, and Eleanor Delveaux was in the clutches of such a suffocating panic that she could neither speak nor act. Then she recovered. 'I don't,' she said, feigning control. 'How long?'

'Say what?'

'How long before they land?'

'Eight minutes, give or take.'

So that was it. Al-Jarrah hadn't taken her at face value after all. He hadn't been willing to wait any longer. They were coming. And *of course*, they didn't have engine problems. The audacity to enter foreign military airspace left no doubt that they weren't here on a peace mission.

'So you know nothing about this?' the ATC-guy insisted.

'No, I don't even know if it's the same people. The jet could have been chartered.'

'Okay, just wanted to confirm. Emergency equipment is on its way, but I guess the Lieutenant Colonel is going to have to scramble some units.'

Eleanor felt her face draining. They regarded it as a suspicious flight movement from a dubious state . . . because that's ultimately what it was. 'Please take my advice,' she heard herself say.

'Quickly then. We got work to do.'

So do I, Eleanor thought. *But my time is up.* 'Go unarmed if you want to prevent a massacre.'

'Wait, what—'

Eleanor ended the call before the ATC-guy could finish his sentence. She wasted exactly seven seconds staring into space, then got going. As she did, a new jolt ripped through her brain, infinitely fiercer than the last, and her eyes momentarily rolled back into her head.

Inside the rising and falling obsidian of her mind, she saw but a single thing, like a sparkling gem in a fabric spun of mycelium.

Fly, a voice from the waves said. *You know where . . . and bring the boy.*

When she came to, she found herself running across the skybridge. The stench of algae was unbearable. The bottle of Stolichnaya was in her right hand, bottom up, pouring a trail of vodka in her wake. With her free hand, she yanked the collar of her maxicoat over her nose and mouth.

'Ms. Delveaux!' Glennis stood up from the sore bunch of people at the bottom of the stairs. They were roughly divided into two groups: Van Driel, Dukakis and the three ops from Belladonna Team gathered next to Glennis and some distance away, the kid's mom, the Adan girl, and the widowed Mrs. Hopman, who were tending to Grim's and Wolf's injuries. They were no longer held at gunpoint, but they didn't look like they were going anywhere. Hopman's body had been dragged aside, out of reach of the shapeless, swelling mass that had once been the *Oracle*.

Eleanor flew down the stairs. 'Jerome, Paul, open up the nozzle. I want it ready for total eradication in three minutes. Dukakis, outside. Tell the pilots to be ready for takeoff in five. A death squad is on its way here, and we're the target. No questions, get to work.'

Dukakis stood agape. 'What's going—'

'*I said no questions! Do as I say, right now!*'

They sprang into action. Paul and Jerome rushed to the fuel truck, and tucking his head, Dukakis ran toward the bashed-in door accessing the tarmac.

Time. Oh Jesus, time was flying. She glanced at her phone: 2:38pm. Three minutes since she hung up. *They were coming.*

She had to control her breathing. She couldn't inhale any more of it. Cramming the empty vodka bottle into Van Driel's hand, she said, 'If you have any other ideas about how to detonate, now's the time to speak up.'

Dumbfounded, Van Driel looked at the bottle. 'Eleanor, this is nuts. You'll blow up the whole building. Give me thirty minutes and I'll fix you explosives and a timer.'

'We don't have that kind of time. Get ready.'

'But the shockwave . . .'

'Goddammit, do what I said! We can't leave anything behind!'

Van Driel's look revealed that he had deduced the entire chain of events leading to this very moment. She saw the contempt in it . . . and yet he would obey her. She was, after all, his superior.

She raised her voice. 'Listen, everyone. Glennis and Sita will escort you to the exit. I want you all in the helicopter in three minutes. Follow their instructions. Anyone who doesn't will be executed.'

She saw that Glennis and Sita were unconvinced and sought each other out but decided to ignore them. The infestation in her lungs. It was swirling. Nestling. *Simmering.*

'The way you executed Wim?' Mrs. Hopman scorned. 'You monster!'

She, the monster? The woman must be mistaken. They had all seen who the monster was. It had tusks and thick fur. And yet another monster was on final approach, the runway lights of 24R likely in sight.

Sita started to gather the captives, but Glennis stayed put. 'Diana,' she said softly. 'She's still in Ward C. So is the family of that Noordwijk cop. What are we supposed to do with them? We can't leave Diana . . .'

Van Driel gave a single, squelched laugh. 'I don't think you need to worry about her anymore.'

Glennis shot him a quizzical look. Eleanor wanted to signal to Van Driel that the less she knew the better, but another flash through her brain seemed to herald the end of time, the end of *her* time, at least, and next thing she knew, she was halfway to the door leading to the tarmac. The tarmac, that meant fresh air. She was vaguely alarmed by her loss of time and awareness, but her panic was too suffocating for her to dwell on it.

Jerome and Paul had torn the spore-covered hose loose and opened the nozzle. Pressurized fuel gushed out. They threw the valve into the fermenting, spumy algae that still vaguely resembled the shape of the gurneys it blanketed. Within seconds, the hangar stank like an airport.

Eleanor snatched her umbrella from the floor. Behind her, Ineke Hopman screamed, realizing now her husband was about to get a premature cremation. She waited for the gunshot. It didn't come. It didn't matter.

She burst through the door, welcoming the lashing of the rain. Eleanor gasped for air. Pointing the umbrella before her like a weapon, she peered across the platform. Fifty yards away, the Cougar was waiting, just as the throb of the turbine roared to life. That was good. To the right, in the thick of the woods covering the F-16 shelters, parts of the runway were visible. At its southwest end, she saw the lights of the fire engines flashing in the rain and a whole battalion of MPs. That was not good. Not good at all.

Further on, a siren was wailing.

No plane was yet in sight within the low-hanging clouds, but as she took her phone out, the digits sprang from 2:40 to 2:41. Five missed calls, all Volkel.

'Come on, come on, come on,' she snarled as Glennis and Sita hustled the others outside. Sita had Hopman by the arm, hunched against the rain. The Wolf kid could walk unaided. Grim was supported by Barbara and Adan. Glennis brought up the rear, looking pale and dejected.

'Lemme guess,' Grim said in passing, his face covered in blood. 'Your buddies are here to say *ma'a salama?*'

That would be food for some serious future discussion with the old fart, but no time now. Eleanor popped her head back inside, just as the three men came hurrying toward her. The kerosine fumes were almost suffocating. Van Driel took up Glennis' forgotten umbrella and opened it to protect the fueled-up vodka bottle from the rain. Eleanor recognized Wim Hopman's torn-off shirtsleeve jutting from its neck. Jerome and Paul readied themselves to join the others, but Van Driel called them back and shoved the umbrella and bottle into Paul's hands.

'That's for shooting the old farmer, pal.' He reached inside his pocket and produced a lighter. 'Don't screw it up. You got one chance.'

Paul went pale but did not venture into protest . . . because Van Driel was *his* superior.

'Hey, are those the jokers you were talking about?' Jerome shouted.

Eleanor followed his finger and felt her knees buckle. In the northeast, low above the trees, hovered the landing lights of a plane.

'Wait until we're ready for take-off!' she shouted to Paul. 'Wait until Van Driel gives you the sign!'

Then she ran. The wind yanked at her maxicoat and flipped her umbrella, so she threw it away. Eleanor ran all the way across the tarmac on high heels and reached the transport bird well ahead of Van Driel and Jerome. By the time she had to cower in the blades' downwash, the landing lights had descended behind the row of trees, and she could no longer see the plane. She did see the battalion standing by at the runway's far end. It looked as if all of Volkel had showed up. Good-natured, unsuspecting Dutch Joe's. Not in a million years would they stand a chance against a band of Mabahith on a mission.

She scrambled inside. The Cougar's cabin had five rows of three seats each with a narrow aisle between the second and third. Glennis and Sita had buckled up the others in the rear, given them safety headphones, and sat two rows ahead. Eleanor chose the jump seat on the bulkhead separating the cockpit from the cabin, but before strapping in, she turned and leaned in to pilots Marcel and Patrick, both Air Force. She tapped Marcel on the shoulder. He looked back, removed his headset, and gave her a curt nod.

'Are we ready to roll?' Eleanor shouted over the turbine's noise.

'No ma'am. Tower didn't clear us. They're dealing with an emergency.'

'You asked for clearance?' Eleanor could hardly believe it.

'Well, yes ma'am. Course we did.' He exchanged looks with Patrick, who was listening to their conversation. 'They specifically asked about you. They want me to keep you on the ground.'

'Marcel, listen very carefully. You know I outrank your air traffic controller. You know I outrank Volkel's entire command staff.'

'I know, that's why I'm telling you, but—'

'So I'll ask you one more time. Are we ready to roll?'

'Yes, ma'am.' At that very moment, Eleanor saw two things in unison. She saw them in her head, and her brain connected them as naturally as would a horse that was accustomed to perceiving danger from two sides at once. On the right, she saw the Gulfstream taxying off the runway, where the MP brigade was blocking its way. On the left, another vehicle was approaching, which she recognized as the Lieutenant Colonel's jeep. Marcel nodded toward it. 'I reckon there's someone who has a different take on that.'

Now, Eleanor, a voice said from the deep.

'*Now!*' she yelled over her shoulder. '*Tell him to do it now!*'

Van Driel, who sat at the exit row with Jerome, leaned out and raised an arm. Eleanor turned back into the cockpit and shouted, 'Get ready! On my order!'

'What's our heading, ma'am?'

'Northwest. I'll brief you once we're—' *airborne,* she wanted to say, but the explosion cut her off. The sound was an ongoing grind, like an avalanche rolling down a mountain side. The cabin of the Cougar glared a brilliant orange. It was so bright it made her shudder, but she still turned to look. A black mushroom mounted the sky, triumphantly rising where Maintenance Hangar 3 had been moments earlier. She saw red and orange blisters pop and dissolve in the cloudburst. She saw the remains of the airplane doors and other debris fluttering down on the tarmac. One of the bouncing pieces was Paul. She imagined how he must have chucked the Molotov inside and run as it spun through the air, propelling a smoke trail. Unfortunately for Paul, it had spun through fumes of jet fuel and exploded before he was even thirty feet away.

'*Jesus fucking Christ!*' Patrick hollered, looking back.

In the back, Wolf leaned over Adan toward the window and lipped an obvious *Whoa!*

'*Up!!*' Eleanor squawked.

'Wait! He's still alive!'

Van Driel called it. *Paul was alive.* He swerved like a drunk and collapsed on the tarmac. Obviously hurt, probably unconscious, but alive. The Lieutenant Colonel's jeep was closing in at high speed.

Wailing fire engines were coming their way from the end of the runway. Behind them, the Gulfstream was surrounded on the taxiway.

'*No time! We need to go!*'

The whir of the blades swelled into a mind-riddling *thwop-thwop-thwop*, but Van Driel tore off his seatbelt and declared, '*We leave no man behind!*'

'*Get back here, you idiot!*'

But out he went, splashing through the rain toward the miserable heap that was Paul. Eleanor cursed and slammed the jump seat. A wave of dizziness flushed over her, and she closed her eyes. Spinning before them were black threads of hyphae, swaying on an invisible tide. How easy would it be to just let it carry her away and not have to think anymore?

Another flash, and the next thing she saw was Van Driel dragging Paul into the cabin. His head was bleeding on both sides and he looked severely whacked. Jerome took his arm and hauled him into an unoccupied seat.

'*What the fuck did you people do back there?*' Marcel shouted from the cockpit.

'*Shut up and fly!*' Eleanor yelled.

Van Driel yanked the door shut just as the Cougar lifted off the ground. They hardly swayed, too heavy to be hindered by the wind.

Eleanor staggered, sat, and buckled up. She looked back as the cockpit window revealed the Gulfstream unfolding its airstairs. They turned, and now she saw the jeep reaching the tarmac in front of the burning hangar. That also disappeared as the chopper rose above the treetops. Soon, she found she didn't care what happened down there.

She got away.

The helicopter swerved around the column of smoke and headed northwest through a veil of rain. Eleanor closed her eyes, leaned back and relaxed. None of the others noticed the corners of her mouth slowly pulling into a smile.

It really was much easier to let the blackness behind her eyes guide her.

No one would find them where they were headed.

And as for that little worm Wolf . . . the sea still had a score to settle with him.

INTERMEZZO

OMENS

1

On February 3, storm Dylan made landfall and sent the country into a frenzy. NOS* weatherman Gerrit Hiemstra said it was the strongest Nor'wester in decades. Pushed by a deepening depression slowly passing south-east across the North Sea, it hurled wind speeds up to 11 on the Beaufort scale, occasionally peaking at over a hundred miles an hour. Gusts like that hadn't been recorded since 1973. Offshore wind farms ceased operations and several oil rigs were pulled as a precaution. The coastal defense service reported surges of up to nine feet above Amsterdam Ordnance Datum at the mouth of the Rhine and put levee managers and Rijkswaterstaat† on highest alert. The media sensationalized comparisons with the North Sea flood of 1953, but good old Gerrit Hiemstra, never the Doomsayer, informed the public that over land, Dylan would soon drop down to a 10 and continue to weaken throughout the night. Rest assured; the situation was far different from that disastrous night of yesteryear. The rivers and estuaries may have been at near capacity due to an overflow of meltwater from the Alps, but the storm surge didn't coincide with a spring tide at its peak and fell six inches short of the critical level that would have closed the Maeslant and Oosterschelde barriers.

All's well that ends well.

2

Since time immemorial, a mother and daughter occupied a small house on the Schouwen-Duiveland polder in the coastal province of Zeeland. Marian was eighty-two but still quite able-bodied. Her mother Betsy was a hundred-and-six and wasn't, but she rode around in a power scooter that got around faster than her daughter. She never missed a chance to point this out this to anyone willing to listen. Not many were, these days, but Betsy and Marian were hardened Zeelanders who had endured the flood of '53 and were therefore an indomitable pair. Not to

* NOS is the Dutch broadcasting organization that provides daily tv, radio and online news.
† The Dutch agency for infrastructure and water management.

mention that Marian still considered her mother to be 'right in the head.' Which was why she was surprised to find her fiddling so solemnly with the old leather laces on the afternoon of the 3rd.

'Why don't you quit mucking about with those filthy things, mother?' she asked.

'They're wind laces,' Betsy pondered. 'Got 'em from my grandfather. He was a merchant on the ships, and he got 'em from an old woman in Saeftinghe, which I reckon was drowned land by then. You're s'posed to tie 'em together with three knots. He wanted favorable wind on his trip across the reach. So he untied the first, and a light breeze got up. When he untied the second knot, the breeze turned into a storm. Nearing the port of Breskens, he untied the third, and a hurricane destroyed all the houses on the dyke. Powerful things, these strings.'

Marian dismissed it. 'Mother, that's just superstition.'

'But that's the thing,' Betsy said. 'The wind today, I don't like it one bit. Makes my bones tingle. I've been trying on and on to tie them knots, but they keep coming loose.'

'Don't be a fool. Here, tie them together and give them to me. I'll put them somewhere you can't reach.'

And so, she stashed the laces with her mother's three knots on the kitchen shelf, between the tea pot and the jar of molasses. But at teatime, she found them untied again. Okay, her mother was old and arthritic and probably messed up the knots. Just to be sure (after all, who wasn't at least a *little bit* superstitious?), Marian tied the laces herself, three times using double overhands, pulling them extra tight. Then she put them away in the pocket of her vest. Only after nightfall, when the storm was howling around the roof, did they cross her mind again. But when she took out the laces, the knots were gone.

Marian's mind wandered off to that fateful night of '53, and she felt something she hadn't felt since: fear.

3

And she wasn't alone.

Mehmet Çelik was a dockworker in transit from the Euromax Container Terminal on the Maasvlakte to the mainland. As he felt the storm building from his Audi, he had a sudden hunch to pull over. He climbed the steep embankment, struggling against the wind. When he reached the top, he could barely stand. Normally, a wide beach would stretch before him, but today, the sea came all the way to his feet. It resembled a roaring monster caught in a jarring hymn with the wind. A sense of dread came over him then, harkening back all the way to his childhood, that an Evil Eye was staring at him from the deep. As he hurried back to his car, Mehmet wished he was wearing the blue Nazar his mother had given to him as a boy, to protect him from rack and ruin.

On a farm near Vierpolders, south of Rotterdam, eight-year-old Noah's grandpa sent him out with an empty jar to catch a weather eel in the ditch. It was a story the old man had made up to keep his grandson busy so he could read his newspaper in peace. *Got a weather eel in a bottle, and it's crooked mad, weather's gonna be wicked bad.* Wicked surprised he was when not an hour later, Noah came back with wind-blown hair, a dripping nose, and the jar full of ditch water, in which a sleek, mean-looking eel was bashing its pale body against the glass. He had never seen such a creature, and its aggressive behavior frightened Noah. Eventually, his grandpa went and emptied the jar back into the ditch, when he was nearly struck by a steel sheet that was blown off the shed. Flinching, the old man considered himself lucky, but then he thought he heard a voice coming from the ditch: *You wish, says the fish!*

In the Erasmus MC morgue in downtown Rotterdam, coroner Marga Hakvoort had just completed a postmortem on three new arrivals. Now they were on the autopsy table, ready to be washed and transported to the funeral home. Marga closed their eyes, but when she returned from pee break and put a fresh pair of rubber gloves on, she noticed all three bodies were staring glassy-eyed at the ceiling. Nothing out of the ordinary, rigor mortis would do that. It just *seemed* a little sinister, because it happened to all three of them at the same time. She shut them again, chuckling as she remembered an old wives' tale that if the eyes of the dead remained open, they were looking for the next person to die. Still, an eerie feeling came over her as she washed them, and when she was done, Marga saw their eyes were open once more . . . wide. Driven by a sudden, foreboding fear, she started to pull out the refrigerator racks, and made the terrible discovery that *all* the bodies, frozen or not, had opened their eyes.

In a pigsty in Berkenwoude, east of the city, a panic broke at night-fall among its eight hundred tenants. The farmer would later state that a poorly closed steel door banging in the wind had induced the events, and that the panic had spread from one animal to the next. But the locals doubted this account. The pigs had clambered onto each other in a frenzy. Many were trampled, but the majority managed to roll over their pen's enclosure, only for more to bash their heads into the steel door before the herd broke through it and escaped. They were found scattered across the surrounding fields. Some drowned in a drainage channel, others simply lying dead with a look of profound terror in their eyes. One pig was found tangled high in the air among the branches of a birch, and no one was quite sure how he got there. But there was one thing on which everyone agreed: the pigs had felt something coming that only a premature death could save them from.

By 10pm, Arnout Waldmann, a maintenance inspector with Rijkswaterstaat, trudged along the hinged south-bank pontoon of the Maeslant barrier. The barrier's storm closing was fully automated, so Arnout's job was merely to monitor its operation and adjust it if required. He had to hold tight onto the rail, lest the storm blow him off the slippery gallery like a paper bag. His rain cape lashed at his face. Arnout didn't report any irregularities that night. He didn't report the colossal flock of magpies that suddenly loomed in the light of his torch, perched on the white steel truss as if the wind were nothing to them. That was strange enough, yet more uncanny was that they all sat with their backs to him, no matter how loud he banged on the beams to shoo them away. It made Arnout sick to his stomach, because as a little boy, he had been told that if magpies turned their backs at you, it was an omen of a great, unholy event to come.

And at eleven that night, as the wind blew unabated, a short break in the clouds over the west of the country revealed pale stars and a watery moon. It was during this time that a bright spark briefly lit up the northwestern sky. Soon, the first dashcam and security footage appeared online: scenes of streets illuminated as if it were daytime, followed by a fireball flashing a tail across the sky. #Meteorite, #falling-star and #ufo were trending. Someone tweeted, *It was bound to happen. The apocalypse has commenced in Rotterdam.*

Because everyone knew what a comet meant.

4

As February 4 dawned on the eastern horizon, the worst of storm Dylan was over. From across the coastal provinces and along the southern border came reports of damaged roofs, ripped fences, and torn out trees. At Every Man's End in Noordwijk, not far from where Luca Wolf and Emma Reich had first discovered the *Oracle*, greenhouses where shattered by flying debris. A man from the town of Kaatsheuvel who had ignored warnings to stay inside, was killed when a giant oak fell on his Volkswagen. There were power outages in the city of Breda, the glass façade of the Winkelhof shopping mall in Leiderdorp was blown off, a crane had toppled onto a Rotterdam office building, and trains came to a halt everywhere. But the dreaded flood didn't materialize. The levees had held.

It was around the time that people were finishing their morning coffee, that they realized it had only been the calm before the storm.

Meteorologists shifted their attention to a new, quickly intensifying depression south of Iceland, in the wake of which developed an even more powerful storm system named Ellen. By the time it passed the Faroe Islands and reached the Scottish isles, it was producing insane wind speeds. An average of 107 miles per hour was recorded between 6am and 6pm over the northern reaches of the North Sea. That afternoon, the NOS aired ongoing updates on distress signals from fishing ships, an entire forest swept away on the Sottish coast, and the protocols for the unprecedented closing of the Delta Works' surge barriers.

But the real sucker punch came when the isobars on Gerrit Hiemstra's weather map were so tightly jammed together that his voice caught live on air, and he was heard speculating that it must be a mistake. But it wasn't. So when viewers saw the color drain from Gerrit's face and heard him utter the word 'superstorm'—yeah, that's when everyone got a little scared.

5

TEMPEST

1

Hyped with adrenaline after what happened at Volkel, Luca would have bet on no sleep for the next couple months. Airborne, however, he was disturbed to find himself constantly zoning out. He tried to fight it. Cling on to whatever sensory stimuli available: the throbbing of the blades, the pain from Jim's beating, the chopper bouncing in unstable air. Anything to stop him from returning to that reduced state of consciousness, where who knows what awaited.

Luca was sick of visions.

Everyone—his mom, Safiya, Grim, Glennis, Dukakis—had gathered around him like he was the messiah or something. No, he preferred Van Driel's attitude, who looked at him like he was a nasty spider and stayed the fuck away.

Talking about it hadn't put it to rest. Instead, it had crawled under his skin, like an itch just beyond his reach, one that could only be relieved by doing what was expected of him: going there. To the rig. To the Mammoth III.

That's what Nunyunnini had told him.

Next thing, they were suddenly on the run. From what? Luca didn't know, but it frightened him. It was Ms. Delveaux. The itch under his skin had become unbearable the moment he saw her.

'There's something wrong with her,' he had whispered to Safiya. 'I don't think she's right at all.'

'Duh . . .' Safiya gestured around. 'Everything's going to hell.' She was right. The *Oracle* was no more. What remained looked like some shapeless, extra-terrestrial life-form. Growing. Festering. Spawning fungi and polyps and all kinds of squirming sea worms. 'That stuff crawled inside her. In me as well, Luca. It's crawled inside all of us . . .'

Her hand slithered around his wrist, but it wasn't a hand. It was a bundle of black tentacles with suckers biting into his skin. He turned to her. Her name died on his lips, as from her grin, fibrils shot out at him . . .

Luca woke with a start and barely stifled a scream. Safiya, to his right, gave him an odd look. All around him was the monotonous throbbing of the turbine, muffled by his headset. Still, his relief was short-lived. The itch was still there. So was the feeling that things were *wrong*.

He was seated in the rear and had a clear overview of the surprisingly large cabin. Safiya was at the window next to him. Across the aisle his mom dozed, her sagging face the ashen color of the clouds. Robert Grim was one row ahead, Mrs. Hopman ahead of his mom. All wore headphones. Conversation was possible if you took them off, but you had to lean into each other and shout to be heard. So they didn't.

Further ahead, Sita was attending to Mr. Hopman's killer. When they hauled him in, he had been bleeding like a stuck pig, and Luca was glad the seats were shielding him from the view. Glennis was alone in second row with no trace of her trademark ice-queen smile. Occasionally she would lean toward the front, where Van Driel, Dukakis, and Jerome had gathered around Eleanor. This was now NOVEMBER-6's makeshift command center.

Safiya tapped his ear protectors, and he took them off. 'Are you okay?' she asked, so close that her breath tickled his ear.

He nodded and she snuggled up against him, so he could smell her hair. Their soaked coats were heavy and cold, but Luca felt her warmth radiating through them. He put his arm around her, and so they sat until Glennis came over, a while later.

She gestured for Grim to scoot to the window and buckled up next to him. Leaning across the aisle, she tapped his mom, who awoke with a start. Her face darkened, but she lowered her headphones and leaned in, as did Grim, Safiya and Luca. The only one who was still staring out the window was Mrs. Hopman.

'I can't undo what went down back there,' Glennis shouted to them over the turbine's throb, articulating slowly for clarity. 'We were facing an unprecedented situation and did what seemed right.'

'If this is your introduction to an apology, you're way off course,' his mom called back. Luca was startled by her tone. She was never this bitter.

'I'm not here to apologize, Barbara. I don't expect you to like us either. Homeland security has always been NOVEMBER-6's priority. After what we saw in the hangar, we understand our need to act.'

'What's your priority, Glennis?' Grim asked. 'How long will you follow her around like a goddamn chihuahua while she takes us all down? That's not very American.'

'The Netherlands is our close ally,' she said perfunctorily, but Luca was of the impression she no longer believed that argument held any water. 'We assist our allies, and I take a pragmatic look at what's required to get the job done. Right now, that's your insights.'

'Here's an insight for you,' Grim said. 'Tell Eleanor that if she had listened to us before, a whole lot of people would still be alive. Including that poor woman's husband.'

Glennis surprised them all. 'You may be right. And I'll support an investigation into the matter. But right now, we need—'

'Why did we have to leave so suddenly?' Safiya interrupted her.

'There was a leak.' Her answer came a fraction too late to sound truthful, and Luca thought, *She's being lied to and she knows it.* Still, she straightened herself and continued, 'But our imperative is to accommodate you, Luca. You said you needed to get to the Mammoth III. So we're taking you there.'

'Seriously?' He exchanged glances with Grim.

'Yes. We believe there's truth to what you showed us. It's our prerogative to prevent that disaster and if we can do so without casualties, it's a win-win. There's been enough human sacrifice already. But Luca, what happens when we get there? What's the plan?'

He hesitated. Again, all eyes were on him. 'I don't know. I just know there's a mammoth skull there somewhere. I think it's the same skull the Doggerland Oracle used to summon Nunyunnini. That's why it's so powerful. It's calling me.'

'Okay. We'll be picking up someone who's been on the rig before. Hopefully he can guide you.'

'Is it even safe to go there in this storm?' Barbara asked.

'Our expert will be the judge of that too. Luca, if the skull is there, and if you find it . . . what then?'

He shook his head. 'I really don't know. All I know is that I need to go there.'

She nodded and got up from her seat, but Luca called to her. She looked back and leaned in again.

'That boss of yours. Ms. Delveaux. There's something wrong with her.'

'What do you mean?' Glennis sounded unmoved, but he was pretty sure he saw her stiffen.

'I don't know. It wasn't there before. In the hangar, I mean. But when she came back and said we needed to leave, it was. I don't know what it is, but I know she's not okay. The same way I know we need to get to the rig.' He hesitated. 'I think she's dangerous now.'

Glennis gave no show of emotion and turned. He called her name again. Again, she looked back.

'Please don't tell her I said anything.'

This time there was no doubt in his mind that she nodded. Right? There was something wrong with Glennis, too. Not the same kind of wrong as Ms. Delveaux, but something was brewing beyond that steel face of hers, and Luca found it impossible to read her. He had no choice but to trust her. At least, she was taking him to the rig. She wanted to *accommodate* him, she had said. But how?

Grim raised his eyebrows and shrugged, then sat back, putting his headphones on. So did Safiya. His mom leaned toward him, so close she could kiss his ear, and asked, 'Will we be okay, Luca?'

How should I know? he wanted to shout, but he didn't. He gave her the most comforting smile he could muster. 'We'll be okay, mom.'

But that felt like a lie.

2

When the ginger guy in the orange coverall saw the passengers in the back, he knew something was wrong. Grim saw the transition on his face from a cursory how-do-you-do to surprise to shock when he realized that not only were they non-service members but there were wounded and children among them. The man made a U-turn in the aisle, only to find himself staring straight into the barrel of Van Driel's Glock. He raised his hands, retreated, and bumped into Eleanor, who had been in the jump seat the entire time.

His name was Vincent Becker, and they picked him up in Den Helder*. Glennis had briefed them while they waited for him to be extracted. 'He's an inspector for Aurora Offshore, the company that owned the Mammoth III at the time of the accident.'

Dukakis had pulled his name from the damage report. The site of the rig too, which turned out to be 165 miles northwest of Den Helder in a shallow on the Dutch Continental Shelf called—drumroll, please—Dogger Bank.

'I'll be damned,' was Grim's comment. Dogger Bank apparently was a moraine deposit dating back to the last ice age, likely the last piece of Doggerland before the North Sea swallowed it up 8,200 years ago. As coincidence would have it, Becker had just returned from an inspection flight to the Mammoth III to gauge whether it could survive the storm. He had left the airport, but one phone call from higher up, and he was intercepted on the highway. Grim wondered what BS they had sold him. Not enough for what he found onboard.

'Whoa, whoa, whoa, what are you doing?' he shouted in an unmistakable British twang to the man with the Glock.

---

* Den Helder is a coastal city and home of the Netherlands Offshore Aviation Mainport

'Ah, Mr. Becker, welcome aboard,' Eleanor said. 'Marco, put the gun away. Our guest has safely boarded.'

'What's going on here? Who are you people?'

'Eleanor Delveaux, General Intelligence. I apologize for the fuss, but time is of the essence, we don't want to land on the rig after dark. Sita, arm the slides, please. Marcel, Patrick, we're taking off.'

Grim was stunned by her openness. During the layover, she had been unusually fazed. She had stared into space, every now and then jerking up as from a dream. Grim wasn't sure whether it was merely a reaction to losing her control of the situation or something more serious, as the kid had suggested.

'Wait, you want to land there?' Becker looked around with a heated face. 'You can't land on the rig! The whole thing is on the verge of collapse. It's too dangerous!'

'Then we'll have to be quick about it, won't we? Glennis, would you mind relinquishing your seat to our guide?'

Glennis gladly complied and slid back a row, and Grim thought, *She can feel it too. She knows something's wrong.*

Eleanor gestured courteously to the vacated seat.

'No way,' Becker protested. 'It violates all safety standards. And you have *children* on board, for God's sake. I refuse to be part of this.' He turned to Sita, who had shut the door and was now blocking it with Van Driel. 'Let me out!'

'Sit down, motherfucker,' Van Driel said.

With rising panic, Becker addressed Eleanor again. 'Why won't you listen? Landing at sea is impossible today, your pilots will tell you the same. Wind speeds are far beyond the maximum—'

In a split-second, Eleanor was in front of him; so suddenly that Becker flinched. Grim hadn't even seen her get up and was convinced none of the others had either. The look she gave Becker was frightening, but what she said was more frightening still: 'The storm doesn't decide if we land. I do.'

No one budged. The only sounds were the pouring rain and the blustering storm. Then the turbine revolved to life. It ended the moment, but Grim was left deeply disturbed. The reason was Eleanor ... but Becker too. The inspector seemed genuinely afraid for his life at the prospect of landing on the Mammoth, and that put the entire operation in a different light.

Eleanor retreated back to her seat, and Van Driel ordered Becker to take his. This time, he didn't protest. The guard dog barked something unintelligible, at which Becker reluctantly handed over his phone.

Grim took advantage of the diversion to quickly move up a row, putting him across the aisle from Glennis. He felt her staring but avoided her gaze.

Hazes of rain washed away the airport below as they rose into angry clouds. The Cougar instantly hit rough air. A sickening swerve-drop bounced Grim's stomach in his throat. He closed his eyes and focused on his breathing. It didn't help. A few minutes later, he dared look out the window and saw they were practically skimming the waves at less than a hundred feet.

He turned away. Looked back. Saw the boy staring past him, straight at Eleanor. Barbara was beyond pale, looking airsick. Ineke had hardly moved and was staring out the window.

Glennis got up, staggered to the front, and conferred with Van Driel. Came back, tapped Becker on the shoulder, and conferred with him. Not masking his reluctance, the inspector rose from his seat and followed her to the back, where they huddled together in the aisle.

'We need to discuss what to do after we land,' Glennis said. 'Grim, I think you should lead.'

He nodded. 'Mr. Becker, I understand? Robert Grim. Let's get this straight: I'm not part of the scum in first class.'

'I figured as much,' Becker said. 'And by the looks of your face, you haven't exactly followed orders.'

'You don't know half of it.'

'Don't I? This is a kidnapping! They said they're general intelligence and wanted to see the Mammoth on a state security matter. I thought it was related to the lawsuit. Nobody said anything about landing there. What's going on? I mean, who *are* these people?'

Grim and Glennis exchanged looks. 'General intelligence is sort of right,' said Grim, 'but that's not the full story. I'm a researcher. I don't approve of their methods, but we *are* on the same mission. And your help is certainly welcome. I'm afraid we must visit the Mammoth III, and you're the only one here who knows your way around.'

'You're working with these knuckleheads? You're an American.'

'Yes, and I apologize for that. But no, I'm not working with them. We've made an important discovery, and they're the executive branch that finally started listening to us.'

Becker shot a glance at Luca and Safiya and shook his head. 'This is madness.'

'It is. Earlier, I overheard you say we can't land there with this storm. Did you mean that literally, or under normal circumstances?' Making air quotes. 'I'm asking because our mission may outweigh the risks. We could be saving hundreds if not thousands of lives.'

Becker shook his head in helpless amazement. 'Listen. This bird is the most technologically advanced piece of equipment there is. It's designed to function in extreme conditions, but even it must obey the laws of physics. The limit for a safe landing on a rig is sixty knots. That's 11 on the scale, which is where we are now. But the wind gusts are off the charts today, and they're the real killers. And that's *before* we disembark. The safety limit for people on a helideck is a 10. You're on the highest point of the platform, completely exposed. You'll literally get blown away. You *will* die if you put us down there. Why would you possibly want that?'

'Robert, this is insanity,' Barbara said. 'He's right. I don't want Luca and Safiya anywhere near that thing. Can't we wait for the storm to die?'

'It won't,' Luca protested. 'Not before it's too late.'

Becker shook his head again. 'I don't know what this is about, but you're right, ma'am. I have children too, and I wouldn't even bring them onto an operational rig with zero wind. This platform is falling apart, and chances are it won't even survive the night. Why take this risk?'

Grim turned from Becker to the boy and said, 'Luca here has a question for you about that.'

Luca, looking solemn, leaned forward. 'Mr. Becker, you went there after the accident, right?'

'Yes, I did.'

'Somewhere on the rig is the skull of a mammoth. Do you know where it is?'

'How do you . . . how the hell do you know that?'

So it's true, Grim thought. *The last piece of the puzzle.*

'I saw it.'

'You talked to the maintenance crew? Or Naturalis? They're the only ones who know about it.'

Luca, Safiya, Barbara, Grim and even Glennis shook their heads in unison. Becker's expression was fascinating to watch. Funny even.

'How did the skull get on board?' Luca asked.

'Divers found it last October on the seabed during an inspection of the tanks. I wasn't part of the crew then; the platform was awaiting decommissioning, and only a handful of men were kept on for maintenance. The chief told me about it later. We often find bones on the sea floor, so it's not so unusual, but the chief said they'd never seen a skull in such pristine condition. So they fished it up for the museum. But then the accident happened, and it stayed where it was.'

'Where?' Grim asked.

'Why is that so important?'

Because an Elder God will speak through it and tell this little boy over here how to prevent a huge human sacrifice to the Seven Seas of Rhye, Grim thought.

'It's complicated.'

'Like I said, this is madness. They wrapped it in plastic and palleted it at the bottom of one of the stairwells. It's impossible to get there. The explosion blew a giant hole in the tower and Stairwell C pretty much collapsed. I saw it for myself during the damage inspection.'

'But still you went there,' Luca suddenly said. 'You saw the skull. Because you were curious. Did something strange happen? Did you touch it?'

Becker blanched.

'Did Nunyunnini speak to you?'

Now he winced. 'What's going on here?'

'I take that as a yes,' Grim said. 'Mr. Becker, you're not alone. We've *all* seen stranger things. But here's my question: can you get us down Stairwell C?'

'I . . . I don't know . . .' The inspector got up and without another word, staggered back to his seat. He shrank down, buckled up, and stared ahead. For Grim, it triggered a sense of déjà vu. He had seen countless reactions like Becker's back in Black Spring, each time it was his turn for bad-news talks with new residents. Truth was people got predictable the minute you pulled reality out from under their feet. Clamming up was first. Here was a man who had only been able to move on from his supernatural experience by bottling it up and dismissing it as a fantasy, only to discover now that it had really happened. Such things needed time. Eventually they all wanted to talk.

'So, Stairwell C,' Grim chirped.

Barbara wasn't convinced. 'I'm telling you, if he says it's too dangerous for the children—'

'Mom . . .'

'Barbara, these aren't normal circumstances,' Glennis said. 'But we're not going to endanger Luca, because we know he's the center-piece in all of this. We'll let the pilots decide if it's safe to land and take it from there.' She got up. 'I'll discuss it with them.'

They flew on.

One row ahead, Paul's condition was dire. During the first leg of the flight, they had bandaged his bloody head and thigh. He had seemed okay (okayish), refusing to get off at Den Helder, but now he appeared to have gone into hypovolemic shock after all. He was slumped across two seats, and Sita and Dukakis were tending to him. Across the aisle, Vincent Becker looked away. For the first time, Grim saw a change in Ineke. She watched with icy satisfaction as the legs of her husband's murderer twitched.

Glennis returned to her seat, looking pale and worn. Eleanor was still staring out the window at the sea. Grim found it difficult to look at her. Yes, there really was something wrong. Her eyes revealed nothing, no compassion, no curiosity. Only eerie concentration.

When he couldn't control his nerves any longer, he leaned across the aisle and tapped Glennis on the shoulder. She took off her headphones.

'I'm worried,' he said. 'About what the kid said. About her.'

Glennis nodded. 'I know. She ordered the pilots to turn off the transponder and data communication, which means ATC cannot detect us. And did you notice how low we're flying?'

'Yes, I did.'

'That means we're under the radar. We basically disappeared when we took off from Den Helder. No one knows where we are.'

Grim's mouth went dry. 'So it's a hijack.'

'The pilots are following her orders; she has that authority. But yes, that's the gist of it. As long as we're headed for the rig, I guess we're okay, but . . .'

He cursed. 'We're not. I don't know her game, but she's not on the same page as we are. The kid's right. There's something terribly wrong.'

'I can't talk too long. Van Driel wants radio silence, and he's loyal to her.'

'If only we knew what's up with her.' He mulled it over. 'Her superior. She's left a holy mess at Volkel. We both know there's a planeload of Saudi commandos on the runway. Not to mention she blew up the hangar. When will they start doubting her judgement?'

'Oh, she lost them with the Bellingcat story and the Yamani connection, but if the Saudis are really there, it will shred any last doubts that she's gone rogue.'

'That's what I'm saying. So why weren't we intercepted by F-16s on the way to Den Helder?'

'Because she anticipated all of it. There's a code she can text in case of emergency to her contact at the ministry. It's basically a stand-down order and means something like, everything a-okay, we'll clean up and contact you as soon as it's safe. Maybe that bought her some time. But that ran out the minute we disappeared from radar. They'll think we either crashed or there was foul play.'

'Goddammit. We're a needle in a haystack out here. And the storm isn't making things any easier. Fucking witch.'

Eleanor suddenly turned her head, and Glennis and Grim shrank back in their seats. But she wasn't looking at them. She seemed to be looking *through* them.

Grim took the cue and leaned toward Glennis. 'Isn't there anything we can do? You have a gun, right?'

'Too dangerous. Van Driel.'

'Any chance we can get Jerome or Sita on our side? They're sturdy. I mean, don't they feel something's wrong, too?'

'They probably do, but they're military. They're trained to follow orders, even to die for them if need be.'

'What caused *you* to come around, Glennis? What happened?'

Grim wasn't convinced she would answer, but before he could find out, Van Driel stood up. 'Tea party's over,' he shouted. 'Asses in your seats. Boss's orders.'

Glennis sat up and gave Van Driel a curt nod. Grim did as he was told and moved back to the rear. He put on his headphones and watched Van Driel return to his seat.

Something terrible is going to happen. And there's nothing you can do.

Outside, the gloom of the sea and the clouds had changed. The light had started to fade and visibility along with it. Soon, the sea would become a black, living darkness.

More déjà vu, this time of his final days in Black Spring.

You'll never forget, will you? No, you'll remember it till the day you die. Just before everything went wrong. It was in the air, foreboding and palpable. Like the charged atmosphere before a thunderstorm. It raised the hair on your arms, it prickled your nerves. The woodland critters felt it too and scurried away into their holes. The bigger animals went berserk. The sheep at Ackerman's Corner. The Grants' horses.

Grim couldn't shake it. He wished they had never come here. Even so, he understood the greatest danger loomed not out there, not on the rig, not in the storm . . . but *here*, aboard this helicopter.

Her hands. There was something wrong with her hands.

They were resting on the hem of her maxicoat, the fingers bony and contorted. Grim tried to focus but couldn't with only one remaining lens in his glasses.

Something wrong with her hands.

She was staring, staring. And suddenly it hit him she wasn't just staring into space. *She was staring at Luca.* Barbara noticed it too and shifted in her seat, eyes wide, face flushed. Grim looked back to see an ashen Luca. Poor Safiya was at a loss, unable to deal with his terror.

The Cougar jolted. Eleanor's scarecrow body shook, and her hands shifted.

That's when Grim saw it.

Algae were growing on her maxicoat.

Precisely where her fingers had been. Her palms. Black, grubby smudges in a glaring contrast to the red fabric.

Evil begets evil, Grim thought. *Of course, you always knew that. How could you have been so blind?*

His mouth opened. He pulled off his headphones. He heard the throbbing of the turbine dwindling. Heard Luca moaning. They were flying slower now.

Do something. Before it's too late.

Grim reached with one hand over the seat in front of him and hoisted himself up. Glennis looked at him, startled. Eleanor too unbuckled and rose. The Cougar swerved, and in front of the cockpit window a massive industrial complex loomed up out of the leaden twilight. Not beneath them, in front of them.

With its four legs and the tall, blackened structure of the accommodation tower, it looked just like a mammoth.

3

Barbara had never been this scared before, and it was all because of Eleanor Delveaux.

There's something wrong with her, Luca had said. *I think she's dangerous now.*

Oh yes, she was. Barbara didn't need a sixth sense to know that was true.

Those ghastly steel eyes wouldn't let go of her son. They revealed fear, but hunger too. They *preyed* on him. They were the eyes of a predator that didn't attack—not yet—because it respected its kill. Except they were trapped inside the same cage with that predator.

If she acted now, they had nowhere to go.

Luca knew it too. He was frantic, and there was nothing Barbara could do to put him at ease. That was the worst part.

'Why is she *staring* at me like that?' he moaned as yet another drop of the chopper nearly threw him into her lap. He was clearly trying to

act brave for Safiya, but she was his mom, and she knew he was on the
verge of tears.

'I don't know, sweetheart.' Squeezing his hand. 'I won't let anything
happen to you, you hear me?'

But what could she do? She imagined a mother doe jumping in front
of her fawn as the lioness attacked. What good would it do? She tried
to convince herself it was ridiculous to imagine Eleanor as some superhuman creature targeting her son. She refused to believe anything like
that . . . but she *did*.

I think she's dangerous now.

The Barbara of three days ago would have waved off such foolish
premonitions. But she was wiser now, and her deep-rooted resistance to
the irrational lay shattered.

A new and terrible thought crossed her mind. *Maybe she wants the
flood to come. Maybe she doesn't care about the casualties. The flood will
deflect attention and erase her tracks. Maybe she doesn't want the Oracle's
message to reach the authorities . . . because she doesn't want a sacrifice to
be made.*

Barbara couldn't move. The skin on her back was crawling.

She's going to make us all disappear.

Robert Grim rose from his seat, his gaze fixed on Eleanor. Eleanor
got up too. The Cougar swerved, and that's when Luca started to
scream. His eyes were bulging. His feet were kicking the floor, and he
squirmed like a worm on a hook.

'Her eyes! *Mom, her eyes! She's just like Dad! Look at her, Mom! She's
just like Dad!'*

All heads turned: Ineke, Glennis, Becker, Van Driel. Instinctively,
Barbara rose and stood in front of Luca. She saw the others, saw their
pallid faces, and sought out Eleanor, who turned to the cockpit, gun in
hand.

Her maxicoat was stained from her shoulders to her rear. Barbara
didn't quite understand what she was looking at. A second later she
did, and terror struck.

The jump seat was teeming with algae.

Then Grim blocked her view when he grabbed Glennis' shoulder
and yelled something. Startled, Glennis looked to the front, where Van
Driel jumped out of his seat and barked, '*Sit down and strap in, dammit!*'

In the rear, Safiya scrambled over Luca and pushed him into her seat
in the far corner of the cabin. His eyes darted, searching between backrests, but couldn't see anything as Safiya was shielding him. Barbara
could have kissed her.

Van Driel's order went unanswered. The helicopter swerved again, then climbed steeply, causing all in the aisle to sway to the right. Arms flailed. Barbara then saw the rig fill all the windows on the starboard side, and the sight of it took her breath away. God, it was immense! A cluster of decks, frames, cranes, and pipes veiled by a haze of horizontal rain and foaming seawater. The explosion had ripped a giant hole through its heart, and the sense of desolation oozing out of it impacted her profoundly. This was no place for life. It was a place of extremes. More terrifying still was that its scale brought home the immensity of the swells ravaging its legs. Coal-colored surges rolled in one after another, towering ruthlessly, spraying swirls of spume. Barbara even imagined she could hear their thunder above the Cougar's throbbing engines.

Screams from the front. The pilots. Glennis shouted to Van Driel, who looked over his shoulder. The green octagon of the helideck swung in and out of sight beyond the starboard windows, topping what looked like a high-rise destroyed by fire. A yellow circle, centered with a white H. Yellow letters spelling MAMMOTH III. A red-and-white windsock, whipping from a bent and twisted aluminum pole. The storm was presenting the pilots with the challenge of a lifetime.

'Sit down!' Van Driel roared again, but Becker did no such thing. He grabbed him by the collar, and Barbara could hear his pleas.

'Please, tell her to abort! I'm married! I have children!'

A violent jolt, and Grim was thrown back into his seat. Glennis yelped as she smacked into the row of seats to the right of the aisle. Safiya yelped too when she tumbled on top of Luca in the rear. Barbara stayed up by pure chance, bracing herself between two backrests. She sat, fastened her seatbelt, and yelled to Safiya and Luca to do the same.

More screams from the cockpit. Van Driel scrambled to the front, steadied himself against the bulkhead, and looked indecisively at Eleanor, who was apparently unaffected by the turbulence.

The chopper started to climb but dipped again to even louder screams from the cockpit. The cause was instantly clear: Eleanor had put her gun to one of the pilot's heads.

'Stop her, you idiot!' Becker roared.

Van Driel stared at her, failing to act. He too had pulled his gun but seemed frozen. None of Eleanor's people acted: Dukakis, Jerome, and Sita were all bewildered witnesses. The gravity of the situation hadn't landed. She was their chief. True, she may be holding the pilots at gunpoint, but that was because *they* had deserted. Not Eleanor.

The pilots attempted a new approach. Barbara saw water whirling off the helideck in the downwash. Saw the landing lights reflected. Thirty feet. Twenty. Suddenly the cabin jerked to the left. Green filled the windows. All screamed. *Barbara* screamed. Did she see sparks fly as the blades scraped the steel, or did she merely imagine it?

They lurched back into position with a dull thud as the Cougar's wheels hit the platform. They bounced, rotated somewhat, and suddenly steadied.

They had landed. Alive.

Eleanor turned around and everyone in the front recoiled, even Van Driel. Dukakis stumbled backward through the aisle and landed on his rear. It was now so dark that Barbara could barely see what was happening, but she could see Eleanor, alright.

She was bigger. Eleanor now filled up the entire front of the cabin, head bent, arms and shoulders crooked against the ceiling. It *must* be an optical illusion. But what of her hands? Her fingers couldn't possibly have grown, but they certainly *seemed* longer than before. Longer and drooping. All kinds of nastiness grew on the webbings between them. Her eyes were dark smudges.

Barbara blinked, and upon second glance, Eleanor had shrunk back to normality. No need to stoop. She must have misjudged her dimensions. An optical illusion after all. But . . .

I'm going crazy.

Eleanor shouted something unintelligible to Jerome, who tried the handle of the exit door. He barely flipped it when the wind ripped it from his hands and yanked the door open. The roar of the blades and the wind bashed inside, penetrating every pore of Barbara's body. Everything was whirling, spinning, screaming *away from here*, but still Jerome clung to the grip above the exit and stuck his head outside. It was like sticking his head into a wind tunnel. With considerable effort he pulled himself back in and shook his head *no*, shook *impossible*, but then Eleanor shoved him so hard he lost his footing and fell backward out of the helicopter.

Barbara saw him hit the deck beneath the Cougar's steel boarding step. She saw him bounce as the wind took hold and swept him across the platform, past Luca's window and away. She couldn't believe it, but she saw it.

She also saw Eleanor swell again.

She was *liquifying*.

And Barbara thought the waves surging below the rig.

Panic erupted. They all knew there had been nothing at the edge of the deck to stop Jerome. Nothing but an eighty-yard drop to the sea below. Dukakis and Becker stumbled backward through the aisle, screaming. Sita, blocked by Paul's sprawling unconscious body, scrambled over the seats behind her to get away from Eleanor. Van Driel, closest to her, recoiled into the corner against the bulkhead, and seemed to have completely forgotten about his gun.

With a jolt, the Cougar lifted back into the air. Unaware of what was happening in the cabin, the pilots had apparently decided they were safer airborne than exposed to the gusts on the rig. It would be the biggest mistake of their career. Furious, Eleanor whirled on her heels and fired three times. The gunshots rang out in the confined space like whipcracks.

What followed was utter mayhem. Barbara saw the pilot on the right smack into the controls. The other roared not to shoot and brought them down again. This time, they hit the platform with much greater force. Barbara was thrown aside and hit her head. People tumbled. People screamed. *Luca* screamed. She could hear him. Now Barbara fought. Grim, Becker, Safiya. They were blocking her way. She had to get to Luca. Had to reach her son . . .

It happened in the blink of an eye.

Eleanor Delveaux had been at the other end of the cabin, *but now she was here too. Liquified.* Her arms stretched, her moldy fingers spread and mineralized like the legs of a king crab. She crashed through the cabin like a wave. She was here. She was there. She was everywhere. Barbara saw the hunger on the floating face above her, the face of the sea, as her hands closed around Luca's shoulders. She saw the black craquelure of algae immediately spreading under her fingers onto his hoodie. She saw the madness on the faces of Safiya, Glennis and Grim. And she heard Luca's scream.

He didn't stand a chance. Eleanor surged back, snapping his seatbelt like a rubber band and dragging him along across the rows of seats. Barbara heard her triumphant shriek. One more flash, the face of her son, a mask of sheer terror, and then Eleanor disappeared with him through the exit door.

Barbara screamed. She couldn't stop screaming.

She flung herself forward. Was caught by Grim and Glennis. Yanked herself free. Crashing onto the next row, she reached a window in time to see an unbelievable vision, an impossible vision: *Eleanor crossed the helideck as if the storm couldn't touch her.* And why not? Wasn't the sea always stronger than the storm? Humanity had been knocked out of that body. And in those drooping, crooked limbs she carried Luca.

She reached the edge of the helideck and flowed down the stairs to the lower levels.

Luca was gone.

4

Robert Grim saw what happened to Luca. He was just in time to grab Barbara by the waist, preventing her from jumping after him and saving her from a fate similar to Jerome's.

She fought him. Barbara Wolf was hysterical and fought with the strength of the insane. 'She took my son! *She took my son!* Let me go, we have to go after him!'

'And we *will*. But not alone. You won't help Luca if you get yourself killed.'

'But she took my son!'

'I saw that, Barbara.'

'That monster took Luca!' Barbara's voice cracked, and she started to cry. With two nods, Grim instructed Safiya and Glennis to tend to her. The girl was in tears but more than willing to be told what to do. Glennis, whose preconceptions about the ways of the world had deeper roots, appeared in greater shock.

Grim himself felt strangely elated. In the realms of pandemonium, for the first time he felt like he was on familiar ground. This too was déjà vu. The exhilaration of the split-second decision in the face of danger, of maintaining order and securing safety where others neglected it. This was his life. Besides, the long haul had done wonders for his body. Sure, his ribs hurt when he breathed, and the cuts on his face burnt like a motherfucker, but the adrenaline more than made up for it. And so, he pushed his way forward along the aisle. Caught the shocked glimpses of folks who didn't understand what kind of nightmare they had woken up in. Grim did.

In the cockpit, the remaining pilot had crawled over the center pedestal and was frantically trying CPR on his comrade. Grim instantly saw it was futile. All the blood. It had sprayed the controls. Van Driel, who made a half-hearted attempt to assist, saw Grim approaching and squeezed his way back into the cabin. He closed his bloody hands on his collar and threw him against the bulkhead. The fire extinguisher crashed to the floor.

'Hey, hey, hey, hey, what are you doing?'

'What the fuck was that?' Van Driel's breath was a mix of mouthwash and acidic fear. 'That thing that came out of Eleanor!'

'Fucking Easter Bunny, happy now? How the hell should I know? Get your hands off me!'

'You know this shit, gramps. So spill it, what was happening to her?'

'When will you get this through your thick head? *One* supernatural phenomenon is what I've experienced. One! I told you people that doesn't make me an expert!'

He shook Grim like a rag doll—okay, his ribs hurt more than he realized. 'You knew! That fucked-up shit with the visions!'

'*Luca* knew! And if you had acted, he'd still be with us! You had the chance to put a bullet between her eyes, but you didn't! Some soldier you are!'

'Shut your mouth or that bullet's yours!'

'Eat a bag of dicks. You still don't get it, do you? Your boss is possessed, that thing from the sea is working through her. You saw what happened in the hangar, didn't you? So quit your egotistical jerkfest and help me think of a way to get us inside. We need to help that kid. We can't afford to lose him.'

Van Driel let go of him and bashed his fist into the bulkhead, breaking the panel. It was a display of sheer powerlessness. Behind his pit bull façade, the man was rattled. Grim might have felt sorry for him if it weren't so dangerous.

He opened a compartment across the aisle from the exit and found a bunch of coiled, orange lifelines in cone-shaped plastic wrappings. He pulled one out of its pack and tossed it to Van Driel, who barely caught it. 'Undo it. Tie us all together. That's the only way.'

He turned to address the others, but then the pilot appeared from the cockpit. His uniform was drenched in blood. He yanked off his headset and looked from Van Driel to Grim with a leaden face. 'He's dead. She killed Marcel. Get that woman, please.'

This—the plea of a fellow soldier—finally got through to Van Driel. He nodded and began to loosen the rope, inquiring with a subdued voice, 'You can't stay here, can you?'

'If I kill the engine, the blades will snap in the wind. It's getting worse by the minute.'

'Can you fly solo?'

The pilot nodded.

'Then fly, radio for backup, and take your friend home.'

'What the fuck happened? Why did she do that?'

'Beats me. *Backup*, brother.'

'I will, but I wanna be in the air first. I'll need my full attention. Wind's fuckin' insane.'

He retreated into the cockpit, and Grim turned to the others. 'Listen everybody, we're going to try and help Luca! It's crazy out there, but if we huddle together and proceed with caution, we should be able to make it. Headphones off before someone gets hurt. Safiya, Barbara, Ineke in the middle. Paul, too. Everyone else, gather around.'

They bunched up in front of the exit door. Grim addressed Becker. 'I'm not going to force you like they did. But we could really use your help to show us the way. You mentioned you have children. Here's a mother who wants to see her son again.'

'This is crazy, you know,' Becker said, but he joined the others regardless. Grim gratefully patted him on the back.

'Paul will slow us down,' Sita said. 'He needs medical attention fast.'

'Then he stays,' Grim decided. 'The pilot will fly back and send reinforcement.'

Van Driel squeezed everyone together and passed along the end of the rope. Grim did a headcount and noticed Ineke Hopman was missing. He found her still seated in the rear of the cabin, staring into space. Grim limped back, but she spoke before he could: 'I'm not coming.'

'Ineke . . .'

'I'm scared. You can't make me, Robert.'

'No, I can't.'

'Good.'

Something was amiss. It suddenly dawned on him that what he had initially taken for mental paralysis was really intense focus. Ineke wasn't staring into space. She was staring at Paul.

Her husband's killer.

Grim considered saying something about her moral compass and karma and deeds, once done, that couldn't be undone, but decided against it.

Ineke Hopman was perfectly capable of making that decision for herself.

He joined the others, grouping around Safiya and Barbara. Glennis gave Grim a gentle nudge. 'You're limping, Grim. If you fall, you want to be in the middle.'

Grim moved up without complaint and folded his glasses into the pocket of his coat. Van Driel tied off the rope and as a conjoined eightsome, they shuffled toward the exit. He and Becker lowered themselves first, then it was Grim's turn.

Outside, it was horrendous. The downwash of the blades and the icy thrust of the storm crippled his senses. The minute he sat on the ramp to relieve his aching leg, the wind blasted into him, and he could barely tell up from down. His face numbed instantly. His lips turned to salted fish. He squeezed his eyes, staggered forward, slipped, got caught by Becker. Clung onto him. Someone screamed. Someone clung onto *him*. So brutal was the wind, that he felt like they were in a tumble dryer. Coordination was impossible, communication senseless. He turtled his neck. Groped blindly, found Safiya, found Barbara, linked arms. Everyone was off the chopper now, shuffling as a collective against the wind.

A steel flight of stairs descended to the entrance of the accommodation tower's top floor. As Becker and Van Driel clasped the rail with both hands, Grim heard the throbbing of the Cougar speed up. There was a strange sound, the almost human shriek of a wind gust through the piping. There was a hint of movement, a shadow falling over him. Grim, huddled against Barbara atop the stairs, was suddenly shoved forward. If they hadn't all clung onto the rails, they would have fallen like dominos. He looked back . . .

. . .and saw the Cougar's tailfin sweep over their heads. And again. At full tilt, the army chopper was spinning on its axis. Then it keeled over. It was sheer luck it keeled over *away* from them. They collectively pushed down the stairs. Grim ducked his head when he heard the blades smash to pieces against the platform. It rained shrapnel. A twisted piece of rotor blade boomeranged past them and smashed through the window next to the entrance. A tremendous crash followed as the Cougar rolled upside down and tumbled off the edge of the deck, plunging eighty yards down into the sea.

Grim's senses screamed, but his thoughts were surprisingly calm: *How's this for a sacrifice? Three people. Four, if you count Jerome. Not a sacrifice of many, but I think the rest of us will follow soon enough.*

Through grilles and frames he could see the enormous swell that had swallowed the Cougar, now a foaming mass of whitewater. He thought he saw the landing gear emerge one last time as the chopper filled with water like a sinking ship. He was appalled to see how far from the Mammoth the waves had already carried it.

Barbara cupped her hands over her mouth. Becker cursed and cursed and cursed. Van Driel's bloodshot eyes were bulging like a grasshopper's.

'Inside!' Grim roared.

In a single push, they scurried between the twisted debris and reached the entrance to the tower.

5

Barbara saw the chopper crash, but she was too shocked to dwell on poor Ineke Hopman's fate. Too shocked even to dwell on what this meant for their ability to ever get off the rig. Instead, a single, scorching thought converged in her brain: *Luca. She took Luca. We need to help Luca.*

As soon as the pneumatic door shut out the wind behind them, Barbara began to probe her way forward. In the sudden dark, she felt the floor heaving under her feet. It sank, rose, sank once more, as if gargantuan hydraulic pumps were keeping the rig in perpetual motion. It was terrifying. It felt like they were in the belly of a living creature going up and down on the rhythm of its breathing.

Pale cellphone lights flashed and Barbara saw they were in a waiting zone for arriving and departing crew. She scanned the lounge and cried out, 'Luca! Luca, oh God, can you hear me?'

'Fuck!' A loud bang as Van Driel unleashed his frustrations.

'It crashed! It crashed, dammit!' Dukakis. 'What happened? Did anybody see?'

'*Luca! Luca, where are you!*'

The room was untouched by fire, but soot still stained the walls. To her right, Barbara saw leather benches that looked well-used by husky roustabouts. A dead flatscreen lay amid a mosaic of shattered glass on the floor, next to a toppled coffee machine. To her left, there was a check-in counter separating the waiting zone from an admin area, strewn with paper.

But no Luca. Where did she take him?

'Paul,' Sita stammered. 'Paul was in there . . .'

'And Ineke, yeah,' Grim said. 'And the pilot.'

'Does anyone have a signal?' That was Glennis. 'We need to call for help.'

Barbara clung onto her. 'Help me, please, we need to find Luca . . .'

Glennis' response was cut short by Dukakis, who was barely able to temper his panic. 'Did he have time to send out a mayday? Did he tell ATC where we are?'

'Didn't your boss tell him not to?' Grim snapped.

'He said he would radio for help as soon as he was airborne,' said Van Driel.

'Why then?' Dukakis again. 'Why not sooner? Isn't that against protocol?'

'*The Boss put three bullets through the copilot's head, you idiot! How's that for protocol?*'

'Fuck!'

Lights flared. Vincent Becker came back from the admin area with three large torches in his hands. 'There's no reception here,' he muttered. 'We used to have an antenna, but the explosion knocked it out. Help me out, will ya? There are more torches here. And helmets, and safety suits. I suggest you all put them on, since we'll probably be here for a while.'

Van Driel snatched one of his torches, causing him to drop the other two. Beams sliced the darkness. In the scattered light on the floor, Barbara saw a black trail. More soot. Or . . .

'Oh no,' Safiya said. 'That's the same stuff that came from the ship . . .'

Glennis highlighted it with her cellphone, and now Barbara saw it too. It wasn't soot; it was algae. The trail on the floor led to an open door in the back and Barbara thought, *She took Luca. She wasn't human and she took Luca.*

Van Driel hadn't noticed it yet. With his free hand, he grabbed Becker's coverall and yelled, 'How do we get out of here?'

'Get your hands off me!'

'I said, how do we get out of here! You know this place, fucker. We brought you here for a job. I suggest you do it.'

'It's because of you and your boss that we're stranded here, *fucker*, so I suggest you show me some respect if you want something from me!'

'Oh, you want respect?' Van Driel let go of him, pulled out his gun and pointed it at the inspector. 'Respect this!'

Becker recoiled and yelped, his hands in the air.

'*Marco, cut it out!*' Glennis jumped between them and cautiously pushed Van Driel's arm down. 'Quit picking fights. We need to call for help and we need to find Luca and Delveaux.'

Van Driel regarded her furiously but lowered the gun. Barbara had taken advantage of the ruckus to slip toward the door. Now she turned and looked through it. It was like the entrance to a mineshaft. Beyond it was a corridor, but left and right, it was pitch dark. Only the wind lived here.

'*Luca! Luca, can you hear me?*'

'You! Stay here!' Van Driel shouted.

She turned to the others. 'Why don't you help me? We have to go after him!'

Grim snagged one of the torches from the floor and joined Barbara, followed by Glennis.

'*I said stay the fuck here!*'

But Grim had already squeezed past her and shone his light into the corridor. 'Oh, Jesus.'

'What the hell is that . . .?' Glennis stammered.

The hallway was choked with algae. Jumbled veins of organic material delineated a gruesome mosaic on the floor, walls, and ceiling. It was like looking into a jet-black spiderweb.

'It's much worse here than—'

A gunshot cut Grim off and everyone flinched. Barbara's ears were ringing. She heard Safiya scream.

'*All of you, get over here, now!*' Van Driel roared.

'Jesus Christ, put the gun away!'

'What the hell are you doing?'

'Have you lost your mind?'

Everyone was screaming over each other in Dutch and English. Barbara frantically scanned the room. No one was dead; Van Driel had aimed at the wall. Glennis and Sita approached him with raised hands. They reminded Barbara of caretakers from a mental institution approaching a dangerous escapee.

'*I want all of you to stay here and do as I say! I won't say it again!*'

'We're here! We're here!'

'Easy, Marco,' Glennis said equably. 'No one's going anywhere. See? We're all here. Put the gun down.'

He did, and Barbara burst into tears. 'Please, stop this nonsense. We're wasting time. We need to help my son . . .'

'Fuck your son,' Van Driel snapped, turning to Becker. 'You. How do we get off this fucking rig?'

Becker's eyes shot daggers. 'Let me clarify the gravity of the situation. I was the last one to set foot on the rig, back in November, and the floor wasn't tilting as much then as it is now. And the construction wasn't creaking the way it is now. We predicted what's going to happen, dammit. I *told* you what's going to happen in Den Helder. The storm has weakened the structural integrity, and if these waves get stronger tonight, it will reach its breaking point. Do you understand that? *It will collapse.* And us with it, thanks to your stupidity.'

There was a deafening silence. Becker's tirade had hit the mark.

'If we want to get out of here alive, for God's sake, let's not lose any more people. Everything beyond that door is destroyed. We're on the top floor of a partially collapsed high-rise. It's a miracle that it's still standing. I don't care who you are or what authority you have, but on this rig, I'm the one giving the orders, is that understood?'

Van Driel made a peevish gesture with his gun. 'Cut to the chase, pal. Where are the lifeboats? The satellite phones, the emergency radios?'

'The lowest deck is fifty yards above sea level. Without an emergency generator we won't be able to lower any lifeboats. The explosion destroyed the entire operational system, and the fire torched the control room. We can see if some of the comms equipment was spared, but I wouldn't get your hopes up.'

'Okay, you and I will go. Everyone else stays here. Glennis, Sita, Dukakis; no wild goose-chases, you heard me? Fuck the boss and that kid. Our sole mission now is to get off this rig.'

Barbara wanted to cry out a protest, but Glennis put a decisive hand on her arm and met her gaze. *Wait*, she signaled. It was almost unbearable as she felt every precious second ticking away, but Barbara understood that Glennis was her only chance.

'I'll take you there,' said Becker, 'but we bring a third or I'm not budging. Shoot me if you want, but without me, you're going nowhere.'

Van Driel gave in. 'Fine. Sita will join us. Happy now?'

'There's a storage locker at the back of Admin. Get everyone helmets and coveralls. They'll protect you from the cold and the wind. Put them on and we can go.'

It was a masterful bluff. As Becker signaled them where to go, Van Driel and Sita pushed ahead of him around the counter and didn't see him pull Grim along by his sleeve and gesture for the others to follow.

He stopped in the doorway. 'Yes, right there. The shelves in the back.' He leaned back into the admin area and spoke quickly and in a muted voice to Grim. Barbara overheard. 'Stairwell C is to the left, at the end of the hallway. You can go down maybe a level or two, but after that, the explosion blew out at least five. Stairwell B is safer, but I have to take it with him, so you'll have to find your own way. If you can save the boy, you'll have to be quick. There *is* a way off this rig, but we don't have much time, and I can't lead that fucker in circles forever.'

Grim was amazed. 'We owe you.'

Becker rushed into the locker room and said, 'Yeah, those are the ones. For seven people. Plus an extra helmet for me.'

Barbara turned around and bumped straight into Glennis and Dukakis, both expressionless. Would they play along? She could only hope.

Sita and Van Driel returned with armfuls of helmets and orange safety suits and passed them around. Becker used Safiya to demo how to get in and zip up, strap the helmet and flick the headlamp. The fabric felt heavy and soothing. Until now, pure adrenaline had driven Barbara along, but she noticed she was beyond exhaustion, her body shaking from the cold.

'Got a smaller one?' Safiya asked, arms spread, slack sleeves dangling. 'This was made for a gorilla.'

'Sorry, love.' Becker cast her benign smile. 'They don't make 'em in your size.'

'Enough,' Van Driel said. 'Sita, hurry up. Glennis, you heard me.'

Glennis took her gun out, zipped up her coverall, and gave him a nod. 'Be careful out there. The hallway is covered with that stuff from the ship.'

Van Driel went visibly pale but followed Becker and Sita to the door. At Becker's direction, their torches turned right. Then only their cautiously receding footsteps could be heard.

'Jesus-fucking-Christ,' Dukakis let out. 'Dude's lost it.'

Finally, Barbara could let go and release her desperation in an outpouring of tears. She was too tired to speak but didn't need to. Grim took her into his arms and said, 'We'll find him, Barbara. Even if we have to comb the entire rig.'

Dukakis was still bouncing. 'It's impossible, right? What happened to Delveaux, I mean. What even was that?'

No one bothered to answer him.

Barbara looked up at Grim. 'What if she's hurt him, Robert? What if we're too late?'

He shook his head. 'I refuse to believe that. Luca's the Oracle. The sea wants him to spread the message. I think Eleanor took him for another reason.'

Safiya's mouth dropped. 'The mammoth . . .'

Grim nodded but before he could speak, Glennis intervened. 'If you're planning on doing something, Robert, now's the time.'

'Alright. How do we do this?'

'We can't all go. If we run into Van Driel, I don't know what he'll do. I think it's better for Zaky and me to be here when he returns, or he'll know we betrayed him.' She shrugged. 'But if one or two of you happened to escape while we waited . . .'

'Good.' He turned to Barbara and held her shoulders. 'Listen, I think I should take Safiya. She's fast. You're in no shape right now, and I don't want you to get hurt. Luca will need his mother when he comes back.'

She dreaded it, but she knew he was right. 'Go. I'll only slow you down.'

Grim looked back. 'Safiya, you ready?'

'Yeah!' she cheered, already at the door. Safiya didn't need coaxing. She was born ready.

Barbara clung onto him one last time. 'Find my son. I beg of you.'

'We'll find him.'

But Barbara thought, *Unless the sea got him first.*

6

Luca came to his senses in a darksome, stinking, rolling hell, and the thing that once was Eleanor carried him along.

Sheer terror had knocked him unconscious, his psyche's merciful intervention to prevent its own ruin. Opening his eyes, he immediately wished he hadn't.

He was dangling from her slimy maxicoat. The body beneath it was a wave. He could feel it swell, rising and rising and thrusting him so high that he could no longer feel the curve of her back. There was a terrifying, claustrophobic sense of getting crushed beneath the ceiling. Then it fell to more human proportions, only to rise again at its lowest. The darkness itself was rolling too: Luca could feel it sway in all directions. He had the impression they were speeding through an endless network of tunnels. Steel groaned like aging joints. A constant thumping arose from the deep. The hollow roar of wind or sea. And Eleanor . . .

Her footfalls were no longer the click-clack of heels. They *squished*, like the pearly feet of a mollusk dragging itself through the surf. Now they splashed through pools of water. Then they echoed against grated steel. She had him thrown over her shoulder, her long, crooked fingers cutting into the flesh of his thighs. Even through his jeans he could feel how cold they were. The old Eleanor could never have carried him so easily. But this creature wasn't the old Eleanor.

He didn't know *what* it was.

But his senses revealed plenty.

He tasted salt on his cracked lips. He heard her gurgling, ravenous breath, like her jugular was choked with seaweed. He smelled her noxious stench, not of the sea but of rotting marine life. As if her body had been left to broil in a dumpster on a seaside dock. Through it, he sometimes caught a whiff of Eleanor's perfume, which somehow made it worse.

Luca knew it was the sea itself that swept him along. The mere understanding heralded the end of reason and the beginning of the end.

A change of atmosphere, a chilly wind. It was the updraft from a shaft. He could vaguely distinguish shapes. Pillars, grilles, twisted steel. They descended a stairwell. His body bumped and rose and fell with the rolling of her back. His cheek bounced against her coat, frothy and nasty and wet with seawater. Something wiggled and stuck to his skin. With a smothered cry, he brushed it away.

It held on, melding with his skin.

Luca screamed hoarse screams, frantically scraping his face. A regiment of ghostly echoes answered. Panic closed his throat, but he couldn't resist it. He squirmed in her grasp, but the Eleanor-thing carried him along into unrelenting darkness.

'Scream, you little worm,' it said with the voice of starfish and barnacles, of dead reefs and drowned, rotting mouths. 'Scream while you still have air in your lungs. It won't be for long. Do you want to know what I have in store for you? What I have in store for everybody?'

Luca's mouth filled up with salt water. He wanted to spit it out but whatever was growing on his face had spun a membrane hermetically sealing his lips. He clawed at it, but it was like grabbing at a jellyfish. His eyes bulged as the water, ever more, pushed up the only other way, forcing his throat open, biting into his nose, penetrating his larynx. A world of pain exploded as his stomach convulsed and his mind shrieked, I'm drowning! Drowning!

The Eleanor-thing cackled with laughter as it jiggled a spongy, cleft finger between his hands and lips and popped the membrane. Luca tasted the disgusting thing in his mouth, tasted pulp and mold. It went all the way into his throat, and Luca threw up water, then spume and slime and bile. He hocked and sucked his lungs full. Tears were flowing down his temples.

'But not yet,' it spoke through Eleanor's mouth. 'First, I'm going to settle a score with an old mothball that should have died a long time ago. And you're going to summon it for me.'

A new corridor. The distant roar swelled into a crushing rumble. With his last strength, Luca screamed for help.

'No one can hear you, little boy,' it thundered. 'Just like no one could hear your little sister when she came to me.'

And then Luca saw. They were teetering on the edge of a giant hole in the tower, a blackened wound that cut right through its heart. In the last of the dying twilight he could see, below a cluster of collapsed decks, the sea. Incredibly grand, unimaginably wild.

'Jenna is among the crabs now,' the Eleanor-thing gurgled as it slithered into the hole and dragged him along. 'She sunk down to us, and as she was sinking, I saw crabs crawling out of her mouth . . .'

'No . . .'

'Oh, yes! Her fragile little body was full of them, and it became their lair. Soon, they'll crawl out of you too. And once they do, you'll sink too, like the rest of us.'

'No, please, no . . .'

'Deeper . . .'

'No!'

'. . . and deeper . . .'

'No, let me go! No, no, no!'

'. . . and deeper.'

Luca screamed, and whatever was with him in the dark screamed along.

7

'Yuckkkk!'

Safiya's cry fell flat against the mold-covered walls. Grim tried to keep up with her dancing light, managing only because she paused. She aimed it all around. AMBERTECH, the casing read, and underneath it, POWERFUL LED TORCH.

'It's growing. See?'

Even with his compromised vision, he did. The corridor looked like a coral reef from a madman's nightmare. The walls were alive, a breathing mass of polyps, mycelium, and anemonean growth, veined with twisting black tentacles that burrowed into them. It reminded Grim of a cancer metastasizing in the veins of a very sick animal.

'I wonder if Eleanor caused it or just made it worse,' he said. 'Because this doesn't look like it just formed.'

'It was in her too, right?' Safiya grimaced. 'She was rotting.'

'Well, yeah, she's been at it for months. Let's hurry. Don't touch it. And cover your mouth and nose, so you won't inhale it.'

They followed the light of their headlamps and Safiya's AMBERTECH through the infested corridor as if they were wading through a spider's nest in a mineshaft. Grim listened to the wailing of the wind through distant pipelines, the pounding of the storm against the outer walls, the singing of the steel that occasionally swelled into a harrowing shriek, and thought, If it's penetrated the rig's very structure, what does that tell you about its stability?

The answer came instantly. Time's running out.

Here and there, he could make out what this place once was. Doors to cabins left and right. Green and red signs, reminders of offshore regulation, evacuation plans. Red casings with glass panels you had to smash to sound the alarm. The hallway led into a deep shaft. Safiya brushed a sign that read STAIRWELL C.

Inside, apparently bordering the outer wall, it felt like an ongoing earthquake. The racket was deafening. Like Becker said, they could descend two levels. After that, the stairs had collapsed. The last land-ing dangled over a gaping void, where only a jumble of twisted steel was visible.

'Luca!' Safiya yelled. 'Luca, can you hear me?'

Only the storm answered.

Their only option was to go back into the complex, but on this level, they couldn't even get halfway down the corridor. There, they hit the upper side of the hole the explosion had gashed through the accom-modation tower, and the floor simply ended. Rain swept inside and Grim had to brace himself against the force of the wind.

'Safiya, back inside!' He grabbed her hand. 'This is way too dangerous!'

'But she must have been here, look!'

She cast her light downward onto a dislodged steel plate that tilted down to the next level, glistening in the rain. Algae festered on the debris. On the ragged edges of the hole, razor-sharp steel fragments clattered from twisted bolts. Safiya's flashlight reached beyond them, showing a panorama of the destroyed facility and the sea beneath it, visible only as a roiling mass. It was deep—immensely deep. Even with only one good eye, Grim could tell. The cavity in the tower functioned as an echo chamber, swirling the racket and creating the impression of a giant maelstrom with them at the center.

Yet there was another sound. A distant hammering on steel walls. It was coming from much lower to the left.

From STAIRWELL C.

Too rhythmic to be an unhinged door.

'Luca!' Safiya yelled again, but the wind stifled her cry.

Then she crouched and let herself slide down the steel plate.

'Safiya, you idiot!'

Grim reached forward in time to see her reach the lower level and stumble over debris. She looked back up at him. 'I can get down from here!'

'What the hell are you doing! Get back here!'

'Can't, the plate's too slippery. If you lie down on it and let yourself go, I'll catch you.'

'Who do you think I work for? Cirque du Soleil?'

'Seriously, it's not that hard! From here, you can reach the hallway to the right!'

Grim cursed, thought about it, then cursed again. He sat down, swung his legs onto the plate and carefully, very slowly, started lowering himself. Cold steel instantly numbed his fingers.

'Okay, here I co—'

But then the plate collapsed under his weight and smashed onto the debris below. Grim was thrown on his side, tumbled down, and knocked Safiya over. That launched the flashlight from her hand, spinning it to edge of the hole, where it landed on a grille.

'Holy fuck, you okay, Mister?'

Grim tried to sit up, groaning. He had hit his elbow, and his heart was still pounding somewhere on the upper level, but miraculously, he didn't seem to have any serious damage. 'I think so. Ow, my chest. Let me catch my . . . *No-no-no-no-no, leave that goddam thing alone!*'

Safiya had crawled to the edge and was reaching for the flashlight. Just for a second, Grim imagined her plummeting into the depths, grille and all. Then she snagged the handle and scrambled back.

'Stop! Stop moving!' he screamed, rain spattering off his lips. 'No more daredevil feats! You're going to give me a fucking heart attack!'

'It's okay. Look, we're safe. Let me get you up.'

She reached and tugged him by the arm, helping Grim to scramble to his feet. About to launch into another tirade, he stopped short when Safiya raised her free hand and looked at him with big white eyes.

'Shhh . . . you hear that?'

The rhythmic boom from STAIRWELL C was louder now. Almost like a tom-tom. And there was something else, a sound that cut Grim to the marrow. A triumphant sound. A voice.

But not human.

'Let's hurry,' he said. 'We'll take the other stairwell and find a way down. But be careful, and not a sound, understood?'

As fast as Grim could go, they scrabbled through the debris and reached the shelter of the corridor. This ran along for another sixty feet, and they had nearly reached its end when Safiya grabbed his wrist and yanked him into the dark on the left. Grim staggered, flailed, and let out a cry, but it was smothered when the girl pressed her hand over his lips.

'*Shhhh! Turn off your headlamp . . .*'

He did as instructed. As he fumbled with the switch, he saw she had pulled him into a side aisle used as a laundry room, arrayed with front loaders and tumble dryers. Then it got dark. He heard Safiya's rapid-fire breathing and his heart hammering his temples.

And voices. A door was opened on STAIRWELL B.

Safiya pushed him deeper into the dark, where they bumped into something. Grim felt the porthole-shaped window of a washing machine, stacked on top of another. There was a space between it and the back wall. She crammed him inside and squeezed against him, trembling.

Three bright lights shone inside, followed by weaker ones. Flashlights and headlamps. 'What's in here?' Moonshine's voice, ill-tempered as always.

'Launderette,' Becker said. 'Nothing useful. There's another storage room one level up that we can check, but I'm afraid we'll have to make do with the flare guns from the depot. Only cabins back there.'

'Fuckin mess.'

It went dark again. The footsteps faded toward the stairwell. Grim felt a brush and Safiya was suddenly gone. 'Safiya, wait . . .'

He glanced around the washing machines and saw her silhouette against the lighter shade of black from the hallway. Quiet as a cat, she stole back to him. 'They went up,' she whispered. A moment later her headlamp flipped on.

'Christ, that was close. If it weren't for you, we would have walked right into them.'

'Dude's totally wacko. He's still waving his gun around.'

'Did you see that?'

She nodded. 'I'm scared. Are we going to get out of this alive?'

Grim didn't believe in sugarcoating, but he did believe in hope. 'A long time ago, I was trapped in a pretty much hopeless situation. It didn't look like I was going to get out of that one either. But whaddya know, here I am. I managed to survive that, so escaping from a collapsing oil rig feels like a walk in the park.'

'Do you mean that supernatural event you mentioned back in the hangar?'

He nodded.

'What was it?'

'Killer clown,' Grim said, deadpan.

One eyebrow went up. 'You're kidding, right?'

He prodded her gently. 'Come on, coast is clear. We got to help Luca.'

Guided by their headlamps, they hurried to STAIRWELL B and started to descend as quickly and quietly as they could.

8

Luca.

The wind carried the voice into his head. She spoke with a serenity and wisdom only millennia of death could instill.

Luca, open your eyes.

He did. He realized he could see. The air itself seemed luminous. *I don't think I'm looking through my own eyes,* he thought. *Not really, at least.* Eleanor was still carrying him through the facility, lower now, but the surge and swell around him had come to a perfect standstill.

Amid that stillness, he saw her.

She was standing before a tangle of twisted steel. A cloak of animal skin fluttered around her gaunt figure. She waved a staff in druidic motions toward the sea. Her lips were whispering the unintelligible rhythm of a prayer.

She was the Oracle of Doggerland, and her voice was in his head: *You must be prepared to welcome him, Luca.*

'Who?' he muttered.

Nunyunnini. You are the vessel through which he will come. Just as she is the vessel that brought the sea. It made her more dangerous. But she also made the sea more dangerous.

Luca was imprinted with an image of dry lichens thrown onto a fire and thought, *Evil begets evil.* Strangely, it was Grim's voice who spoke these words.

'But why me?'

Because you are pure of heart, Luca. Nunyunnini is an indomitable god. Let there be no doubt about him in your heart, as there was in mine. The burden has been heavy, and the price high. But the debt can be settled.

The image he now saw before him was the Oracle raising her fist and cursing the skies, after which the tsunami came and swept the mammoth away.

'But how am I supposed to do that?'

Make them believe in you, the Oracle spoke. *Make them worship you.*

There was so much he didn't understand. So much he wanted to ask. But the priestess returned to her prayer, and he couldn't see her any longer among the rubble. The breath of the sea grew stronger once again, but something had changed. He could *see.* His brain perceived the slightest glimmer of light hitting his pupils with the ease of an owl or a weasel or another creature of the night.

She carried him through another corridor and down a stairwell. Everywhere her feet landed, obsidian bouquets flourished on the grilles, shooting out mycelia into the very grains of the steel.

They arrived at a small, sheltered area at the bottom of the stairwell. Luca had a sensation of falling backward. The arms that had held him were no longer there, but before he could panic, he splash-landed into a shallow pool of icy water. The shock of cold took his breath away. It instantly drenched his clothes and he started to shiver. Backwards he sloshed, scrambling on hands and rear and feet, until his head bumped into something.

The Eleanor-thing came for him, and for a single mad second, he caught a glimpse of it. She filled the entire lower hallway. The face was hers, yet it wasn't. He could see the glimmer of tiny black eyes. Her limbs, much too long and jumbled. She was completely covered in mold.

And indeed she was surging. Rising and falling, like the perpetual tide beneath their feet.

She grabbed him by the waist, knocking his head back. Upside down, Luca stared straight into the eyes of the mammoth skull.

The thing he had bumped into was one of its curling tusks.

So there you are.

With her spare hand, she heaved the tusk, and the skull hinged backward. She shoved Luca into the resulting space, scraping his shoulders against an underwater pallet. If it weren't for his soaked hoodie, it would have ripped the skin off his back. Then the skull came down on top of him. Luca stifled a cry, afraid it would crush him, but the skull's weight was supported by its cheekbones and the curves of its tusks. What pressed down against Luca was actually rather comforting.

She started to pound the walls, as if to provoke a wild animal, and the sea spoke through Eleanor's mouth, *'Your time came long ago. Don't you know that?'*

Clang-DENG-clang-DENG-clang-DENG . . .

'Get up, vermin, show yourself if you dare. I am Time! I am Mankind! I am Warming! I am Crisis! I am Death! I am Extinction!'

Clang-DENG-clang-DENG-clang-DENG . . .

The Eleanor-thing drummed her tom-tom, and inside the hollow of the skull Luca began to smile.

This mask fit him like a glove.

9

'Glennis, we can't stay here,' Dukakis said in a choked voice. 'It's inside the steel now. Look, they're like veins. Poisoned veins.'

Barbara, dazed, looked up from her hands and didn't initially understand what she was seeing. Dukakis was sweeping the floor with a broom he must have found in the storage locker, but it was pointless. The algae were spreading everywhere, carpeting the floor, walls, and ceiling.

'I think you better get off that, Barbara,' Glennis said.

She turned and saw it was also staining the leather couch. The cushions looked like pumpkins beginning to show the rot within. She leaped up faster than she thought she was capable of.

Mangled and wracked with nerves, Barbara was counting down the minutes. She felt frightened and hopelessly inadequate. Worse still was having to go through these emotions in the presence of Glennis. She had hated the woman from that first night in the dunes, but amid all this madness, Glennis had somehow become a voice of reason.

'Why did you flip?' she asked her on impulse. 'You were so loyal. But then you deceived Van Driel. What happened?'

Glennis' face hardened. 'My loyalty is to my country, not to Van Driel or to Eleanor Delveaux. Long ago, I got involved in something I strongly regret. Eleanor knew about it and used it against me.' She hesitated before she continued. 'There was a woman who worked for her and whom I regarded as a mentor. Her name was Diana Radu. Eleanor murdered her.'

Dukakis: 'You're shitting me!'

'Van Driel blabbed. He was the one who disposed of her body.'

'Fucking hell!' He threw his broom to the floor.

'And that was well before she was under the spell of—'

'Footsteps!' Barbara called, raising her hand.

They listened. Yes, they were quickly approaching through the hallway. Torch lights entered first, followed by Vincent Becker, Van Driel, and Sita. None of the others. No Luca. Hoping against hope, she wanted to ask if they had found him but then saw Van Driel shining his torch around the room. Saw the look on his face.

'Where's Grim?' he asked in a soft voice. 'Where's the girl?'

Glennis shrugged. 'They ran away.'

'Ran away? How's that possible, Glennis? There were only three of them. You and Dukakis were armed.'

'I don't shoot children, Marco.'

'What about the old fart? Is he a child, too?'

'It happened really fast. The girl was in front of him. I had to choose: leave these people here alone and endanger myself or wait here like you ordered. I decided to wait.'

'One job. I gave you one job, and you can't even do that. Or maybe you let them go?'

'Marco, don't sweat it,' Sita intervened. 'You saw what it's like. If they're roaming around down there, that's their problem. It's not like they're going anywhere.'

'It's a problem if I fucking *say* it's a problem!' Van Driel hollered, making Sita flinch. 'I have the authority around here! And I fucking said that no one was allowed to go *anywhere*!'

'And who gave you that authority?' Glennis objected, but before Van Driel could answer, they were all startled by a deep rumble, followed by an awful, ongoing crunch. The floor dipped, buckled, then recovered. They all looked at each other in frozen shock. Barbara saw the fear in Becker's eyes, confirming her worst suspicion: *This is far beyond what it's supposed to do.*

'*Fuck!*'

Van Driel was losing it. He kicked the trashcan, the flatscreen, the coffeemaker. Just in time, Becker yanked at Barbara's sleeve to get her out of his trajectory.

'Fucking freakshow! I'm not gonna die here, you hear me? Not for this fucking shit!'

'Let's keep it together and discuss what we can do,' Glennis tried to calm him.

'We can do jack-shit! A fucking flare gun. That's it. That's all we've got. An who's going to see that?'

'After the storm, we can—'

'There is no after the storm, don't you see that? We won't be here tomorrow! It's all going to hell! And that fucking ghost shit . . .' His voice broke into a sob, and he squirmed, scratching his head with both hands as if he were suddenly itching all over.

He's truly scared of it, Barbara realized. *He of all people. The most dangerous one.*

'Grim,' Van Driel said. He strode up to Glennis and stopped a few inches short of her face. 'Where's Grim? He knows this stuff.'

'I told you, he's gone.'

'Go find him.' He gestured his gun to the door. 'Now.'

Glennis tried to remain calm. 'What do you think he can—'

'*Go get him right the fuck now, bitch!*'

The group was paralyzed by his erratic behavior. Only Becker was bold enough to speak up . . . making a fatal misjudgment. 'No! We're not breaking up any further. Let's all go and find the others together. If we do that, I might be able to get us out of here.'

'*What* did you say?'

Van Driel had lapsed back into his soft voice, which was much more terrifying than his rage. Becker realized he had said too much, but there was no going back now. 'There's a way of getting off the rig. The Mammoth had three freefall lifeboats. One was damaged in the explosion, and another was used during the evacuation. So the last one should theoretically still be operative.'

'And you're telling me *now?*' Again, the soft voice. He was like a tiger stalking its prey through tall grass.

'Mr. Van Driel, the lives of children are at stake. You may be able to make choices that disregard that, but I cannot.'

Van Driel crossed the room in the space of seconds and put his gun to Becker's temple. The latter winced and yelped, as did Barbara. She tripped and sprawled across the couch—realizing only moments later what she fell *into.*

Van Driel was now behind Becker and seized him by the collar, holding him at gunpoint. 'You've all been conspiring against me. No more. You're going to take me to that boat right now and you and I are going on a little cruise. The rest of you can rot in hell for all I care.'

Before Barbara could even begin to hurl herself up from the contaminated leather, the rig came to life. The rumble accumulated into a thundering roar. For an instant, the waiting area seemed to shrink. To twist. To turn. There seemed to be a release of pressure, like something humongous was finally able to exhale. All the windows exploded, and a blast of wind howled through the room. Cracks shot through the overgrown walls, shaking off the algae like a dog shaking off water.

We're collapsing, Barbara thought. *We're falling. Oh, Luca . . .*

For a second they did fall. The entire rig toppled backwards . . . until it slowly rocked back in place. *And Barbara could have sworn she heard an exuberant trumpeting over the pandemonium of the storm.*

Not an elephant. Bigger.

'*What the fuck!*' howled Van Driel. '*What the fuck! What the fuck!*'

Glennis and Dukakis knelt by the check-in desk, grabbing each other's shoulders. Stunned, Sita stood frozen in the doorway.

'To the lifeboat! I'm not asking again!'

Van Driel pushed Becker ahead, but Becker resisted. 'Let go of me! I refuse to—'

'You want a put a bullet in your face?'

'You can't shoot me. You need me to take you to the lifeboat and you need me to release it!'

Van Driel didn't hesitate. He aimed the gun at Sita, who had the time to open her mouth but not to utter a denial, and shot *her* instead.

Barbara woul never forget how Sita's head—or what was left of it—jerked backward before her body followed.

'Walk, or the next one goes in three seconds!'

'Okay-okay-okay-okay!' Becker yelled.

An awesome tremble now shook the platform, and Barbara knew that if Van Driel disappeared with Becker and the last lifeboat, they would all perish. She acted on impulse. Her eyes met Becker's and then Glennis'. *I'm going to give you a second. Please use it.*

Barbara wriggled her hands from her sleeves and brushed her palms across the pillows. It was nasty and greasy and it made her quiver, but she persisted. She scrambled up and ran to the doorway, where Van Driel was forcing Becker to step over Sita's body. She reached out her smudged hands and began to shake like she was having a seizure. She thought Luca would have appreciated her gurgling like a zombie too, so she did exactly that.

Van Driel turned to see a woman afflicted by his worst nightmare, coming for him. The gun swayed from Becker to Barbara, and she had the time to think, *Luca, I love you.*

In that split-second of confusion, Becker dropped to his knees, yanking Van Driel out of balance and back into the waiting room. Glennis jumped at the chance to snatch the torch from the floor and smash it into his skull.

Something cracked. Van Driel went down with a dull thud.

'Jesus-fucking-Christ!' Dukakis shrieked, his voice pitched higher than ever.

Becker gazed in disbelief at the two bodies at his feet. A pool of blood was forming around Van Driel's head. Glennis decided it safe, crouched beside him, and felt his neck. 'Out but not dead,' she said matter-of-factly. 'That was very brave of you, Barbara.'

'Someone had to stop that bastard.' She grimaced and wiped her hands on her coverall.

'Let's find the others and beat it,' Glennis said. 'Mr. Becker? Good reaction.'

'Thank you. But I think you better call me Vince from now on.'

She got up. 'Make sure you get it all off, Barbara. It's all over the back of your coverall. Stuff's dangerous.'

'Is Sita . . .'

'Yes. Come on, let's go find Luca. I don't know what's happening down there, but whatever Delveaux' plan is, I think it has started.'

Barbara was convinced she was right. The Mammoth was now in constant motion. Again she had the feeling that it was alive, no longer swaying with the rhythm of the sea but with the breathing of a wild animal.

That trumpeting. What was that? Please let Luca be safe.

Vince went into the corridor, followed by Dukakis and Glennis. Barbara tiptoed around Van Driel's unconscious body. The pool of blood was growing, and she was horrified to see the algae absorbing it. Tiny, polyp-like tentacles on the floor were sucking it up and swelling like leeches.

She thought about how he had slapped Luca in the face, when they were forced to sign the NDA. Then she remembered Jenna's body floating in the carp pond. In an impulse she picked up the torch, knelt beside him, and raised it above her head.

A hand grabbed her wrist.

'Don't be like them, Barbara,' Glennis said, surprisingly sympathetic. 'We can still be civilized.'

'Will that bring back Jenna?' she asked. 'Will it bring back Alexander?'

'No,' said Glennis. 'But maybe you.'

The hand let go.

Barbara lowered the torch.

10

Clang-DENG-clang-DENG-clang-DENG-clang-DENG . . .

Eleanor's tom-tom pounded ruthlessly through STAIRWELL C, but all cosmic, rallying powers aside, Luca was in a state of bliss, and it no longer intimidated him.

Clang-DENG-clang-DENG-clang-D . . .

Inside the mammoth's skull, he bathed in an aura of energy that appeared to emerge from the rig itself. It was coming to life around him; a life spindling around him, Luca Wolf, the Oracle of Katwijk. He felt its ancient, benevolent power enter him and he soaked it up like a young animal basking in the spring sunshine for the first time. The salutary warmth dried his skin and awoke a hidden wisdom. All at once, Luca knew as much about the juicy grasses on the coastal drylands as the strawberry Rip Rolls he and Safiya liked so much. All at once, the ice sheets of the Northern Land held as little mystery for him as the *Game of Thrones* wiki.

'Nunyunnini,' he laughed, enthralled. 'Come to me!'

Nunyunnini came.

11

The lower levels were beyond destruction. One look at the level-zero control room and Grim understood that Becker, Van Driel and Sita hadn't been able to find anything useful. Outside was even worse. Once, the ironwork had been painted yellow; now the dripping skeleton had taken on the colors of fire, water, rust, and storm. In the heart of this, the explosion had occurred. It had blasted out entire decks, and the pyramid-shaped derrick had collapsed in on itself. Any debris that hadn't plunged into the sea was strewn across the shattered jumble of tanks, installations, compressors, and pipelines. If they wanted to reach the bottom of STAIRWELL C, this was what they were up against.

The storm down here was murderous. 'Hold on!' he yelled to Safiya, the minute they exited STAIRWELL B onto a gallery of grilles. 'To the rail or to me, I don't care, just don't let go!'

'Gotcha!'

Step by step, they moved away from the door, Safiya clasping both the railing and a handful of Grim's coverall. Corrugated metal barriers provided more shelter from the wind here than on the helideck, but the majority of the plates were twisted, ripped, or blasted out entirely. The wind sang a harrowingly dissonant song with the sea beneath their feet.

Grim was about to tell Safiya this was nuts, that they should go back, that there were plenty other boyfriends to choose from, when it happened.

He only had time to grab the rail and hold Safiya close to protect her when the rig not only pitched up—and *kept* pitching up—but expanded. High above them, crossbeams snapped like twigs and spun into the sea.

'What's happening?' Safiya yelled. 'Is it collapsing?'

'I don't know! Hold on!'

But then Grim did know.

This wasn't the rig's demise, it was its triumph. Robert Grim saw an image before him that was unimaginable but real: though anchored in concrete, the facility reared up and crashed down with a mighty splash on its forelegs, like a large animal waking from hibernation stretching and shaking its fur.

And above the sea and storm sounded an unmistakable and deafening trumpeting.

'It's him!' Safiya yelled. 'He did it! Luca did it!'

Luca? thought Grim. *Wasn't this Eleanor's plan?*

But suddenly he wasn't so sure anymore.

Safiya froze. 'Over there . . . what's that?'

The gallery looked out onto the destroyed heart of the complex. To the left was a single flight of stairs leading down to the lower decks. And yes, there was something there, just beyond a charred collection of tanks and sealed wellheads. Something large. Safiya's light managed to catch it only for an instant before it was gone. A surging body, like a giant snake surreptitiously gliding through the water.

'*Safiya! Run!*'

He grabbed the girl by the waist, but dropping the flashlight, she held onto the railing with both hands. 'No! We're supposed to stay here!'

Says who? he wanted to shout, but then he saw her light had attracted the attention of whatever was haunting the lower deck.

Grim saw what was coming for them.

12

Luca sat up and found himself surrounded by a white light that filled the entire lower hallway. The light rippled, but not like the sea. It rippled like woolly fur. Luca looked back and a brilliant tusk of twisted light burst through the safety glass of the exterior door. A second cleaved like a scimitar through the debris on the first landing.

Nunyunnini had descended upon him. The fog of birth was still in the air. He was composed entirely of light.

Time to look for Eleanor, he heard the voice of the Oracle say.

The mammoth skull was gone. Luca stood up and saw Ravinder's dripping wet jeans and hoodie, and he saw the palms of his hands. And he saw something else: a millennia-old perspective on the passing of ice ages and the life cycle of the universe itself. Amazed, he wondered how it was possible but then remembered the spyglass, and it dawned on him. He wasn't just looking with his own eyes. He was looking through the eyes of the mammoth, and the mammoth was looking through his.

A Task awaited him.

But where was Eleanor?

Eleanor is your Task, Luca. Eleanor and the sea, through whose eyes she is looking. Be careful, because she wants you dead. Because the sea wants Nunyunnini dead.

'Then let's end this,' he whispered.

Luca walked into the night and Nunyunnini followed.

On the lower deck, the storm no longer bothered him. He still heard the drone of the sea, but within Nunyunnini's light he could see each individual wave that broke onto Dutch shores miles away. He could sense the minute currents released by tendrils of deep-sea life making love in dreamless depths. And he could hear the last bubbles of air escape from the lips of three hundred and fifty lost souls, who had made their last voyage centuries ago on a *fluyt* ship named the *Oracle*.

He could smell better too. He smelled the wind now and the sooty steel and the brine. But above all, he smelled *her*. A scent only partially human—her sweet perfume, her putrid flesh—but mostly the smell of algae.

The lower deck was festering with them.

Luca understood the danger. As they ate away at the rig and weakened its structure, they weakened Nunyunnini as well, because the mammoth and the rig were essentially the same.

You need to hurry, Luca. And you need to be prepared for her to strike you where you are most vulnerable.

Yet Luca felt supreme. He reigned over land and ice and wind, so why shouldn't he be able to defeat the sea?

'*Eleanor!*' he cried out, and from another era, a triumphant roar trumpeted into the world, rising above the wind. '*Eleanor, I'm coming for you, coward! Come and get me, if you want me so badly!*'

Luca ran through the destroyed equipment on the lower deck, basking in indomitability. The mammoth galloped along, sweeping away debris left and right with tusks of pure light. He could smell she was near, just beyond a forest of vertical pipes. He braced himself for the moment when he could fling her into the air with a toss of his head . . .

. . . and jerked to a halt, slipping on steel. The wind stole his breath away.

She was standing on the rim of the explosion hole. The sea beneath was surging with a nocturnal glow, her body rising and falling to the rhythm of the waves. Her cloak and hair were fanning like seaweed. Her eyes were foaming. Algae had eaten the flesh off her face and what was left had taken on the color of dead coral. She looked at him . . . and smiled.

Safiya was in her arms.

Safiya's eyes met his. Tears were rolling down her cheeks. Luca could smell her fear and desperation.

'Leave her out of this!' he shouted, his voice now shockingly small and human. 'She doesn't have anything to do with this . . .'

But he knew she did, because Nunyunnini could only be as strong as him, and Luca's weakness would be *his* weakness too.

'My *pleasure*,' the Eleanor-thing gurgled.

She leaned over the rim and dropped Safiya.

13

They were halfway down STAIRWELL B when all hell broke loose. *Earthquake*, Barbara thought, but she knew it wasn't the earth that was shaking. She had to grab onto the banister to keep from falling and on the next landing, Glennis, Becker and Dukakis did the same.

'What's happening?' Glennis screamed.

'It's not supposed to move like that.' Becker was slurring his words, like he found himself trapped in a dream. 'Even with the damage to the pillars, it's impossible.'

Then, they heard elephantine trumpeting again. But this time, it didn't sound triumphant. It sounded like a cry of pain.

'Oh God, Luca!' Barbara yelled and flew down the stairs. 'Luca, I'm coming!'

14

When the creature that was once Eleanor washed over them and yanked Safiya from his hands, Grim was thrown backward onto the gallery. The smack to his aching ribs forced the air from his lungs. He watched powerlessly as it carried her to the edge of the hole and held her out over sea. The swells underneath surged so high that their crests were mere yards from reaching the rim and their troughs seemed immeasurably deep.

Only when Luca entered the scene did he understand why she hadn't dropped the girl right away. But this and any other rational thought died immediately when he saw what was behind Luca. A woolly mammoth bull made out of pure light. Its majestic tusks swirled sparks framing the kid like smoke in the wind.

We need to talk about the elephant in the room, Grim thought, releasing a single mad laugh. Before him stood Nunyunnini, or at least Nunyunnini's spiritual projection, a totem animal for the Oracle. *My God, he's magnificent! No wonder Luca wanted to bring us here!*

He stared in awe at the two gods of the old land facing each other on the lower deck. Nunyunnini's posture of supreme confidence faltered as the sea held hostage what was closest to Luca's heart. Luca shouted something, swallowed by the wind. The mammoth growled and stamped its foot, blasting sparks of light.

And then Grim understood.

The Eleanor-thing dropped Safiya. Driven by Luca's desire to save her, Nunyunnini jumped after her. Grim saw him leap straight through the kid, who collapsed to the ground. Behind him, a fossilized mammoth skull clattered onto the debris, suddenly shrouded by darkness.

The rig shuddered. The accommodation tower shook. Grim moaned, dragging himself to the edge of the gallery to look.

Luca knew he had been tricked. This had been her plan all along. Now, the Eleanor-thing grinned.

Lying before her was nothing but a little boy, unmasked.

'Luca, watch out!' Grim shouted, but too late.

Her claws landed on Luca's shoulders, digging into his flesh and drawing blood that darkened his hoodie. Her hideous face twisted into a hungry grimace from which a regiment of tiny black crabs emerged, scurrying sideways across her arms, engulfing the boy. Luca didn't stand a chance. The sea swelled as she pulled in her prey, only to toss it away like a useless piece of driftwood. Luca crashed into a mountain of twisted steel and disappeared out of sight. Eleanor sloshed back, readying herself for another wave.

Grim lay defeated on the gallery. Cold and wet and spent. The storm lashed at the lower decks, numbing him. He didn't want to be here, yet he was, and the struggle was over. They had failed. Nunyunnini was mighty, but the sea was cunning. Such was the law of darkness: it ripped your heart out. The heart that anchored us all to life. That's how it had ended in Black Spring, and that's how it would end here.

Grim's heart? It was now old and frail.

Footsteps approached. Grim looked up and saw his worst nightmare.

He hadn't seen her since that day in 2013 when he had pulled dirty socks out from under his bed in his Atlantic City penthouse; the day before he had replaced the bed with a low-framed box spring, under which nothing could hide.

Robert Grim saw two emaciated and mud-stained feet.

15

It's cold and dark where Luca is, but he doesn't feel the cold. The night sky is alive with floating colors. Safiya's face lights up in greens and blues and violets and purples. It's beautiful. After a while, she realizes he is watching her and smiles.

'Wow,' she says.

'Wow?'

'You've never been this sexy.'

He looks down at his body and grins. 'So you got a thing for hairy?'

'I got a thing for confidence. And if anything emanates confidence, it's this.'

'Nice save.'

She laughs and looks up at the lights in the sky. 'It's so beautiful! Are we flying?'

No, flying doesn't really capture it. Luca thinks it's more a state of being, although that doesn't do it justice either. They aren't really here, and at the same time they are the light, and the firmament onto which it shines, and the time that makes it last. But he doesn't really know how to say it, so 'flying' will do. Safiya is sprawled along the cushion of his curved trunk. Her knees hang across his right tusk and her feet are dangling. She seems to love the bed he has spread for her.

'I think I caught you,' he says. 'Don't worry, Safiya, we're not dead. In some way, we're still on the rig. We never left. That's because—'

'Omigod, are you mansplaining our astral trip to me right now?'

'Alright, alright, I'll stop.'

'I know, Luca. Nunyunnini is an old god. He's almighty.' She smiles blissfully. 'Bummer I didn't bring my phone. This would make such a dope TikTok.'

Stars sparkle in her eyes, yet something dark descends upon Luca. 'Sorry you were thrown off an oil rig because of me.'

She laughs but can see he's serious. 'Boy, if you'd told me this would happen at the Christmas gala, I would totally have friend-zoned you. But know what? I wouldn't have missed it for the world.'

'You're just saying that.'

'I am.'

Far below is a gathering of tents made of hides. Smoke rises from the opening of the largest. It smells of herbs and Luca senses that he's being invoked by the tribe. They are chanting his name, Nunyunnini, Nunyunnini, Nunyunnini . . .

Fleetingly, he recognizes their voices.

This ritual, the simple act of devotion, pumps power through his veins.

Suddenly Safiya frowns. 'You must go back, Luca, or Eleanor will kill you. You're the Oracle. Without Nunyunnini you're unprotected.'

'I know. But I don't want to go back. I want to be here with you.'

'What can we do to defeat her?'

He peers at the horizon, where the aurora glistens above the sea. 'Long ago, there was an Oracle who didn't believe in me. I told her, "Trust me," *but she doubted my wisdom, so I couldn't protect her against the oncoming sea. Before the waves took their sacrifice, the Oracle cursed me, and the land was swept away, and I was forgotten.' A trace of sadness washes over him. 'That was a pity. The world would look different today.'*

'Of course!' Safiya calls out. 'We don't need a sacrifice! And we don't need punishment either! Wasn't Nunyunnini a god of indomitability?'

Luca nods. He speaks with the inflection of a god, but his heart is that of a boy. 'Believe in me,' he whispers.

'I believe in you, silly, don't you know that?'

'Promise?'

'I promise. I believe in you.'

'I need it, Safiya.'

'I believe in you.' And as every spell is true when spoken thrice, her belief empowers him. 'I love you, Luca. Saying it the first time sounds cheesy, but it's true, I think.'

'I think I love you too.'

If they weren't already flying, then Luca is flying now. An excited trumpeting escapes his trunk. He can't help it.

'Yo, show-off!' Safiya laughs. She stretches like a cat. 'Now go, there's an old bitch waiting for you down there.' She waggles her eyebrows and says, 'Attaboy . . .'

'Oh my god, you're evil!'

'You know it!'

He is afraid of what will happen when he gets back to the rig, not knowing how seriously Eleanor has mauled him. But he thinks he is ready for it now, and for the rest of his life, no matter how that will turn out.

Because he has a worshipper.

16

Grim looked up from the grubby, bruised feet to her ankles and to the hem of her dress—and got a shock.

Not who you expected to see, Grim.

'Are you . . . real?'

The woman was old; there was little flesh on her bones and her face was dry like bark. Her cloak was made of animal skin and flapping in the wind. She wore the skull and antlers of a caribou.

What an irrelevant question for a clever bird like yourself.

'Alright, I know who you are. But how did you know I was expecting someone else?'

I know many things. When you are as old as I am, you know almost everything.

'Do you know how *she's* doing?'

The old woman didn't answer, and for a moment, Grim thought she wasn't going to. Then she turned away from the storm and her expression became contemplative. *Those who harbor grudges in death shall never be at peace. It is not good. Look at me. I'm still waiting for . . .*

She spoke a strange word, and Grim knew it was close to 'liberation' . . . but not exactly.

'Me too, I think,' he said.

She raised her staff. *Up. You still have a role to play, Grim.*

'What do I need to do?'

Invoke him. Worship him. Idolize him.

Grim hoisted himself up on the rail. 'In Luca's vision, you were wearing mammoth skin. Shouldn't you be wearing that now?'

No, the old woman said. *The Oracle is.*

17

Luca smacked against the remains of the wellheads and folded in agony, his shoulders and upper arms bleeding from Eleanor's claws. Still, he managed to roll away just in time before the next wave flung the mammoth skull after him. Both tusks snapped as it washed through the debris. The massive cranium cracked. Luca knew it wouldn't take long before he drowned. Each time she came at him, he tumbled through her foaming darkness, pushed onward by the sensation of her tidal power. And each time she withdrew, he came up spluttering and gasping for air.

'No more,' he moaned, trying to crawl away behind the wellheads. 'Please help me, I can't, I'm so tired . . .'

But Nunyunnini didn't hear him. Luca had a vague sensation of floating on the breath of time through a distant universe. He saw Safiya through the totem's eyes, sprawled between its tusks. The mammoth had saved her, but Luca's relief was short-lived. It looked like an animal washed ashore after an oil spill. Its fur was smudged with algae and the sea's fingers were crawling all over it.

She's poisoned it. It's dying, like I am.

Then he looked through his own eyes again and saw her flood toward him. Searching for him through the dark with lobed eyes. Then she broke over him.

Luca was swept along, moaning with pain and exhaustion. She was simply too strong. She was going to throw him into the depths along with Nunyunnini's skull once and for all. Then, Safiya and his mom would follow with all the others when the rig collapsed.

'Help me!' he screamed. 'You gotta help me before it's too late! If I die, you'll die!'

That he heard it, borne on the wind: an amalgamation of sounds from this or another world. The crackling of a fire. An unearthly drum, weaving emphatic, exotic rhythms into music. And above it all, a mantra of human voices: *Nunyunnini, Nunyunnini. Nunyunnini . . .*

He felt uplifted.

He felt empowered.

And Luca understood.

Nunyunnini is a god of indomitability, the old woman had said. *Let there be no doubt about this in your heart, as there was in mine. The burden has been heavy and the price high. But the debt can be settled.*

As all gods, Nunyunnini existed only by the grace of belief.

But the Oracle's belief was the most important.

Through the dark, the Eleanor-thing came for him again. Luca saw her flushing mouth, her foaming whitecaps, her triumphant, dehumanized face.

'I believe in you!' he suddenly yelled, his voice cracking. 'Nunyunnini, I believe in you!'

And he didn't just say it. He believed it, with all his heart.

The Eleanor-thing shrank back with a tormented cry, washing away through grated steel to the lower deck.

Nunyunnini, Nunyunnini. Nunyunnini . . .

'I believe in you, Nunyunnini! I believe in your might! I believe in your indomitability! I believe that you've saved Safiya! And I believe that you can beat this old bitch!'

And with each word woven into the mantra, Luca's belief grew stronger. He scrambled to his feet, looked around and couldn't see the mammoth—not yet, at least—but he could *sense* it getting up too, unsteady at first on wrinkled forelegs, then onto its hind legs. He sensed it shaking its massive fur from head to tail and heared lumps of black sludge splatter everywhere.

Nunyunnini, Nunyunnini. Nunyunnini . . .

'I believe in you,' Luca whispered.

And as he turned to look for Eleanor, he wondered why the voices sounded so familiar.

18

Barbara doesn't get a heads-up before she's pulled out of her body. One minute she's running down STAIRWELL B *shouting her son's name, and the next, there's a little tug at the back of her head, and she lands in front of a crackling fire in a tent, nice and comfy. She's not alone. Three figures are gathered around the fire. The man on her left wears a headdress of brown feathers and a beaded necklace with the skull and talons of an eagle. It's Robert Grim. The girl on her right wears the back fur and skull of a feline. This is Safiya. She doesn't recognize the woman across the fire. She is wearing the antlers of a large deer.*

The Mother's worship is the strongest, *the deer woman speaks in a language Barbara doesn't know yet somehow understands.* She protects her young.

Barbara looks down and sees she is wrapped in the fur of a bears. Above her head, she can feel the sow's snout and teeth. She feels comfortable in her skin.

The bird and the cat take her hands. The deer woman throws something into the fire, sending up sparks. It smells spicy, reminding Barbara of a meal she once ate with Alexander at an Afghan restaurant in Amsterdam. Then it's gone, and the priestess starts to thrum a strange, irregular rhythm on a drum with her thumbs and palms, chanting, Nunyunnini. Nunyunnini . . .

The cat and the bird join in, and Barbara understands she's expected to do the same. So she does.

Before long, she feels light-headed.

Barbara thinks of Luca. She also thinks of Jenna and Alexander, but right now, she mostly thinks of Luca. Her heart fills with love, sadness, and hope. Their voices rise into the night, and after a while, Barbara isn't sure whether she's invoking the name of the mammoth or her son.

19

Luca found her on the mid-deck. She stood in defiance of the storm, monumental, terrifying, waiting. The sea was a whirling black mass, her perfect reflection.

'There you are,' the water spoke. 'Have you come to sacrifice yourself? Perhaps it's for the best. You are the last of your kind. Your death will be lonely.'

'No, Eleanor. I've come to trample you. I'm here to send your rotting, stinking soul straight to the depths it came from.'

She roared with laughter, spattering up water. 'You're old. You're crippled. And you've sent a child.'

'You should have left my sister out of this,' Luca said. 'That was your mistake. And using Safiya to get to me?' He snorted with disdain . . . and wasn't that insecurity flashing behind her superior disguise? 'That's just low.'

She was replenishing. Retreating like the sea before a tsunami would wash over the land, sweeping away everything in its path. Luca braced himself. He knew this. It had happened before, and then it had brought the end. But there was one significant difference now.

She came. She rose and rose and crested and broke . . .

. . . and only then did she hear the mantra of his name.

'I didn't come alone, bitch,' Luca said.

Her expression changed into a stormy mix of surprise, rage, and hate. From an explosion of light the mammoth erupted, galloping forward with might and pride. It lunged, and they collided, not in water, not on land, but in the air. It swept up the Eleanor-thing with fiery tusks and flung her into the air, smashing her against the grille ceiling of the upper deck. She shrieked with pain as she splashed onto the gallery, breaking apart and washing away from him.

Nunyunnini leaped at her, and they fought.

She clawed deep into its fur, tearing out sparks of light and ripping the skin underneath. He crushed one of her surging, skeleton limbs under his hooves and heard bones snap like razor clams on a beach. She tried to drown him in waves of cold, salty water, but he clamped his jaws around her emaciated frame and violently shook his head. Luca heard something rip and saw her dissolve into a retreating wave.

She attacked again, but she was weakened now. Nunyunnini swooped her up and tossed her into the air. Again. And again. It was frightening even for Luca, because the cruelty that possessed him was primitive and savage, but it was *his* all the same. It had to happen, and he couldn't stop it. Every blow that Nunyunnini dealt, knocked the sea further out of her, diminishing Eleanor to more human proportions. And every blow he dealt her brought more of the beast out in Luca. He realized he was crying. For his dad and Jenna, for Emma, for his mom, but mostly for himself.

Finally, Nunyunnini flung her off the mid-deck. She tumbled down through the steel remains of the derrick and came to a stop on the lower deck, broken and bleeding.

A strange silence descended upon the world. The storm and the sea had calmed to a standstill. The rig seemed afloat in a vacuum where everything had returned to its normal shape.

Luca walked over to the edge and stood next to Nunyunnini, who snorted softly.

Down there, in her filthy red maxicoat, lay Eleanor Delveaux. Ruined, she seemed small and insignificant. Reflected in her eyes Luca saw a woolly mammoth made of nothing but light.

'Kill me,' she begged. 'Monster . . .'

'No,' Luca said. 'I'm not like you.'

Her face twisted with horror. Only at the last moment did Luca see the silent wall of water approaching them. The Mammoth III wobbled as the massive swell washed over the lower deck.

Nunyunnini stood indomitable.

When Luca looked again, Eleanor was gone.

20

Grim opened his eyes just in time to witness the tidal wave. Initially, he was disoriented, but soon realized that he was on the gallery at the foot of the accommodation tower and no longer in a nomadic tent on some strange, astral plane. Maybe he had never really been there at all.

Did he do it? Did Luca do it?

A shattering rumble. The rig shook and Grim jerked up his head. His eyes needed a moment to adjust, but thanks Nunyunnini's light he could see enough to want to scream in one choked breath, *Wave oh god oh god oh god it's close!*

It looked like the wake of some giant sea creature. The wave was too powerful even to break when it found the rig in its path. It merely submerged the lower decks for a moment as it passed. The hand of a god collecting its own.

Everything was swept away. Piping. Steel debris. And Eleanor.

Grim watched as the sea fell once more and the storm reignited. There was a new sound now, of waterfalls raining down from the Mammoth's frame. On the rim of the hole in the mid-deck stood Nunyunnini in all its glory. Its trunk caressed the shoulder of the antler woman by his side, who stroked it with love and devotion. The expression on her face was one of quietude, as if something knocked out of balance thousands of years ago had finally been restored.

On his other side stood Luca.

Grim heard a sound and looked over his shoulder.

'Tell me this isn't real,' Vince Becker shouted over the wind. His face was a mask of bewildered disbelief. Joining him were Glennis and Dukakis, whose expressions mirrored Becker's.

'*Luca!*' Barbara yelled. She pushed Dukakis aside and ran down the stairs. Maybe it was the simple act of a mother calling out her son's name that restored normality, because when Grim looked again, the mammoth and the antler woman were gone. On the mid-deck now lay a broken skull with splintered stumps where the tusks had once been. Two jeans-clad legs jotted out from under it, diminutive by comparison.

From the dark on the mid-deck emerged another savior: Safiya. As she and his mother reached Luca at the same time, Grim turned and stepped beside Becker. 'Did you see them disappear?'

'Huh?' The inspector seemed to be waking up from a dream.

'The mammoth. The old woman. Did you see them go?'

'I . . . I don't know what I saw.'

Grim put a reassuring hand on his shoulder. 'Don't sweat it. You've got one hell of a story to tell your wife and kids.'

But Grim suspected he wouldn't. Already, Becker was doubting what he had witnessed. A mirage. An illusion. It would be easier to come to terms with something like that. Which was a good thing.

Glennis joined them. 'Is it over, Grim? Whatever it was?'

'Yes. She's gone.'

She nodded. 'Then let's get to the lifeboat. See that?'

She aimed her light at one of the four steel pillars shimmering through the grilles at the far side of the explosion hole. Grim paled when he saw the black blotches forming there, spreading like ink on paper. They seemed to be crawling up from the sea.

'We won the battle, but not the war,' Glennis said, then turned to Becker, surprisingly calm. 'I need to ask you a favor. We need to evacuate, and you're going to lead us.'

Becker nodded, relieved. This was something tangible, something that he knew. Grim straightened up and said, 'Get it ready. I'm going to collect our Oracle.'

He descended the stairs as fast as his joints permitted. Leaning against the wind, he rushed toward the heap of people on the mid-deck. Barbara and Safiya had pulled Luca out from under the skull and were holding the shivering boy. Barbara embraced and rocked him, eyes shut, unable to stop saying his name, 'Luca, Luca, oh God, Luca . . .' Safiya sheltered him on the other side, rubbing his arms. Luca himself looked small, beaten, and pallid. His hair stuck to his forehead, the upper half of his hoodie was drenched in blood and his eyes were sunk in dark hollows. The mammoth had taken its toll.

All three were in tears. Grim got close enough to hear the boy stammering to his mom as she kept soothing him. He cleared his throat, and

Barbara and Safiya looked up. 'Sorry guys. I don't want to intrude, but this thing is going to collapse. It would be a shame if this were all for nothing.'

Luca turned to him. 'Th-th-there was no other way, I s-s-swear. If there was, I would have d-d-done it. Really. B-b-but she would have k-kept on coming. She would have k-killed us all.'

'Oh, we know, sweetheart,' Barbara said. 'We know.'

Grim crouched. 'Hey. Well done, kid. When we're back ashore you're getting a Chupa Chup.'

'S-s-seriously,' he shivered, wiping the tears from his face. 'You're an old d-d-dude and you're offering me c-c-candy?'

'How're you doing?'

'C-c-cold.'

'Can you walk?'

Luca shrugged and winced with pain. Grim stood, joints creaking, and smiled. 'If you can't walk by yourself, your mom can certainly assist you. She has the strength of a bear.'

They helped Luca up and supported him across the mid-deck and back to the stairs. Had the rig's stability worsened, or was it just his imagination? Grim couldn't tell. But shining his light around, he did see algae were now covering the wellheads and other surfaces. It spread faster now. The spirit had left the carcass, and the sea was a scavenger, ready to feast on its bones.

Glennis was waiting for them atop the stairs. 'Is the boy okay?'

'He's hurt, but if there ever were a place with a first aid kit, it would be a lifeboat, huh?' Something occurred to him. 'Aren't we a few people short? Where's Sita? Moonshine?'

'Sita didn't make it,' Glennis said, a shadow passing over her face. 'Van Driel . . . do you really care where he is?'

He didn't.

She led them to a walkway that orbited the accommodation tower on the outer perimeter. Conditions there were downright nasty. Exposed to icy winds and the lashing of briny froth, the little band of survivors found it difficult to stay on their feet. Luca moaned and huddled against Grim.

'*One hand on the railing at all times, alright?*' Glennis yelled. '*It's just this part, there's cover on the other side!*'

They crowded around the boy and inched ahead on slippery grilles. The rail numbed Grim's hands even more, but the roar of the sea rising and falling beneath their feet reminded him there was no time for hesitation. Onwards, onwards, no other option. This side of the facility was untouched by fire and in the light of his headlamp, Grim saw red arrows signaling LIFEBOAT STATION and STAIRWELL A.

Reaching the other side, a flight of stairs descended to a sheltered landing. If Grim's sense of direction was right, the helideck must be somewhere up there, far above them.

'Jesus Christ!' Barbara yelled. 'This is insane!'

'This way!' Glennis pointed to Dukakis, who was waving his flashlight at the rear door of a vessel that hung suspended from a steeply inclined framework of white steel bars and cables. In Grim's mind it looked like a giant orange suppository, pointing downward at the sea.

'Hell yeah!' Safiya cheered as the meaning of 'freefall lifeboat' apparently sunk in.

Hell no, Grim thought, when he looked inside. A windowless, cramped cabin, jam-packed with at least twenty back-facing seats on both sides of an aisle. The seatbelts weren't of the airplane-kind but the rollercoaster-kind. Grim hated rollercoasters.

'I'd rather die here,' he muttered to Glennis, as Barbara, Safiya and Dukakis assisted the boy inside.

'Drama queen. You survived Eleanor, and she wasn't even your first witch. I think you can manage this last hurdle.'

'Is it the last hurdle, Glennis?' he asked. 'Is it really?'

She gave him an odd look, but before she could reply, Grim climbed aboard.

21

Luca Wolf was drenched, dazed, and exhausted from the pain, but even so, entering the lifeboat he felt a flash of excitement. This reminded him of the Speed of Sound, a rollercoaster in Walibi Holland that bulleted backward along the entire length of the track. He rode it last year, during a visit to the theme parc with his soccer team. And the icing on the cake? A splashdown, like in the Crazy River. Not bad.

'Everybody to the front!' Becker directed. 'All the weight in the nose, please.'

The inspector sat in one of the two cockpit seats in the rear, elevated on either side of the aisle. The cockpit was in fact a hump with portholes, facing Becker forward to look out over the nose.

Shivering, teeth chattering, Luca slumped into a seat next to Safiya. Glennis carefully wrapped a golden space-blanket around him. It crackled when she folded a thicker, woolen blanket over it. That was nice.

'We'll take care of your cuts first thing when we're out of here, alright? Hang in there.'

He nodded and yawned. With his mom across the aisle, he had a strange déjà vu of the chopper, except this cabin was darker, with only headlamps for light. The cold had numbed him so deeply that he barely felt the pain anymore. More than anything, he wanted to doze off. Maybe he did, as Glennis was buckling up his shoulder straps. Whatever. He was just so tired.

He shook awake as she strapped a helmet on his head, clipping it under his chin. 'Ready,' she said, buckling up a row ahead.

'Everyone seated?' Becker called.

'Are you sure this is safe?' Grim called back. 'Won't the storm smash us against the pillars?'

Becker lowered his head into the aisle. 'Got another plan, Robert? The wind and the waves are tricky, but this is it. With all of you upfront to dive as straight as possible, we should be okay.'

Grim muttered something unintelligible. Luca felt sorry for the man but was too far gone to worry about it himself.

'Fingers crossed, I'm firing up the engine now. Normally the battery is kept fully charged, but the place has been out of power for a long time, and I don't know what condition it's in. There are two handles on the seat in front of you. Grab 'em, hold on tight, and don't let go until we're in the water. You too, Luca.'

Luca wriggled his arms from under the blanket to grab the handles. That bumped up the pain—badly. He winced and waited for it to fade into a dull, tolerable throb.

The engine roared to life, like the old diesels of the tulip scoopers plowing the Katwijk fields in summer. Luca could feel the handles vibrate.

'So far, so good.' Becker grabbed a throttle next to his seat. 'I'll pull this lever a few times. That's the release mechanism that will launch us. Your seat cushions are designed to absorb the impact, but it's going to be rough, guys.'

'Spare me the inflight safety video and get us out of here!' Grim shouted.

'Alright, alright. Everyone ready?'

A chorus of unconvinced yesses.

'Don't let go!'

Luca felt a tingling in his stomach that wasn't unpleasant at all. He saw his mom bracing herself and briefly met her anxious gaze. Safiya had braced herself too, but she was blooming with cheerful anticipation. Despite everything, Luca smiled.

Becker pulled a safety pin from the lever, pumped it twice, three times, and they were loose. Luca relished the sudden acceleration, the sensation of weightlessness, and the brief, baffling moment of full disorientation. His mom and Dukakis yelled, Safiya screamed with laughter, Grim turtled his head, and Luca thought, *Now we're really flying*.

The impact was massive. First, he flew into his shoulder straps, then smacked back into his seat. The blankets softened the blow on his cuts, but he still screamed with pain . . . and roared with laughter. They lurched forward like a rocking horse, capsized, then bobbed up and clung to the waves.

'Whoohoo! I wanna go again!' Luca shouted, kicking his feet.

'Goddamn-mother-fuck!'

'Awright, haha!'

They were all laughing now, even his mom. Even Grim. Everyone needed to let off a little steam, he supposed.

'Okay folks, that went pretty well,' Becker said. 'Now prepare yourself for the part that won't be fun.'

Luca realized what that meant only when the inspector got the lifeboat moving. The waves were worse than the fall. Much worse. The surges overtook them from the rear, which meant that they were constantly pressed against their seats as they rose on the crests then flipped forward as they fell into the troughs. Before long, Luca's stomach churned.

When Becker had put enough distance between them and the rig to safely send out a distress signal, he killed the engine. By then, the excitement of the launch had been wiped away. At the mercy of the waves, the vessel began to turn into the wind, causing them to rock sideways and upsetting Luca's insides even more.

In the rear, they cooked up a plan. Luca shut himself off from their voices. He closed his eyes, but that just made the dizziness worse, and he moaned.

They came to tend to his wounds. Glennis and his mom, looking quite green herself, removed his wet clothes. The antiseptic bit into his cuts and momentarily cleared his head, but then he saw their bloody hands, thought, *That's coming out of me*, and got light-headed.

'I think I'm gonna be sick,' he mumbled.

Glennis pushed a screw top storage container against his chest. The plasticky smell was all it took, and Luca puked, unable to resist the spasms in his guts. It was awful. When it was finally over, he was shivering and dripping with cold sweat but felt a bit better.

'Yuck,' he groaned to Safiya. 'I wish you didn't have to see me like this.'

'So you're human. Big deal.'

They dabbed him dry and wrapped him in bandages from the waist up. They were swaddling him in blankets when Grim and Becker came up.

'It's going to be a bumpy night,' the latter said. 'I'm not going to risk sailing. The EPIRB is low on battery and if we abandon the place from where we sent the SOS, we'll be a needle in a haystack.'

God knows what an EPIRB was, but Luca didn't have the energy to inquire. Safiya did.

'It's an emergency locator beacon. The signal is detected by satellites that pass on our GPS and ID. The Coast Guard then sends out a search and rescue, but I'm afraid they can't do anything in this storm. So it could be a while before they find us.'

'Aren't we drifting off with the waves?' Glennis asked.

'Yes, but they can calculate that. I'll send out a signal every now and then for as long as it's up. The good news is that we're completely safe here. In the compartments on your right-hand side, you'll find emergency rations, water, and pills against seasickness. I highly recommend you take them.'

They did, but if they had any effect, it was only on Safiya, Grim, and Becker. Over the next hour, his mom, Dukakis, and Glennis were not so lucky. At least there were plenty of screw tops on board.

The sea kicked up crests, the sea dug out troughs. Luca became numb to the monotony of the bobbing, unable to adjust, still growing into it. His misery gave way to submission. He slept and he dreamt, he jerked awake and dozed off again.

In the wee hours, he was sluggishly staring out at colors illuminating the cabin from the cockpit. A searchlight? A rescue chopper? Nah, the light was fluttering too strangely for that. And the colors were . . .

'Luca. Come here a second.'

It was Grim. He was sitting alongside Becker in the second navigator seat, inviting him with a nod of his head. His mom and Safiya were asleep. So were Glennis and Dukakis. Luca fashioned his blanket into a cloak, got up, and staggered his way to the front. 'What *is* that?'

'Wait.'

Becker slipped out of his seat and landed in the aisle. He helped Luca up to take his place behind a basic dashboard with a steering wheel that looked more like it belonged in a truck than a seagoing vessel. But his gaze was instantly drawn to the sky.

The storm hadn't dwindled, but the clouds had retreated to the horizon, where they piled up to massive heights. A cosmic eye had opened across a painted sky, fluxing and pulsing with deep pink-purples and occasional bursts of green. He could now see how the lifeboat mounted what could only be called the swells of the gods. They loomed up like towering mountains, forcing them to tilt backward in submission, facing the sky until they reached their crests, only to flip forward in a burst of fairy-tale colors that seemed to illuminate the entire North Sea. Then they rode the waves like Hawaiian surfers, down into their valleys, before the next swell would come.

Luca searched for words that could express the grandeur of this display of powers, but he was speechless. He just stared at it in silence.

'It's so beautiful,' he eventually said.

'*Aurora borealis*,' said Grim. 'The northern lights. That's the scientific explanation, at least. But tonight, who can tell?'

'I've seen it before,' Luca said. 'Not here. I don't really know where it was.'

'It usually only occurs around the polar circle,' Becker said from down in the aisle. 'It's rare on the North Sea. You're witnessing something special tonight.'

Luca nodded. Becker didn't understand what he had meant, and never would. Grim did but didn't need words to acknowledge it. Instead, he pointed at the horizon.

'See that? There, wait until we reach the crest.'

On the horizon, in stark contrast against the reflected colors of the clouds, rose the skeleton of an offshore rig.

'Is that the Mammoth?'

Grim nodded.

'But how's that possible? I thought we would have drifted much further by now.'

'We did. Whiloe you were asleep, we sailed back to the GPS location of our distress signal.'

Vince tapped Luca's seat. 'The two of you probably have lots to discuss. Someday, I'd love to hear the full story over a pint, but I can wait. If you don't touch anything and strap in, you can sit here for a while and watch the sky.'

Grim cast him an appreciative nod. 'I owe you that beer. The story too.'

Grim and Luca watched the stormy lights for a while and the mammoth on the horizon. Then they saw it go. It happened unannounced. Its front legs simply buckled, as if finally giving in with a sigh of relief. Its shoulders swayed forward. The lifeboat disappeared into a trough and when they mounted the next swell, they just caught a glimpse of its humped back sinking beneath the waves. At the third crest it was gone, as if it had never been.

Tears burned in Luca's eyes. He wiped them away, but they came anyway. Grim saw it and reached across the aisle, placing a bony, but surprisingly warm hand on his shoulder.

'Just a seedpod,' he said. 'It's done. It's fulfilled its purpose. This is nature's way.'

That might be true, but for a while, Luca's life and that of the mammoth had been intimately entwined. He wasn't ready for that to be over just yet, because he instinctively understood it would never return. Maybe he had hoped for a more meaningful farewell, a message that would reveal how he was supposed to carry on alone. But it didn't come, just as he hadn't gotten the opportunity to say goodbye to his dad and Jenna and Emma. If this was nature's way, it was incredibly cruel.

Luca Wolf felt lonely and orphaned in his grief but was relieved to be sharing this moment with Grim, not his mom or Safiya.

'Why do you think the sea let us go?' he finally asked, when the worst was over.

'You're still the Oracle,' Grim said. 'Eleanor may have been defeated, but whatever worked through her isn't. You still have a message to pass on.'

'But to whom?'

'I suppose Glennis and Dukakis will take you to the proper authorities. The ones with executive power now that Eleanor's gone. I'll corroborate your story, of course. So will Glennis, and she'll back it up with evidence.'

'And then what?'

'Then we'll have to see whether they believe you or not. And if they'll act upon it.'

Luca looked at him in surprise. 'Why wouldn't they?'

'Why do you think? Picture it. Some psychic kid gathers the entire top of the Dutch intelligence services, the army and the government and tells them that within the next twenty-four hours, a massive human sacrifice needs to take place on the North Sea. Right? Because yesterday you said, two days before the flood. And if they don't heed this warning, a major disaster will claim many more lives. They'd laugh you out of the room. Except, their own intelligence service then comes in with a huge stack of evidence that shows something very sinister really *is* going on.

Hours of footage. Witness statements. Verifiable physical evidence. The disappearances, the dead families, the messages on the walls. Not to mention the specimens of that algae shit. They'll be uncomfortable. Not uncomfortable enough to act, because what rational person would sacrifice anyone based on a supernatural presumption?'

'But then they'll find out that it happened before,' Luca said. He was starting to see where Grim was going.

'Exactly. A historically documented case from the eighteenth century, when a sacrifice *was* made. And an eight-thousand-year-old, geologically documented tsunami on the North Sea when, according to the psychic kid, a sacrifice was refused. Suggestive at best, but still a flagrant coincidence, and it will bug the hell out of them. Suppose meteorologists then come in to warn them of a storm coming, the worst ever recorded. A storm of biblical proportions. That's going to shake their worldview. And suppose then another thing you predicted happens. A bunch of storm surge barriers fail to close. A serious flood is imminent. What will be their tipping point? What's the moment they'll start to believe?'

'I think they'll be peeing their pants,' Luca said.

'No doubt. There's always a tipping point. But that's only the beginning. Because then what? Will they act on a blatantly supernatural premise? And what about the ethical consequences? Is it morally justifiable to kill a group of people in order to save a bigger group? And who would we choose to sacrifice? And *how?*'

'Alright, Chidi. My mom always says you can work anything out.'

Grim sighed. 'Your mother is probably referring to your homework, not mass murder. And even so. Suppose they manage to get past all the moral and practical objections, and they do make a sacrifice of many. They give in abundance. And the disaster doesn't happen. How can they ever be sure it was the sacrifice that prevented it? Who says that if they *hadn't* made the sacrifice, a disaster *would* have occurred? Would they be able to live with that?'

Luca looked at the horizon, where the mammoth had stood only moments ago. 'I'm scared,' he finally said, softly.

'That they won't act?'

'That they *will*.'

Now it was Grim's turn to be perplexed.

'The sea was working through Eleanor. I could never have beaten her on my own. It was the mammoth who did it. I think Eleanor was supposed to kill it through me. But she didn't succeed. Instead, we lifted an old curse.'

'The Oracle of Doggerland,' Grim said.

Luca nodded. 'Nunyunnini is mighty, but only when he's believed in. The old woman told me that if she'd kept her faith, the tsunami would never have come.'

Grim sighed and leaned back. The northern lights shimmered in his remaining lens. 'That's not your responsibility, Luca. Your responsibility is to deliver the message. What they do with it isn't for you or me to decide.'

'Isn't it, though?' he asked, a bit heated. 'If this is what I know, shouldn't it be my responsibility?'

'So what do you want to do? What do you think they'll say if you tell them a major flood disaster is coming, but that it's no biggie as long as we collectively start worshipping a woolly mammoth and say our Hail Marys?'

Luca shrugged. 'We could keep quiet.'

'You mean not deliver the message?' Grim looked at him incredulously. 'You dare to take that gamble?'

Luca motioned to the sky, alive with reds, purples, and greens. 'Looking at that, wouldn't you?'

Grim mulled it over, considering the universe's sparkling display. Finally he said, 'I would, I guess. But not Glennis. People are pragmatic, Luca. She'll have to give them something better after the mess Eleanor left behind. She won't be convinced that one boy's belief is enough to hold back a sea. She's not authorized to bear such a responsibility. She's going to have to leave it to the Dutch authorities.'

'That would be a mistake,' Luca said.

Wistfully, he stared northwest and let the conversation slip away, and then the wistfulness too. In the face of the miracle unfolding before him, such inconsequentialities would only act to diminish it. The lights knotted on the breath of the cosmos, and if you looked at them in a particular way, you could see all sorts of images. A human head with soft, sparkling eyes, wearing an AC Milan cap. It faded away, and now Luca saw a terrestrial animal with swirling flashes for tusks trudging across a prehistoric horizon. That too faded, and all that was left were his own thoughts enfolding the light, as if it had always been so.

EPILOGUE

GRIM

1

On a day in May, a man exited the lobby of the Lily Arcade Residence in Atlantic City, New Jersey, and walked into the bright sunlight. He paused on the plaza and squinted. From behind his marble front desk, the concierge watched him, seeing a completely different man than the disheveled hermit who had until recently dwelt in the penthouse. *That* man would almost never come down to the lobby, ordered in his groceries—usually from the Ocean Liquor Store on Pennsylvania Avenue—and had the constant air of a thundercloud that might unload at any time, if you dared to speak to him. Frankly, the concierge had always feared that man a little. The housekeepers too. How had a reclusive alcoholic ended up in one of the city's most expensive condos? And what was the point of having the panoramic ocean view, if you persistently instructed the housekeepers to keep the curtains drawn?

It all became even more mysterious when early in December, that man was picked up by strangers in a blacked-out car. For almost three months, he disappeared from the face of the earth. The rumor mill ran rampant among the Lily Arcade staff. He was a distinguished diplomat. A spy. Whatever the case, his absence appeared to have done him some good, because when he resurfaced in late February, he looked reborn. Granted, he had a limp now, stitches on the top of his head, and a little scar on the bridge of his nose which he tried to hide behind his horn-rimmed glasses. But *this* man was smartly dressed, clean-shaven, bright-eyed, and lo and behold, even *greeted* you.

And that was an understatement. Swaggering toward the desk, waggling his eyebrows, he would say, '*¿Qué pasa?*'

If he wasn't carrying bags—he did his own shopping now—he might flash both index fingers at you and say, 'Whoop, whoop!'

And just now, the worst yet, 'All Gucci?'

It was embarrassing for a man his age—ludicrous even—but at the same time, the concierge found it endearing. So he repaid him with the same cheerfulness every time. Here was a man who had shaken off the weight of the world and was sending a little love back. Who was he to ruin it?

Seeing him scan the plaza left and right, then walking down the street with his jacket draped over his shoulder, he thought, *Someone got him good, wherever he's been. But whatever it was that weighed him down, it lifted his curse.*

2

Robert Grim crossed the boardwalk and strolled along the sun-drenched promenade, past the Hard Rock Hotel & Casino. It was just a short walk to the car park at the northeast end. He enjoyed walking nowadays and wouldn't let the opportunity pass on a day like this. The doctor said he would make a full recovery from the whiplash, it just took longer at his age, and any exercise was good. Some days, Grim paid for his hubris. Like that afternoon in March, when he had walked along the beach all the way to Longport and had to drag himself up the steps. He was forced to take an Uber back and could barely stand for four days.

Today, his disability didn't bother him. Today was a good day. He eased on past the Revel and down the path to the parking lot. It was midmorning and the lot was already jam-packed, but Grim instantly singled out the obsidian Dodge Durango waiting with its engine running.

He opened the rear door and got in.

'Hello, Grim,' Glennis said. 'Are you ready?'

'Yes,' he said. 'Today's the day.'

3

Of course, not all days were good. There were days when he was plagued by his physical ailments, and there were days when he was haunted by his memories. Those were the bad days.

On such days, he would often stare out his panoramic windows at the sea. Nowadays, he kept the curtains open because what he saw in their reflection no longer scared him. The sea didn't scare him either. But sometimes, when the wind whipped up the water into a boiling cauldron, he remembered the surging creature with the searing black eyes that spread mold and algae wherever it went. Then he would stare at the horizon, imagining what slumbered in the deep—not dead, no, not dead.

You may have crossed an ocean, but all seas are connected, he would think.

Admittedly, on such days it was tough not to reach out to his old pal Blue Label, or his newer friend Xanax. What kept him going was talking. The Point had offered him a therapist, but Grim found a better alternative: a social life.

He stayed in the Netherlands for the better part of February, even after Glennis left for America. He didn't know what he hoped to find there, but he had nothing to return to either. And in the end, he found it.

Every three or four days, he would meet with Vince Becker. Their go-to was Brouwcafé De Hofnar, a harbor pub in The Hague. A risk, perhaps, to expose himself to the temptation of such a wide selection of quality brews. Vince had repeatedly and thoughtfully suggested to go someplace else to ease his torment, but for Grim, it wasn't torment. It was a test. If he could stay dry there, he could get through the bad days as well.

He enjoyed Vince's company and liked to listen to his stories about the offshore industry. A strange thing had developed: a friendship, that they maintained even now, albeit low-key and via FaceTime. It was an arrangement that benefited them both. Vince had been amply compensated for his silence. But he had seen enough on the Mammoth III that night for that silence to swell inside him like a balloon that would eventually burst. By sharing his experiences with Grim, he could let the air out in small bits before that could happen.

And Grim, after all, had promised him a story.

His newly discovered social life wasn't limited to Vince Becker, though. Luca Wolf had insisted that he install WhatsApp and Grim acceded. He couldn't be bothered with the superficial back-and-forth and hated the annoying emojis, but he had a soft spot for the kid, so he indulged him. Initially, Luca mostly sent pics of kitlers (cats that looked like Hitler), closeups of quokkas (a species of Australian guinea pig that appeared to be on a constant heroin high), and once, a particularly ugly deep-sea anglerfish captioned *Eleanor*.

Occasionally, he sent brief updates that lead Grim to believe he was doing well, as well as could be expected, considering the circumstances. In late March, the boy wrote, *Omg safiya calls me dumbo!! Not bc I'm dumb. Bc the flying elephant.* And a whole stream of scrunched emojis with steam blowing from the nose. Grim sent back, *There isn't a single species of animal where the female doesn't have a certain dominance over the male. Worship her, Luca, that's your only way to repay her.* And, *(Otherwise, immuring her will do the trick).*

As time progressed, Luca appeared to use him more and more as an emergency hotline, sharing aspects of his life that at first seemed trivial, but which in the eyes of a teen amounted to the whole world. School.

Soccer practice. His girl. Topics he perhaps would have discussed with his dad. Or maybe it was the physical distance between them, having shared that single brief but terrifying ordeal on the North Sea, that had built the foundation for his trust.

Rarely did Luca touch upon what had happened. But one time he wrote, *I keep thinking about the people. All those poor people. Should we have kept quiet after all?*

Yes, that had been a bad fucking day.

4

Glennis Sopamena had stepped out of Eleanor's shadow for good. It began when she turned against her during the Cougar's flight to the rig. The circle was closed with her testimony and recommendations for the NOVEMBER-6 interim team. Opportunistic? Maybe. Grim hadn't forgotten her resumé of odd jobs carried out for that rotten organization, albeit with her back against the wall. But he wanted to believe there was more to it than that. He wanted to believe that even on this level, people could change.

She joined him in the back seat, and the driver headed north. Since the events on the North Sea, he had seen Glennis only once, in early March, when she had come to Atlantic City to arrange the first part of his payment. The financial part.

Now she had come for the second part.

'I assume they put a statue up of you at West Point,' he said as they turned up the Garden State Parkway, leaving Atlantic City in the rearview.

She trilled a laugh without even a hint of contempt. *But she's always had a poker face*, Grim thought.

'It won't surprise you how few people know where I was last winter.'

'Not even in *Open Your Eyes*? You have a hell of a story to tell them. And they'd believe you.'

'That's the way these institutions work, Robert. We exist by the grace of silence. It's our burden to bear. You should know that.'

Glennis would have to bear that burden, too. She got herself promoted. She was running the Black Spring file . . . for life. It was the price she had to pay for leaking to Delveaux and compromising the entire operation. A fine piece of reverse psychology from her supes, but it worked.

'So NOVEMBER-6 will continue to exist,' he said.

'Of course, what did you expect? They'll reorganize, but their existence was never exposed in the Netherlands. Just particular aspects of the *Oracle* file. Yamani, mostly. More than anything, they are testament to the importance of their existence. They're not that different from us. Except that in an ideal world, no autocrat should ever rise that far through the ranks.'

'So The Point put you in charge,' Grim said, gently sarcastic.

'Voilà.'

'And in the Netherlands? Are they doing penance?'

'Maybe,' Glennis said. Grim suspected that he was looking at her poker face again. 'I like to tell myself it's not the work that creates the monsters. We just hide them, so we can all sleep at night. But sometimes you don't know who the monsters are.'

Grim thought, *I know a boy who would agree with you there.*

His thoughts drifted back to the morning of February 4. By the time the coastguard picked them up, light prickled the eastern sky, and the storm had waned. They could consider themselves lucky, the captain told them. 'The gods are poopin' out a new one already, and this time it's a primo dump.'

Grim wouldn't hand him a Pulitzer, but with these words, the last piece of the puzzle fell into place. Storm Dylan's timing hadn't coincided with Luca's prediction. Storm Ellen, now building above the Faroe Islands, was the real monster, and heading straight for the Dutch coast.

'And it's a spring tide first thing tomorrow,' the captain added. 'They say the barriers will close, or it'll be 1953 all over again.'

Glennis explained he was referring to the Dutch national trauma of the North Sea flood that claimed 1,800 plus lives—wondering out loud if *that* had been the result of a missed sacrifice, too.

Both Grim and the kid needed urgent medical attention. Once the adrenaline wore off, Grim had trouble breathing again. No wonder, with two broken ribs pressing against his right lung, as it turned out. But there was no time to lose, and upon making landfall, Glennis and Dukakis took them straight to the Ministry of Defense HQ in The Hague. They appeared before a crisis team whose sole purpose was to clean up the mess Delveaux had left behind. Dukakis said they were absolute top-tiers within the Dutch secret service, police, and armed forces.

An audio call was also set up with a man named King, who sounded particularly ordinary and asked particularly few questions as Luca recounted his story.

Later that day, the Maeslant barrier failed to lock when the water reached critical levels. There was an attempt to close it manually, but it simply refused to work.

As did the IJssel barrier east of Rotterdam.

The cause of the glitches was never discovered. The following day, a superintendent with Rijkswaterstaat had run tests on the system, and everything had functioned properly. The metaphor he used in his report stated that it had seemed like there had been a 'ghost in the machine.'

Trees and buildings flashed by the car window. The New York City skyline was shining in the east.

'I always wondered what happened with the Saudis,' Grim said. 'I mean, I know you threw them under the bus, that was fucking hilarious. But Eleanor must have had her reasons to rush out of Volkel like that. It seemed rather . . . explosive?'

'Correct, except the bomb had already gone off, of course. They were too late. There was immediate deliberation on the highest level to de-escalate, because it was still an infiltration of an army base by a nation the Dutch are technically friends with, but only because a lot of oil money is involved.'

'What a clusterfuck.'

'Of course, the Saudis played innocent. They were detained, the plane was searched. Turned out they were armed to the teeth, but Mabahith always are. Dukakis said they explored the possibility of linking them to Yamani, but the evidence just wasn't there. Since they had diplomatic immunity, they were sent home.'

'And then you nudged the Dutch to run that press conference,' Grim chuckled.

'Diplomatic immunity my ass. This was retribution. By selling her soul to them, Eleanor inadvertently gave us the perfect scapegoat.'

The press conference was a hastily put-together, joint effort by the Dutch AIVD and the British SIS, identifying a number of Saudi individuals as responsible for the attacks with a previously unknown nerve agent. It explained the physical deformities and eventual deaths of Abdulaziz Yamani in London and two Dutch informants in Noordwijk, who had been onto their plot.

'Didn't you consider it risky to draw attention to the Noordwijk cops?'

'We had to do something after what Bellingcat published. You know how it works. Press conferences are the opposite of what we want. So why do we call them? To reclaim the narrative. The masses jump, thrilled to get a rare peek into the shadow world of spies and counterspies. They never imagine it's designed to distract them.'

Grim peered outside. 'That creates a dangerous precedent. If it leaks one way or the other, it's fuel for the conspiracy truthers. The QAnon believers, the antivaxxers, that Klan Mom from Georgia . . . you're feeding their lies.'

'That's why it rarely happens.' She looked at him candidly. 'And how is that any different from what you did in Black Spring, Grim? You veiled a bit of truth, because if you hadn't, the consequences would have been worse.'

But Grim wondered, not for the first time, if they had made the right choice, given how things turned out.

The press conference took place at 3:30pm on February 4. No one paid much attention, and that too was orchestrated. That afternoon, the Dutch were preoccupied with the approaching hurricane. At Schiphol Airport, flight cancellations over the past twenty-four hours had resulted in chaos. When air traffic slowly returned to use the brief window between storms, it led to long delays and overbooked flights. KL689 was a commercial flight to Vancouver, with 323 souls on board. It took off at 5:24pm, more than four hours after its scheduled departure. Exactly twenty-six minutes later, when the Triple Seven had reached its cruising altitude over the North Sea, it collided with a Dutch F-16 participating in a last-minute training mission, taking advantage of the unique weather conditions. Later, it was revealed that a series of miscommunications between civilian and military ATC and an error made by the fighter pilot had led to the tragic accident. The latter had disengaged his proximity warning system, likely because they had been flying in formation. He botched a last-ditch attempt to avoid the collision, clipping the Boeing's wingtip. Several hellish minutes ensued for the passengers in the doomed plane. The sole consolation for the relatives was that their misery had ended instantly on impact with the sea.

That night, the country was in shock. The prime minister declared a week of national mourning. The Secretary of Defense resigned, but Grim suspected she wasn't the only one who had been sacrificed as part of this affair.

No one gave a damn about Noordwijk anymore.

Or about storm . . . even though meteorologists were unanimously dumbstruck as to how suddenly and inexplicably it had subsided over the North Sea.

They all concluded the country had dodged a bullet.

5

Luca turned fourteen on April 12. Grim got a WhatsApp message: *Mom told me to invite you. I know you probably can't but we have meringue cake.* And a drooling emoji.

Grim bought a ticket and flew commercial for the first time in his life. The two remaining members of the Wolf family had moved across town, now occupying a nice and spacious home Barbara undoubtedly hadn't financed herself. It was jazzed up for the occasion with party streamers and balloons. Family would arrive for dinner, so Grim visited in the afternoon. Barbara texted that a few of Luca's peers would be around, but that didn't bother him. It was the adults who asked the questions.

On the way from the airport, he asked the taxi to detour through Every Man's End, where he got out. The land was unrecognizable, a glittering kaleidoscope of hyacinths, peonies, and tulips. Lots of tulips. Nothing to remind Grim of what had happened here four months prior. The fallow corridor where steel road plates had formed passageways may just as well have been mowed for farm equipment, and the wasteland in the middle, where the *Oracle's* replica had burned, was practically invisible from the road.

When the taxi driver asked if he wanted a picture, he turned and noticed the realtor's sign reading TE KOOP in the front yard of a modest farm across the road. Robert Grim didn't need an interpreter to understand what it meant.

'No thanks,' he told the driver. 'There's nothing here I need to remember.'

How different it was in Katwijk. It was a sunny and pleasant afternoon, so Barbara led him into the backyard, where the children—two boys, two girls—were having cake. With a cry of joy, Safiya jumped up and threw her arms around him. Luca looked good. He had grown in the brief amount of time since February and his voice had deepened. When he unpacked his present, his eyes grew wide.

'Is that . . .?'

Grim nodded.

The boy held it up. A leather necklace, its pendant a diamond-shaped, fossilized piece of bone.

'So . . . you in the ivory trade, then?' Luca's smart-ass friend asked.

'No, I only deal in human bones. This is a piece of my ex-wife's cranium.' That cracked them up. 'Kidding aside, it's a piece of mammoth tusk from a sunken land in the North Sea. It once belonged to a beach-comber from Katwijk.'

He gave Luca a quick and almost imperceptible wink, but it was enough for the boy to understand. On an impulse, Grim had broken it off from the splintered stump of the skull on the rig. He had carried it with him ever since, but he always knew it had a more deserving home.

Luca put the necklace over his head, letting the pendant slide under his T-shirt. You couldn't see it anymore, but it was where it was supposed to be. Close to his heart.

'Thank you,' he said softly.

After cake, the children went further down the yard to make TikToks: lots of laughter, bedlam, and surprisingly well-synchronized dancing. Grim could see Barbara pressing her lips together, having a hard time. She looked better than in February, but the traces of mourning were etched on her face. He leaned over and put a hand on her arm. 'How are you coping, Barbara?'

'We're coping,' she said with a sob, rubbing her face. 'I'm dragging along, truth be told. Thanks for coming, Robert. You've made his day.'

She told him about the impossibility to close the hole in her heart left by Jenna and Alexander, and about the paradox of allowing brief moments of happiness like today, when Luca had a good day. Such moments threatened to bury her sorrow and made her feel guilty instead. And she knew that it would eventually get easier, but it was taking so damn long.

'What did we witness that day, Robert?' she asked against the backdrop of the children's carefree laughter. 'What really happened on the rig that night?'

Those who harbor grudges in death shall never be at peace.

'A kind of cosmic liberation, I think.'

What he really meant to say was the word the old woman had used. The word that wasn't exactly *liberation* but close. He remembered its sound and wished he could repeat it. That word expressed it better, he supposed.

'The skull you gave him a piece of,' Barbara said. 'It had power.'

Grim shrugged. 'You saw what it did to Luca. But don't underestimate your own role. You gave him that power. You and Safiya.'

She considered this. 'I just keeping wondering, if there really were higher powers in play that night, does that imply it was all meant to be? If so, then Jenna and Alexander were just pawns in some cosmic game.'

Grim could have told her that he didn't know how such powers worked or why they sometimes suddenly erupted. What quirk of fate caused nature to sometimes bend against all understanding and answer only to the laws of pandemonium? But he didn't say that. He didn't want to burden her with questions he himself had struggled with for the past ten years, ever since his own liberation. Because sometimes there were no answers. And sometimes it was better to stop asking.

That too was liberation.

6

Those who harbor grudges in death shall never be at peace.

It was just after midday, a full circle of the clock before the witching hour, when they reached the Bear Mountain Bridge. Grim noticed that his hands were trembling. It wasn't gloom, and it wasn't fear, but they still trembled. The hills to the west of the Hudson were slumbering in the sun like ancient secrets, pushed up by the same glaciers that had exposed Doggerland as they retreated, until the sea had come to reclaim it, thousands of years later. These hills had been reclaimed too. Not by the sea, but by silence.

Robert Grim had never returned here. He was shocked to see it was all still there. The same jammed toll plaza, the river shimmering far below through the leaves, the way Route 9W suddenly swerved north-bound, opening a panorama across the Popolopen Creek of the Hudson and the bridge's pillars.

One thing had changed, though: the road signs didn't read BLACK SPRING anymore.

You know damn well that's not the only thing that's changed. Everything is different. Can't you feel it? Fifty-seven years of your life, and time has erased them like they never existed. Just like the memory of the almost three thousand people who used to live here. It's creepy when you think about it, and it's even creepier to consider you're the only one still thinking about it. So don't fool yourself. Nothing here is the same as it was.

But the mystery hidden among the hills was still there. It may not be the witching hour, but the veil between the worlds had always been thinner here.

The driver passed the Highland Falls and West Point exits, turned off at the golf course and flashed his taillights at a military checkpoint. That was new. You used to turn onto the NY293 here, locally known as the Storm King Highway, which wound southwest and uphill through the Black Rock Forest where it crossed the Black Spring town line. Now, there was a guarded fence, and you could only go back past the golf course and down into the valley.

Unless you produced a pass with the appropriate clearance, which they did. Two armed soldiers cast jittery looks into the car but opened the barrier and let them through.

The Storm King Highway was now an anonymous, deserted road, no longer maintained. Glennis saw he was having a hard time and left him with his thoughts. Less than three miles further, they reached a concrete roadblock, beyond which the road simply dead-ended.

Remember standing here at the town limits, that night? You were trying to signal the residents of Upper Highland Falls. No matter how loud you screamed and honked the horn, they couldn't hear you. Didn't even see your fireworks display. You, Claire Hammer, Warren Castillo—God, how long since those names have crossed your mind!

Where the town line once was, there were dense woods.

No, he thought. *The last building before town was the Army's MWR Lodge. The Christmas lights were still flickering that night, remember? This isn't the town line yet. It's at least half a mile away. Of course. They would have considered this too close.*

The Dodge stopped by the wayside, and Glennis and Grim got out. The Black Rock Forest was full of secret life. Grim stood there for a moment, taking it all in. He thought about things he had suppressed for years. Small things, whose memories had faded without attention, but resurfaced here, so close to the source. The barrel organ at the Market & Deli's plaza. The old leather armchairs in the Point to Point Inn, smelling of home and age. The little bell above the door of Griselda's Butchery & Delicacies. The rolling fields of Ackerman's Corner, where John Blanchard kept his sheep. Philosopher's Creek, disappearing beneath the road at the Grant's house.

His vision went blurry. Grim crouched and hung his head between his legs.

'Are you alright?' Glennis asked. She put a hand on his back.

'Yeah. Just give me a few. It'll pass.'

It did, and they headed into the woods. There were young pines, but forest giants too, which must have been transplanted roots and all to have grown that much in the ten years since these woods had been cultivated. It was thoughtfully executed. Dense undergrowth of blackberry bushes impeded their progress and if Glennis hadn't come prepared, they would never have gotten through it. Grim stood perplexed as she produced hand pruners from her purse.

He didn't see the MWR Lodge anywhere. They must have torn it down when they took out the access road and let nature run its course.

After what could well have been half a mile, they hit a path around a perimeter fence. The fence was at least thirteen feet high and topped with an abundance of razor wire. A sign read: UNITED STATES MILITARY ACADEMY AT WEST POINT—MT. MISERY TRAINING AREA. DANGER.

LIVE FIRE. KEEP OUT. Below it, another sign: AUTHORIZED PERSONNEL
ONLY.

Beyond the fence there were more woods and a narrow trail.

Grim noted with a sense of irony that his long-cherished wish for Black
Spring had finally and posthumously come true: locked, wired, and gated.

They followed the path uphill until they reached an unguarded gate.
Or was it? Glennis pointed to the cameras and motion detectors hidden
in the trees on each side of the fence. She said they were placed along
the entire ten miles of the perimeter. Grim hadn't noticed them, and
that, of course, was the point. If uninvited guests were ever to penetrate
the cordon sanitaire spanning almost the entire Black Rock Forest, this
would be the last opportunity to keep them out.

Glennis produced a keyring from her bag and flipped the locks. Then
she opened the gate . . . just a little.

'Alright, Grim. This is it.'

He took a deep breath. His hands were still trembling, but the dizziness was gone. 'Thank you, Glennis.' He cleared his throat. 'Thank you
for everything.'

He walked inside. Glennis shut and locked the gate behind him.
Then they said goodbye. He watched her go, and when he could no
longer hear her footsteps in the undergrowth, he turned around.

He had come alone.

*Come and gone. You remember it like yesterday. This part you'll never
forget, because it's your curse to bear. The price of your liberation. Because
by the time the sun came up, you were the shadow that haunted the town.
Black Spring had become a ghost town, just like in 1666. Just like in 1713.
But not you . . . you were alive. Why? Even Veldheimer and Cox couldn't
wrap their heads around that one. But you know. One last act awaited you
before you were free to go. There, by the accursed Grant house, in the water-
course of Philosopher's Creek. So that's where you went, and when you got
there, you knocked, because the power was out for good. You thought you
saw something move in the hallway, behind the panel curtain. But nobody
came. Nobody answered the door. So you knocked and you knocked, until
you finally picked up that rock from the front yard and bashed in the lock.*

All those years, he had kept her hidden.

When he found her on that final night, he had whispered one word
to her.

Mother.

Robert Grim followed the trail toward Black Spring. He didn't know
what he would find there, but whatever it was, he would tell it a secret.

Acknowledgements

Copy to follow

Copy to follow